SHALA

SHALA

MILIND BOKIL

Translated from the Marathi by
Vikrant Pande

HARPERPERENNIAL

HARPERPERENNIAL

First published in India in 2014 by Harper Perennial
An imprint of HarperCollins *Publishers*

Building 10, Tower A, 4th Floor, DLF Cyber City, Phase II,
Gurugram Haryana – 122002, India
www.harpercollins.co.in

2 4 6 8 10 9 7 5 3 1

This edition published in India in 2019 by Harper Perennial

P-ISBN: 978-93-5302-667-7
E-ISBN: 978-93-5302-668-4

Typeset in 11/14 Adobe Caslon Pro
by Jojy Philip, New Delhi

Printed and bound at
MicroPrints India, New Delhi

The main road leads to my school, but I prefer the winding path through the fields. There is a long stretch of grassland behind our house, beyond the Mhatre chawl lines, barren except for a few date palms and tufts of grass growing between the rocks. The village of Kanhe begins where the grassland ends. On the right are paddy fields, overlooked by massive rocks, and on the left is Nana's jungle. The road to school begins beyond the rocks.

I never had to come this way earlier. Till eighth standard, that is. Our school, till Seventh Standard, was at a different place. Back then, I'd take the road opposite Ganesh Provision Store which joins Kanhe Road near Mokshadham, winds past the railway station through Dattawadi and Pendse Colony, and then goes straight on to Nandi Talkies. Most students and teachers took this route to school. Pawar from the Tiloda building came along with me till last year, but has left school since. In any case, these days, I prefer to walk alone.

In the month of Shravan, the skies are a lovely blue, scattered with white clouds, and the fields are drenched in warm yellow sunshine. Now, the rains are nearly over and the Ganapati festival, too, got over a few days back. The paddy fields are still water-logged and it gets quite muddy at times, but I prefer this route except when it pours really hard. I love the rain. It is fun walking barefoot through the slushy fields. The air is cool and crisp, you can hear frogs croaking in the fields, and the sweet smell of ice-candy tells you that the paddy crop is ripe and ready.

These fields belong to Shankar Bhoir of Tenth Standard. During the planting season, the entire family, including Shankar, is out in the fields. His father knows me and greets me with a cheery 'So, off to school, are you?' Sometimes, he plucks a few young ears of paddy and shows me how to eat the milky grain without hurting my tongue.

In the afternoon, the fields are empty except for Shankar's father and a few egrets. The faint, sweet smell of ripening rice wafts in with the breeze. How happy and contented the fields look in the mellow sunlight—like a painting. I have a favourite spot, a rock on the way down from the road, from where I sit and watch the fields. I can sit here for hours! And then I think of Shirodkar. Of course, I think of her all the time; morning, evening, at school, at home, everywhere! But all the more when I see these green and yellow paddy fields… And then I'm left with an aching feeling of emptiness in the pit of my stomach.

School begins at 12:40, but I usually leave home by eleven. It takes only thirteen minutes to reach school, but we—Chitre, Phawdya, Surya and I—get together for our adda at Surya's place en route. Of course, Aaisaheb and Ambabai do not know this. Ambabai is already in college by the time I leave for school; Aaisaheb doesn't have a clue anyway. The one time Aaisaheb asked me, I had a readymade excuse: that Takalkar sir helped us with difficult sums in maths either in the morning or in free periods. This was true, except I never attended his classes! And if that wasn't convincing, there's always the excuse of band practice, which takes place an hour before school. In any case, my leaving early suits Aaisaheb because she can catch up with her friends before Ambabai returns from college.

Surya's father is building this new place, conveniently enough for us. The construction began in May. By the time school reopened, the first slab had been laid; that's when we began to have our adda there. Once we were nearly caught by Surya's father. Thankfully, we saw him coming and quickly pretended to be busy studying Maths. 'Don't you have school today?' he growled at Surya.

'Yes. We are doing Maths.'

Chitre added, 'We don't have a place to sit, so we thought we'd stop by here for some time.'

Our legs were trembling with fear. Surya's father, a tall and well-built man with perennially bloodshot eyes, can be quite a terror. He thrashes Surya every now and then. Surya does not fear anyone in the world except him. He has gifted an acre of land to our school, hence even Appa, our otherwise strict Principal, always gets up from the chair reverently, saying, 'Come, come, Mhatre sheth.'

Somehow our excuse worked and he merely rolled his eyes, saying, 'Oh, studying, is it? Good, good. I'll have a proper room made for you here, with tiles and all, okay?'

'Not here,' piped up Surya. 'The room above this.'

'The one above?'

'Yes, it is too noisy here, with people coming and going all the time.'

'But you guys had better study hard, okay? If I ever find you wasting time, I'll break your legs!'

Soon, the next slab was laid; walls and tiles followed. Surya brought a dhurrie. We have our adda in the room upstairs, but we ensure that we spread out our books as an alibi first. The walls are sprayed with water, so the rooms are always cool and fresh and smell of cement.

The construction workers live in shacks behind the building. We often see a dark-complexioned woman feeding her child out in the open. Sometimes she doesn't even bother to button up her blouse properly afterwards. We just smile at each other then.

From our room upstairs, we have a clear view of the road to school that comes straight from Mokshadham. No one from the main road can see us, but we can see everyone clearly. Phawdya and Surya stand by the window, commenting on the girls passing by, each of whom they have a nickname for. Bibikar and Shembe wanted to join us but we refused. Bibikar is a scaredy cat, and Shembekar a dimwit who gets thrashed by each and every teacher. Who would want such boys around?

The passers-by know that there is someone up there who makes wisecracks, but we are careful not to get caught. Once Phawdya called Randive sir 'Prem Chopra'. Randive sir stopped in his tracks and shouted, 'Do you want me to come up there?' as we stood stock-still, peeping through the holes in the wall where the bamboo poles are placed. He finally left after what seemed like an eternity, turning around and glancing upwards several times.

'Phawdya, why can't you just shut up, bhenchod?' Surya had shouted. 'We'd have been screwed if he had come up here. We wouldn't be able to sit here ever again!'

Ever since, we decided not to tease the teachers. Earlier, Surya and Phawdya would tease each and every girl too, but not anymore. We just sit there and have mindless conversations, resting our backs against the walls. And of course, I wait for Shirodkar.

That morning, I reached our adda to find Chitre sitting against the wall, fiddling with an old torch. His bag lay near him; a couple of battery cells and a few lengths of wire with clips were strewn on the floor. Chitre arrives as early as nine o'clock sometimes! Both his parents work. They leave home early and return late in the evening. There is a maid called Devaki who is supposed to look after them, but all she does is sleep. Chitre's younger brother Raju leaves for school early in the morning, after which Chitre is free to do whatever he wants. Whenever Raju has a holiday, though, we are in trouble, because he follows us around like a pet dog, asking inane questions from time to time. He is a pain in the ass!

Chitre tells us that his mom and dad often quarrel in the evenings, but I think his mother is a gem. Her fair, soft midriff peeps out through her saree; Surya loves to gawk at it. We get to eat cakes in their house. She always asks us to stay back and play. But what can we play indoors? And then there is also the fear of that Raju trailing us once he sees us!

'What are you up to?' I asked Chitre, hanging up my bag on one of the bamboo poles jutting out of the wall.

'Experiment.'

'What about?'

'Arre, I'm trying to create a torch that works both ways.'

'Both ways?'

'Yes. It'll light up on this side when I push the button that way and then on that side when I push it this way,' explained Chitre.

It was beyond me, so I kept quiet. Chitre is always up to some experiment or the other. I know him since Fifth Standard. He loves to try out stuff not mentioned in our textbooks, and always manages to get the first prize in the science exhibition at school. Even the kids tease him, calling him 'shyntist' in their Marathi accent! Last year he stole some sulphuric acid, poured it into a fused bulb, added copper sulphate and heated up the mixture. The bulb exploded with a loud bang, singeing his hand, and an acrid smell spread all over, but that hardly deterred our ever-curious Chitre. In fact, he went and asked Manjrekar sir why the mixture exploded!

'Hasn't Surya come in yet?' I asked.

'No.'

'Phawdya?'

'No.'

Phawdya (his two front teeth stick out like a spade, a phawda, hence the nickname!) would be late for sure. His father passed away when he was very young, and his mother runs a vegetable shop. Phawdya helps his mother buy vegetables at the mandi every morning, cleans them while his mother prepares lunch, and then comes running all the way. In the evenings, he minds the shop. We hang around too, sometimes, watching the women bend down to select the vegetables. Surya says Phawdya is a lucky scoundrel who gets to see melons every day! His mother frets if we crowd around Phawdya, but Surya soothes her saying, 'We won't disturb him, mavshi. We're here to keep an eye on the melons and other vegetables!' How we all laugh then! But of course the pun is lost on her.

Phawdya's mother is a simple soul. She feeds us local

figs and seasonal fruits. She has a straight green line across her forehead. Phawdya says when his father was alive she would put sindoor in it, though Chitre, with his scientific mind, wonders how the sindoor could ever stay put in a horizontal line!

Phawdya hates selling vegetables. His passion is cricket. He is the best fast bowler in school. Chitre and Phawdya are the kings of the game. If Chitre decides to stay put, no one can bowl him out. Last year we defeated Tope High School and Subhash Vidyalaya in the inter-school cricket tournament. We lost to the South Indian School in the finals, though. They had a prejudiced umpire!

Surya *has* to be in the team each time, irrespective of his skills. His dadagiri comes in handy, especially when playing against other teams in town. They can't leave me out so I usually stand behind the wicket-keeper as I have butter fingers! If Chitre and Phawdya play their natural game, we have nothing to worry about. But last year we lost to Ninth-A. A boy called Aire bowled out Chitre on the very first ball! Had it been some other team, Surya would have created a ruckus calling it a 'trial ball', but it was our own school, so we had to eat the humble pie.

Surya is the next one to join the adda. (His real name is Suresh, but no one calls him that.) He wears the tightest pants, and his biceps bulge with all the exercise he does each day. On the very first day of school, Zende sir had taken one look at his pants and quipped, 'You may as well not wear anything!' Surya ignored the taunt. He loves to buff his hair and gives it a quick brush with his comb when no one is watching. He doesn't carry a school bag; he just ties his books together with a thick rubber band.

Most boys in our school carry their books around in this fashion. I wanted to, as well, but Ambabai made a bag for me after she learnt some stitching. It is quite nice actually, and many teachers have asked me about the design. Only I don't like it at all. Some of the boys know how to twirl a notebook on their forefinger. All of Surya's books have a small hole in the centre. He can spin the books for nearly ten minutes at times on the tip of a divider.

'Ichibhana, what are you up to?' Surya drawled, entering the room. Ichibhana is Surya's favourite term of endearment. No one knows what it means, but people in the villages around here use it all the time.

'Some experiment,' I explained.

'I am trying to make a torch which burns at both ends,' elaborated Chitre.

'Torch? Ichibhana, can you feel the current? Come, I will show you how to get some current!'

Surya is always up to some prank or the other. He is a little crazy, and raring to pick up a fight with anyone in the classroom. There are other guys like Dashrath Bhoir the six-footer, whom Surya never tries to mess with. They are distantly related to each other too. Surya's cousin Harishchandra is also in our class. A quiet fellow, he does not interfere in anyone's work and merely smiles if you tease him. He never gets angry. But last year, when some of the boys from Sonarpada came to beat up Surya, one shout from Harishchandra was enough to stop them in their tracks. If any outsider challenges any one of us, our entire gang comes together. Hence, even a wimp like Sadu Kale can afford to strut around like a dada.

'Hasn't Phawdya come in yet?' Surya asked.

'No. Must be busy cleaning the vegetables,' I said.

'Is Barve ma'am likely to come in today?'

'God only knows!'

It had been a week since Barve ma'am had come to school. We were not sure why. The daily Hindi class was thus a free period for us. But since it was the second period, we were not allowed to go out. If only it had been after the mid-break, we could have gone out into the playground. Some teacher or the other substituted her class.

'I hope Bendre ma'am does not come in that period,' Surya said.

'I am doomed if she does,' Chitre said.

'Ichibhana, she doesn't get married and tortures us!'

No one likes Bendre ma'am. She's unmarried and a terror. Her tongue lashes out like a whip. And, of all subjects, she teaches English! All are scared to attend her class. Phawdya says it is because of the collective curse of all the students that she's still unmarried. She insists that we speak in English in her class. I'm fine with that. Naru mama has taught me good English and in fact, I'm the one who answers most of her questions. But that does not make me her favourite student. She does not like anyone in our class!

Phawdya walked in just then, lumbering noisily up the steps.

'Why are you late?'

'The rotis took some time,' he said, trying to catch his breath.

'Come, sit here,' I said.

'I saw Paranjpe ma'am.'

'Where?'

'Near the station. She was coming this way.'

'Was she alone?' Surya asked.

'Yes.'

'Come on! That's not possible. That Zende must be somewhere close by. Are you sure?'

'Yes. She was alone. I overtook her on the way. I suppose she came in a little early today.'

'Sleeveless?'

'No. No sleeveless blouse today.'

It is Surya's firm belief that Zende sir and Paranjpe ma'am are having an affair because they walk down together from the railway station. Paranjpe ma'am comes from Bhandup and Zende sir comes in from Ghatkopar. Ma'am said that she comes by the 11:20 local. I had asked her whether Zende sir came by the same train. She was a little surprised and said, 'Yes, there is no other train at that time. We both come by the same train.' Ever since, Surya has triumphantly concluded that they are having an affair.

Surya is always scouting for such alliances. The most well-known affair is Sathe-Mohite's. Sathe ma'am and Mohite sir have been around for years and years. They teach all subjects; though we are not being taught any subject by them this year. A junior college for the Eleventh and Twelfth Standards had been opened in our school premises. Those classes are held in the morning and all the senior teachers, including Sathe and Mohite, teach them. The Sathe-Mohite episode is quite notorious, and known to all outside our school too. Our school is called 'Sukhdev Namdev Warhadkar Madhyamik Vidyalaya' or in short, 'Warhadkar High School', but the children from other schools have nicknamed ours 'Sathe-Mohite School'. Just as we call Tope High School the 'Dighe-Pandit School'!

Surya believes that all ma'ams and sirs are up to something and, if not, there ought to be something to make them have an affair. Last Sunday, he wrote in bold letters on the blackboard outside school: 'Paranjpe-Zende Shubh Vivah'. Everyone saw it and Ganoba, the watchman, had to hurriedly wipe it off. Surya is confident that if he writes this every day, it will result in them actually having an affair some day!

The school children were trickling in now. I moved closer to the window. As usual, the first ones to arrive were those silly Achrekar and Deshpande girls. They stay in the same chawl, share the same bench, spend their mid-break together under the neem tree and whisper animatedly to each other all the time, oblivious to all else. No one disturbs them; not even the teachers bother to ask them any questions.

The sun shone brightly now. There is a flat stretch between Mokshadham and Surya's building. My earlier school, the one up to seventh standard, was on the other side of Mokshadham. How scared we were of that place then! The road skirts its tall walls and the smell of burnt flesh permeates the air once in a while. From time to time, you can see a procession carrying a dead body to Mokshadham. We would stand on one side, allowing the funeral procession to proceed.

There is a jhopadpatti right next to Mokshadham where children shit out in the open. A few shacks have come up along the way. Santu from our class stays there. His sister

Sundri too is in our class. Santu is a good bowler. He often plays with us, but the girls do not talk to Sundri much. She sits alone on the last bench.

'Surya, what time is it?' Phawdya asked.

'*Bara ku dus kum*,' Surya said in his Bombaiya dialect, looking at his watch. 'Ten minutes to twelve.'

Only a select few, other than Patil, have a wrist watch. Chitre could have easily got one, but he never felt the need for it. Aaisaheb has promised to get me one once I move into the next class. Of course, Baba's old Favre Leuba has been lying idle ever since he bought a new Henri Sandoz, but we have such strange rules at home and so I wouldn't be given a watch of my own till I get to Tenth Standard!

The eighth standard girls arrived in a group next. They normally arrive early. I don't know most of them, except for one Pangarkar from our neighbourhood. Anyway, they are way too young for us, so we do not bother them much. We were all waiting for Kevda, especially Surya.

The road was now crowded with girls in blue skirts and boys in brown pants. Surya and Phawdya stood waiting near the other window, hidden from outside view. Chitre was busy, as usual, fiddling with his experiment.

We spotted Sakhardande from Tenth Standard. She walked alone today.

'Look at the way she struts!' Surya said.

'Why don't you whistle?' Phawdya suggested.

Surya promptly put two fingers into his mouth and let out a loud *phityooo phitttt*. We all moved back instantly because we knew that Sakhardande would look up the moment she heard the whistle. She did look up but could not see anyone. She merely smiled and continued walking.

'Saw how she smiled? Bhenchod!' Surya muttered.

'She's real clever.' Phawdya agreed.

'Look at the way she juts out her tits!' Surya exclaimed.

When Sakhardande was canvassing for the post of Student Representative, she had come to our class for a speech. Sawant from Tenth-D was another aspirant, as was Deshpande from Ninth-A. Everyone knew that Sakhardande was a carefree girl, but we were surprised to see her in our class. Rajguru sir was teaching us when she came in asking for permission to speak. She came up to us and announced, 'There is no reason why boys cannot vote for girls. If I win I will ensure that the playgrounds are utilized well. I will get bats and balls for each class.'

'Oh we all have bats all right!' Phawdya said loudly.

The entire class was in splits. The joke was lost on the stupid girls, who kept asking, 'What happened? Why are they laughing?' Shrewd Sakhardande understood the pun, but chose not to react. The girls may have voted for her, but we all voted for Sawant. Deshpande is from our grade and was hoping he would get the support of the ninth and eighth graders, but he is too arrogant. No one would vote for him. Sawant won the election. Sakhardande wasn't too perturbed when she lost the election, and continues to strut around jutting out her boobs as before.

Manjrekar sir came in, holding his bicycle in his hands. Rajguru sir and Borhade ma'am walked along with him. We let them pass without making any comment. Bibikar came by. He knows we sit up here. He looked up and let out a shrill whistle. Surya replied with a whistle. Prem Chopra walked past, followed by Ghasu Gokhale. Ghasu has an irritating habit. He often waits near the walls of Mokshadham for some teacher or the other to come by so that he can show off by walking along with them.

The girls were streaming in continuously by now. Kevda came in. Kevda is the Gupte girl from eighth standard. She joined school this year and the entire school wants to hook up with her. She's slim and tall and wears flowers in her hair each day, and also a leaf of fragrant kevda; hence the nickname. Surya fell for her on day one, but doesn't know how to progress further. Earlier he used to wait by the roadside and stare openly at her. But we were worried that she'd complain to her father, or at school, and get us all into trouble. So now Surya contents himself with shouting 'Kevda, Kevda' from the window. I told him what Naru mama had advised; that you should never tease a girl in this fashion. It would only upset her and then you can forget about wooing her. Naru mama gives me such tips which I pass on to these guys. I don't tease the girls or call them names. I just sit there, restless and helpless.

'Chitre, look, your jaatwaali is coming this way!'

'Let her,' Chitre said. 'I am not interested.'

'You may not be, but we are!' Surya said. 'Saale, why don't you introduce us to her? I'm sure you'll have some connection in common.'

Surya's guess was right. Chitre had told me once that Gupte's mother goes to the same mandal as his. Their family had visited Chitre once, but he stupidly hid inside a room and never came out. Of course, we haven't told Surya this lest he rag Chitre to death.

'How the hell do I win her over?' Surya wailed, looking at her. 'What should I do?'

We said nothing. There was no point.

Sukdi and Bakre followed Kevda.

'Joshi, Sukdi is here,' alerted Surya.

'Is she?' I asked. I saw her coming our way. I allowed her to come as close as possible and then, stepping back a bit, shouted, 'Ae Mahesssshhhh!'

Sukdi is four or five years elder to us. She joined our school when she was in seventh standard. She was probably in Tope High School earlier, and before that in Subhash Vidyalaya, close to her home. She was thrown out of various schools as she kept flunking and has now landed in our school. She has been having an affair with Mahesh Sutar for many years. One would think they've been together since birth! Mahesh often visits our school on his Speedking bicycle and they both talk to each other without a care of those around. Sukdi's affair is known to everyone, including the sirs and ma'ams, even Appa. We often tease her, especially me, but she never gets ruffled. She's very gentle.

The girls in our class do not let go of any opportunity to tease the boys, but not Sukdi. She's the tallest in the class and sits alone. She has a sweet voice, and is often asked to sing in free periods and in all our school programmes. Mahesh has been beaten up by our boys a few times. Once when Surya was beating him up, Sukdi intervened and held his hand to stop him. Surya was too dumbfounded to react. Ever since, everyone has accepted their affair and no one troubles them now. Mahesh has a hardware shop in the market. He sits there the whole day.

They both roam around the town and go together to the movies sometimes.

Sukdi did not react to my catcall and continued walking along with 'shorty' Bakre, royally ignoring us.

Kendalkar sir followed them. We saw him and fell silent. He is our supervisor and although Appa is the Principal, it is Kendalkar sir who runs the show. Appa is strict but doesn't shout at anyone. The whole school calls him Appa though his full name is Appasaheb Ramchandra Tuljapurkar. That's not the case with Kendalkar sir, though. He is one of the seniormost teachers in the school, and no one dare speak in his presence. Once he starts thrashing someone he loses all control. He used to stay in Kanhe village earlier and is familiar with the locals. People like Surya's father like him a lot. Last year, one of Surya's distant cousins was thrashed by Kendalkar sir for throwing ink on Halbe sir's shirt. He was half-dead at the end of it but Surya's uncle remarked, 'You should have broken his hand so that he would dare not repeat such a prank.'

It is good that Kendalkar sir is not teaching us anything this year. He can teach any subject—Maths, Physics, whatever. We have to be very alert in his class. He would suddenly spring a question on one of us; if you didn't answer, he would drawl, 'Where's your mind, you rascal?' and then pound you on the back with his fists. He should have retired long back, but god knows when he actually will. We all eagerly await that day. He has six or seven students who go to his house for tuition, free of cost. If the student is weak in Maths the parents send him there. But the very thought of going to Kendalkar's house is enough to make anyone an expert in Maths!

I spotted Shirodkar from a distance. My heart was pounding loudly and there was that familiar feeling of emptiness in the pit of my stomach. I looked around; Chitre was fiddling with his 'battery experiment' and Surya and Phawdya were busy helping him. I peeped out to see Shirodkar walking down with Kanvinde and Watve. I knew the guys would pass some comment or the other seeing them. If I objected, that would be enough to create suspicion. I would be dead then!

I quickly tried to distract them before they could spot the girls.

'Hey guys, have you finished Bendre ma'am's homework?'

'Homework?' Surya asked, a little surprised. 'Ichibhana, did she give us some homework?'

'Of course! She had given us some words for which we had to write the synonyms.'

'Oh god I'm dead! Joshi, have you finished it? Give me your notebook.'

I gave him my notebook. I could now go and sit at the window undisturbed. Chitre had done his homework, but he sat there comparing his notebook with mine. Surya and Phawdya had obviously not done anything and were busy copying from my notebook. The words were not difficult. I had to refer to the dictionary twice for words like 'gallant' and 'penetrate'. The rest were quite easy. It was from a chapter on Robin Hood. I had got Naru mama to explain the story to me when he had last visited us.

Shirodkar had reached the foot of the building while the boys were busy copying. As usual, she sported a bunch of aboli flowers in her hair. Ambabai says the flowers are called kanakambaram in south India and firecracker in

English. She loves to wear these flowers but is unable to find them. I wonder where Shirodkar gets them from! She has curly hair, which creates a sort of nice pattern around her face; just the way the hair falls on my mother's face.

I held my breath while she passed by. It was good that I was sitting down because I felt weak in my knees. It felt good though! A great start to the day.

'Anyone passing by?' Surya asked, looking in my direction.

'No one we know; some tenth standard girls,' I replied.

'Any good-looking chick to ogle at?' he asked.

'No. You finish your work. And remember the correct pronunciation. It is 'forest' and not 'faarisht', okay?'

Shirodkar had left. There was no point in sitting there any more. Most of the children from our class had gone by now.

We ran down the steps to the rear. We never walk out of the entrance on the main road lest we get caught. We exit from the rear, circling the school to reach the back gate. We spotted the labourer woman getting ready to suckle her child and Surya wanted to ask her to finish before we left, so we would not miss anything! The fence behind our school has been bent low by the boys from Kanhe village. It is convenient to reach class that way.

Earlier, it was okay to reach school after the assembly had begun. But, ever since the Emergency was declared, there is a lot of stress on discipline, and we are forced to attend the assembly. These days, if you arrive late, you will not be allowed to attend classes. What's more, you will have to bear some caning on your palm. And to add insult to injury, they are administered by Appa himself in his office. He would chant, while caning the students, 'Should you not come on time, huh? Should you not come on time?' We take care to arrive well in time, but we too have tasted the spanking once. Earlier there was just a single prayer in the assembly followed by '*Jana Gana Mana*', and we were done. But now we are forced to sing '*Hum Honge Kamyaab*'. It was fun initially, but now we find it boring. Luckily we sing just the first stanza. If we sang the whole song we would never be kamyaab! School authorities now ask us to sing such songs even in the P.T. period! There are no such rules in Tope High School. Nana of Subhash Vidyalaya, in any case, supports the opposition party. I wonder why Appa is enamoured of all these things.

We scampered up the steps and reached the classroom just as Paranjpe ma'am entered. The prayers began, and I got busy watching Shirodkar. I had a clear view of her face—the yellow ribbons, the flowers in her hair, and those earrings. That's one good thing about the prayer assembly; everyone looks straight ahead, allowing me to stare freely at her. The boys in the row ahead act as a shield, thus preventing any ma'am from catching me staring at Shirodkar! The dumb girls in my class sing '*Hum Honge Kamyaab*' so earnestly. God only knows what inspires them so. The boys, of course, shuffle about restlessly. Bibikar tries to act smart at times, mumbling 'umm, umm' a tad too loudly. A piercing stare from ma'am is enough to shut him up, though.

The classrooms in our school are built in a row, like the bogies of a train. Our classroom has two doors; one in the front and the other at the rear. A few steps lead us directly to the playground.

I sit at the back of the classroom, near the door. Desai sits next to me while Surya and Phawdya occupy the bench behind. Desai is a simple soul. He never utters a word, sits quietly in all the classes and copies whatever the teachers say in the class. Chitre was my neighbour earlier and would chat away all day. Paranjpe ma'am noticed that and moved him to the front bench, asking Desai to sit beside me. It turned out to be a blessing in disguise; I can now stare at Shirodkar unhindered.

I get a good view of the playground from where I sit. No other school has such a huge playground. Tope High School has a large one, but it is on hire for plays on most days. Ours is twice their size thanks to the largesse of donors like Surya's father. Our Appa is a smart fellow; he got the local villagers to contribute a lot of land free of cost when he built the school. He also managed to get them to build the fence.

There are toilets at both ends of the ground; one for boys and another one for girls. There are no separate ones for the teachers. Anyone using the toilet has to cross the playground, giving the person sitting at the door a clear view. In one of his classes last year, we asked Zende sir the meaning of the word 'vulgar'. He said 'vulgar' meant having to go to the toilet in full view of the school! Since then we have a code for peeing; we say, 'Let's do the vulgar thing!'

When it rains, there is green grass everywhere in the playground. The grass grows coarse and dry within a few weeks, but it is still fun to watch the field. Our school is on the outskirts of the town, in Kanhe village, hence there are no houses on this side. You can see the tiled roofs of Umbarpada in the distance. The paddy fields begin where the playground ends. The hills of Sonarpada are visible in the distance on a clear day. Surya tells me that the local fair is held in the month of May there. The road on the left leads to Nana's jungle while the one on the right leads to paddy fields belonging to Surya's cousins. If you cross over you reach the Mohpada bay where Surya's father has his business of sand-digging. We all plan to visit the place one day.

I spend most of my time in school either watching Shirodkar or looking outside at the playground. On a sunny day, the sky looks like a steel plate reflecting the sunlight onto the mountains, the grass and the trees. There is a sort of warm silence when school begins in the afternoon. I divide my time looking at Shirodkar and at the sights outside, ensuring that the teachers do not catch me. If they look at me I just stare ahead at the blackboard. I have realized that no one bothers you if you stare ahead vacantly. And I have learnt the art of stealing glances at Shirodkar while looking straight ahead. To be honest, I don't need to look at her to see her at all; she's visible to me wherever I look, whether I look out into the playground or when I close my eyes.

Paranjpe ma'am took the attendance and began the lessons. She's our class teacher and hence takes the first period. The Marathi period is a good way to begin the day. She's a good teacher and gets into form, especially when explaining poems. She loves to give extra information. She begins by saying, 'Children, do you know...?' She has a habit of glancing at the front door from time to time while teaching. Surya, ever alert for such things, is of the firm belief that she's on the lookout for Zende sir! He is such an idiot!

No one creates any trouble in the Marathi period. School would have just begun and the boys are silent; the girls too. Shirodkar listens to the teacher with her face resting on one palm. She does not look anywhere else. She sits in the third row. Sometimes she talks to Sarwate sitting next to her. If she turns back, she will find me staring at her. But she rarely turns towards the boys' side.

The girls and boys in our school do not talk to each other. It is like a crime to be seen talking to the other sex. One might be torn to pieces for doing so. The girls never take the initiative, but then neither do the boys. All we do is pass snide remarks. Girls like Sukdi can retort without a care, but she is a rarity. The other girls keep to themselves. They cover their mouths with their handkerchiefs and giggle if the boys crack a good joke. They cover their mouths even while talking to each other.

Shirodkar never tries to act smart. Kulkarni and Dongre sit on the bench ahead of her. Rege and Mirikar sit on the first bench. We call the four of them 'birdies'; they chatter the whole day. They love to fight over petty things with the boys. Shirodkar joined our class last year, but I don't remember the bench on which she used to sit then. She was in the dance group last year, but in the last row. The 'birdies' are short and are always in the first row for the dance.

Ma'am asked a few questions on the lesson. I knew all the answers but did not raise my hand; I have decided there is no point in showing off. Some boys and girls love to answer; especially people like Bibikar, Ghasu Gokhale, Teredesai amongst boys, and the four birdies who are constantly raising their hands shouting, 'Me, Ma'am!', 'Me, Ma'am!' They are in ninth standard but behave like fifth standard juveniles, clamouring for the teacher's attention.

Barve ma'am did not turn up today for the second consecutive day. I don't know what is wrong with her. I attend her classes diligently. After all, Hindi is one subject which everyone understands well. You can do whatever you want in Barve ma'am's class as long as you don't speak and disturb the others. Usually, we finish our pending homework in it. Bendre's class after hers. But you can even read novels sitting right on the first bench! Like Surve on the second bench in the corner. He is a bright fellow but lives in his own world of detective fiction. He carries old novels with exotic names like *Kala Pahaad, Jhunzaar, Dhurandhar*, etc. in his bag all the time. He has even lent me a few once.

We were hoping to have Barve ma'am's period off, but Manjrekar sir came in. We requested him to give us a break, but he decided to teach Social Science with an excuse that we could finish off the syllabus. Manjrekar sir is our hero. In Surya's words, he is a 'bindaas' character. He is the only one who tucks his shirt in and buttons up his sleeves, wears a steel bracelet and has long hair that falls over his forehead. He is unmarried and a jolly good fellow. He loves theatre and even directed a play for us last year. When he is in a good mood, he recites the dialogues from his plays. He speaks his mind and says he lands up in many an argument in the staff room thanks to his outspoken nature. But he is a first class M.A. B.Ed, so no one can challenge him.

He teaches us SS, that is, Social Science, which includes History, Geography and Civics. But he does not take History—that's Pethkar ma'am's subject. He should have, in fact, taught us History. For that matter, he should have taught us everything. Alas, our school administration has a policy of giving the tough subjects to boring teachers and easy subjects to good teachers.

Manjrekar sir believes that History, Geography and Civics are the most important subjects, and that all students should be taught just these subjects. He says language is learnt naturally and the other subjects are not worth learning. Earlier, he would express such thoughts freely. But blabbermouths like Ghasu Gokhale conveyed this to the other teachers, who in turn complained to Appa, and Manjrekar sir has been careful ever since.

The next class was Bendre Ma'am's. The children were happy in Manjrekar sir's class despite the fact that he sometimes uses difficult words. But now there was pin-drop silence. The moment ma'am entered, she wanted to know if there was anyone who had not done the homework. Lucky for Surya and Phawdya, who were reminded by me in time! But Dashrath, Harishchandra, Santu, Bhaishetye and a few others were caught. As usual Sundri was the one amongst girls.

Ma'am asked Bibikar to fetch his thick wooden ruler. I have told him a thousand times not to bring that thing, but that fellow does it just to impress the teachers. She rapped each of the offenders on their hands twice. Sundri got an extra one on her arm for not oiling her hair. They stood there silently bearing the punishment. Dashrath could have easily gripped the ruler in his hands and not let go. She could have done nothing! But he too silently bore the punishment. The poor souls were lucky Ma'am did not insist on keeping their hand on the desk and hitting them with the thin side of the ruler.

She then checked the notebooks. Ghasu Gokhale the smartie had written ten extra words, over and above the ones given by her.

'Who asked you to be oversmart, huh?' she shouted. 'You want to show off ...?'

Gokhale made a sour face and went back to his bench. She did not say anything to Phawdya but caught hold of Surya. 'Have you written this yourself or copied from someone else's notebook?'

'No, ma'am. I did the work myself.' Surya pleaded.

'Really? Tell me, what does "gallant" mean?'

Surya was in trouble. She asked the meaning of a few more words, but Surya was tongue-tied. She took out the wooden ruler screaming, 'How dare you lie to me?' Surya got a couple of raps on his arm and screamed out loud, though he was not really hurt. He went back to his seat rubbing his arm.

Bendre ma'am began her class. She began conversing with us in English. The whole class was silent. I could follow a little better than most but for the rest, it was beyond comprehension. All of us sat there like mice, scared to death. It was sunny outside. The playground was baking in the bright sunlight. There were no fans in our classroom and it was hot and stuffy inside.

I was busy watching Shirodkar, oblivious to the class, the

teacher and all else. She sat there with her eyes focused on the blackboard as she listened in rapt attention. I realized her hair was not jet-black but slightly brown. The flowers set off their brownness. And it blew gently in the air. No other girl has hair like hers. The birdies oil their hair so much it looks all wet and greasy. Even Ambabai does that. They do not realize how foolish they look with such oily hair. Shirodkar is wise. She must have a wise mother, I guess.

I do not know her exact address. I know she stays somewhere in the direction of Sathewadi, which means her house is quite far. I realized Misal too stays that side of the town. He surely knows where her house is. I need to find out discreetly. I cannot afford to be direct in such matters; the boys would rag me to death. Shirodkar has been with us since last year, but I had not noticed her earlier. We normally know the addresses of most of the boys. I don't know whether she has any siblings; probably none. I need to find out from Misal.

I turned gently to find Misal sitting on the third bench next to Gaitonde. Both of them are quite dim-witted. We never mingle with them; being friends with them is out of the question. But I will be able to extract some information out of him.

The next class was Maths. Halbe sir, though absent-minded, is good-humoured and does not shout at us. He starts teaching the moment he enters, and doesn't stop to check whether we understand or not. So we are in a fix. I heard someone say that of all the subjects, Maths of ninth standard, in the run-up to tenth standard, is the toughest. Only Bibikar, Ghasu Gokhale and a few others understand the subject well enough. I can, if I try, but I don't feel up to it most of the time. Chitre too is good at it. He, in fact, likes it. He is usually busy copying everything diligently. So the responsibility of teaching Surya and Phawdya lies with him. But that doesn't always help. Algebra and Geometry are such topics that everyone flounders.

To put it in the language of set theory, which we were taught in Maths class last year, our class can be divided into three sets. The first set is that of intelligent and oversmart boys. There are around five or seven such boys, like Bibikar, Ghasu Gokhale, Surve and Teredesai. The other set consists of us—our gang, and boys like Dashrath, Harishchandra, Santya, and so on. There are some like Chitre who could have, in fact, been part of the first set. The third set comprises the general crowd who are neither in set one nor set two—people like Shembekar, Gaitonde, Misal, Memane, Khandagle, Sadu and so on. They are the biggest set. They are there to fill the classrooms. Their presence or absence makes no difference, but they are needed for a school to run. There are such groups in every school.

The girls too have such sets amongst them. The birdies and a few others form one set. They think they are smart but are such idiots. Then Sukdi, Rairikar and few form another set: the chalu girls. There are not many in that set of girls. I mentioned this to Chitre once but he said that you never know how many belong to that set in reality. Then there are the rest who form the general set—to fill the classrooms. All the dumb and stupid girls are in this set. Shirodkar, quite obviously, is not part of any of these sets.

She forms an independent set of her own. Singleton. Just like me. I wonder when our sets would, if ever, intersect.

It was time for mid-break after the Maths class.

We ran to drink water and then did the 'vulgar' task. We do it quickly. No one bothers to waste time on such activities. We eat at home before coming to school, hence there is no need to carry a lunchbox. But a few boys, like Gaitonde and Ghasu Gokhale, carry tiffin boxes. They huddle together in one corner and eat. The birdies too bring lunch. Stupid people like them waste the entire mid-break eating. Ambabai insists that I carry lunch every day but do I care? Sometimes I carry peanuts in my pocket; they are good to munch on when I get bored in the fourth period.

We sit in the shade of the woods during the mid-break. That's one remarkable thing about our school. The woods are literally a mini-forest. It belongs to Surya's kaka, hence no one can ask us to leave. We allow Dashrath, Santu, Bhaishetye and such boys to come there. We sit on the big branch of a tree that bends down low, almost touching the ground, before it curves up again. In summer, it is full of a kind of sticky fruit. There are other trees too. Surya can identify all of them. There are many like palash, hirda, jamun, etc. There is a mango tree, but it never bears fruit. But the trees provide a cool shade, however hot it may be outside. There are huge rocks over there and we have enough places for everyone to sit. The paddy fields skirt the wooded area, but I don't quite enjoy looking at them from there.

'Joshi, let us go and have some ice-candy.' Surya said, after drinking water. 'It is so hot today.'

'No, you carry on.'

'Come on, bhenchod. Why are you acting pricey? Chitre, come on.'

Surya has money in his pocket at all times, and is always buying something or the other. Whenever Phawdya mans his vegetable shop in the evening, he manages to snitch a few coins. Chitre's parents give him pocket money. I am the only one who never has any. The ice-candy costs five paise; the milk bar is for ten. But my parents do not give me any pocket money. It's very embarrassing. To add insult to injury, Ambabai keeps harping, 'Your friends treat you every day. One day they'll ask you to treat them at a good restaurant. What will you do then? Never take such favours, okay?' But Surya does not appreciate this logic. He drags me while Chitre and Phawdya follow.

The ice-candy seller comes in the afternoon. We hear his bell in the fourth period. Earlier he would come right into the playground, but Appa drove him away. Now he stands below the tamarind tree outside the gate. Then there is an old lady there, who sells berries and guavas. A few days back, a lady came selling some batata wadas, which she carried in a steel box. She met Appa first, asking for permission to sit in the school verandah, but Appa promptly refused. She then sat below the tamarind tree for two days. Her petticoat, peeping out of her saree, was frayed at the edges. Surya started his usual nonsense, asking her, 'Your wadas seem nice. Are they hot?' She caught Surya's pun but replied coolly, 'Son, I have children of your age. They go to school too. I sell these to earn some money for their books.' That shut him up. He treated us to the wadas. She was there for a couple of days but could not sell much. We did not see her later.

We cannot get the ice-candy to thc playground. We have to sit in the grove and eat.

'Chitre, you need to teach us Maths, okay?' Phawdya said, sucking on the ice-candy. 'Else we are doomed.'

'We need to do something about Bendre,' Surya muttered. 'Worse, she does not seem to be getting married any soon.'

'Who'll marry her?' Chitre asked. 'Anybody would run away seeing her face.'

'What about her big boobs?' Surya remarked. 'Isn't that reason enough?'

We sat there in the cool shade of the woods, enjoying our ice-candy. There was a damp, greenish smell all around. We could hear someone chopping wood somewhere. Someone must be cutting the branches. I thought of Shirodkar and wondered what it would be like to sit here with her, all alone.

'How nice it is to sit here, isn't it?' Chitre remarked. 'It would be great if we could have our classes here.'

'You bet!' Surya said. 'We'd even understand everything then.'

An image formed in my mind. The rocks were large enough for our entire class to sit on and we could have the blackboard resting against the big tree trunk. We could sit in a large semi-circle, unlike the straight rows in the class. Shirodkar would be right across from me and catch me seeing her then!

'Joshi, Ichibhana, your ice-candy is dripping.'

That broke my reverie. The ice-candy had left a big stain on my shirt. I would have to wash it off before reaching home or hear a mouthful from Aaisaheb.

'Surya, when shall we visit the bay?' I asked.

'Anytime. Shall we go now?'

'No. Not today. But we should visit soon.'

'Whenever you say.'

We saw Bhaishetye coming towards us sucking on his ice-candy. He has come to our school this year from some remote village in Konkan. He stays with his sister and calls her husband jijaji. 'My jijaji got transferred here, you know. So I had to come with them, you know.' He speaks in a typical Konkani sing-song accent, and did not quite seem our type, until the day he told us about Bhaween from his village. God, that was unbelievable! We were stunned to hear of her exploits. Surya could not believe his ears. We realized this fellow was far beyond his age. We stopped teasing him from that day onwards. We wouldn't have minded if he had joined us at our adda, but he is always running late. In fact, he just about manages to reach in time for the assembly every morning.

'Come!' Surya said, making space from him on the big rock.

Surya allowed Bhaishetye to lick his ice-candy and said, 'Ichibhana, Shetye, can anyone visit this Bhaween girl of yours?'

'Anyone,' Bhaishetye said, without looking at him. 'All she needs is a maund of rice.'

'Even boys like us?'

'In fact, she prefers boys like you. They don't last long, you know!'

'What fun, bhenchod,' Surya said loudly, jiggling his knees. 'Have you ever visited her?'

'Me?' Bhaishetye looked at all of us. Then he confessed,

'No. I could never dare. My mother would have broken my leg.'

No one said anything for a while. Surya broke the silence asking, 'Joshi, what's the next period?'

'Physics; followed by Biology, Drawing and PT.'

'Ichibhana, what the hell is this Physics all about? I cannot make head or tail of what that fellow teaches.'

'Me too,' Phawdya added. 'He simply drones on and on and on.'

We sat there for some more time. Our Physics teacher, Redkar sir, mumbles and lisps so much that we cannot understand anything he says. What's more, two lower teeth are missing from his mouth. When he reads out a formula or a theorem, it is total chaos. The other day, he was teaching some properties of liquids and gases, when Teredesai decided to play a prank. While explaining the property of gases, Redkar sir drew a big circle and another oval one, more like a balloon. Teredesai asked, innocently pointing to the elongated shape of the oval one, 'Sir, what does this look like?'

The whole class began to laugh as everyone knew he was referring to the shape of a condom. We expected Sir to get angry and give him a tight slap, but he bowled a googly.

'You'll understand it well when you grow up. If you don't, come to me.'

Teredesai did not know where to hide his face.

'Oh, we have Biology following Physics, is it?' Surya asked. 'At least ma'am will teach us something interesting.'

We have Potnis ma'am to teach us Biology. She's a simpleton. Her son is in the eighth standard. Her subject being Biology, the onus of teaching all the 'vulgar' stuff is on her. Guys like Surya just love that. In her very first class, ma'am was teaching classification of living organisms. She explained the difference between those with vertebrae and those without. She explained phylum protozoa. A snigger spread across the room. The girls started looking down at the floor. Potnis ma'am realized that something was amiss, but she continued, 'These were the first organisms to inhabit the Earth. Most of these organisms are microscopic in nature and are found in moist, damp soil. They are found in clusters.'

'And they have only one occupation the whole day', interjected Surya.

The whole class burst out laughing. The teacher was at a loss for words. She skipped to the next chapter.

The second half of the day is not bad. We normally have one period assigned for Physical Training or Drawing. The sun is down and it is not so hot. There is always some class or the other playing in the ground. Cricket helps one to while away time well. Just watching them play is fun.

Physics is boring. The chapter in question was on calculation of molecular weight. It was beyond anyone. No one could understand the structure of C12 atom and the method of calculating its mass. Chitre was the only one listening carefully. We were all waiting for the class to end. Surya was hoping Potnis ma'am would teach us various reproductive organs in the next class. But it turned out that she was on leave. Zende sir took the class instead.

Zende sir is our favourite. 'Popatrao Manikrao Zende! Does anyone else have such a name?' he challenges. No one else sports a pointed moustache like him. He chews paan all the time. He could pick any subject, but he chooses to teach us Chemistry.

He talks incessantly in the class, chatting with the students, sometimes in English or in Hindi. He always has some joke or the other up his sleeve for each students based on their names. He tells Sadu Kale, who sits quietly in one corner like a scared mouse, 'Why are you so silent, Kale? Say proudly "*Hum kale hain toh kya hua dilwale hain!*"' To Bibikar he taunts, '*Bibi kar aur baith ghar!*' To me, '*Joshi hai par josh nahin hai*,' and to Teredesai he quips, '*Woh tere desai toh tum mere desai!*' Bhosale is just referred to as '*Maharaj*'.

Next came Rajguru sir's Drawing class. This is the only class when Surya is at his best. He loves to draw and does not like to be disturbed then. He is Rajguru sir's favourite. He not only shows Surya's paintings to all in the class but very often displays it on the school notice board.

That class is pure fun. We can draw whatever we like; we can walk across to any person's bench; we can chat with anyone. Sir sits on his chair, ready to help any student. And of course, he draws really well. With just a few simple pencil strokes, he can create a masterpiece. And the way he paints is simply amazing. Whenever he paints for someone, that student takes the painting home and shows it to each and every one he meets on the way.

I love the class because it affords me a closer look at Shirodkar. She moves around the class, chatting with her friends. She does not talk to the boys though. I love to watch her draw. It reminds me of a Hindi song, which Ambabai hums very often—'*Woh kaun chitrakaar hai, woh kaun chitrakaar*'.

The last period is Physical Training, PT. This is normally held for all the classes together. Students from each class streamed out into the playground and then lined up; girls on one side and the boys on the other. Pethe ma'am emerged with her harmonium to teach us a song on discipline. This is how it has been ever since the Emergency came into force.

'Ichibhana, what the hell is this discipline all about?' Surya enquired loudly, much to merriment of all boys around.

'Hey, shut up. Don't laugh.' Redkar sir yelled.

After the song, Appa stepped forward to give a lecture on the concept of discipline. Standing right in the front, we were forced to keep quiet and listen. Appa earnestly went on about how indiscipline had become rampant and why the country needed good, disciplined citizens. We had no choice but to suffer the lecture in silence. The PT followed the lecture, followed by the singing of '*Vande Mataram*' after which the school ended.

I was having my tea with toast when Aaisaheb announced, 'Naru mama is coming.'

'When?'

'I suppose in a day or two. I got his letter today. He is coming to Mumbai for some work and he will be here any day.'

Naru mama is a lot of fun. He is Aaisaheb's only sibling. There is a lot of age difference between the two, hence a darling of the family. Naru mama changed a lot of jobs and is now teaching English in a college in Aaji's town. We are great pals. Earlier, he used to spend a lot of time with Ambabai, but ever since I came to high school, he has become my buddy.

'Waah!' I said. 'I will go for an English movie with him.'

'An English movie, is it?' Ambabai taunted, cutting vegetables. 'What about your studies? Remember you are going to be in class ten next year.'

'Isn't that next year? We will see when it comes.'

'Yes, but you need to start preparing from now on. And what about your tuition classes?'

'What about them?'

'Mukund! Don't act like a dunce. Aai, this fellow has not joined tuition classes yet.'

'Why do I need tuition? Don't they teach me in my school?'

'Everyone knows what they teach you in your Warhadkar school; all ghati folks!'

'Let them be ghati. I am not bothered. We know what they teach in your college.'

Ambabai studied in Subhash Vidyalaya. We call that a Brahmin school. It has produced some rank-holders. That's why the students there strut around with their noses up in the air. Ambabai used to nag Baba to put me in Subhash Vidyalaya, but luckily Baba ignored her. She's very proud of her school and ever since she has joined that fashionable college in Matunga, she considers every other school ghati.

'You have to join the tuition classes the moment your half-yearly exams are over, okay?' she announced. 'Aai, don't listen to him one bit. He just whiles away time after school.'

'I don't need your advice.'

'Why? Is she saying something wrong?' Aaisaheb joined in.

I thought it was best to keep quiet. These folks had made up their mind to make me an engineer and the preparations were to start now. Ambabai has been harping on these extra tuitions ever since I came into class nine. Earlier, Aaisaheb was of the opinion that we needed to have extra tuitions only in class ten, but the constant nagging has changed her mind. On top of it, Ambabai gives examples of toppers—useless folks—who have joined the tuition classes. I just hate these classes, especially the ones that are held in the evenings. Who in his right mind would want to study the same thing after learning it all afternoon in school? Moreover, the classes are held in small, cramped rooms with three or more students sharing a bench under a dim, yellow light. Who would want to spend one's evenings there?

That does not solve the problem of spending time in the evenings, though. One can do a lot if one wishes to. Depending on how you see it, you could call my home part of a chawl or a building. It's an L-shaped structure. There is an empty space in the middle with four houses on one side and four on the other. Ground-floor houses have a verandah in front and the first floor people have balconies. The first floor guys can just stand in that balcony, but the ground-floor folks spend all their time in the open space. Sukhtankar and Ponkshes have actually moved their beds outside. Many sleep on the verandah at night.

Our landlord, Kudalkar advocate, does not stay here. He is an old man who comes once a month to collect rent. He does not take much care of the building, hence the tenants are at constant loggerheads with him. He has a stock reply for every complaint—'Are you willing to pay a higher rent? I will take care of the repairs then.' But the tenants do grudgingly admit that the construction is very strong;it is impossible to even drive a nail through the thick walls.

Most of the tenants go to Mumbai for work; by the suburban train, of course. They return only late in the evening. Upasni aaji stays home the whole day as she's alone. She makes papad, pickles and such items, and sells them in the local shop. Nikam kaka works in our Municipality and does not have to board the daily train. Except for the ladies, there is no one in the building at daytime. The building comes to life in the evening. In the morning you hear the sounds of pressure cookers whistling, radio news, and Marathi songs. Each door on the ground floor has curtains with floral prints. But most of the doors remain open throughout the day; except that of the newlyweds, the Mayekars! Sudhakar Mayekar stayed aloof even as a bachelor, and did not mingle with the rest of the tenants. In the evenings, inviting smells from various kitchens in the building waft into the open courtyard. The Shenvis love fish. The Upadhyes get fragrant rice from their village in Konkan, which they refuse to sell to anyone despite eager pleas from all. The Nikam household eats mutton for dinner every Sunday.

Kudalkar advocate has gifted the courtyard with a partially covered, tiled floor. It has proved a great blessing as everyone can assemble there in the evenings, thus escaping the heat of the cramped rooms. Ponkshe kaka continues to sit bare-chested despite repeated nagging from kaku.

There is an open space where some grass grows. Once in a while, some of the enthusiastic members of the building clear the space and play badminton over there. They put up a makeshift pole on which a naked bulb dangles at night for light.

The boys play underhand cricket during the day. But evenings are meant for chess and carrom. Baba introduced the chawl to chess and it has now become an addiction for many. At any given point, there are a few games happening simultaneously with enough 'advisors' around each. Ponkshe kaka got a carrom board and now there are two such boards to play on; the 'advisors' are present there too! Everyone assembles here after dinner. The womenfolk get busy cutting vegetables or chatting and exchanging gossip. The tenants from the first floor are come too. In one corner of the first floor are two rooms kept locked by Kudalkar. He gives them on rent for wedding celebrations or other such functions. The other corner is occupied by a threesome—KT, Ashok and Vijay. No one knows what they do for a living. We see a group of men and women come into their room once in a while. They close the door and we are unable to make out what they discuss. Then they join the crowd, playing chess on many evenings. They also participate in the children's underhand cricket. They are a nice gang to hang out with.

Baba comes home sharp at seven, unless his train is late. He comes in, goes for a wash, changes into his pyjamas, has a cup of tea, and then sits down to play chess. He has to finish one game before dinner and one afterwards. He then goes to sleep. If you want to speak to him you have to find time either when he is having tea or when he is eating dinner. He does not like to talk while playing chess, only gesticulates because there is a wad of tobacco tucked away in his mouth. But that is only before dinner. Not afterwards.

Baba is of no use in the evenings, much to the chagrin of Aaisaheb. He does household chores only on Sundays or on the second and fourth Saturdays when the office is closed. He does not play chess on those days, but that does not stop Aaisaheb from getting upset. 'I feel like throwing away your chess board!' she grumbles. But would she dare! In fact she takes care to search, the next morning, for the pawn or any other chess piece fallen under the bed. She's happy that I am not addicted to chess. It is not that I don't know how to play. In fact, I play quite well and have defeated Baba a few times. Baba says he taught me chess when I was in fifth standard and had I continued I would have been very good by now. But he did not force me. Some people come to him to learn. He does not believe in participating in tournaments. He says one should play for personal satisfaction and not for winning matches.

I don't like to be at home in the evenings. I love to spend time walking down the roads, especially after the street lights come on. The soft, friendly glow of the streetlights makes the town warm and affable. I like that hour when no one can recognize you walking by. I spend my evenings visiting either Chitre or Phawdya or go to the Municipal library. I did the same when Ambabai started her discourse on the benefits of extra tuition. I picked up a book and made my way to the library.

We had assembled at our adda as usual. Surya was fine until he saw Kevda, which is when he grew desperate. He was keen to speak to her, but did not know how to get started.

'Ichibhana, Joshi, come on! Give me some idea,' he pleaded, seeing Kevda pass by. 'How the hell do I woo her?'

'It'll happen, don't worry,' I said, winking at Chitre.

'Don't you see, the days are just passing by? She goes by and I just sit here looking at her. She needs to know, no?'

'Bloody fool', I muttered under my breath. But when Shirodkar passed by, and I sat there with my heart pining for her, I could empathize with him. I realized the days were flying and we were doing nothing except sitting there watching the girls walk past. Shirodkar needed to know! I wondered how I would ever be able to tell her. The familiar feeling of emptiness in the pit my stomach deepened.

I decided to seek advice from Naru mama. He had arrived by four o'clock, and when I returned from school, he was chatting with Aai, a tea-cup in hand.

'Mukund, how are you?'

'Fine,' I said.

'Not *phine*,' he corrected. '*Faieeeen*...that's the way to pronounce it. The person hearing you should feel you are really feeling fine.'

'*Faieeeen*,' I repeated.

'Yes. Say, Fine, thank you sir,' he said.

'Fine, thank you sir,' I repeated.

Aaisaheb watched us with admiration. I had nothing to worry as long as Naru mama was here with us. Ambabai had gone visiting some friend. We went out. The English movies are screened only on Saturday and Sunday mornings. We did not want to see some stupid Hindi movie, so we decided to go to the place where the new bridge is being built.

'So, how are your friends?' Naru mama asked.

'They are all fine.'

'No girlfriends yet?'

'They are trying. But they haven't found one yet.'

'What about you? Haven't you found anyone?'

'No!' I said. 'I don't have time for all that.'

To be honest, I was about to blurt out Shirodkar's name, but I checked myself. I could not afford to confide in him. What if he blurted it to Aaisaheb? I'd be doomed.

'There is this boy in my class,' I began carefully. I knew that Naru mama was sharp, so I created a fictitious character. 'Manoj Desai. He is in love with a girl. But he does not know how to tell her that. The girls in our class don't talk to us boys, you know.'

'That's easy,' Naru mama said. 'All he needs to do is to impress her. Then she'll automatically start reciprocating.'

'But how does one do that?'

'That's for him to decide.'

I did not pursue the discussion further for I knew Naru mama would smell a rat. I knew Naru mama would broach the topic on his own later. He had a few affairs in college. He is full of stories, but I am not sure which ones to believe.

Aaisaheb has seen a few prospective brides for him, but he has not shown any interest yet. I suspect he has some girl in mind. He has not confided in me though, and that's quite all right. These things are private. Unless, of course, you are an idiot like Surya who goes about telling the whole world.

I mulled over Naru mama's advice but was unable to decide the next move. Bendre ma'am caned us again in her next class. We remembered her teaching us 'past participle' the previous day but she had not asked us to write a few examples of it on our own as homework. But she thought she did. So she decided to punish the entire class. She started with the front bench and continued till each one had received their quota. Bibikar tried to object and got an extra one in return.

She then began the class in her usual monotone. The whole class was silent after the caning. It was hot outside and there was no one in the playground. Naru mama's advice echoed in my head. I wondered what I should do.

Bendre ma'am began writing on the blackboard, and I took the opportunity to stand up and do an elaborate namaskar. For a moment, no one said anything until the boys sitting behind my desk began to giggle. Some of the girls had a vague idea of what I had done, but most of them looked askance as the boys sniggered away.

Bendre ma'am turned around to face us but could not put her finger on what had transpired while she had been busy writing on the board. The whole class was silent. She turned to write when Chitre, who was sitting next to me (for Desai was absent that day), stood up and mimicked my action.

The boys behind were expecting it; this was our regular pantomime. Earlier we used to show the middle finger, touch the tip of the tongue, and point it at the backs of teachers who were either tyrants or bores. But that was very risky. Once someone had tried to do that to Prem Chopra but got caught and was hammered badly. Then we discovered the relatively harmless namaskar gesture, where chances of a harsh punishment, if caught, were low.

The boys behind us laughed out loud seeing Chitre stand up and do the namaskar. Sundri, Sukdi and a few girls too giggled, covering their mouths with their handkerchiefs.

Ma'am turned around and asked in Marathi, 'What is so funny?' She lapses into Marathi whenever she's angry. But no one answered. Other boys were ready to mimic the namaskar as soon as they got a chance. There was an air of anticipation in the classroom now.

I waited for a few minutes. The moment ma'am turned, I stood up and repeated the gesture. The boys giggled again, and this time Chitre and I joined the laughter to avoid any suspicion. Ma'am turned around, fuming. 'What is it? What is happening? Looks like you haven't had enough of the caning.'

There is a fatso Shembekar who sits on the third bench right in the middle of the classroom. He is a little oversmart and loves to show off. He decided to mimic the namaskar next. Chitre and I knew that ma'am was alert now. But Shembekar stood up and the moment he folded his hands in a namaskar, ma'am turned around and caught him.

'Come, come,' she said, moving towards his bench. 'So you want to do namaskar, is it?' She came near him and hit him with her ruler. He tried to dodge. He gets caned a lot by the teachers and is an expert at dodging the blows. Luckily for him, the bell rang just then and he was spared. The moment ma'am left the classroom, he came charging at me.

'Saale, Joshi! I got caught because of you.'

'Hey, hold your horses,' Surya cut in. 'Bhenchod, who asked you to try a prank on her?'

He went back to his seat, but I felt bad for the fatso. I was happy that the girls were giggling at my prank, but I was not sure whether Shirodkar had joined in.

The Physics period was free and Manjrekar sir came in to substitute, much to everyone's delight. He announced that he would teach Geography, but we all clamoured for a free period and he relented.

'Okay, so what do you guys want to do?' he asked, sitting on the chair.

One of the birdies said, 'Let's play word games on movie titles.'

'Yes, sir, it's been so long!' Another one added.

The girls and boys do not talk to each other much, but they love to play games. One of the favourites is a word game based on movie titles. We have outgrown the 'name, place, and town' sort of word games and none of the boys know the ones based on film songs anyway. Some of the ma'ams ask girls like Sukdi, Deodhar, Nangre or Deshpande to sing songs in a free period, giving themselves time to sit and knit sweaters. Sukdi hesitates at times, but the others can barely wait for a cue to burst into song. They are stupid enough to sing songs originally sung by male singers. That Nangre is willing to sing some Marathi folk tunes too while most of the boys laugh and make fun of them. That Deshpande has joined us this year from Gwalior or Bhopal or some such place. She has a favourite Meera bhajan—'*Sukh ke sab saathi dukh mein na koi*'. She dwells long on the last word, *koiiiiii,* and the boys join in, mimicking her. That's when she usually gets annoyed and stops singing. She got badly ragged once and ma'am had to intervene. Since then most of the girls don't volunteer to sing. But everyone is ready to play word games.

One of the teams has to write the first and the last letter of the title of the movie with blanks in between and the other side has to guess. We win all the time and the reason is yours truly! Our neighbour Nikam kaka, who is fond of listening to film songs, has a book with movie titles listed in it along with the songs. I have read the book many times and that's why I can quickly guess the title.

It is easy to arrive at the name of the movie if the first letter is '*shree*' and the last letter is '*s*'. It has to be *Shree Char Sau Bees*. Similarly if the first letter is '*la*' and the last one 'yo' then it has to be *Love in Tokyo*. We boys are especially good at this and guess them promptly. I come up with tough ones and the girls invariably lose. But we still enjoy playing the game.

'Okay, let us play the game,' Manjrekar sir agreed. 'But I don't want any noise. We should not disturb the other classes, okay?'

'Don't worry, Sir. We won't make any noise.' The girls chorused.

The game began. The girls, it seemed, had done some homework this time, for they seemed to be referring to a notebook.

As usual, it started with some simple names which we guessed immediately. Bibikar, Ghasu Gokhale and Teredesai were trying to impress the girls while Deodhar and shorty Bakre tried to impress the boys. I was quiet. Chitre was bored and started reading his Physics book. Surya and Phawdya were busy with some prank or the other.

Ghasu Gokhale wrote on the board, '*ja*', followed by eight blanks and then '*hai*'. Sukdi promptly guessed, '*Jab Pyaar Kisi se Hota Hai*'.

'That's correct!' Surya exclaimed loudly. Phawdya added, 'Kisse hota hai?'

'Mahesh se,' someone answered loudly.

The boys burst out laughing. Manjrekar sir knew about their affair and smile slightly. Sukdi made a face and sat down without saying a word.

Then the girls continued with some stupid names like *Kati Patang, Tumsa Nahin Dekha* and so on. Bakre tried *Sant Tukaram*, which was too easy. Then Bibikar wrote, '*ma*' followed by four blanks and then '*ya*'. The girls were at a loss. Bibikar started jumping with joy. Sir looked at the girls and when he found that they were unable to guess, he hinted softly, 'Bharat mata ki jai.'

Mirikar was quick on the uptake. She said out loud, '*Mother India*.'

Bibikar complained, 'Sir, you are being partial to the girls.'

'Shut up and sit down.'

The game continued without anyone losing and the boys looked at me for some help.

'Joshi, come up with some tough name, buddy,' Ghasu Gokhale said, trying to be friendly.

'Joshi, Ichibhana, why don't you give them a really difficult one?' Surya said, poking my back with his pencil.

I thought for a while and told Surya, 'Go and write "*de*" followed by seven blanks and then "*di*".'

Surya promptly went and wrote the same on the board. It was a googly for the girls. They were lost.

'What is this? *De...di*?'

'There is no such movie,' Sukdi claimed.

'You will be the first one to see it when it releases,' I tried to keep my voice low, but Sir heard me. He said, 'Joshi, don't try to be oversmart.' He too looked at the board and thought for a while. He did not know the answer either.

The girls were busy scratching their heads. They huddled in groups but to no avail. Sir waited for some time and then announced, 'Okay, the girls lose this round. Joshi, tell us the answer.'

'*Destination—Post Office Dhebewadi*,' I said. It was a Marathi movie.

'There is no such movie,' one of the birdies piped up.

'Sit down,' Sir intervened. 'I have seen the movie. It is nice and has good suspense.'

Then slow worm Deosthale stood up. She took ages to write the words, taking some ten hours to finish. She had written the first letter, '*mou*' and, before she could complete the endless row of blanks, I said, 'Don't write further. It is *Mughal-e-Azam*.'

She just stood there holding the chalk in her hand. Then with an 'Issh!', she stomped her way back, muttering that we could identify every damn movie on earth.

The boys were having fun.

It was bright outside and inside as well. I wished that the class would never end. The girls were desperately racking their brains to come up with a difficult title.

Shirodkar got up to write.

'I will try,' she said. She went to the blackboard and started writing.

The boys were busy looking at the words, but I could not take my eyes off her.

The name seemed to be enormously long. The first letter was '*ja*' followed by a train of never-ending blanks. The entire class fell silent. There were twelve blanks after the first letter. The last one was '*li*'.

No one had a clue! Someone muttered, 'What is this '*ja…li*?'

I had not noticed the clues as I was busy looking at her. My heart was pounding away. The boys clearly were unable to search for an answer and were on the verge of accepting defeat. The girls chorused, 'Now tell us! Do you know the answer?'

The boys looked at me for support.

'Joshi, come on, man! You ought to know!'

'Hey, come on, fill in the words quick.'

My mind was numb. I tried to desperately search for the right connection between the letters. There were quite a few films whose name began with '*ja*' like '*Jab Jab Phool Khile*', '*Jis Desh Mein Ganga Bahti Hai*', '*Jab Pyaar Kisi se Hota Hai*', etc. but they did not match the letters. This title had twelve blanks….

'Have you written it correctly?' Ghasu Gokhale raised a doubt, asking the girls.

He had a point. It happens many times; the opponent goofs it up and we rack our brains in vain, searching for the right answer.

Shirodkar looked at the board and counted the number of letters again. She confirmed, looking at Manjrekar sir, 'Yes, sir. It is right.'

The girls were baying for an acceptance of defeat from our side.

'Joshi, we are going to be mauled. Come on!' Surya pleaded.

My body was trembling. It seemed like I would have to accept defeat—and that too at the hands of Shirodkar. I looked out at the playground glimmering in the hot sun. The girls were making a din inside the classroom. Shirodkar stood smiling, knowing that victory was very much hers. What could be the word beginning with '*ja*'? My mind raced...*jab, jawan, jahan, jameen, jal.*

'So are you guys ready to give up?' Manjrekar sir stepped in, looking at me. He moved to the blackboard to mark the points.

'Wait, Sir. I know.' I blurted out.

Shirodkar stared at me in disbelief. There was complete silence in the class. Everyone looked at me while Shirodkar's eyes bored into me, burning like two lovely lamps. I allowed the moments to pass, enjoying them. She continued staring into my eyes, blinking a few times.

'Tell me,' Sir said.

'*Jal Bin Machli Nritya Bin Bijli*,' I said, enunciating each word slowly for effect.

'Wow!' The boys erupted in joy. Surya and Phawdya drummed the bench to announce victory.

I turned to look at Shirodkar. The lamps in her eyes had gone out. She went back to her bench smiling wanly and sat down without saying a word. There was no sound from the girls' side. Within a few minutes, the bell rang and the free period came to an end.

My body continued to tremble until school got over. I

did not feel like going back home taking the main road. I excused myself telling Phawdya that I had some work and walked back silently through the paddy fields.

The fields were serene as usual. The crops stood still without swaying in the breeze. Shankar's father was nowhere to be seen. The water had receded and there was a sort of dry smell of ripe paddy in the air.

I sat on the rock for a while. I felt a deep sense of achievement. Shirodkar had looked at me for eternity, it seemed. She continued staring at me without a care in the world. I was sure she would remember those moments too. Perhaps she would recount the episode to her family when she went home. I am sure I had left an impression on her.

Then I stood up with a start. She must have gone back home disappointed and dejected. Would she not have written the words being sure that no one would be able to guess? The thought struck me like a bolt of lightning; her eyes had been pleading with me not to reveal the name. Like an idiot, I had read her all wrong and gone ahead. What an ass I had been! How could I ever hope to impress her again? She must be so mad at me.

I had been a bloody idiot. Naru mama would have advised, 'You should allow the girl to win. That's how you impress them. You win even as you are defeated.' I had lost a golden chance. All I could do now was sit and brood over it. I lost the energy to walk back home. A deep sense of sadness engulfed me.

I promised myself that I would never make the mistake again. If ever we played the game again, I would refuse to participate. But such an opportunity did not arise, for Barve ma'am returned the next day.

It was Warhadkar Jayanti a few days later. The day is celebrated to remember Shri Sukhdev Namdev Warhadkar after whom our school is named. He was a great freedom fighter and, sometime in the 1940's, he had sabotaged a train by removing the fish-plates from the track. He had also captured a post office for which he had been imprisoned for a few years. Each and every student knows this history only too well, for it has been narrated a hundred times over by the teachers, especially Appa.

Even a passing reference to S.N. Warhadkar makes the teachers eulogize his heroic deeds and describe how he once ran twenty-three miles to escape the police, how his feet were cut and bleeding and how he spent an entire night in a dry well, and so on. The story is quite fascinating and the first time a schoolboy hears it in class five, he dreams of becoming a revolutionary. But when you have heard it a million times, it ceases to motivate you. There are a few thousand copies of his biography in our school. The teachers sometimes get a bundle of it to our class when there is a free period and give it to each student to read. The book costs ten rupees and is given to us at a concessional rate of three, but no one is interested in buying them. On Warhadkar Jayanti, we are called to the school to celebrate the founder's day. We would rather have a holiday, but they insist on us coming to school. No classes are held that day, and the morning and afternoon batches are called together in the morning itself. We have a big hall on the first floor which doubles as a laboratory. Debates and speaking competitions are also held over there. We sit in the hall, girls on one side boys on the other, with the benches acting as a divider. We are asked to enter the hall in single file to avoid any confusion.

The students from the tenth and eleventh standards were made to sit in the front. The teachers kept a hawk eye, but the students made a ruckus as usual. We rushed in to grab the aisle seats and it was only later that I realized that Shirodkar and the girls were sitting very close to us. Phawdya and Surya were right behind me and, when I turned back to speak to them, my eyes met Shirodkar's. She was, quite obviously, not looking at us, but I could see her every time I turned back.

It was nice. Such programmes are meant for fun and we were least concerned with what was being said on the dais. The children who had volunteered to participate in the elocution competition were sitting in the front. There were speeches by the teachers, the chief guest and many others. We were busy with our own pranks. After all we had the girls sitting next to us—especially Shirodkar!

The topic for elocution was the usual 'my favourite freedom fighter'. All the oversmart boys and girls clamour to participate in the contest. From our class, Bibikar and Mirikar are the regulars. They are always ready to participate in any competition. Ghasu Gokhale is intelligent, but he does not have the nerve to face a crowd. The birdies participate in all competitions except elocution; they are a little shy when it comes to speaking in front of the boys. They know that if they falter, they will be teased to death for the rest of the year.

Redkar sir coordinates such events. He came near the mike and, snapping his fingers, said, 'Hello, mike testing, one-two-three-four...one-two-three-four.'

'Who asked him to test the mike?' Surya quipped as usual.

'What else can he do?' Phawdya answered.

'The mike can be tested only with English words,' I commented, looking back to see if Shirodkar had heard my repartee.

The boys around laughed, but none of the girls joined in. They continued to stare ahead.

'The students participating in the contest may please come and sit in the first row,' Redkar sir's voice echoed through the hall.

The participants stood up and moved towards the front. Bibikar was sitting right ahead and he stood up dusting his trousers' seat.

'Guys, please do clap when I get up to speak, okay?' he said, looking at us.

'Let us first hear your speech, smartie,' Surya quipped.

The programme started with the Jayanti celebration. It was being chaired by the local Doctor Shetty while the chief guest was our mayor. This fellow has been the mayor for many years now. The state may have a Congress government, but the Opposition always manages to bag the Municipality elections. We hear that this fellow is a corrupt guy. I get to hear some of his escapades when the elders sit around and chat in our courtyard every evening. Nikam kaka works in the Municipality and has lot of information on him. He is a fair, plump, paan-chewing sort. Other than those two, the only other guest on stage was our own Annasaheb Surve. He is the secretary of the school trust and hence an attendee by default.

Appa began his speech when the guests settled on the dais.

'You children may be wondering why we need to have this function each year,' he began. 'It is important to remember our heroes every now and then. They have sacrificed their lives for us and borne a lot of pain and trouble for the future of this country. If we don't remember them, who else will?'

Just then the mike emitted a loud '*koooooon*' kind of sound, echoing across the hall. That happens when someone speaks very close to the mike or speaks out loudly. Appa glared at the mike technician and then continued, 'Today's topic is "my favourite freedom fighter". You may ask why this topic was chosen. Because we hope that you will be inspired by your favourite freedom fighter and employ some of those values in your own life.'

'Okay, let us become revolutionaries then!' I said.

'Super! Then we can throw bombs wherever we wish,' Surya hissed.

'You'll be hanged, you idiots!' Phawdya opined.

'We are ready to go the gallows,' I said, looking back to steal a glance at Shirodkar. 'At least then you guys will celebrate some jayanti in our names.'

'You guys will get one more extra holiday,' Surya added.

'Good idea,' Chitre said. 'Ensure that you are hanged on different dates so that we get two extra holidays.'

'Shhh...silence!' Barve ma'am hissed from the bench across the girls.

A ceremony of garlanding the statue followed. The guest did their needful and the mayor stood up to deliver his opening speech waddling his way to the microphone.

'Respected Chairman, officials of the school, Principal sir, all the teaching staff and my dear girls and boys,' he began.

I knew the rest. I had heard many of his speeches.

'As the first citizen of our town,' I said, trying to sound gruff.

'As the first citizen of our town,' he repeated.

The boys burst out laughing. I turned back quickly to see how the girls had reacted to my wisecrack. Shirodkar tried to stifle her laughter, pursing her lips. Even Barve ma'am was trying to suppress a smile.

'Shh…Joshi!' She raised her eyebrows and put a finger on her lips motioning me to be silent. I ignored her.

'What is this "first citizen" business?' Surya muttered.

'It means he has the right to be first at all places,' Phawdya said.

'At all places?' Surya asked.

'Yes. Even at public latrines. He gets to go first.'

We all laughed.

'Shh…' Barve ma'am hissed again.

We were silent for a while. The mayor continued his lecture, recounting the sacrifices made by the freedom fighters, how we were indebted to them and why we children should learn from them, as we were future citizens, and so on and so forth.

I stole a glance at Shirodkar to find her listening earnestly to the speech. All the girls in my class pay attention to such boring speeches. Some are stupid enough to take notes! I was hoping she would look at me. No one would have noticed. But my fate! She continued to stare straight ahead.

'Our freedom fighters swallowed bullets,' the mayor continued, using the Marathi term for sacrifice. He drawled on, 'And what do we eat now?'

'Money,' I answered.

The boys joined me in the laughter, but I turned to see that Shirodkar was not amused. I was silent for a while. The mayor spoke for ten more minutes followed by Doctor Shetty. He has recently joined the town hospital and cannot speak fluent Marathi.

'My dear boys and girls,' he started in English, pulling his trousers up a little. 'Today is an important day.'

He continued his speech in English. I was able to understand most of it, but it was difficult for the others to follow. Chawre, sitting ahead of me, said a tad loudly, 'Not samazeeing!'

The boys laughed and I turned back to see Shirodkar holding a handkerchief to her mouth to hide her laughter. I felt dejected. I should have been the one to quip. I had lost another golden chance. Appa heard Chawre and indicated with his forefinger to pick the villain out of the crowd. Prem Chopra immediately came over and asked Chawre to follow.

The elocution contest began once the guests had done their duty and had been duly escorted out. It began with the eighth standard students. They mug up their speech at home and recite like a parrot. In fact, most of the students do that. Some stand with their hands behind their backs and speak. But we do not tease these young kids. In fact, we encouraged a few by actually clapping for them.

Then we were in for a shock. Kevda stood up to deliver her speech. It took a while for Surya to register. He was busy polishing his belt's buckle with a handkerchief.

'Surya, look ahead,' Phawdya nudged him with his elbow.

Surya's mouth was agape.

She began in a soft voice, standing a little away from the mike. None of us could hear her properly.

'Sound please!' Someone shouted.

'No breakfast?' Bhaishetye teased.

'Hey, just shut up, okay?' Surya erupted. 'If someone interrupts, I will break his teeth, bhenchod.'

Everyone was quiet until someone from the back called out, 'Hey, Pendse! Look, your sweetheart is on stage!'

Surya could not take it any more. He turned back to ask, 'Which one is Pendse? Who is he?'

'Boys, stop talking!' Barve ma'am shouted from across the room. 'Mhatre, keep quiet.'

Surya was silent. Kevda did not speak for long, but she spoke well. Everyone was watching her intently. We clapped loudly to cheer Surya up. In fact, we overdid the clapping and some people turned around to stare at us.

There were more speeches and we kept busy with our pranks. I was at my wits' end trying to impress Shirodkar. I commented on each and every speaker. Barve ma'am continued to warn us intermittently, but we ignored her. Manjrekar sir stared at us once, but no one bothered.

Bibikar stood up next, but none of us clapped. He started off in Marathi using words like *bandhu, bhagini* and *adhyaksh maharaj*. He then recited an English phrase, presumably learnt and memorized at home, 'Fame is the fragrance of heroic deeds,' he said. 'The flowers of chivalry and not of weeds.'

I knew the meaning as I had read it in one of the books Naru mama had given me.

'Ichibhana, what the hell is he blabbering?' Surya asked.

Bibikar continued, 'Our country has always been one

step ahead when it comes to sacrifice and valour. One name which leads in this category is Bhagat Singh's. He is my favourite freedom fighter. I like him because...' Bibikar fumbled. He tried to recall the words... 'I like him because...'

'Because he used to wear a hat,' I completed the sentence on his behalf.

The boys around laughed out loud. The girls joined in. But Bibikar continued without getting perturbed. I glanced to find Shirodkar listening attentively.

'What did Bhagat Singh do when Lala Lajpatrai was attacked by the British?' Bibikar asked theatrically.

'He cooked subji and rotis,' I retorted.

The boys laughed, encouraging me to go on.

'Bhagat Singh gathered his friends and told them, come on....'

'Come on, let us have wada-pav!' I said.

'Come on, let us teach them a lesson. His heart was filled with...'

'The fire of revenge,' I added.

Suddenly I realized my ear was very hot. I turned back to see Zende sir bent over me, twisting my ear.

'Your tongue is wagging too much, eh?' Zende sir said, continuing to yank my ear. 'You want to give a speech, eh? Why don't you go on the stage? You need guts to do that. Did you hear what he said? Fame is the fragrance of heroic-deeds. Got it?'

He twisted my ear fiercely. I would have burst out crying but somehow managed to hold on. My head was reeling. I looked down, knowing well everyone—especially the girls, especially Shirodkar—was staring at me.

Zende sir continued his 'ear treatment' for a while and then left without saying a word. No words escaped my lips for the rest of the function. I was feeling dead. I dared not look up while Phawdya and Surya continued their pranks. I felt crushed. It would have been far better if Sir had marched me out like Chawre.

It was well past one o'clock when the function got over. I sneaked away like a thief and took the road through the paddy fields. I had been holding back my tears, but they were now threatening to burst out. The fields stood silent in the afternoon while the sun burnt brightly. I sat on my rock resting my back against the tree. The tears flowed freely.

I knew it was finished. It had been my own doing. There was no way I could impress Shirodkar now. She would, in fact, be more impressed with Bibikar. I sat there sobbing like a baby for a long time.

On reaching home, I could hear a heated argument at the base of the staircase. Ponkshe kaka was arguing with Ashok and Vijay. Nikam kaka joined in.

'Do you have any freedom during this Emergency?' Ashok asked Ponkshe kaka.

'What do you need freedom for?' Ponkshe kaka hit out, scratching his back. 'Aren't the trains running on time? Is work not being done promptly? What else do you need?'

'Is that enough?' Vijay asked. 'What about *your* rights?'

'Are you not getting your rights?' Nikam kaka said, in his hoarse voice. 'Chaila, earlier no one would reach the Municipality office on time. Now they are all punctual. See how they come on time now!'

'Rights are different, kaka,' Ashok explained. 'We don't

need to declare Emergency for employees to come on time. We can teach them discipline.'

'Impossible! Just impossible,' Nikam kaka repeated.

'Mukund!' Ambabai had come out looking for me.

I gestured at her to keep quiet. I was enjoying the discussion. Such arguments take place often and they are fun. Nikam kaka and others have heated arguments. Ponkshe kaka speaks in a low voice but somehow manages to provoke the other person. And ever since Emergency had been declared, such arguments had become more frequent. Besides, those guys upstairs keep having meetings very often. I wish I could attend them once.

I was hoping Ambabai would go back after calling out once, but she stood there waiting for me. Vijay looked at her once and continued, 'During Emergency no one is allowed to express any opinion. Don't you agree?'

'No,' Ponkshe kaka said. 'Nothing has been hampered. Everything is running smoothly, better than ever before!'

'There is no point in speaking to you,' Ashok said.

They started climbing the stairs when they noticed me.

'Mukund, are you not going to the library today?' Ashok asked.

'No.'

'Mukund goes to the library, is it? Which one?' Vijay asked.

'Don't you know? He goes to the Municipal library. It is a great place to ogle at girls.'

'Come on! Don't joke,' I said weakly.

'Hey, Mukund; tell me the truth,' Ashok said, putting his arm around my shoulders. 'Do you get to see some good chicks there?'

'No,' I said, brushing his hand away. I was blushing by now and turned to go back. They ruffled my hair and walked away laughing.

'What were they saying?' Ambabai asked, suspicious as usual. She stood with one hand blocking the doorway.

'None of your business.' I said, ducking below her hand to enter the house.

Surya was itching to find Pendse and teach him a lesson. I reached our haunt the next morning to find him on the ground floor, waiting, as he stood behind a wall of bricks. Phawdya and Chitre were present while Surya was accompanied by Chandya, his cousin. Chandya was in our class until class eight but had had to repeat the year when he failed.

'Chandya, point out Pendse to me when he comes, okay?' Surya said.

A few girls passed by, but Surya was too preoccupied to tease them. In a while, Chandya spotted Pendse coming along with some boys. He went to him and then accompanied him to the building. He was a very fair, decent-looking fellow; a little on the heavier side. He became alert when he saw Surya and the gang blocking his way. Surya stood there like a hero, his fingers hooked into his belt.

'I am told that you have an eye on Kevda. Is that true?' Surya asked, walking towards him.

'Kevda?' Pendse was at a loss.

'Tell me the truth. Do you have an eye on Gupte?'

He nervously shuffled his books from one hand to other and said, 'No. I don't have an eye on her. Not me.'

'Tell me the truth, bhenchod,' Surya growled grabbing his collar.

'I mean it. I am telling the truth,' Pendse pleaded.

'Listen. I need to hear the truth, okay?' Surya said, changing his tone all of a sudden and sounding friendly. 'If you tell me the truth, I will let you go. But tell me honestly.'

Pendse relaxed a bit.

'Tell him the truth. What are you waiting for?' Phawdya cajoled him. 'Are you feeling shy?'

'Yes, I do fancy her. But nothing serious, you know,' Pendse confessed.

Surya jammed his fist into Pendse's stomach.

Pendse doubled up, clutching his stomach. The books flew out of his hand. He stood up but Surya hit him again.

'Will you look at her again, bhenchod?' he growled.

'No, I won't, I promise,' Pendse said, sitting down and clutching his stomach. That spared him another blow.

'Keep that in mind,' Surya warned him. 'If I see you even as much as stealing a glance at her, I'll bury you at the same place, okay?'

'Yes, yes. I understand,' Pendse said, shivering.

'And tell everyone in the class—Kevda's mine. No one dare look at her.'

'Yes, yes,' Pendse said, getting up hurriedly. His eyes were watering and he was trembling with fear.

Chitre and I helped him gather his books. Surya stood there, his face red with anger. We grabbed our books and proceeded to school.

The classes started on time, but the previous day's episode rankled in my mind. In the Marathi class, Ganoba the clerk came in to hand over a notice. Bibikar and Kevda had got a certificate of appreciation. Paranjpe ma'am clapped and we were forced to join. We clap whenever anyone in the class gets an award; even for someone like Bibikar! The awards are handed over much later in a prize-giving ceremony.

Surya and Phawdya were, as usual, in their elements. I missed Naru mama. I wanted to ask him many questions. Shirodkar never looks at me. She looks straight ahead in all classes, even during the drawing class. The birdies are busy all the time chirping away. They argue with the boys, but no one bothers much about them. But girls, in general, are idiots. They never look at you. How the hell do I then convey my thoughts to her? Perhaps we need to do what Surya does; proclaim your love openly. Write it on the school walls, maybe. But then I might as well be dead!

The first few classes are a real bore. And History tops it all! Pethkar ma'am keeps on droning in her monotone. I think she's not interested in teaching at all. She has her notes ready and all she does is read out from them. We have a huge syllabus this year; the dominion of the French and English, the rise and fall of the British Empire, feudalism, colonialism, what not. The boys doze off during the class. It is difficult to concentrate when Pethkar ma'am is busy delivering her sermon. We have to be very alert in Bendre ma'am's English class though; we cannot afford to be caught napping. But History is one subject where one is tempted to shut one's mind. Today she was busy teaching the French revolution. Unfortunately she has no sense of humour. She does not scold or hit us. She just goes on teaching. She would look at you once if you tried to crack a joke and then continue speaking. There is no point in saying anything in her class. We are lucky that Manjrekar sir teaches us Geography and Social Science.

The next class was that of Zende sir's. He looked at me, but I avoided his gaze. I was afraid he might rake up yesterday's episode, but luckily he focused on the subject at hand. There was a strange ache in my ears, though.

Getting bored in the evening, I decided to visit Chitre. He was, as usual, busy with some experiment in the verandah.

'Come, let us go inside,' I said. I like the inner room, which is always cool and cosy.

'No,' he said. 'Daddy is busy having his drink and Aai is just back from office. They had a fight a little while back.'

Chitre tells us that this happens often. His daddy comes home from office and likes to enjoy a peg or two in the evening. We do not understand what exactly that means, but his mother does not like it and they end up having an argument. Chitre had once found the key to his father's wooden cabinet and shown us the coloured bottles lined up inside; bottles of amber, green, brown and other colours. There was one in the shape of an eagle.

Chitre says after the argument his daddy shuts himself in the room and doesn't open it for a long time. He is quite a gentleman actually and never shouts at us. In fact, he entertains us once in a while, playing some old vinyl records.

Chitre was referring to a book to make a magnet-powered car. The parts lay scattered around him. I could not spot his younger brother Raju. His mother was probably busy in the kitchen and I could hear their arguments out in the verandah.

'Joshi, do you promise me not to tell anyone?' Chitre asked, while tying the battery cells with a rubber band.

'What about?'

'Kevda had come visiting our house last evening.'

'Don't tell me!'

'Yes. But don't tell anyone; especially Surya.'

'Why did she come?'

'She came with her mother. They had some errand in this part of the town.'

'Did you speak to her?'

'But of course! I had no choice you see. She was sitting right there! She asked me whether I liked her speech.'

'What did you say?'

'I said it was quite nice. I also told her that we clapped for her.'

'Did you tell her that Surya pines for her?'

'Of course not! Are you a chutiya? And promise me not to tell anyone. Surya will kill me if he finds out.'

'Did she stay for long?'

'Yes. Her aai is a chatterbox. They were here for quite some time.'

'What all did you talk about?'

'Nothing in particular. I don't remember anything.'

'Come on saale. Tell me!'

'I swear on my mother! I don't remember anything. Time just flew. We spoke of everything and nothing, actually!'

'Saale, you like her, isn't it?'

'Come on!' he said, trying to brush me off. But I knew that his voice lacked conviction. He avoided my eyes and I knew. I was about to probe him further when his mother came out and sat down to read the newspaper. The discussion remained incomplete and I left soon after.

I was jealous of Chitre. How I wished Shirodkar would come to my house someday? Chitre was a lucky bastard. Kevda had visited his house on her own accord.

I then decided to make friends with Misal. One day when Desai was absent, I asked him to sit next to me. We can sit wherever we wish during Redkar sir's class. I casually approached him saying, 'Don't you stay near Natyamandir?'

'Yes, that's right. But not near it,' he clarified. 'I stay near the road leading to the big stone well.'

'Does anyone we know stay towards your house?'

'No one from our class. Dhande stays that side, but much ahead; closer to the other village, in fact.'

'Good. No girls living that side,' I added, hoping he would talk about girls.

He was quiet for a while as he was busy copying some equation, which Redkar sir had written on the board.

'Actually; Mande does live near my house and so does Shirodkar.'

I suddenly sensed the hollow in my stomach. Despite knowing for a fact, hearing him say so made me nervous. I had to tread carefully now.

'No. I don't think she stays there,' I challenged him. 'Does she not stay near Kanifnath temple?'

'No. That's in the other direction. She stays quite close to my house, in fact,' he clarified.

I did not want to pursue the line of conversation further lest he smell a rat, and changed the topic.

'I would like to see that old stone well. I am told it's massive.'

'Yes, that's right. It is really a big one.'

The big stone well is one of the key attractions of our town. No one knows when it was built or who built it, but it has been around for ages. Earlier, everyone used to draw water from the well, but ever since the Municipality has laid water pipes, it has been out of use. It is rumoured the well never goes dry. I had seen it long back but did not tell Misal so.

'Will you show me the well some day,' I asked, 'if I ever come that way?'

'Yes, of course. There is nothing much to see, though. It is just a well.'

'When shall we go?' I asked, not allowing the opportunity to pass.

'Any day you wish.'

I was eager to go the same day, but unfortunately he had tuition classes that day. We decided to meet the next day. I asked him for his address and he gave me the directions: 'Come down Subhash Vidyalaya and turn left at the Dhekne Laundry'. Next to the laundry was Sumangal Store followed by a narrow lane where his house was.

I came home and gulped down my tea. Luckily Ambabai was not at home to ask unnecessary questions. I had carefully noted down the directions and had no difficulty in locating his house. It was the oldest part of our town. The houses had tiled, sloping roofs. There were many mango and coconut trees around. Despite the rains having ended some time back, the entire area was lush with big trees extending a cool shade.

Misal's house was part of a chawl with five or six rows of houses. Each house had two rooms. There was a tiled area in front of every house with a small garden adjacent to it. A few children were playing outside Misal's house. It was getting dark. When I got in I noticed his mother wiping the floor, her saree tucked into her waist.

'Aai, this is Joshi, my class fellow,' he said. 'He wants to see the stone well.'

'Then show him,' she said, continuing to wipe the floor. 'But have your tea first. And don't come into the house now. Your feet will leave stains on the floor.'

'We will have tea when we come back,' I suggested, winking at Misal. 'Let us see the well first.'

The well was really enormous. Its wall was more than three feet wide, with three places for drawing water. It was full of water, a little greenish black in colour. The shadow of the walls made the water look darker. It was scary to lie down on the edge and look down at the water. There were fish inside. 'Are there turtles too?' I asked. A few women were drawing water. The pulley made an eerie creaking sound, which echoed from the bottom of the well.

We hung around for a while. I was, quite obviously, not interested in the well itself. Misal took the road leading to his house when I suggested, 'Why don't we go for a stroll?'

We walked along the narrow lanes. There were a few independent houses hidden partially by trees. Misal continued to tell me some facts about the well, and about how some people performed animal sacrifice at it. I was least interested. I looked around the locality, but I couldn't find what I was looking for. I knew that Shirodkar stayed in this part of the town. I wondered how I would react if she were to come and stand before us. As usual, the hollow in the pit of my stomach grew.

'Are we not likely to come across that Mande or Binde or whoever stays somewhere in this part of the town?' I asked casually.

'No. She spends her evenings studying,' he said. 'She borrowed my notebook. She did not come to school today, you know?'

'Does she speak to you?'

'Yes, of course! We were together in the other school earlier. She bunks a lot and then borrows my notebooks.'

I had no knowledge of this arrangement. Boys like Misal do not reveal all this to the rest of us in class. So Misal does not speak to any girl in school but exchanges notebooks with Mande! Smart cookie!

'Doesn't Shirodkar borrow your notebooks?' I asked, trying to sound casual.

'No. I don't know her well enough. She just smiles at me when she sees me. Besides, I don't try to make friends with her. They are rich folks, you know.'

'Does she not stay this side of the town?'

'A little further up. They stay in a bungalow of sorts.'

'Bungalow?'

'Not their own. They have rented it.'

I continued to look at the sign boards of the bungalows we passed, hoping to see her father's name. We passed by a two-storeyed bungalow. 'Devgiri', said the nameplate. A lady in a white saree stood there, hanging some clothes in the balcony. She looked at us. I got nervous. Perhaps it was her mother!

After some time, Misal stopped near a gate and, pointing towards the house, he said, 'Shirodkar stays here.'

My heart was pounding. A brick wall, partially covered in green moss, surrounded the house. The gate at the entrance did not have a board proclaiming the name of the occupants. The house was not clearly visible from the gate, hidden partially by a tree. It was a two-storeyed house. There was a big garden with a cement stand for the tulsi plant in the middle. A yellow bulb burnt in the verandah with a window partially covered by a curtain. I could not see the door from the road.

Not wanting to sound too curious, I kept quiet. Two coconut trees stood adjacent to the gate intersecting each other at the top. It was a good landmark. One could see them from a distance.

'She has two sisters and a younger brother,' Misal said. 'Her elder sister is in college. The younger brother Pintya plays with our neighbour's son sometimes.'

I was relieved to know that she did not have an elder brother.

'God knows where her father works.'

'He is a hapisar.' He meant officer. 'Works for some big firm,' he said. I wondered how this fellow knew so much, but I kept quiet. The road ended in a square flanked by Phadke Hospital on one side. There were a few shops, a Shrikrishna Bhawan hotel, a medicine shop and a huge tamarind tree. There was an open library around the tree, where a few old men sat reading newspapers. I observed the place carefully. Shirodkar's house was clearly visible from the tamarind tree.

We turned left and reached Misal's house. I was not keen on having tea, but I did not want to raise any suspicion, so I sat down. I was hopeful that Misal would share some more information about Shirodkar, but the idiot continued to blabber on about the well.

'Which tuition class do you go to?' I asked, changing the topic.

'Saraf sir's classes,' he said. 'He is from Subhash Vidyalaya. He does not have a formal tuition centre. He just teaches at home.'

'Are there a lot of boys?'

'About seven or eight of them. Nobody from our school. All of them are from Subhash Vidyalaya, except one from Tope.'

I decided to leave. Misal seemed to have enjoyed my visit and said, 'Do come again.'

'Come again. You can study with Sunil,' his mother added.

'Sure. I will,' I said. I meant it—from the bottom of my heart.

Saturday afternoons are usually reserved for Scouts' practice. These days they have made Scouts and NCC compulsory for eighth standard and above. I was actually keen to join NCC, but I was unwell on the day the list was drawn up. Boys shorter than me are in NCC! But Chitre had his own views and volunteered on my behalf to enrol me in the Scouts' list. He says Scouts is brain work while NCC is just brawn work where you are expected to simply follow rules.

He is right. We can hear the NCC practise when we play in the ground. *Parade! Agey badhenge agey badh; peeche mudenge, peeche mud. Parade, aisa karange. Parade, waisa karenge!* They are led by a pot-bellied Sergeant who shouts out such crazy orders. And the uniform they give never fits anyone. The boys looked like jokers when we saw them wearing their NCC dress for the first time. Earlier the cadets were given glucose biscuits in each session. Now they get a stipend to polish their boots and starch their clothes.

Most of the big girls are in NCC. They wear funny brown pants and a grey shirt. Surya says the dress suits the girls a lot, even though he would have preferred them a little tighter! Surya and Phawdya are, quite expectedly, in the NCC. They consider Scouts sissy. They say we look girlish in those funny caps and with the handkerchief tied around the neck. I love the red pompom that the NCC cadets sport on their berets. Most of the girls are in the Guides. They have a blue dress. The Scouts and Guides practise together in the grounds in the afternoon. Rajguru sir is in charge of the Scouts and Adhav ma'am looks after the Guides.

It's fun to have these sessions in the grounds. Rajguru sir is sometimes joined in by Manjrekar sir. They are our favourites. Sometimes they invite people from outside to teach us things like tying different types of knots, signalling using the whistle, identifying insects, climbing trees, and other such activities. There is a book by Bedon Powell which Rajguru sir reads out to us. Then there are songs like '*Lord Bedon Powell, tere chele hum*' and '*Ooncha sada rahega jhanda, ooncha sada rahega*'. We are divided into groups based on names of animals and birds. I am in the Eagle group. We have our own scout notebooks. Chitre got a few stickers with a picture of an eagle, which we have stuck on our notebooks.

The other day Adhav ma'am was absent and Manjrekar sir asked the girls, who otherwise march ten miles away from us, to join us. Manjrekar sir made us sit in mixed rows. He began with the usual recitation of the oath and our motto. Surya says the Scouts and Guides may be sissies, but he loves our motto—*'Be Prepared!'* Always ready, he says, adding his usual 'bhenchod' for effect. He is eager to join us for the *khari kamai* when we are supposed to go to a few households and do some chores and earn our own money. But that is still quite some weeks away.

While we were reciting the oath, I managed to steal a glance at Shirodkar. She and I were sitting in the last row, meant for the team leaders. I was not aware that she too was a team leader. The playground was enveloped in warm, yellow sunshine. There was greenery all around and a cool breeze blew. We were wearing our usual blue cotton handkerchiefs around our neck while the girls had a pink silk scarf. Shirodkar sat there fiddling with it. Her hair blew in the soft breeze. She looked like a goddess.

Shirodkar did not initially realize I was looking at her. I had read in one of Naru mama's psychology books that if there is silence all around and you concentrate on an individual's back, that individual is bound to look back at you. I looked at her from the corner of my eyes, but I was sure that she was aware. Someone cracked a joke and all the boys laughed out loud. She turned to look at the boys and saw me staring at her. It is natural for anyone, finding the other person staring at him or her, to assume it must have been a coincidence. The person is tempted to check out once more to confirm whether it really was a coincidence. I was sure she would check. So I continued to stare. She turned and, finding me staring at her, quickly turned away.

I knew that she would not turn to look at me again. Not so quickly. I kept my face straight but, through the corner of my eyes, I was keenly looked her.

There were a lot of fruit flies buzzing overhead. One had to swat them or shoo them away. Shirodkar waved her hand to shoo away the flies and took a chance to look in my direction. From the corner of my eyes, I caught her checking on me. She did the same once again, but I did not try to catch her. But the next time she turned around, I looked straight into her eyes. She quickly turned away, knowing she had been caught.

The game was getting enjoyable, despite the emptiness in the pit of my stomach refusing to go away. I played with grass and made a makeshift doll out of it. I could make its arms move by pulling its legs. Then I made the doll walk a few steps on the ground. My eyes, all this while, were constantly on the alert to catch her sight.

She was watching me for sure. Listening to the entire oath of the Scouts and Guides is boring and one cannot help getting distracted. She must have seen me making that doll. She turned to glance at me and I could see a slight smile playing on her lips. She probably wanted to say the doll was cute. Her eyes, her face—they had lit up. A lightness filled me—it was like the feeling you get when you have a sweet, soothing ice-candy on a hot summer day.

'Joshi, what is going on over there?' I heard Manjrekar sir's voice.

I looked ahead with a start. Thankfully he did not seem

angry. His raised his eyebrows in question. I quickly threw away the grass doll. Some of the boys turned back to look at me.

'Nothing at all, Sir,' I blurted. We were usually not intimidated by him and I was more surprised than afraid.

'What do you mean nothing? Are you listening to what I am saying?' he asked. 'Okay, tell me the last rule which I just read out.'

Had he asked me to repeat what he had just said, I would have been in trouble. But he had framed the question differently asking me to repeat the last rule—the tenth rule. I knew it by heart. I said, 'A Scout is clean in thought, word and deed.'

He gave me a knowing smile. He knew I had managed a narrow escape but did not say anything. The other children could not guess, but it was enough for me. I dared not look at him despite having given the right answer.

We were left free once the Scouts' anthem had been sung. 'Go and observe the nature around you,' sir said. The two of them sat down on the chairs, and we were free to roam around. We could hear the parade practice of the NCC cadets going on amidst incessant whistling. We boys too had our long, narrow whistles with us and we blew them whenever we liked. The sky was clear and blue just the way described in the Scouts' song, 'the blue sky spreading the love of brotherhood'. Wildflowers bloomed in the grass and the blue hills beyond the tiled, sloping roofs of Umbarpada village looked inviting. The girls looked like flamingoes in their pink silk scarves.

My heart went wild with joy and I wanted to dance around. We had the entire ground to ourselves; our two favourite teachers sat on the chairs and chatted; the woods were green and dense and the sunshine was warm and friendly. Shirodkar and her gang were a little away, but I could spot her from any distance. She looked like a fairy queen. Her image seemed to fill up the entire playground. The grass and the woods around reminded me of the African grasslands in Lord Bedon Powell's stories. I was not concerned with other characters in the story. All that mattered was her presence. Everything else was irrelevant.

We were sitting in the mid-break in the woods when Dashrath suddenly announced, 'Chaila, my bottle burst yesterday.'

We had just finished our ice-candies. For a change, I had got some money from Aaisaheb and had bought one on my own. Surya sat on a rock while Santya was hanging on a branch when Dashrath made the remark.

'Don't tell me!' Surya said, getting down.

'Really, bhenchod,' Dashrath said, looking down at the leaf he was busy tearing into pieces. Chitre and I looked at each other.

'What happened?' Surya prompted. 'Were you watching some photos?'

'No. Nothing of that sort,' Dashrath said, looking at us sheepishly. 'It was in my dreams. I slept off at ten and when I woke up in the morning, I discovered this!' he said, pointing at his groin.

'Better be careful,' Phawdya warned. 'If you lose too much of your juice, you may die.'

That scared Dashrath. Earlier Harishchandra and Surya had confessed of their 'bottles' bursting, but they seemed relaxed. They were not worried. Dashrath was petrified hearing Phawdya's warning.

'Don't worry. There is nothing to fear,' Chitre said. The nonchalance with which he said so made us wonder whether he knew much more.

'What do you mean nothing to fear?' Phawdya erupted. 'Do you know each drop of that thing is made up of millions of blood cells?'

'There is nothing of that sort,' Chitre continued authoritatively.

'How the hell do you know all this, bhenchod?' Phawdya challenged.

'My Kaka is a doctor. He had explained everything to me and even gave me a book to read. He said it is good if the bottle bursts once in a while. It is quite natural. In fact, you need to worry only if it doesn't.'

We looked at him with newfound respect. Dashrath moved closer to him. Santya came down from the tree branch.

'What if the bottle bursts every night?' Dashrath asked.

'It won't happen every night,' Chitre said. 'And don't bother even if it does. But don't play around deliberately. I will give you the book to read if you wish.'

'No need. I am fine as long as you are telling me the truth.'

'Yes, of course. This happens to all of us.'

'Just don't go about fingering girls,' Surya said, getting back to his elements.

'Who the hell is asking for your advice, bhenchod?' Dashrath said, flinging a stone at him.

'Arre, Arre. Don't hit me, saale,' Surya said, dodging the

stone. 'Hey, Joshi. Why don't you get that magazine from the library? What is it called *Apsara* or something?'

'No,' I said firmly.

'Saale, why don't you get it?' He pleaded. 'It is fun to read. When was the last time we read it?'

'Joshi, get the magazine, please,' Phawdya said. 'Remember that serial? That fellow Govindrao and that woman Leela!'

'Yes!' Surya said. 'Let us read what they are doing now.'

'No way,' I said. 'I would be damned if I bring it again.'

I had made the mistake once in the beginning of the year. The magazine was issued from the Municipal Library. Aaisaheb does not care, but Ambabai does not allow me to read it. She does not mind my getting it home for her from the library; she loves to read it. I had carried it to school the next day to show it to my friends. We read it first at our adda. In Pethkar ma'am's class, Surya poked me in my back with his pencil and took the magazine away. For some time, he and Phawdya read it without making any noise, but then he got excited and whispered a tad too loud, 'Hey, just see, bhenchod, what is written,' he said and then read out; 'Govindrao lifted Leela off the ground and threw her on the bed and then with his rough hands, started to paw at her ample bosom...'

The boys around us giggled. The girls too must have heard as they sniggered. Pethkar ma'am, otherwise quite absent-minded, quickly identified the source of the disturbance. She came over to Surya's bench. Surya did not see her coming. It was too late to hide the magazine by then.

'Oh, so this is what is keeping you busy, is it?' she said.

'No wonder you are not interested in History. Why would you be, when you have such interesting stuff to read?' So saying, she snatched the magazine and put it on her table and her purse on top of it.

I was in deep shit. It was a library magazine. If I confided at home, I would be thrown to the wolves. I had to find a way of retrieving it. I asked Surya to go and get it from the staff room, but he just laughed out stupidly and walked away. I had no choice but to go the staff room myself. I went in with an excuse ready: how I had got it for my mother from the library the previous evening but had forgotten to remove it from my school bag; how Surya had seen it in my bag and had started reading it. I was prepared to plead the magazine belonged to the library and was on the verge of tears, but I soon discovered there was no need for concocting a story. To my surprise, I found ma'am engrossed in the magazine! She asked me to come and collect it after school hours.

That taught me a lesson. No more magazines to school. Of course, I still enjoy reading the magazine when there is no one at home. A frisson of excitement runs through my body when I read the stories. Once Chitre had got an English film magazine with awesome photographs. He says seeing is not as much fun as reading. I agree. But these days nothing gives me as much pleasure as thinking about Shirodkar.

The much acclaimed *Sholay* was finally being screened in our town. We were familiar with all the dialogues, having heard them on radio for months on end. Our town did not have a seventy mm screen but then something was better than nothing. Having seen the movie, Surya went about singing '*mehbooba, mehbooba*' all the time. Santya had bought the audio cassette and it was fun to ask him to repeat the dialogues in our free time.

Except for a few such diversions, school continued as before. It was the month of October and the sun burnt brightly. The paddy fields were dry and the crop had turned yellow. The frogs had vanished long ago. It was no fun watching the playground in the harsh sunlight of the afternoon. The roofs trapped the heat inside, making the rooms hot and muggy. What was worse, we had to deal with dreary lessons and boring teachers. Marathi was okay except for some dull songs and abhangs. Hindi was easy. The French Revolution in the History class seemed unending. Geography was luckily being taught by Manjrekar sir, but the portions were tough including different types of winds, moving of continents, types of rocks and what not. Algebra had simultaneous equations and division of whole numbers. We had the entire classification of plants and animals in Biology. Simple trees and plants were given complicated names like coelentrata, plantohelianthis, and echinodermata. It was difficult to even pronounce them! Chemistry had its own share of difficult equations. Newton and Edison's experiments made our life difficult in the Physics class. We were at our wits' end.

Bendre ma'am continued to torture us as before. One day, on a whim, she decided to check our notebooks. As expected, they were not covered. Most had photos of filmstars like Rajesh Khanna, Dharmendra and Hema Malini or cricketers like Wadekar, Engineer, Bedi, etc. It enraged her. She issued instructions to get our notebooks covered the very next day. The paper had to be specifically brown. We were left with no choice. Santu, poor fellow, did not know where to buy the paper. He seemed petrified.

I took his notebook home. Baba had got the paper from his office long back. I used that to cover our notebooks. Phawdya's mother was upset; she had to spend money to buy the paper. Surya loves such tasks and covered all his notebooks with brown paper. Chitre, meticulous as always, had had his notebooks covered with wax-coated paper since the term began.

Ma'am inspected the notebooks the next day. Amongst the boys, Dashrath, Memane and Kadam were caught. They were given the usual 'cane treatment'. Santya was grateful I had saved his day. Sundri, amongst the girls, was not spared. Ma'am, disappointed at having caught only a few offenders, was itching to catch more. She decided to inspect each and every notebook carefully. Seeing Shirodkar's notebook, she commented. 'This is not brown colour. It is yellow. I had asked for brown, don't you remember?'

'Ma'am, it *is brown* paper,' Shirodkar asserted.

'Do you think I am colour blind? Stand up.'

Shirodkar stood up, fearing the worst. She was clutching her handkerchief tightly in one hand while the other hand covered her mouth. The whole class watched her silently.

'My dad covered the notebook for me,' she said in her defence.

'Are you arguing with me? It is *not* brown paper,' she said, mercilessly tearing the cover off the notebook.

'Get it covered properly by tomorrow. And if you don't know what brown is, ask the shopkeeper. He will tell you.'

Shirodkar was sobbing softly. The class was silent.

'My father personally covered them, staying awake till late night,' she said.

'There is no need to cry now. Get it done tomorrow.' Turning towards us, she said, 'Class! Open the page to lesson number nine.'

I was fuming at Bendre, but I realized I could do nothing. I cursed her that she may never get married and suffer from TB and get no water when she lay dying and die begging on the streets. The boys too were fuming but were silent. We vented our anger in the mid-break. We wanted to teach her a lesson.

Next day one of the teachers was absent. Manjrekar sir came in the free class. We normally get the last five minutes in his class free. He taught us Civics that day and wound up dusting the chalk dust off his palms. Surya prompted me, 'Joshi, ask him something terrific.'

I thought for a moment and then raised my hand. Sir raised his eyebrows questioningly.

'Sir, what is the meaning of Emergency?' I asked in a clear, loud voice.

'Shabbash!' he exclaimed. 'Someone has finally had the guts to ask this question. I was waiting for the day when at least one of you would get up and ask.'

He moved his books away and sat on the edge of the table. 'Emergency means difficult times,' he began. 'A nationwide Emergency declaration heralds difficult times for the entire country. But that's just one part of it. Emergency, in reality, means a curb on freedom of the citizens of this country. I am, in some sense, a government servant and I cannot say much. You guys are a little too young to understand all this. Hence I won't elaborate.'

'But why do they declare Emergency in the first place?' I asked.

'To make us sing songs,' Surya interjected.

'To make people more disciplined,' Ghasu Gokhale added.

The other boys were silent. I managed to glance at Shirodkar. She was waiting for Sir to answer.

'It is true it helps to get people disciplined,' Sir explained. 'But the fact is there is a lot of discontent amongst the people. The ruling class is afraid the people may throw them out. They are scared and they declare such measures like Emergency to prevent people from revolting.'

'But Emergency is also called *Anushashan Parva*, trying to create a culture of discipline, isn't it?' Bibikar asked.

'That's what is said in public,' Sir explained. 'The people in power use such terms from texts like the Mahabharata. But you children need not worry about it. You must concentrate on your studies and do well.'

'But people are unable to express their views openly during Emergency,' I continued.

'That's right,' Sir agreed. 'That's why it is called Emergency.'

The bell rang just then.

'So I hope you guys have got some understanding of the Emergency,' Sir said, while leaving.

'Yes. It means Bendre ma'am's class,' Surya quipped.

The whole class burst out laughing. Sir glared in mock anger but left with a faint smile on his lips.

The next class was Bendre ma'am's. The very thought of

the previous day's episode made me angry. I had an idea. Everyday a student was supposed to volunteer to write on the blackboard the subject of the class to be held next. No one bothered to do the same for Bendre ma'am. She preferred to write that on her own.

I glanced at the ground. She had not yet arrived. I quickly stood up and picked up a piece of chalk from the desk. I rubbed out the earlier subject 'Social Science' and quickly wrote, 'Period four: *Anushasan Parva*' in bold letters. The birdies were shocked beyond belief and gaped open-mouthed. Even Shirodkar seemed a little surprised at my audacity.

I went back to my seat and sat with an air of nonchalance.

Ma'am came in wearing a starched saree, jutting out her chest. She kept her books and purse on the table and picked up the duster to clean the blackboard when she stopped in her tracks. The words were clearly visible—Period four: *Anushasan Parva.*

She kept staring at the blackboard for a long time. She then turned and asked, 'Who has written this?' she asked quietly. There was pin-drop silence. Normally she would have raved and ranted to the high heavens. While her tone was controlled, there was an unmistakable underlying threat.

No one dared utter a word.

'Who has written this?' she repeated in the same tone.

The class was silent. There was no movement.

'I say who has written this?' her voice held a sharp edge now. I could feel the hair on the back of my neck rise.

Some of the girls murmured amongst themselves. No one dared glance at me. The boys on the first bench are in any case meek and would not have dared turn around. It had happened once. Someone had made the mistake once of turning around to look at Surya, and Surya had taught him a lesson he never forgot.

'Okay, so you guys are not going to volunteer so easily,' she said, pursing her lips. Her anger was about to explode.

'Get your ruler here,' she said, pointing at Bibikar and, before he could step forward, she came to his desk and picked up the wooden ruler.

'So are you going to tell me or not?' she asked, tapping the ruler in her other palm.

The discomfort in the class was evident. My palms were sweating. No one likes Bendre ma'am. The memory of her rude behaviour with Shirodkar was fresh in everyone's minds. No one was going to speak out despite her warning. But the threat seemed real. Her ruler moved menacingly. No one had the nerve to bear the brunt of her lashings for the sake of protecting someone else. After all, it wasn't a simple punishment like standing in the class for the rest of the time. The girls were losing patience.

'I don't want to unnecessarily punish the entire class,' she said calmly going back to her desk. She turned to look at the boys and said, 'The culprit must step forward. There is no point in hiding like a coward. Else the entire class will bear the punishment thanks to one individual.'

The arrow hit the target. The girls were clearly agitated. One of the girls turned back and muttered, 'Why should we suffer?' Teredesai glanced back at the boys.

I was shivering by now. I had not anticipated my act would lead to such a situation. I knew she wouldn't like what I wrote, but I had not expected her to get so angry.

I was petrified and had no choice now but to get up and admit to my crime. The moment they got the first caning, people like Teredesai and the girls would have blurted out my name in any case. Some did not even need that prompting. We had teased girls like Sukdi so much that she would not lose this opportunity to take her revenge.

I looked out at the playground for a moment. The hot breeze blew dust all around. The distant mountains were lost in a haze. I knew there was no other option. I may as well get up before I was exposed by someone else. It was a do or die situation. I remember Zende sir pulling my ears. The words of the speech rang in my ears—'Fame is the fragrance of heroic deeds'.

I got up and said, in a calm voice, 'I wrote it, ma'am.'

Stunned for a moment, she looked at me. She had not expected the culprit to admit on his own accord. She thought I had stood up to point out the prankster, but here I was, confessing in the presence of the whole class. She recovered, her anger erupting with renewed intensity.

'Come forward', she growled.

I went and stood before her.

'Stretch out your palm,'

I stretched out my left palm. 'Both palms,' she said.

I stretched out both palms.

She hit out with the ruler on one palm with all her force. I could see her face contorted with anger. A stinging pain travelled from my neck down to the toes. I felt hot tears bubbling up, but I was determined. I gritted my teeth and was ready for the next one. I had decided to not show my weakness; not a whimper escaped my lips.

'*Anushasan Parva*, is it? *Anushasan Parva*?' she repeated

as she continued to hit me with the ruler. 'Do you have any shame? Take this! Take this!' She continued battering me.

My mind went blank, filled with a warm darkness. A reddish haze blurred my vision. The assault on my palms continued, but not a moan escaped my lips. I had noticed Shirodkar looking straight at me when ma'am hit me for the first time.

Ma'am continued to hammer blows on me without mercy; one after another. She had expected me to beg her to stop. But I was like a man possessed! I imagined I was Lokmanya Tilak or Bhagat Singh. I imagined I was being taken to the gallows, my hands were being nailed to the wall, but I was unperturbed. I was standing tall and proud. I challenged them to continue hitting me. Let the blows fall! I am ready to take them. The reddish curtain blurred my vision, but I could see Shirodkar through it. She continued to stare at me while I stood like an undefeated hero.

Finally, tired of her own assault, ma'am stopped.

'Go and sit at your place,' she said, throwing the ruler on to the table.

I went back without uttering a word. Sensation returned to the palms. They were red and swollen. My fingers ached miserably. I put my palms upwards on my thighs and placed my head on the bench. No one bothered to disturb me through the rest of the period.

The bell, mercifully, announced the mid-break.

The boys gathered around me even before ma'am had left the classroom.

'Ichibhana, this Bendre…!' Surya started, fumbling for the right words. 'We need to throw her out of school.'

'Chaila! Look at the way his palms have swollen up,' Teredesai observed. 'Must be aching like crazy, isn't it?'

'I salute you, Joshi,' Bibikar said. 'I could not have dared.'

'You are the bloody sissy-type first-benchers!' Surya erupted. 'And that ruler of yours! I've told you a thousand times not to get that thick ruler to school. If I see that again, I'll break it, bhenchod!'

'I won't get it again, I promise.'

'We ought to go and complain to the Principal,' Ghasu Gokhale suggested. 'Shall we?'

'What is the point in complaining?' Phawdya said. 'They are all the same. Is this a school or some kind of jail?'

I realized the girls were also looking at me. They were watching me from a respectable distance—the birdies, Mirikar, Sukdi, Bakre, Sarawate, and Deodhar; Shirodkar too.

'Look at the way she has battered him, poor soul!' one of them said.

'I swear! She has become a terror these days.'

'No one can afford to say anything in her period.'

The boys held my palms and inspected them. They felt as if they were on fire.

'Joshi, don't just sit here,' Chitre said. 'Come, let us go down. We need to put your hands under cold running water. You may feel better.'

We stood up and went out to the taps. I cringed when the cold water fell on the palms, but after some time I felt a little better.

'Do you want to drink some water?' Chitre asked.

'Yes, but how do I drink?' I asked. 'I cannot do anything with these hands.'

He ran and got a tumbler from Balu, the watchman and held it to my lips.

'Phawdya, go and get some ice-candy,' Surya said. 'Here, take this money and get four.'

'You will feel better eating that,' he said, looking at me.

'We have a special oil at home,' Santya suggested. 'Shall I get it? You smear it on the area where it hurts. It gives a lot of relief.'

'Then why don't you go and get it? Don't sit here and ask!' Surya said.

Santya rushed home. Chitre got another tumbler full of water. Phawdya got the ice-candy. Chitre helped me suck on it. I had held back my tears in the classroom, but now I could feel them brimming over.

Santya got the oil before the break ended. The oil was blackish-red with a pungent odour. He gently rubbed it onto my palms.

'It is an ancient remedy,' he whispered. 'Ekdum bestest!'

'How come you have it at home?' Phawdya asked.

'My dad got it,' he said, sharing a secret. 'It comes in handy whenever he gets beaten up by the police.'

The oil smelt horrible, but I felt a little better. The next period was Drawing. I sat at the back doing nothing. Rajguru sir asked me the reason and I was forced to show him my palms.

'Bendre ma'am hit him, sir,' Teredesai said.

Sir inspected my palms but kept quiet.

The next class was Manjrekar sir's. He asked us to draw a diagram. I tried holding the pencil, but it was impossible. Sir asked, 'Why are you not drawing?'

'Just look at his hands, sir,' the boys in the front bench

said. 'Bendre ma'am hit him because he wrote *Anushasan Parva* on the blackboard.'

Sir came near me and held my hands at the wrist to inspect the palms. He kept looking at them for a while. The entire class was silent. I was desperately trying to hold back my tears. Then he gently ruffled my hair saying, 'Grow up!'

Chitre and Phawdya wanted to accompany me back home, but I refused and took the route back through the paddy fields. I stopped near the trees. The tears were waiting to burst. I did not fight them. My palms were burning, but there was a strange sense of elation too. I felt good. It was like flying high in the air.

The sky was azure. The paddy fields stood silent in the warm sun. A patch of land on one side had been cleared out; they had probably started harvesting. The smell of ripe corn hung in the air. The breeze from the woods carried the scent of the trees. The oil on my palms smelt strange. But the fragrance all around me more than made up for it. I felt like a feather floating on fragrant waves.

I had decided not to say anything at home, but when Aaisaheb put the cup of tea before me, I wondered how I could possibly drink it. I tried curling my fingers around to pick it up but couldn't.

'Can you pour it in the saucer for me?' I finally asked Aaisaheb.

'Why? Are you a two-year-old toddler?'

Then I showed her my palms. Seeing them, she exclaimed, 'You rascal! What prank did you play this time? Got punished, isn't it? Great!'

Ambabai came running out of the room. I recounted

the entire episode before they had a chance to start their sermons.

'Who asked you to act oversmart?' Aaisaheb shouted. 'You think you're a big revolutionary, eh?'

Ambabai was silent for a while. She kept looking at my palms, wide-eyed.

'You are such young children. Why should you get involved in all this politics-volitics? Who taught you all this?' Aaisaheb continued.

I was expecting Ambabai to add insult to the injury. But surprisingly she kept quiet and did not toe Aaisaheb's line.

'Just look at the way she has hit him!' she exclaimed. 'This is akin to the brutality shown by the police. Why should she beat anyone like this? You must tell Baba to lodge a complaint in school tomorrow.'

A strange fear enveloped me. A complaint against Bendre ma'am would give her an excuse to hold a grudge against me forever. I could not risk that. I preferred to silently endure the pain instead.

Luckily Baba did not do anything. He was told about the entire episode when he returned in the evening. The lead was taken by Ambabai, of course. Baba merely said, 'The fault is his, isn't it? So he has to bear the punishment too. And in this case, it is better for a government servant like me to not interfere.'

Aaisaheb was initially upset with me, but after hearing Ambabai, directed her anger at Bendre ma'am. She kept quiet after hearing Baba's point of view. After dinner, she smeared fresh sandalwood paste on my palms, followed by the mandatory lecture. That night KT had come down to play chess with Baba. I was lying down with my palms facing down, hiding them, but he noticed. He quietly took me upstairs where his friends Ashok and Vijay were chatting. They asked me to recount the whole incident. They were impressed and, patting my back, said, 'We thought you were a kid. But you turned out to be a brave man! Shabbash! Yeh hui na baat!'

'What is the name of that sir?' Vijay asked. 'The one who told you about Emergency?'

'Manjrekar sir.'

'Would he come here if we invited him?'

'Yes, I am sure. He is a bindaas character.'

'Then we'll invite him one day. You did a good job today.'

'We should include him in our group,' Ashok suggested.

'What do you mean include him? He is already in our group,' KT said, looking at me. 'Isn't it so?'

I could not make out head or tail of their discussion, but the fact that I was part of their group made me feel very good. I felt I had suddenly grown up. I had grown in respect amongst the boys in my class and the girls too looked at me with a renewed sense of pride.

They believed that I had done something for the country. But only I knew the person for whom I had borne the punishment.

Chitre had arrived before me when I reached the building. He was reading a book titled *Biographies of Great Scientists*.

'When did you come?' I asked.

'Early,' he said. 'Ten-thirty or so.'

'That early?'

He pursed his lips and kept quiet. I realized something was amiss.

'What happened? Did your parents fight again?'

'No yaar. That saali Devaki!'

'What did she do now?'

'She asked me to lie down on top of her!'

'What?'

'She finished her work and then lay down on the cot. She then asked me to lie down on her saying her body was aching.'

'What did you do then?'

'What could I do? I just left the house and came here.'

Devaki, their housemaid, is a horny character. Whenever we go to Chitre's house, she hovers around us, sometimes dropping her pallu deliberately. She giggles for no reason to attract our attention. Surya says she is itching for some action.

'How does she get so much time?' I asked.

'That's easy. She comes in at eight-thirty. She finishes her work and my parents leave at half past nine. She's free then and tries to flirt with me. She even said she would help me undress.'

'Really?'

'She tries to fondle Raju. Raju does not understand; he is still a kid. But he mentioned that she fiddles with him.'

'Why don't you tell your Aai?'

'What can I tell her? She is Aai's favourite. And Aai pampers her knowing she cannot get a replacement easily.'

I visualized Devaki and a shiver of excitement ran through my body. I felt a little jealous of Chitre.

'I cannot concentrate on my studies, yaar,' Chitre confided. 'And the way she tries to hug me, I am scared my bottle may burst some day.'

I did not know how to advise him. For a moment, I missed Phawdya and Surya's counsel. But then I realized had they been present here they would have ragged him to death.

We sat there lost in our own thoughts.

The work at the building was temporarily stopped. There were piles of sand and bricks, but all the workers had left except for the couple staying there. Surya said that his father's money was stuck elsewhere. That was good news for us, because it meant his father would not visit us too frequently; we were free to use the entire building now. We used to reach there at eleven o' clock. It was an addiction.

Paranjpe ma'am finally came in one day, wearing a sleeveless blouse. We had spotted her from the building. Surya got excited seeing her. It was his lucky day. By the time we reached the classroom, the girls had already written the day, date, period etc on the board. We then asked Dashrath, the tallest in class, to rub it off and write the previous day's date a few inches higher. Those dumb girls could not understand why anyway.

The bell rang and ma'am entered the class. All of us waited with bated breath. Ma'am started a new chapter and, when she turned to write on the blackboard, she spotted the previous day's date. She picked up the duster to rub it off. She had to lift her hands and stand on her toes to rub what Dashrath had written. We had achieved our objective and were enjoying the sight, winking at each other and smiling. Ma'am must have realized something was wrong and looked at us suspiciously.

'The boys do it deliberately,' Sukdi volunteered. She was a little older than the other girls and understood the real reason behind the prank. 'They deliberately wrote the lines high up.'

It did not take much time for ma'am to understand what Sukdi meant. But it was not our fault. We had not asked her to wear a sleeveless blouse. She continued her class as if nothing had happened.

We were all pissed off with Sukdi. We could never do this again. Ma'am was teaching us grammar that day. The topic was figures of speech. She gave an example, 'Ram hit Ravan.'

She asked me to give another example and I promptly said, 'Suresh hit Mahesh.'

'Correct,' she said. 'Suresh hit Mahesh.'

The boys laughed out loud. Some of the girls tried to stifle their laugher with their handkerchiefs. I turned to look at Sukdi. She was cursing under her breath, looking down at the bench. Ma'am, quite obviously, was unaware of our prank.

The boys had got the hint. For every example we had Mahesh as the subject now. Ma'am continued, explaining some other parts of speech and said, 'Boy drinks milk.' She asked Bibikar to give another example. He said, 'Mahesh drinks milk.'

For some other example, the response was, 'Mahesh gets beaten.'

Ma'am could not understand why we were using Mahesh as the only subject. She asked, 'You seem to like Mahesh very much; don't you?

'Yes, Ma'am,' Chitre said. 'We all love Mahesh, Ma'am. And some of us love him too much.'

The class erupted in laughter. The girls did not know

how to react. They wanted to laugh but were not sure. Sukdi was fuming with anger, but she had no choice but to put up with it. She had been taught a lesson.

I decided to visit Misal that evening. I didn't inform anyone at home. I hadn't told Misal either. Had I met him on the road, I would have said I was coming over to visit him. I knew he would not be at home as this was his time for tuition class.

I took the road from Subhash Vidyalaya. I did not go towards the stone well. It was getting a little dark, but there was enough light. I could not dare walk directly into the lane leading to Shirodkar's house. I was worried I would be tongue-tied if I ran into her on the road. I went around the block, turning at Radheshyam Dairy. A few men sat reading the newspapers at the free library near the tamarind tree. Two tongas stood waiting for customers.

The two coconut trees at the gate of Shirodkar's house were visible from where I stood. My chest was pounding now. I could feel the hollow in the pit of my stomach growing. I realized standing there on the road would arouse suspicion and bravely decided to walk into the lane that directly led to her house.

The lane was silent. An old man walked by, carrying a small cloth bag. I ignored him. Old men are prone to start talking, especially seeing young boys. I reached Shirodkar's gate and had made up my mind not to look at the door but could not resist. The iron gate was ajar. A lamp burned in the verandah, but I could not see any movement inside the house. I stared at the house for a moment. It felt good. Then I continued walking and reached the end of the lane.

A lane there led to Misal's house. For a moment, I thought of visiting Misal but then decided against it. He would not have returned from tuition and visiting him without any reason may lead him to suspect me. A few people walked by. I lingered for a few moments and decided to return the same way.

I walked around casually, looking at the houses as if I was an outsider in that locality. I passed the Devgiri bungalow and was stunned to see the same old lady in a white saree standing in the balcony. She seemed to be looking straight at me. Luckily, it was getting dark and I was sure she couldn't see my face clearly. I was worried she would begin to wonder why a young boy was pacing the lane in the late hours of the evening. In all likelihood, she would have seen me go the other way only a few minutes back. I quickened my pace.

Shirodkar's house was enveloped in silence. I walked a little slower, but there was no one to be seen. I observed the house carefully but decided not to stop on the road. Then I walked all the way back to the tamarind tree.

I could not go back. There was the danger of that lady at the Devgiri bungalow spotting me again. I decided that it was enough for the day. In any case, it was unlikely I would meet Shirodkar on the road. I was happy I had been able to spot her lane and house.

I was feeling light. The place, unknown to me till the other day, seemed very familiar now. It felt like home.

I was keen to go back the very next day, but I knew I needed to be careful lest the people there suspect my movements. I allowed a day to pass and then decided to go for a walk the next evening. I was carrying a notebook and a Mathematics textbook in hand. A school boy, and that too carrying a few books in his hand, is left alone and no one doubts him. One needs to carry something in one's hand—a book or even a bag would suffice. People have a habit of staring at anyone walking empty-handed. That jobless old lady at Devgiri bungalow; she would be sure to notice. I had an excuse ready for Misal if he spotted me—I would tell him I was on my way to his place.

I walked into Shirodkar's lane with confidence. A rusted iron name-plate, secured to an electric pole, proclaimed the name of the lane. There was an overflowing garbage dump nearby. It was a good landmark, unlikely to be missed.

I entered the lane and glanced at the Devgiri bungalow. Luckily the old lady was not around. I felt relieved and stopped opposite Shirodkar's house. There was a young boy playing with a cricket ball in the garden. I was sure he was her younger brother. He must have been in class four or five. I stood for a while at the gate watching him play.

The thought of engaging him in conversation by asking him for directions to some fictitious address flitted across my mind. I had learnt this from Chitre. He says it is a good way to strike up a conversation. He advises that one should carry a chit with some incomplete address. There should be some landmarks like 'near the station,' or 'across the hospital,' and so on. It makes the address look authentic. When you ask someone for directions with a written note as reference, people take you seriously. Chitre has tested his hypothesis with many people. He can keep a straight face and the fact that he is fair-skinned acts in his favour. People normally trust fair-complexioned boys. Phawdya and I would simply burst out laughing. No one would trust Surya seeing his face! And in any case, he does not care about such pranks.

I realized I did not have a piece of paper on me. There was no point in asking a small kid for some address. He would immediately call out for his 'Aaiiiiii!' Mothers are still manageable as they do not suspect you easily, but if there were an elder sister, that would make things quite difficult. Elder sisters have been coached not to talk to strangers. I would be dead meat if Shirodkar herself were to come out! I dropped the idea.

I did not linger for long and continued walking up to the tamarind tree. I turned to go for another round of the lane. Shirodkar's brother was still playing with the ball. I hoped that the ball would fall outside the gate and I would get a chance to speak to him. Luckily for me, he was her younger brother. Elder brothers take it upon themselves to protect their sisters. I could have brought Surya along to thrash an elder brother, but then if you thrash the brother, you cannot expect his sister to fall in love with you, can you?

The child continued to play with the ball, which refused to fall outside the gate. I had a good look at the house. There was a small verandah outside the main door with three steps leading to it. There was a longish window covered by a curtain. A flight of steps from the side led to the top floor. The house looked big but was probably narrow and long. There were a few trees in the garden outside—hibiscus, firecracker and other flower shrubs. The garden was well-kept. The grass too had been trimmed.

I walked upto the garbage dump and turned back immediately. I could have paced the lane many times, but unfortunately I spotted the old lady in white saree standing at the gate talking to some other lady. She peered at me as I walked by. I reached the tamarind tree but lost the courage to turn around. The two women were still chatting away at the gate. They were sure to have accosted me if I had gone past them one more time.

I was at a loss. I did not know what to do. If only there had been a few shops around, I could have spent some time roaming around. I looked at the open library below the tree. Men sat there immersed in newspapers as usual. A board at the library proclaimed 'Shrirang Library'.

An idea formed in my head. I had solved the problem of whiling away time. I went to the library and picked up a newspaper kept in the wooden pigeon-holes. I kept the books on the side and pretended to read the newspaper while holding it across my face. The paper was a local one, full of notices and tenders. There was nothing to read in it. I could see the lane clearly from my vantage point. The ladies continued to chat, standing at the gate. It was a perfect place to wait.

I picked up another paper after sometime. There were all kinds of newspapers kept there—*Navakal, Navashakti, Loksatta*, etc. Each person read his newspaper, and keeping it properly folded at the rack, pick up another one. No one spoke to another. One man, sitting next to me, shuffled his paper and loudly exclaimed, 'These bastards should be skinned alive!'

I turned to see he was muttering to no one in particular. No one paid him any attention. He was wearing a striped pyjama and a baniyan. He had white stubble on his chin and reeked of alcohol. I moved a few seats away.

I was enjoying myself. I felt like a daredevil detective. I had a vantage point to observe the lane. I could sit here for as long as I wished, and spot Shirodkar the moment she arrived.

It was getting dark. The shops had switched on their lights. There was not much light below the tree. The people reading the newspapers too had left one by one. The municipal lamps were switched on in the lanes. I could see a faint silhouette of the gate now. I realized I had to leave. But I was feeling good. I now had a place to wait. No one would suspect me of anything even if I sat there for a long time. After all, school children are supposed to read newspapers. I returned home with a spring in my steps.

The half-yearly exams loomed large after Dusshera. Surya and Phawdya wanted us to meet at our adda before the exam to study together. I helped them with English and Chitre, as usual, would solve all problems in Maths beforehand. But it was impossible to study for long when we were together. Surya talked of Kevda all the time. We whiled away most of the time chatting, whilst the books were mute spectators to our activities. I would come home and study. But it was not easy to concentrate there either.

The exams began. For the language papers, we were made to sit with the eighth standard students, stoking Surya's hopes of being in the same room as Kevda. But to his dismay, we were with Eighth-D, while Kevda was in Eighth-A. We are made to sit in alphabetical order, so Chitre would sit ahead, followed by me, Phawdya and finally Surya. Surya's neighbours were Dashrath and

Harishchandra, and of no use to him. If he was lucky, he got to sit in the row next to mine. That's when he could copy at least the 'fill in the blanks' and 'match the following' type of answers from me.

But Surya needed help in all the papers. We could help with the answers in Maths, but how could one help him copy the equations? Halbe sir once wondered how he had got the answer right when all his steps were wrong. Anyway, it all depends on who the exam supervisor is. If it is Bendre ma'am, then we are screwed. There is no point in having Manjrekar or Zende sir either. They may be friendly, but they do not allow us to talk when the exam is on. Our best bet is Rajguru sir or Halbe sir. Even Prem Chopra is fine. He likes to believe pacing the aisles is a sufficient deterrent; but then we know how to copy.

Since Shirodkar's name begins with 'S', she sits far away from me; in fact most of the time in the next classroom. The eighth standard rooms are cramped and stuffy. But things changed suddenly before the social science paper. We were asked to move to the laboratory, which had been converted into a makeshift exam room. A row of cupboards, lined up in the centre of the room, acted as a divider. But there were just three cupboards. The teachers arranged them in such a manner that they left wide gaps between them. The benches on either side of the divider faced each other.

I came in early. I was on the first bench while Phawdya and Surya were far behind. An eighth standard girl shared my bench. The bell rang and all the girls and boys streamed in to occupy their respective seats. I could not believe my eyes when I looked ahead. Shirodkar and I sat facing each other. It was unbelievable!

I was conscious of the hollow in the pit of my stomach. The tension before the exam added to it. A tremor passed through my body. She saw me staring at her and quickly looked down.

Paranjpe ma'am was the supervisor. I was on the first bench so there was no question of helping anyone copy from me. I had no such plans in any case. Ma'am distributed the question paper and answer sheets. The nerds started scribbling the moment the teacher gave the signal to begin.

Shirodkar glanced at me once before she began writing. She quickly put her head down when she found me staring. I realized this was too good an opportunity to lose. The next exams, the finals, were six months away. There was no guarantee we would be seated this way again. I was not going to let this godsent opportunity go waste.

I continued to stare at her. She must have guessed and did not look up again. Ma'am came to sign the answer sheets. Normally teachers do not converse with students during an exam but, seeing my pages blank, she asked, 'Why, what happened? Haven't started yet?'

'I will,' I said, muttering under my breath.

I continued to look at Shirodkar after ma'am moved away. Her face radiated freshness; as usual she was wearing aboli flowers in her hair. Her uniform was neatly pressed while her hair was tied into two plaits with yellow ribbons shaped like flowers. The ribbon flowers shook as her hand moved on the paper. Her earrings too moved gently.

I continued to stare while she continued to write without looking up even once. She knew I was staring at her so there was no question of her looking up. No girl would ever do that.

I then decided to concentrate on the question paper. Normally I would attack it with great gusto, but this time the questions were weird: reasons for formation of Prussia, special rights given to the French aristocracy, differences in opinion between Mazini and Garibaldi and so on. We had to write the name of the person who said, 'If they do not have bread why don't they eat cake?' I would have answered these easily on any other day, but today I could not remember a single answer.

I then decided to attempt the 'fill in the blanks' section. That turned out to be easy. Manjrekar sir says we should always attempt the best answers first. The examiner is impressed if he or she finds correct answers in the beginning of the answer sheet and then does not bother to check the rest of the paper with the same alertness. If you impress with the first few answers, you are likely to get good marks.

But I was unable to write much. I was worried she may look at me while I was busy writing and I would miss the opportunity. But she never did. The girl next to me seemed to know very little and had a huge blot of ink on her answer sheet. Chitre and I used to help the duds in the senior classes especially in Language or History examinations. But she did not seem to be the kind that deserved help.

The bell rang indicating the end of the first hour.

The paper was for a total of three hours consisting of History, Geography and Civics with forty, forty and twenty marks respectively. The first hour and a quarter were meant for History and all I had answered so far was a ten-mark question. I was sure to fail if I continued at the same speed.

I had a final good look at Shirodkar and decided to attempt the paper with all seriousness. I attacked the

History section first and completed it as quickly as possible. I then tackled the Civics paper, answering questions on formation of government, types of governments, etc.

I looked up once and was taken aback. She was looking at me and the moment our eyes met, she looked down. It meant she too was looking at me! My heart began pounding again and the familiar feeling in the pit of my stomach returned. I knew that I should not look up. Else, she would not dare look at me again. I concentrated on the Geography section at hand when the bell sounded, signalling the end of the second hour.

The first question was regarding the different types of layers forming the structure of the Earth. I recalled the coloured picture in our textbook and wrote the answer. Then I looked up to find her looking at me again. As usual, she quickly looked down the moment I caught her.

Our game was getting interesting now. I was thoroughly enjoying it. I was not aware of what I wrote in the paper. There were some topics related to the shifting of continents, the various topographies in India, etc. Our game of glances continued for the rest of the hour. I saw her smile faintly just before the final bell rang.

On the way back home, I was in seventh heaven, floating all the way. I was least bothered about the marks I would get. It was a half-yearly exam in any case. Just a bloody drama to keep the teachers busy correcting answer sheets during their Diwali holidays. Her eyes and those lovely irises floated in front of me. Nothing else mattered. Now I had three weeks of Diwali holidays. 'French Revolution Zindabad!' I shouted with joy as I walked my way back home through the paddy fields.

The Diwali holidays began; but, really, no one likes holidays. 'There is no school to go to,' Chitre complained, 'I do not know what to do. There is Raju on one side and that Devaki on the other!' Phawdya was worried he would have to sit in the subzi mandi each day and that his mother would buy extra vegetables to sell now. Surya dreaded staying at home lest his father find some reason to spank him. I had no such problems, but there was the issue of passing time during the day. There were no children to play with in our building; the adults would be back only in the evening. Even KT and Vijay were not around until sundown.

I could go visiting Chitre or Phawdya, but that was possible only once a day. What did one do with the rest of the day? We did meet a few times at our adda, but that was no fun. There were no school children passing by. The road was empty. The irony was we would pray for a free period during school hours to escape classes, but a whole vacation with no school was turning out to a burden. We could not even play cricket between just the four of us. Finally, on the third day, Surya said, 'Ichibhana, this holiday is a pain in the ass. Why don't they have holidays interspersed with school days?'

I had my own little plans though. I decided to visit Misal. I invited him to my place first, lest he doubt my intentions. I visited him the very next day, but it turned out to be a waste of time. He was keen to visit other parts of the town while I wanted to roam around the lanes next to his house. I realized visiting him was not of much use. He would sit on the steps of his verandah and bore me with stories of farming and other village activities. It was clear; visiting him would not serve my real purpose.

I went to that side of town the next day and spent time sitting below the tamarind tree and reading the newspaper. But I was unable to see her. I tried going up and down the lane a couple of times, but the house seemed to be enveloped in silence. There was no one to be seen. I feared they had gone away in the holidays. In that case, it would be meaningless to roam around, hoping to catch a glimpse of her. I did not linger any longer and returned home.

But Shirodkar had not gone away, for I saw her at Phawdya's shop the very next day. We sat on two makeshift benches made of wooden boxes and covered with old gunny bags. There was not much crowd. Phawdya showed me how he could easily cheat some women by randomly raising prices or weighing vegetables incorrectly.

A fat Gujarati lady came in and haggled a lot. Phawdya winked at me saying, 'Just see how I fool her now.' And he passed off half a kilo of cauliflower as three quarters of a kilo. He did the same with cabbage. We laughed a lot when the lady waddled away, unaware that she had been duped.

The crowd picked up as the evening progressed, and women returning from their offices stopped by to purchase vegetables. I was about to get up and leave when Phawdya nudged me with his elbow. 'Wait. I can see Shirodkar coming this way.' I thought he was pulling my leg. I followed his line of sight and there she was! For a moment, I was worried Phawdya might have guessed I was falling for her.

She came and stood there. I kept staring at her like a zombie, unable to believe my eyes. She was not in her school dress, and it took me a moment to recognize her.

She was wearing a lovely floral-print dress. She looked so different.

She flashed a bright, friendly smile at us.

'So what all do you have today, Pandurang?' she asked in her sweet, melodious voice. And then turning towards me, she enquired, 'What are *you* doing here?'

I continued to gape at her. Phawdya, on the other hand, was a cool customer. He replied, 'I have some nice ridge-gourd and fresh guar beans too.'

'Give me half a kilo of both. And add a kilo of tomatoes, some coriander leaves and green chillies.'

Phawdya weighed the vegetables. She gave her bag and he poured the vegetables from the weighing scale into it. He added a liberal quantity of coriander and green chillies.

'How much?' she asked.

'One rupee for the ridge-gourd and one and half for the beans,' Phawdya said. 'And three for the tomatoes.'

She took out a five-rupee note from a small purse along with a fifty paise coin.

'No lemons today?'

'No.'

'Oh.'

She turned to go, but not before looking at me to give a sweet smile. She disappeared before I could say anything.

She had come in and gone away like a breeze. And she had spoken to me! Actually spoken! I had roamed around her house a zillion times but without getting a glimpse of her. And here she was, standing right across and asking me what I was doing in Phawdya's shop.

'What are you thinking, buddy?' Phawdya asked me, nudging me with his elbow.

'Does she come here often?' I asked.

'Yes, why?' he asked, gathering the guar beans into a heap. 'Not just her—most of our school girls do.'

'Most of them?'

'Yes, most of them. You think people don't buy vegetables?'

'Do you give them for free?'

'Why would I give them for free? Just because they happen to be in my class?'

'Do you give them a discount?'

'No. Many of them bargain a lot when they come with their mothers. In that case, I don't haggle and agree to whatever they say.'

'Shirodkar did not ask you the price before buying, isn't it?'

'Yes. She's nice. That's why I gave her the chillies and the coriander leaves for free.'

I was jealous of Phawdya. And angry at my parents! Why couldn't they own a shop like this? Any shop for that matter: vegetables, stationery, kirana, cosmetics, or whatever! Even a shop selling pooja items would do. I could sit at the counter the whole day and give away the entire shop for free to Shirodkar whenever she visited us.

'Saale, you never told me.'

'Told you what?'

'That all the girls come visiting your shop.'

'What is there to boast about? In fact, you don't know how embarrassed I feel when I see them.'

What was there to feel embarrassed about? I was not embarrassed to sit there and, in fact, I went there on a few more occasions. But she didn't come. I could not ask

Phawdya about her as he would then surely smelt a rat. He was not an idiot like Misal! I would have to find some other way.

I invited Surya, Phawdya and Chitre to my house on the first day of Diwali. Normally Aaisaheb is not keen on calling my friends home, but on Diwali she does not mind. I wanted to invite Santya too, but he was not at home. Later, I sent across a parcel of sweets to his house.

Surya and Phawdya are happy to come home. They love the laddoos made by Aaisaheb. But she does not have the finesse with which Chitre's mother prepares the dishes. Her chaklis never turn out right; they are either too soft or too hard. Ambabai is the one to be blamed. She hovers around in the kitchen trying to help but causing only trouble. But I have to praise whatever is prepared.

Naru mama came over for the bhai dooj festival and stayed back for a few days. I do not miss my gang when he is around. He is the equivalent of four friends. As always, Naru mama had got a lovely saree for Aaisaheb. Aaisaheb was thrilled and had kept the saree prominently displayed for Baba to see on his return from office. He, as usual, gave a packet of money to Aaisaheb on the Padwa day. It must have been the same amount each year. Aaisaheb seemed a little upset that evening. But Naru mama's presence made the house lively. Baba had given me some money to buy Ambabai a gift. I decided to get her a book of poems. I had wrapped it in coloured paper, and she was happy to receive it.

The next morning was a Friday. A new movie was being screened in the theatre.

'Naru mama, shall we?' I asked. 'There is a new picture in town.'

'Which one?'

'*Diamonds are Forever*. James Bond. It is on in the morning show only.'

'Let's go,' he said in English.

'But are you not already late for the show,' Aaisaheb asked.

'You won't get tickets.' Ambabai, as always, had to have her say.

'You need not curse us. We will see what we have to do. Diamonds are for ever,' I said, repeating each word carefully.

'No, that's not the way to pronounce the words. The 'R' is silent. You should say diamonds aa foh eveh,' Naru mama said, as he zipped up his trousers.

'Diamonds aa foh eveh…,' I said, trying to imitate him.

We reached the talkies to find a huge crowd there; clearly, there were many like us who wanted to see the movie on day one. The queue for the balcony and the first class stall extended right up to the road. A huge poster of James Bond with his gun in his right hand greeted us. Two ladies, one black and the other white, stood with their backs to each other, flanking him. Now I wanted to see the movie even more. But there seemed hardly any chance of getting the tickets. I could not spot any of the usual black marketeers.

'I don't think we are going to get tickets today,' I told Naru mama. 'Ambabai cursed us.'

'Hmm,' Naru mama said, looking around.

We stood there wondering what to do when I heard a

familiar laughter. I turned to see Sukdi with two boys. She walked towards us.

'Aiyaa, Joshi?' She exclaimed. 'So you too have come to see the movie, eh?'

I was at a loss for words. We teased her in the class, but I had never actually conversed with her. And here she was, talking to me as if we spoke regularly.

'Yes,' I managed to reply. I looked at Naru mama who raised his eyebrows in question. I was praying she would leave me alone, but she continued.

'Who is he?' she asked, looking at Naru mama.

'My mama.'

'Oh, is that so? Namaste,' she said, sounding very well-mannered.

Naru mama was impressed and I was taken aback for a moment. She looked stunning in a purple sleeveless dress, which showed off her slender arms. The dress was knees-length and accentuated her height. She was wearing a big, white hair clip.

'And she's…?' Naru mama asked, looking at me.

'This is Geeta Shenoy, my classmate.'

Naru mama seemed a little surprised. Sukdi does not look like a school girl and in that dress, particularly, she looked much older.

'So are you also here for the movie?' Sukdi asked.

'Yes. But it seems your theatre here will not give us tickets,' Naru mama said.

'Oh, is that so? Wait here for a moment. Let me see,' Sukdi said. Then she called out to someone in the queue, 'Mahesh! Get two more!'

So Mahesh was there too. I looked in the direction of

the queue and saw him standing there. He waved back, acknowledging Sukdi's request. I looked around to see if there were any more known faces. But Sukdi continued talking without a care.

'So what are you up to in the vacations? 'Sukdi asked. 'Studying, I suppose.'

'No. I haven't started yet,' I said. 'What about you?'

'I went to my village for a few days and have not yet looked at the homework.' Looking at Naru mama she asked, 'So what does your mama do?'

'I teach English in a college,' he answered.

'English? Oh god! Ask him to teach us. Our Bendre ma'am is a terror.'

Naru mama did not reply but smiled at her, glancing at his wristwatch once. The crowds were increasing but luckily I did not spot any known faces.

'Is English such a difficult subject?' she asked Naru mama.

'No. Not at all. In fact, English is a lovely language,' Naru mama said, speaking the last line in English.

'But this Bendre ma'am makes it so difficult,' she said. 'What do you say?' This was directed at me.

'Yes!' I said.

Mahesh came with the tickets. He did not say anything, but just arched his eyebrows. I was embarrassed but kept quiet.

'Meet Mahesh,' Sukdi introduced Mahesh without any hesitation.

'Glad to meet you,' Naru mama said, extending his hand stylishly.

Mahesh was impressed with Naru mama's style. He

shook hands and gave him the tickets. Naru mama paid him.

'Thanks so much,' he said. 'Hope it was not a bother. Now we can see the movie thanks to you.'

'Come on! That's no big deal!' Sukdi said. 'Mahesh was buying the tickets in any case. Luckily he was right there in the queue.'

The bell rang and it was time to go in. I was worried Mahesh and Sukdi may be sitting next to us, but luckily they were a little further away. I was waiting to tell Naru mama about them.

'Sukdi and Mahesh are having an affair, you know?' I told Naru mama.

'So what?'

'Did you see the way they come for the movie together? Without any fear.'

'What is wrong with that?' Naru mama asked.

'Things are really hotting up, you know?'

'Nonsense,' Naru mama said. 'Don't blabber anything you feel like. She's quite a decent girl. I liked her.'

I kept quiet. I wanted to tell him everything: how we teased her, how Mahesh was beaten up once. But seeing Naru mama's reaction, I decided to not volunteer any more information. The movie began soon enough.

We came out in the interval.

'See if you can spot her,' Naru mama said. 'We will buy ice-cream for all of them.'

Now this was getting dangerous. Naru mama was going beyond the ordinary. I would be dead meat if my school mates found me sharing an ice-cream with Sukdi.

'They will buy it themselves, Naru mama,' I tried. 'I will

be teased to death if the boys find out I shared an ice-cream with her.'

'Nonsense,' Naru mama dismissed me.

We went about searching for her when she landed up with a packet of popcorn.

'Please!' she offered the packet to us.

'Come on, let us have some ice-cream,' Naru mama said, pointing at the ice-cream counter.

'No, it is fine. We just had tea.'

'I will not take any excuse. You are with us, isn't it? Then please come.'

'No, I mean, we are fine,' she pleaded. 'Joshi, why don't you tell him?'

Naru mama was not in a mood to listen. He seemed to be impressed with her and bought expensive Chocobars for all of us. I had begun to enjoy the interaction.

'This nephew of yours teases me a lot in the class,' she said, taking a bite of her ice-cream. She was smiling. Mahesh too smiled. I did not know where to hide my face.

'Is that true?' Naru mama asked, a little angry. 'This is not good,' he added in English.

'Anyway, leave it!' Sukdi said. 'But he is really good in playing word games, especially those with film titles. You cannot beat him to it.'

I forced a smile on my face.

We walked back home, trying to keep in the shade. It was hot. I told Naru mama about her affair.

'You should not tease her, 'Naru mama said. 'I admire her. You tease her yet she's not afraid. She comes out to see the movie with her friend caring two hoots about the world. That's real love. I must say: hats off to her. I liked her.'

Naru mama had a point. Sukdi was being honest about her relationship. I was worried Mahesh would bully me and I may have to resort to taking Surya's help, but he had smiled and said nothing. My fears had been unfounded.

'Listen! Remember one thing,' Naru mama continued. 'It is such progressive thinking people who take the nation ahead. Not the bespectacled, bookworms who are just buried in books. You need to support such people instead of teasing them.'

I did not understand what he said then but later on realized he was right. We used to tease her in the class all the time. I was told her father would beat her up regularly. Even the teachers taunted her often. Mahesh kept to his own affairs yet was beaten up by Surya and gang. But they did not bother about what others thought or said about them and that was remarkable. How would I feel if people teased me and Shirodkar? I promised myself not to tease Sukdi any more.

Aaisaheb had been on the lookout for a suitable bride for Naru mama and took the opportunity of his visit to show him one of the prospective brides. They visited her house. I was keen to tag along, but no one asked me. As per the original plan, Baba was to go, but he was happy to pass it up. Besides, Aaisaheb was superstitious and believed 'three may spoil the party'. Ambabai suggested we call them over to our place, but Aaisaheb preferred not to. She did not want the people around to gossip. She preferred secrecy in such matters.

Naru mama did not like the girl. We had gone for a walk around the MIDC area when he confided he found her a sort of 'kakubai'. Luckily Aaisaheb did not like her much either. Naru mama was safe for a while.

'I am going to look for a Christian girl,' Naru mama said. 'You know the smart, bob-cut type? How impressive they look!'

I liked the idea.

'Yes, Naru mama. You should find someone like that,' I concurred. 'But then, why are you going through this rigmarole of seeing girls. Why don't you find one yourself, Ichi....?'

I was about to say Ichibhana, just the way Surya does, but checked myself. I prayed Naru mama would fall in love with a girl and then confide in me. I would get to meet her secretly a few times and after the wedding, I would proudly boast to Aaisaheb and Ambabai of having known about it all along. What fun it would be to see their faces then!

'Sure. But for that I have to meet one first!' Naru mama said.

'Don't you have good looking girls in your college?' I asked.

Naru mama started laughing.

'They are all my students!' he said.

'So what? What is wrong with that?'

'You are too young to understand these things right now. It is not that easy.'

I knew that these things were not easy. Naru mama need not tell me that. In fact, I wanted him to tell me how to make these things easy!

'There is this Manoj Desai in my class,' I began, bringing up the fictional character to tell my story. 'He is unable to confide his love to the girl he loves.'

'He needs to be relentless. He should not give up,' Naru mama advised.

'He goes towards her house each evening. But it has not helped him.'

'Why does he go there?'

'In the hope of seeing her.'

'Patience, my dear friend. Patience!' Naru mama said.

'But what is the point in just going around the house? Does it help?'

'I don't think it does. And who knows, she may be in love with someone else.'

I had never thought on those lines. What if Shirodkar was interested in someone else? Naru mama had mentioned once that girls generally avoid falling in love with someone from their locality or their class as they fear their affair would become public knowledge. The boys, unaware of their affair elsewhere, keep hoping. Sukdi was a good example. So was the case with Gopujkar in tenth standard, or Sule, for that matter. There was no girl I knew who had an affair with a classmate.

I was mortally scared. But I brushed away the thought. Shirodkar was a nice girl who did not have an affair with anyone. Had it been so, Misal would have told me. She was not like that, I assured myself.

'Ask Manoj to visit her house,' Naru mama continued. 'He should go to her house, play with her younger siblings, eat whatever her mother offers, and have a good chat. That way you become good friends and no one suspects you.'

The idea was fantastic! And flawless! That was the case with Chitre, wasn't it? I imagined a scenario: Shirodkar had invited me to her house. I was being introduced to her mother and her sister. 'He's Joshi from my class,' she was saying. 'He is very intelligent.' Then her Aai said, 'Oh is that so? Why didn't you come earlier?' Her sisters sat around and talked to me. I played underhand cricket with her younger brother and deliberately got out a few times. And then they fed me something I had never eaten in my house. And as I was about to leave, her Aai said in a sweet voice, 'Do visit us once in a while.' Shirodkar came to the gate to see me off and smiled sweetly. I was lost in my dream.

'What are you dreaming about?' Naru mama asked, patting me on my head. 'Looks like you too are trying to get something going.'

'No way! I am not interested in such things.' I said.

'Good,' he said. 'Focus on your studies.'

I was waiting for the holidays to get over so that I could tell the gang about our encounter with Sukdi. We all assembled at our adda, as usual, and I recounted the entire episode, including minor details like the colour of Mahesh's shirt. I told them what Naru mama had advised me and then I declared, 'I am not going to tease Sukdi any more.'

I was expecting Surya and Phawdya to growl at me, but surprisingly Surya said, 'You are right, bhenchod. If tomorrow Kevda and I are together, I don't want anyone to tease her.'

'I have never teased Mahesh,' Phawdya declared.

The school children were passing by, but none of us seemed to be in a mood to tease them. I kept an eye out on the road for her.

'There should be a separate school for folks like me,' Surya said.

'What do you mean by folks like you?' I asked.

'Folks who are in love. There should be a school for such people. Others like you would not be allowed there.'

'Great idea.'

'Of course, bhenchod! A couples-only school. And each couple will have a separate bench. No one disturbs anybody. It would be fun.'

'Even the teachers should be couples,' Chitre added, winking at me.

'You are absolutely right, bhenchod!' Surya said, getting excited. 'That's the kind of school, which is worth being called a school. What a horrid school we go to!'

I loved the idea but did not show much enthusiasm; I was scared they would ask, 'What about you?' But the idea was fantastic. I imagined myself and Shirodkar sitting on the fourth bench. There were others like Surya and Kevda, Sukdi and Mahesh, and others. Ghasu Gokhale and Mirikar were sitting on the first bench. The teachers were Sathe ma'am and Mohite sir or Paranjpe ma'am and Zende sir.

No one would tease any one. Everyone would be focused on studies as there was no reason for any distraction when the one you wanted was sitting next to you.

I was thrilled with the idea. That day while coming out of the classroom in the mid-break, I saw Sukdi. We did not talk, but her knowing smile said everything. I returned her smile.

The half-yearly results were announced a few days after school reopened. I had come tenth while Chitre stood fifth. Bibikar, as usual, came first, followed by Ghasu Gokhale and Mirikar. I had slipped two ranks since last year. Teredesai and Deshpande had moved up. I was scared of my performance in the Social Science paper but luckily had managed fifty-five per cent. Shirodkar stood twelfth. I was happy I stood close to her. How I wished they would arrange the seating in the same order as the ranks.

The school atmosphere was a little relaxed. The next two or three months were going to be fun. We would have our annual trip, guest lectures, sports and annual gathering—there would be many such programmes ahead. One good thing about our school is the constant stream of extra-curricular activities. Appa loves these things. It is not the case with the folks at Tope High School or Subhash Vidyalaya. They have their usual annual programme and that is it.

The activities around the Emergency continued. Appa came up with a new song, '*Maa tere beeson sapne sakar karenge hum*'. It had something to do with the government's twenty-point programme. It included work for the unemployed, good wages, equal rights, homes for the poor and so on.

The meetings between Ashok, Vijay and KT had intensified. Earlier they used to play cricket with us, but nowadays they were busy holding meetings. Earlier they used to keep the door open, but now the door stayed shut. There was a constant stream of people coming and going.

Ambabai threw a fit seeing my results. I had planned to show it to Baba in the evening, but she was all set to pounce on me the moment I entered the house. 'Show me your progress report,' she said the moment I stepped in. I handed it over to Aaisaheb and while she searched for her spectacles, Ambabai snatched and started reading it.

'Wow! He has a good rank in two digits,' she said, sarcasm pouring in. 'Aai, our prince has managed a rank among the top ten.'

Aaisaheb did not get her taunt.

'What is his rank?'

'Tenth! Earlier his Lordship used to come in the top five. He is improving in geometric progression—five, ten, twenty, forty. So it would be great if he manages to pass in the tenth standard.'

'Marks do not mean everything,' I said. 'Aai, give me something to eat.'

'What do you mean marks do not mean anything. Then why don't you get the first rank?'

'What do you mean *get*? Is it some kind of a vegetable that I can buy in the market?'

That incensed her further.

'Aai, do you see how rudely he speaks? He says there is nothing great in getting a rank. Then can you explain doing what is great?'

I realized there was no point in arguing with her. I left the snacks untouched on the table and quickly put on my sandals and stepped out. Aaisaheb tried calling out to me, but I ignored her. She would go back and shout at Ambabai. That would serve her right. I knew the way to upset Aaisaheb and make her shout—ask for some snack and not eat it. In any case I was not interested in her bland upma.

I returned home by dinnertime. Ambabai was waiting for me to hand over the report card to Baba.

'Baba, my report card.'

'I have already signed it,' he said, without taking his eyes off the newspaper. 'It seems you have gone down by a few ranks.'

'Yes,' I admitted. 'I didn't do well in one of the Social Science papers.'

'Which one?'

'Civics. Even the History and Geography portions were absurd.'

'Fine. Just ensure that you do not fail, okay?'

'Yes,' I said, putting the report card back in my school bag. Ambabai looked at me and I made a bulldog-like face, but she was waiting to have her revenge during dinner time.

'Baba, Mukund should join tuition classes now,' she announced.

Baba looked at me with raised eyebrows.

'There is no need for extra tuition in class nine. My finals are not over yet,' I said.

'That's the reason you should join now,' she persisted.

'I know Maths and English well.'

'Knowing is not enough. How much have you scored in Maths?'

I had got a hundred and ten out of one hundred and fifty, if you included Geometry and Algebra. It was quite okay, but Ambabai was a difficult customer.

'You should join the classes immediately,' she said.

'Let us see,' I said, using Baba's favourite line.

She persisted. 'Don't you want to be an engineer?'

I did not continue the argument. Aaisaheb was certainly not on my side, but I was not sure if Baba would support me. I decided to keep quiet. I got up, washed my hands, and went out to watch a carrom game in progress.

I went the next day towards Shirodkar's house and sat at the usual place below the tamarind tree reading the newspaper. The regulars were there, including the man in the striped pyjamas. There was no point in speaking with anyone, so I kept to myself reading the papers.

I was not expecting to see her and was about to get up when my patience bore fruit. I saw Shirodkar stepping out of her house along with another girl. She couldn't have been her sister as she was quite dark. They both walked in the direction of the tamarind tree. My heart was beating loudly. I hid behind the tree, using the paper as an additional cover.

They went to the Suyog General Store behind the tree. It struck me that I could go in there on the pretext of buying something. But I did not have any money in my pocket. But one could always ask for a graph notebook unlikely to be found in a general store; it was another of Chitre's ideas. But my heart was beating wildly and the hollow in my stomach was getting deeper. I could not move an inch and continued to sit there. There was, of course, the problem of the other girl accompanying her.

They bought something from the store and started walking back the way they had come. They did not look around else they could have spotted me.

I was angry at myself. I had sat here for days in the hope of seeing her. I had seen her now and I could have easily gone in there and spoken to her. There was no need to worry about the other girl. I had missed a huge opportunity. Now I could sit there until eternity without achieving anything! I cursed myself.

But there was no point in getting upset. I knew I got

mortified and tongue-tied, and my body went limp, the moment I saw her. I returned home with a heavy heart. But the fact that I had seen her was something to feel good about.

As the days passed by, I found myself constantly thinking of her. It did not take much effort anyway; it came about naturally. It was better in school when I could watch her while pretending to look ahead at the blackboard. But she was with me even while returning home, in the paddy fields, while watching carrom at night, at dinnertime and even while drinking water. I would feel her presence around me all the time. It was a warm sensation, which left me thirsting for more. I knew something was happening to me but could not put a finger on it. I was floating and feeling suffocated at the same time. I could feel her close by when she was absent, but she would seem lost in the distant clouds when I could see her.

Surya too was probably going through a similar phase. He would sit in the building and, putting his hand to his chest, keep repeating Kewda's name. Phawdya once teased him saying he was probably just waiting to paw her. Surya flew into a rage and shouted at Phawdya.

'I'll break your jaw, bhenchod! It is nothing like that. To me she's a pure goddess—my queen. I don't have any such thoughts for her.'

Then he sat by the window, closed his eyes and said, 'I imagine Kevda as the goddess on the Mumbra hill. I am her devotee waiting at the foothills for her visitation. It is such a nice feeling to think of her. It is like going to a temple.'

After watching *Sholay* for the third time, he said, 'You know what I dreamt last night? I was sitting out in the verandah playing the mouth-organ while Kevda watched me, closing one door after another.'

I liked the dream. Chitre said the dream was fantastic. But he had no need to dream. Kevda was, in reality, knocking at his door and visiting his house. He had progressed a lot during the Diwali holidays, he confessed to me one day.

The paddy fields were barren now. Sometime during the Diwali holidays, Shankar's father had harvested the crop. The bundles of harvested crop lay in a corner for a while. They too were removed later and nothing remained in the fields except the stubble. Animals from the nearby fields came in to graze and after a few days the stubble too vanished. The land was dry and there was no need to go along the fringes. Shankar's father had flattened a part of the field to thresh the rice. That became a temporary pitch for boys to play cricket on. The small boys could not play for long as the fields were occupied by the elder lads from Kanhe village, who would spend the whole day playing cricket and other games there. There were no Test matches happening during that time except for the visiting Sri Lankan team. They were no match for us Indians. They had not even achieved Test match status yet.

Ambabai continued to harp on my need to join tuition classes. The scene would be repeated each evening and, while Aaisaheb had not yet firmed up her mind on the subject, it would not take much time for Ambabai to influence her.

I had no plans to join the tuition classes—in ninth or

ever! None of us in our gang wanted to take tuitions. Surya, unfortunately, had no choice as Bhadbhade sir went and taught him each evening. His father had given him a place at a lesser rent on the condition that he would teach his son. Surya would have loved to go out each evening in search of Kevda but had to sit and study instead. Bhadbhade sir was newly married and in dire need of a place; he was unlikely to let go of such an opportunity. Chitre had no need to join a class and Phawdya had no time for it. The tuition classes in our town were the most boring places of all. They did not have large, airy rooms like those in our school. They were held in cramped, stuffy rooms. And the worst part was to listen to the same stuff, which had been taught in school. The same equations, the same theorems—how boring!

Chitre has a point—he says if you don't understand something in school, you can always refer to the books, or else you can ask the teachers. You cannot clarify your doubts in tuition classes. They run like trains, one batch after the other. I would rather go to Kendalkar sir's classes. He may shout, but he will go to great lengths to explain until your doubt is clarified. But who would explain this to Ambabai and Aaisaheb? They believe tuitions are the panacea. They would be happy to have tuitions morning, noon and evening. They do not understand our need to go out and experience the world. They believe we don't need to play or do anything else once we get to class nine.

The next day I was at the free library, whiling away my time, when I met Pingle. He had been in our school earlier but had since joined Subhash Vidyalaya.

'Joshi? What are you doing here?'

'I had gone to the library,' I said. 'What about you?'

'Tuition!' he said, looking at the notebooks in his hand.

'Where do you go?' I asked.

'To Deshmane sir's classes,' he said.

I had heard of this Deshmane sir. He was in Subhash and was known to teach well. Earlier he used to teach at home after school hours, but when some of the parents complained, he left his job and started taking classes full-time.

'Are you taking classes for all subjects?'

'No. Just English and Maths.'

'Is anyone from our class attending the tuition with you?' I asked.

'No. No one from our class,' he said. He thought for a moment and then said, 'But there are two girls.'

'Which ones?'

'Shirodkar and Mande.'

A bolt of lightning hit me. Shirodkar was attending tuition with this guy. No wonder I had not seen her in the evenings. Here I was, sitting like a fool waiting to see her, while she was busy attending tuitions!

'What are your timings?'

'Six to seven in the evening.'

'Does he teach well?'

'Okay. Not great but at least he does not shout. That's the good part.'

I returned home that evening forming a plan in my head. The moment I saw Ambabai, I said, 'I had gone enquiring about tuition classes. I have found a good one.'

'Which is....?'

'Deshmane sir's. Do you know he was in Subhash Vidyalaya earlier?'

'Really?' she said. 'When do you intend to join the classes?'

'I will go and meet him one of these days,' I said, trying not to sound too eager.

The next day I dropped my bag at home and rushed over to the tuition classes. I knew the place. One batch was just getting over. I looked around but could not see Shirodkar anywhere. I decided to meet Deshmane sir before the next batch began.

'You are most welcome,' he said, dusting his hands. 'But there is no place in this batch. You can come for the next batch or for a batch in the morning.'

'No, sir. I need to come for this batch,' I persisted.

'Where will you sit? There is no place. The batch is full. And what is so special about this batch? You can come in the morning. Or the next one too is fine. Do you have any constraints?'

As if a bulb lit up in my head, I said, 'Yes, sir. I work,' I lied through my teeth, 'That's why I cannot come for the later batch. Or the morning batch.'

He pondered for a moment and then, picking up the duster and chalk, said, 'Okay baba. You may try. Someone or the other is absent each day. Try your luck.'

I silently bowed before the blackboard and decided to join the class right away. The classes were held in his house. The otherwise large room was stuffed with benches. There was very little space in the aisles to walk. There was one window on the girls' side and a single tubelight for the entire room. The students shared the bench, three to one. Pingle asked his partner to move to the other bench and invited me to join him.

Shirodkar came in a little late and sat with the girls. She did not notice me. She continued to look straight ahead at the blackboard and was busy making notes. I felt good. Deshmane sir's teaching was similar to our Halbe sir's, but who cared. I was not there to learn! We were sitting three to a bench and the classroom was getting stuffy, but it was all fine. All that mattered was that I could see her.

When the class got over, I deliberately came out of the class along with the girls, hoping to catch her attention. I turned back and shouted out loudly for Pingle. I had plans to follow her after class, but unfortunately Pingle came in and, putting his arms around my shoulders, said, 'Come. Let us go over to my house. It is nice to meet an ex-classmate after a long time.' I had no choice but to go with him. But it was fine. I did not resist. I had found a way to see her again every evening, and that was enough.

Ambabai was happy at my having finally joined the tuition classes. That the teacher was from her favourite Subhash Vidyalaya was a double bonanza. That day I understood the real meaning of the phrase, 'to kill two birds with one stone.'

The next day we gathered at our adda and I told the gang about the classes.

'Joshi, saale! You said you wouldn't join any classes, didn't you?' Chitre asked.

'Yes, but what could I do? My sister was making my life miserable.'

'Chaila! I too should join some classes,' Phawdya muttered. 'But I don't have time either in the morning or evening.'

'I am not going to join any classes,' Chitre said. 'What they teach here is enough to tire the brain out.'

Surya was already stuck in a home tuition. He asked me right away, 'Anyone from our school there?'

I was expecting it and had prepared an answer for the same. They would come to know about Shirodkar sooner or later, so there was no point in hiding the fact. I said, without any hesitation, 'There are a few girls, but I could not see them well. It's a very cramped, crowded room, you know. You remember Pingle who was with us earlier? He is there.'

'I hope you are not going there after someone you fancy?' Surya wanted to know.

'What are you saying? I had to join the class to keep Ambabai at bay,' I said. I spotted Kevda passing by and immediately distracted him with, 'Look, your heartthrob is going by.'

'Is she? Ichibhana, should you not tell me earlier?' Surya went over to the window and peered down, muttering, hand on chest, 'Hai meri Kevda! What do I do? Bhenchod, Chitre, I keep asking you, but you won't ever introduce me to her, will you?'

Kevda looked pretty with flowers in her hair, her dress neatly ironed.

'But I need to know her before I can introduce you, isn't it?' Chitre responded.

'Hai meri rani! I must do something soon,' he sighed, looking down at her.

That day when Manjrekar sir was in the class, Appa entered without any warning. The students stood up and said 'Namaste sir' in unison. Appa had a girl accompanying him. He came in and addressed the class,

'Sit down please. You have a new classmate joining you from today. She's from Mumbai. Her father got transferred, hence she's joining school in mid-term. Please introduce yourself.'

'Anita Ambekar,' she said in a clear, confident voice.

We all looked at her with a mixture of surprise and awe. Girls are girls, but this one was different. She was a dish! Most of the students who join school are shy and look down at the floor, but she looked at us, straight in the eye. The girls were impressed and gaped at her open-mouthed. Even Manjrekar sir fell silent.

Appa guided her to one of the benches in the front row and asked her to sit there.

'Who is your class teacher?' he asked. 'Oh, yes! Paranjpe ma'am, isn't it? She'll come and write her name in the register. Please continue with the class.'

We relaxed a little after Appa left, but the air was full of anticipation.

'What a lovely chick she is!' whispered Surya.

I did not reply.

'So, which school do you come from?' Manjrekar sir asked her.

'Saint Mary's, Bandra,' she replied in the same confident voice.

We were all stunned. Bandra! Wow! We rarely hear the anglicized version of Bandre. We knew Dadar, Mahim and Bandre. But Bandra! And that too pronounced as Band-ra! This was rare. Chitre's mavshi stays there and he visits her sometimes. What's more, she was coming from an English-medium school. A convent! We would have ragged a newcomer to death but this case was different.

The Ambekar girl was quiet on the first day, but the next day she created a tremor of sorts.

She walked up to Bibikar and said, 'Bibikar, would you lend me your notebooks?' She had found out he was one of the better students.

Bibikar was dumbfounded and didn't know what to say. Never before had a girl borrowed his notebooks. She did not wait for him to answer and asked Ghasu Gokhale. He was quick on the uptake and retorted, 'Why don't you ask one of the girls?'

'Do you have any problem in lending me your books?' she asked. 'The girls act pricey. Do lend me yours. You come first or second in the class, isn't it?'

He lent her one of his notebooks. She did not stop there. Within a few days, she knew the names of all the boys. She realized quickly that the nerdy guys on the front bench were not of much use and turned to make friends with us back-benchers. One day, when we had a few free classes and held a cricket match with nine-d, Phawdya took five wickets and Chitre hit three fours back to back. She walked up to us saying, 'Congratulations, Pawar. You played a great game. Chitre, you too played well.'

Chitre was a cool cucumber. He was used to the girls from Bandra and just nonchalantly brushed his hand through his hair. But Phawdya was clean bowled. He asked after she had left, 'What did she say? Congress session? What does that have to do with cricket?'

We laughed heartily. That day onwards, we teased him to death on the subject.

I consciously kept my distance from Ambekar but Dashrath, Harishchandra, Santya, and others fell for her. Sometimes she cycled to school and once, when the tyre was punctured, asked Dashrath to get it repaired. He not only got the work done but also delivered it to her house. She asked Harishchandra to get a rose plant and requested Santya to get a stone pestle and mortar for her house. Her house was in Kanhe village where Surya lived. She didn't spare him either.

'Mhatre,' she approached him one day. 'Would you take care of that guy who sits in the laundry shop—the one in the corner. He whistles whenever I pass by.'

'Who are you talking about?' Surya asked.

'The one who sits in that Ganesh Laundry—that dark fellow.'

Surya had been waiting for such an opportunity. He took Dashrath along with him. There was no need really because the fellow pissed in his pants the moment he saw Surya. Surya warned him and returned elated, with his collars turned up. He boasted, 'If you have any trouble with any guy, just tell me. I don't allow anyone to mess with any of the girls in my class.'

Surya decided to put his offer into action. He targeted Thombre from eleventh standard. Ever since Ambekar had joined, the boys from tenth and eleventh standards had started making rounds of our class. Surya had seen her smile at Thombre. He was a body builder and had won a few competitions representing the school. We boys believed some of the ma'ams too flirted with him, especially that shorty Pawaskar ma'am. She was unmarried and was a temporary teacher in the laboratory. Thombre had bulging biceps. But he was a decent fellow who minded his own business. He used to sometimes come over to our classroom in the mid-break. He commented once, a tad loudly, 'You guys have got some nice mangoes ripening this season in your class, isn't it?'

Ambekar had smiled hearing him. But Surya, along with Harishchandra, decided to challenge him.

'I heard you are eyeing the girls in my class, bhenchod.'

'Mhatre, you don't get into this. And don't use foul language.'

'So, what will you do? Huh?' Surya challenged him.

Thombre could have easily punched Surya unconscious. He had arms of steel, but he did not want to stretch the argument. Luckily, the bell rang and the scene ended. But Surya was keen to pursue it and tried to get his relatives in the tenth and eleventh standards on his side. Unfortunately for him, he found they too had an eye on Ambekar. One of them said, 'Oh boy! I would love to take her to the woods and suck those mangoes!' Surya decided to drop the matter.

Ambekar was popular with the boys, but the girls decided to boycott her. She was not liked by any of them because she talked freely with the boys. She was very good in English and became a favourite of Bendre ma'am's. That irritated the girls further. Sukdi, otherwise a cool girl, had an argument with Ambekar within a matter of days.

It was only later that we came to know of Ambekar's real preference. While she would give a sweet, coy smile to the boys from higher classes, her heart was set on Manjrekar sir. She would sit quietly in other classes but become very vocal in Manjrekar sir's class, raising her hands and chanting 'sir, sir' for every question asked by him. She would sometimes rest her chin on her palm and giggle to herself. Manjrekar sir too liked her and would often ask, 'Understood?' directing the question at her alone. Soon the news of him being partial to her spread. We had never scribbled any comments against Manjrekar sir in the toilets because he was our favourite, but Teredesai's sister told him that the girls had written about both of them in the ladies' toilet. The message read that a particular teacher really loved *Ambe*, which meant mangoes in Marathi. It had to be a prank played by some girl from our class. It was obvious. A fresh round of gossip began in school.

I started attending the tuition classes in earnest. Shirodkar too was sincere. But within a few days, I realized that this was just another form of school. At least in school, we had enough time to play some prank or the other, but in this class there was no time at all. Moreover, I had no friends here. My school would get over at 5:20. I would have just enough time to go home, drop my bag, gulp down a cup of tea and leave for tuition class. Shirodkar too must be experiencing similar problems. We had no time after the class. It would be dark and she would head home with the other girls.

It dawned on me that this was taking me nowhere. It was just a waste of time. She would never know the real reason for my joining the class. She never looked at me in the class. She seemed to have forgotten all the things I had done for her sake—the beating I got in Bendre ma'am's class, the grass doll in the Scouts period and the way I had stared at her in the Social Science exam—everything! She did not show any interest, even if she harboured it.

As Naru mama rightly said, 'No one can fathom a girl's thoughts!'

I knew each day was being wasted. There was no point in continuing in this fashion. I thought of the long road ahead. We had to clear ninth, tenth, go to college, find a job…I had to make a start! I knew I would not get any time or opportunity next year. Class ten was no joke! Ambabai and Aaisaheb would sit on my head and not allow me to breathe. And then we had eleventh and twelfth standards, too, to boot! The pressure would only escalate. What is the guarantee she would be in my class then? She would, in all probability, opt for Arts. If by then we were going steady, I could ask her to join the same college as mine. Colleges normally have both Science and Arts streams. Even if she did not join my college we could meet every evening. I would study all day and spend all evening with her! I would get into engineering. And then I would not care if everyone came to know of our affair. I could tell them proudly and roam around without a care in the world.

I could see the road ahead with clarity. The problem was solving the issue at hand. Now! But Shirodkar seemed immune to all this. I had no clue how to let her know. I was tempted to write to Naru mama seeking advice. I could use the fictional character of Manoj Desai, but I was worried he may say something to Aaisaheb. So I dropped the idea.

One day I decided to excuse myself from Pingle saying I had to go to Misal's house. I left the moment the class got over and moved towards the lane leading to Shirodkar's house. I stood near a shop. It was getting dark and she would not see me standing there.

I spotted Shirodkar walking along with two other girls. One of them was Mande from our class; the other girl was not known to me. I began to follow them at a safe distance, walking slowly. They turned near the temple and walked along Gandhi road. The other road led to the stone well and I knew that they would not go that way. They turned again near the kirana store. There were a few lights on the road, but it was not bright enough. Mande turned and went into a lane and the other two continued walking. The road led to Phadke Hospital and further to the tamarind tree. I knew Shirodkar's house would come soon. There was a small lane next to the road. The two stopped there for a moment and then, seeing her friend off, Shirodkar walked ahead, alone.

My heart began to throb. My lips went dry. The Municipality lights had been lit, but the overgrown trees blocked most of the light. She was wearing a dark skirt and a white-and-yellow floral print blouse. She walked at her own pace, unaware I was following her.

As expected, the lane turned towards her house. The lane had a row of houses, most of them covered by big trees. There were no shops on the road, nor any traffic. She could have easily spotted me if she had turned around just once.

I was expecting her to reach the tamarind tree and then turn into the lane leading to her house, but she jumped over a narrow drain near a house and vanished. Probably this was a short cut.

I followed suit, jumping over the drain. She came into sight again and I realized the road ended right in front of the Devgiri bungalow next to her house. So this was her route; no wonder I had never seen her while waiting under the tamarind tree.

Before I could reach the road, she had gone inside the house. The Devgiri bungalow stood silently in the darkness. Waiting there any further was of no use. But now I had discovered the route she took. I returned home, floating on air.

The next day I was trying to think of an excuse to shrug off Pingle, but luckily he did not turn up. What a relief. It would be great if he were to be absent each day. I had decided I would follow her the moment the class got over.

As expected, the three girls took the same route. The other girl did not turn into the lane leading to her house but continued walking with Shirodkar. I had a fleeting doubt Shirodkar had seen me following them. I kept a safe distance. They both went into Shirodkar's house. Maybe the other girl needed to borrow a notebook. I lingered and on my return encountered the girl accompanying Shirodkar. I wondered whether she recognized me. She might have wondered what I was doing in that part of the town, but I coolly ignored her and continued walking past. I had expected Shirodkar to come see her off at the gate, but there was no one there. The lamp in the verandah burnt brightly.

I analysed the situation carefully. It was not possible to excuse myself from Pingle every day. Following the girls too seemed a waste of time. They went together most of the way and, after seeing off her friends, Shirodkar, briskly walked through the lane leading to her house giving me hardly any time to speak to her. It was not worth the while to let her know I was following them. Girls don't like being followed. It scares them off.

I had to create a situation where I could meet her coming in from the opposite direction. It had to look like a chance meeting.

I realized I had been a fool to take the same batch as hers. A total idiot! Had I taken the next batch I could have easily met her before the classes began. Deshmane sir had been asking me to take the next batch. But there was no possibility of changing batches now. I could sit and curse my luck forever.

I thought hard and came to a conclusion. There was no need to change the batch. All I had to do was to bunk the tuition classes and meet her on the road.

I was a little scared about my bold decision. I was not nervous about Deshmane sir. He never asked anyone why he or she was absent. He never took attendance, in fact. But the question was—where to wait for her?

Then it struck me that the best place to meet her was on the way back home. I had to meet her either in the narrow lane or on the road leading to her house where she would be alone. The lane was normally empty and would serve as a good place to meet her.

I had to plan it to the last minute. The classes got over at five past seven. The girls would spend a few minutes chatting and then they would walk back home. It would take them say ten or fifteen minutes to walk the distance. I had to meet her after she had said her goodbyes. I realized I had to while away an hour at least. But I did not have a wristwatch with me. How would I know the right time?

'Baba, I need a wristwatch,' I asked, when we sat down for dinner.

'Watch?' Baba asked, arching his eyebrows.

'Yes. How do I keep track of the time? I go for the tuition classes these days.'

Baba looked at Aaisaheb. Ambabai focused on her food. She's a smart cookie and does not want to give her opinion in such situations. Aaisaheb did not say anything either.

'Else, give me her watch,' I said, looking at Ambabai. 'I need it only in the evening.'

My trick worked. Ambabai looked up and waited for Aaisaheb to respond. Aaisaheb came to my rescue.

'You have a spare one, isn't it?' she said. 'Why don't you allow him to wear it? You have kept it for him in any case.'

'Okay,' Baba agreed. 'Don't forget to wind it up every day.'

The watch was old but functional. It had a steel strap. I would have preferred a black leather one, but since I had got what I wanted, I decided to keep quiet. I wore the watch to school the very next day.

The classes went on as usual, but I was there only for one reason—Shirodkar! I was unable to concentrate on anything else. We boys used to meet, as usual, at our adda, but there was no fun now. We had stopped teasing Sukdi and I would be very quiet if Shirodkar passed by. Surya too would just gaze at Kevda. There was a science exhibition in school and Chitre was busy with his experiments. He was making a railway signalling system, so he would come in late, sometimes carrying yellow and red wires with him. Phawdya would arrive as usual, huffing and puffing his way up the stairs.

I had planned to bunk the tuition classes that day, but then it dawned on me that I needed to time the entire activity of following Shirodkar. I managed to give Pingle a slip and then noted the exact timings, minute by minute. The class got over at 6:56 and we were out at 6:58. The girls left at two minutes past seven and reached the temple at five past seven. They went into Suvarna Novelties and spent around six minutes there. They left the place at eleven past seven reaching Gandhi road, fourteen past seven at Dedhiya Kirana and then stood for a few minutes at the entrance of the lane leading to Shirodkar's friend's house. I was noting the timings as I followed them. It took half an hour for her to reach home. Had she come in directly she would have taken fourteen minutes. It meant she was likely to arrive anytime after ten minutes past seven.

The next day I bunked the classes. I left home and wondered how I would spend an hour. I deliberated if I could spend time at Phawdya's stall, but then it would make him suspicious. He knew I had tuition classes at that hour. I went to the free Municipal library. Anyone can come and read there. The building is quite old and has a high ceiling. A few large trees outside it provide shade. There are a few fans and some large relaxing chairs inside. Several people simply come there to take a nap. You can spend a thousand hours there without anyone bothering you.

I whiled away my time and left at quarter to seven. I could have left at seven o' clock as it would not have taken more than five minutes, but I did not want to take any chances. What if the clock in the tuition class was running a bit slow?

I wandered around for a while and reached the tree

five minutes before seven and stood under its shade. I had around twenty minutes to spare. I was willing to wait for twenty thousand minutes. There was a huge peepal tree on one side. I recognized the tree from the shape of its leaves. We used to keep them pressed in our books. I had a vantage position as I could see both the lanes leading to her house. There was a huge yellow lamp across the street so one could clearly see a person approaching. The lane was silent.

Small flies buzzed around the lamp while mosquitoes hummed overhead. I could hear the chirping of crickets too. I had willed myself to take this chance, but there was a deep sense of fear—the kind of feeling one gets before the beginning of an examination, or just before the announcement of the results. My eyes and ears were alert and the body was tense. For a few moments, I had a strong urge to run away. And yet, I did not feel like moving away from that place. Time crawled and, when I looked at the watch, it was ten past seven. She was expected any moment now. My body was tingling with excitement. I wanted to quickly run and pee at the edge of the road, but I could not make myself move from the place.

Then I heard a cycle bell. I got nervous for a moment and thought it would be nice if I walked about a little to show I was not lying in wait there, but the cyclist did not notice me. He pedalled away vigorously and I continued standing there.

It was quarter past seven now. My eyes darted to my watch every other second. It had a radium-coated dial, which glowed in the dark. The seconds hand ticked away rapidly. But Shirodkar was nowhere to be seen.

I was getting a little worried now. Did I make some

mistake in my calculation? Was Shirodkar likely to have crossed the lane earlier? But that was not possible. I was there at seven. And no one had passed by. She was probably chatting with her friends and would arrive by 7:30.

I decided to hold fort. A man accompanied by two small children walked by. I was tempted to move, but then they had already seen me, so I continued to stand at my place. The children looked at me, but they did not say anything.

It was getting dark now. The mosquitoes were biting me and the breeze turned cold. The winters here are not as cold as at Naru mama's place, but it gets dark pretty early. It was getting colder now and the days were getting shorter. The smallest day of the year would arrive soon.

It was half past seven and then it was thirty-five minutes past. There was no point in waiting any more. I decided to go back, checking the tuition class en route. There was a chance I might meet Shirodkar on the way.

I walked down the road looking carefully. Although there was no need to do so as there was no one on the road. Besides, the street lamps were bright enough. Two old ladies went by, followed by a few men returning from office. But Shirodkar and her friends were nowhere to be seen. I crossed the lane where her friend stayed. I could smell the dinner being cooked in various kitchens. But there was no one standing there.

I walked all the way to the tuition classes, but there was no one outside. The next batch was in full swing.

My plan had failed. Possibly Shirodkar had taken another route. Perhaps she had some errand to run. Or she was sitting at some friend's house. Anything was possible.

It was eight by the time I reached home.

Shirodkar came to school as usual, blissfully unaware of my efforts for her. Paranjpe ma'am was teaching the poem 'Chitraveena'. She was wearing a blue saree with a matching blouse and looked beautiful. I was listening attentively. One could imagine the rain falling listening to the poem.

'The cloud forms a black shadow on the blue waters
The rice fields burst forth with their ripe grains
The rains drizzle coolness
On the dense bamboo forests'

I knew every word of it. I could imagine a black shadow formed by clouds in the waterlogged paddy fields. I had tasted the ripe grains, thanks to Shankar's father, and we had experienced the cool shadow of the bamboo trees in our mid-breaks. I felt as if the poem had been written exclusively for me. The poet somehow knew I would love it. The words kept ringing in my ears the whole day.

I wanted to bunk the tuition class that evening. It is convenient to bunk few days at a stretch as the same excuse holds for all the days of absence, but I was keen to find out what Shirodkar was up to.

Shirodkar came in a little late just as our batch was entering the room. Her friend asked, 'What happened yesterday? I did not see you.'

'I will tell you later,' Shirodkar whispered.

I felt like a fool. She too had bunked!

Pingle asked me the reason for my absence. I was tempted to say something about guests at home or a stomach ache but thought otherwise. These excuses could come in handy some other day.

'I had a toothache,' I said. 'And the doctor's place was too busy. I may have to go a few more times. I hope you will lend me your notebook.'

He nodded his head, falling for my words.

I bunked again the next day. I spent time in the free library. I wanted to go and stand below the tamarind tree because it was closer to her house, but it was a bit risky. Someone may ask why I was standing there for such a long time. I whiled away my time reading a few newspapers. There was not much to read though. Thanks to the Emergency, the papers have become very careful and do not publish anything sensitive. Earlier it was fun reading the editorial column that carried criticism of the ruling party. But now things were different. The government was clamping the voices, they said. In one paper, there was a dark black patch of ink striking away a news item. Perhaps that's what they meant by 'clamping the voices'.

I reached the peepal tree sharp at seven. I was on the lookout for the people whom I had encountered the previous time. If they saw me again they would wonder why I was standing there so often. But none of those people turned up. The lane was quiet but not desolate. There was adequate light and yet there were a few spots where one could stand in darkness. No one from the bungalows would see me standing there. It was perfect.

Then I became aware of the mosquitoes around. I could feel them biting me. Our town is known for its mosquitoes. Someone had joked we should rename our village Mosquito

Nagar! The guests who come to our house complain about them all the time. Each house tries its own methods of driving them away. Some burn neem leaves while some of the others burn dried cowdung. Earlier we too used to try such tricks, but now we simply sleep under mosquito nets. Some mosquitoes are so big they leave a blood stain when you swat them. One Jagdale from Baba's office is looking out for mosquitoes all the time, often ignoring his tea or his hosts. He does not mind swatting them on someone else's back too. Aaisaheb does not like him at all because he once cried, 'Vahini, look! A mosquito on your stomach!' People wearing trousers are spared to some extent. But boys like me wearing shorts are in trouble. You would find boys constantly scratching one leg with the other. If you spot any boy in the world doing that, you can be sure he belongs to our town.

I stood there scratching my legs. I was quite sure I would not see her today. When one is desperate for something one does not get it. That's the way the world is! I had a trick in my childhood—think of the worst. For example, I would imagine losing a match or not getting movie tickets. That way, if it actually turns out so, you don't feel bad. And if it does not, you are elated. I convinced myself that I would not see her today. She would have bunked or she would have gone over to some friend's place. She would not come today. She would not come today. I repeated the mantra.

But then she came! I saw her in the light of the street lamp. I would have, of course, recognized her from a mile away. I realized she might get upset seeing me hiding in the darkness, waiting to pounce on her. I decided to walk in her direction.

I met her halfway. As I had expected, she looked surprised.

'Aiyaa, you?' she said, her hand on her mouth.

'What are you doing this side of town? You didn't come for the class today, did you?'

I could not believe my eyes and ears! Here she was. She had actually stopped and was talking to me. In the silence of the lane, with no one around, she and I were actually having a conversation. With no one there to disturb us! My ploy had worked.

'Umm…no,' I managed to mumble. But I was at a loss for words. She must be wondering why I was not saying anything.

'Sir taught us well today,' she said, moving towards her house. 'Don't keep bunking like this.'

And then she was gone!

I stood stuck to the place. I remembered the phrase, 'kimkartavya vimoodh'—someone who is stunned and does not know what to do next. I should have gone home straight, but I walked back towards the tuition class and then took a long route to reach home.

My mind was blank as I walked back. Ambabai remarked during dinner time, 'Where are you? You seem to be lost in thoughts.' I did not reply but continued eating. The chess games were on, and Kudalkar advocate came in to play with Baba. No one prefers to chat when a chess game is on and I could sit there without having to talk to anyone. Baba likes it when I sit and watch him play.

A plan formed in my mind as I watched them play. It was superb! I could meet her every day. The place was ideally suited. It was a narrow lane forcing the person to acknowledge the other person passing by. She had spoken to me without being prompted. What else did I need?

I soon realized the foolishness of my plan. Shirodkar had spoken to me. But she would have spoken to anyone—Chitre or Bibikar or Teredesai or Misal. Her questions had been innocuous; 'What are you doing here?' 'Why did you not come to the class?' It was a question she would have asked anyone from our class. There was nothing special about it. She would never guess I had bunked class so that I could meet her.

She would be blissfully unaware of my situation. She would speak to me the way she did this evening—anywhere, anytime. There was no need to find a rendezvous for such a conversation. I knew Shirodkar was a simple, straightforward girl unlike Mande or Sukdi. She would not understand what I was attempting to do.

Naru mama had told me long back that one should be upfront with girls when it came to expressing one's feelings. There was no point in beating around the bush or trying to flirt. One should express one's emotions directly and face the consequence. At the worst, she would say no. OK. 'Tu nahi toh koi aur sahi' was Naru mama's philosophy.

The thought of writing to her crossed my mind, but I quickly dismissed it. Letters lead to mahabharata. It had happened in every school around town. Last year, when we were in class eight, there had been a huge fuss over Paradkar and Sontakke of tenth standard. They were writing letters to each other and someone discovered a whole bunch of them. Both of them had to leave school. They were hell-bent on committing suicide on the railway tracks, it is rumoured. Ponkshe kaka keeps on saying never give anything in writing. You are doomed when you put things in writing. Say whatever you feel like, but don't write it down.

I decided against writing any letters, even though it was far more convenient to speak one's heart through them. One could re-write, too, if there was a mistake. One cannot do that while speaking. I had to steel myself and speak up. There was no other way.

'What do you say? How was my move?' Kudalkar advocate exclaimed, breaking my train of thoughts. 'See how I have trapped your father, Mukund.'

Kudalkar had trapped Baba's bishop and was gloating over it. Baba examined the board and answered, unruffled, 'I am fine with giving up my bishop, but are you prepared for a checkmate in three moves?'

Baba was right. Advocate saheb was in trouble. This was Baba's favourite trick. Sacrifice an important piece, sometimes even the queen, and then checkmate your opponent! We laughed out loud looking at each other.

I let the next two days pass by. One was a Sunday in any case. I diligently attended tuition classes during that time. Shirodkar would not look at any of the boys, as always. I would sit there and simply gaze at her. Deshmane sir taught earnestly, explaining the problems on the blackboard, but no one asked any questions. In school, some of the oversmart guys like Bibikar would raise doubts just to impress the teacher, but that helped us to understand the problem. Watching the playground from the classroom was a great way to spend time in school. There was nothing of that sort in the tuition classes.

Had Shirodkar not been present, I would not have come anywhere close to this dump.

I bunked classes again on Tuesday and spent my time standing below the peepal tree. It was five past seven. It was okay to stand there for a few minutes. My chest was not thumping as loudly as before. I was feeling a bit better. I had braced myself just a bit.

I stood waiting for her when I saw a man walking slowly down the road. He must have been very old, for he wore the dhoti in an old fashioned way. He had a walking stick in hand. He was wearing a black woollen cap and, seeing me, he came over and asked, 'Beta, who are you?' His voice was quivering and he probably could not see clearly. I was taken aback. Most of the people in our village have a queer habit of asking such questions. They invariably start a conversation with school children, asking unnecessary questions. They may also ask you to run errands. An old lady once asked me to deliver her bag from the atta chakki. I was a little annoyed at the old man's question, but I told him my name. He asked further, 'Whose son are you?'

I thought for a moment and then answered, 'Mr Joshi's.'

'Where do you stay?'

For a moment, I was tempted to lie and say I stayed nearby, but that was dangerous. He may ask more questions and it may lead to trouble. He would be familiar with most of the households in this area and would know them on a first name basis.

'I stay near Dhaparewadi,' I said.

'What are you doing here?' he continued.

This old man was not willing to let go. I could land in trouble if he had a habit of taking this route every evening.

I looked at my watch. Shirodkar was likely to come in any moment. I should have walked away seeing him come in the first instance. But I could not do that now. I said, 'I am waiting for a friend.'

'Oh, a friend, is it? I see,' he said. 'But be careful, okay? It is dark here and you need to be alert. There may be scorpions, who knows?'

'Yes, ajoba,' I said.

He left, hobbling slowly.

I heaved a deep sigh of relief. It was sixteen past seven now. I saw him walk away, his head shaking a little. I did not feel any anger towards him. In fact, I felt that I should have had a grandfather like him. I had never seen either of my grandfathers. Both Baba and Aaisaheb had lost their fathers when I was very young. This old man was a friendly, loving person. No one would have doubted me seeing me chat with him. He would have actually helped me. I would be glad if he came by every day.

Shirodkar came in at twenty-five minutes past seven. I saw her enter the lane and walked slowly towards her.

'You? What do you do here every day?' she asked. It was clear that she was confused seeing me in her part of the town.

'I was waiting,' I said. The aching emptiness in the pit of my stomach had reappeared and my chest thumped loudly. I was not sure if I would be able to say it.

She did not wait for long. She started moving when I said, 'Wait!'

'What for?'

'I…' I took a deep breath. My heart was threatening to explode. I was finding it difficult to speak.

'I wanted to say something to you,' I blurted.

'What?' She quickly glanced at both sides of the lane fearing that someone may spot us there.

I kept looking at her. I was hoping she would stay, but she seemed to be in a hurry to leave.

I looked around. The lane was silent. There was no one around. It was an opportune moment and an opportune place. But I was losing my resolve. For a moment, I thought of telling her to meet me at the same place the next day. But then I knew I could not afford to lose the moment. I had to act now.

'I...I like you.' I blurted out, at last.

I was not sure if she heard me. She did not say anything. She continued looking down and then glancing this way and that, she turned to leave.

'Will you meet me here tomorrow?' I asked, seizing the moment.

'Na re baba! I don't think I can do all this,' she said and then left, walking away briskly.

I was drained of all energy and somehow managed not to collapse on the road. I held on to the tree trunk and waited. I was scared and my chest continued to pound. I had finally said what I had to. Now I was not worried about what might happen. She may get upset, angry or even stop speaking to me. I was quite sure she would not use this route any more. Perhaps this was the end of it all. But having told her my feelings brought a great sense of relief to me. The load was off my chest.

The next day, I bunked the tuition class and stood below the peepal tree again. The old man whom I had encountered the previous day was not to be seen, but I saw a group of old ladies coming my way. I was worried they too may accost me and started walking to avoid a conversation. A few men passed my way and some school boys walked by as well. There seemed to be more than usual activity in the lane.

Shirodkar had said she would 'not be able to do this'. I knew it was an immediate reaction. She would return by her usual route. But it was half past seven and she was nowhere to be seen. I waited until forty minutes past seven and then walked back towards the tuition classes. I did not see anyone on the way. It was almost time for the next batch to be over.

I realized my foolishness then. The very fact that I had not gone to the tuition class was enough for Shirodkar to guess I would be waiting for her in her area. Quite obviously, she would not take that route. Normally she does not glance at the boys' side, but since our conversation she would have definitely checked if I had come in.

I realized she would find a different way to reach home whenever I was absent from class. She would either take the other route or spend time with her friend, chatting. Either way, I would not be able to meet her. I could keep sitting until eight or even ten o'clock!

Ambabai was waiting for me at home.

'What happened? Why are you coming home late these days?' she demanded.

'I was with my friends. Have I not told you earlier?'

'But why so late? It is past eight, you know?'

'So?'

'What kind of friends are these? And what were you

doing in the Municipal library? Padma told me she saw you there.'

My mind did a million calculations in a second. I had to come up with something credible.

'Sir came in late,' I said, without getting perturbed. 'So I decided to spend time in the library rather than wasting time elsewhere. Aai, I am hungry. Give me dinner.'

I was quiet at dinner time. In Naru mama's words, I had not 'factored' in such eventualities. Ambabai's friends are spread all over—school, college, embroidery class and that committee or samiti, or whatever they have. One can never be sure where one will run into one of them. Many of these friends come home. I always go out whenever they come, but they recognize me. They are all 'aunties' like Ambabai, with oily hair. I like that sharp-nosed Marathe though. I heard Ambabai telling Aaisaheb once that she resembles Nargis. I like seeing her and, whenever she comes in, I get butterflies in my stomach. She should have been in my class. It would have been so nice then. Or I should have been Ambabai's elder brother. But these girls are all idiots; they treat Ambabai's brother as their own. So they take it upon themselves to keep an eye on me. God knows where that Padma landed from. I need to be careful henceforth.

I decided to attend the tuition class earnestly.

The classes were full as always. Shirodkar behaved as before, not looking towards any of the boys. But I felt light. There was no stress now. Earlier I used to feel stressed whether in the class, in the playground, in the building—everywhere. As Naru mama would say, it was a lot of 'tension'. But now I felt relaxed.

But after five or six days I got a little worried. It was different earlier. My thoughts were mine. But now I had spoken them out. And that too directly to her. God knows what she would be thinking. She may be upset or angry—or both. She had clearly said it was not possible for her to do this. What if she continued to remain upset?

I was tempted to wait there every day. But I knew it would be foolhardy. She would think I was trying to block her way like some lout. And it was quite right for girls to think that way. I needed to come up with some other idea. I had to find a way of meeting her every day either in the lane or on the road, or sometimes near the temple. It did not matter whether we spoke or not. I had made the mistake of accosting her in a dark lane. I would be a dead duck if she told this to Mande or some other girl. The news would spread around town in no time.

I had no other choice now. Naru mama would have advised the same. He had said you need to sow a seed in their minds. He said that the seed would sprout and become a tree and then the tree would flower and there would be fruits. But the seed had to sprout first. And for that one needed patience. You cannot reap until you sow, can you? Our duty is to sow; whether it sprouted or not was another matter.

I decided not to bother anymore. The arrow had left the bow. Whatever had to happen would happen.

It was Pethkar's ma'am's class, but she had not turned up. More than five minutes had passed since the earlier class got over, but no teacher was in sight. Most of us were getting restless.

'Ichibhana, shall we push off?' Surya asked.

'Come on, let's go,' Phawdya added.

'Joshi, you also come, bhenchod,' Surya said, looking at me. 'Chitre, are you coming along? What are you going to do sitting here? What is the next period?'

'PT.'

'And the one after that?'

'Rajguru sir's—Drawing.'

'That's it, bhenchod! We will return for the drawing class.'

By the time we could decide, we saw Dashrath and Santya coolly walk out of the classroom without looking at anyone. They turned back once before leaving the class. This was a common occurrence. They did not scamper or run. They just walked out and disappeared into the woods. Harishchandra was absent else he too would have followed them.

Surya got restless seeing them leave.

'You guys can sit here, bhenchod,' he said, from the door. He glanced back for a moment and then ran off behind the other two.

'I too am leaving,' Phawdya said, getting up.

I looked at Chitre. He was sitting on the other bench.

'Come on, let us push off,' he said, getting up. 'What are we going to do sitting here? In any case, if they declare an off period, everyone would be out in the ground.'

I peeped out of the door. The ground was silent. There was no teacher in view. Ganoba, the watchman, was not to be seen anywhere. I walked down the steps and ran through the playground towards the woods. Chitre followed me.

The trees had a cool shade. Phawdya, Santya, Surya and

Dashrath had already taken their respective places. Surya, as usual, was sitting on the huge branch while Santya dangled from another one. Phawdya and Dashrath sat on the ground.

'See! I knew you too would follow!' Surya said. 'Why were you acting so pricey then?'

'We were not acting pricey. We were just making sure,' Chitre clarified.

We selected a rock and sat down. The area was getting dry now. The earlier dampness had given way to a dry patch. The paddy fields on the other side had been reaped sometime back and were barren. The sun was mellow and there was a nice, warm feeling all over. A lot of dry leaves had gathered on the ground.

'When is the sports competition?' Surya asked.

'Fifteen days from now,' I said.

'And the gathering?'

'Following the sports meet.'

'I am going to be a volunteer there,' Surya said. 'You guys should volunteer as well.'

Surya loves to volunteer in the gatherings. He can strut around wherever he wishes. He does not participate in any of the events like plays or songs but does his job sincerely. He gets a chance to go around at will—the girls' make up room included. I had participated in a play last time, but I found it to be the domain of nerds like Bibikar. The play, on top of it, was quite boring. I decided I too would join the volunteer group this time.

We saw Bhaishetye coming our way. He must have left the class following us.

'Abey oye, seth ke chamche, munim ki aulaad-idhar

aa,' Surya called out to him. Ever since he had seen a recent Dharmendra movie, he would try this dialogue on someone or the other.

'Aaya, aaya,' Bhaishetye replied in Hindi.

'Come, saale. Looks like you too pushed off from the class.'

'I had nothing to do sitting there.'

'Did anyone take the off-period?'

'No,' Bhaishetye confirmed.

It was evident why Surya was engaging Bhaishetye in a conversation. Ever since he had told the story of the Bhaween lady, the god's mistress in his village, Surya was keen to know the details. Chitre believes Bhaishetye exaggerates a lot, but listening to the stories is exciting.

'So tell me what happened in her house then? You left the story mid-way,' Surya, said, referring to the conversation they were having in the class.

'I told you. Both Bhikusheth and Dadya went to her house together. That's all.'

'That's all? They must have bickered over her—who would go in first, isn't it?' Phawdya added.

'No. Nothing of that sort,' Bhaishetye said. 'They are idiots. They went in together. They did not fight.'

'She must have been fraught,' Phawdya said.

'She can handle ten such fellows.'

'Must be fun for her, bhenchod!' Surya drawled.

'Yes. Bhikusheth and Dadya were sweating it out,' Bhaishetye added.

'Were you there to witness it?' Chitre asked, nonchalantly. I doubled up with laughter, hearing that. Bhaishetye made a face.

'Shetye, don't you bother about them,' Surya cajoled. 'You sing that song.'

'Which one?'

'Remember the one you sang yesterday?'

'Ah! Leave that be!'

'Hey, come on! Don't act pricey.'

Shetye pondered for a while.

'I will sing just one stanza, okay?' he said, feeling a little shy. Then he cleared his throat and looked around. Santya, sitting high up in the trees, was all ears.

'One two three four
Aunty says close the door
Grab tight, hold right
I want once more'

We all laughed out heartily.

'Waah! It is really nice, bhenchod! Will you write it down for me? I want to memorize it.'

We then sang a very raunchy song, which has become our unofficial school anthem. No one knows who wrote it, but it is immensely popular. All the boys, including the new ones, learn it within days of joining. Surya may not recall a single poem from his textbook but knows most of the stanzas of this one. Chitre knows twelve. I am told Sonar from class ten knows seventeen of them.

Phawdya said, 'I know a new one.'

'Tell us!' We chorused.

'It is not a song, just a sort of a abhang. I learnt it from one of the boys from Tope High School.' And then he went on to recite it in all sincerity.

'They say there is nothing wrong
To find a girl tall and strong
Listen to what the wise men said
Find a tree with ample shade'

He then paused and looked at us.

'What next?' Surya said. 'What happens next?'

'I am trying to recall the words…'

'Arrange the leaves to make a bed
The girl is waiting to be laid
Gently open her blouse's knot
And then you know how to start!'

'Waah! Shabbash!' Surya said. 'They should have such abhangs in our textbook too. What is the point in having those dull, boring ones? What do you say, Joshi?'

'I agree. Boring ones talk of soul and salvation!'

'We should write our own textbooks,' Phawdya said.

'Right,' I said. 'We can easily do that. We need not write everything ourselves. We can get others to do that. We can select the songs we want and the chapters we like.'

'We can copy from *Apsara* magazine.'

'Yes.'

'And we need to include our favourite school song,' Surya said.

'That's the anthem. It has to be there. We will make the school sing it each morning,' Chitre said.

'The girls will not sing,' Surya doubted.

'We will create a new one for them,' Chitre continued. 'We will have a committee for selecting such songs. Ambekar will lead the one for girls. The committee will decide on the books too.'

'It will be fun, bhenchod,' Surya said. 'Ambekar will create a raunchier one than this.'

We loved the idea of asking the children to select their school curriculum. No one would be bored of studies. No one would complain. We would learn our lessons in a day!

We kept talking in the shade of the trees. Phawdya was lying in dry grass. Santya had climbed to the higher branches. Dashrath, as always, got up to pee in one corner. He returned to boast of how his pee had reached a distance of five feet.

'Hey, you know the latest about Rairikar?' Phawdya asked.

'What about her?'

'That girl is going around with a guy from Tope High School.'

'Rairikar? No way! What are you saying? She does not even look at boys.'

'I am telling the truth,' he said, getting up. 'I saw her last evening. She's too clever. She came over to buy some vegetables and then wasted a lot of time asking about this and that. I wondered why she was not leaving when she had finished buying.'

'Then?'

'That hero came in after a while. They went into the lane near Mathura Sweets. Luckily Aai came in and I got free. I followed them to find the two standing there and merrily chatting away.'

'In that crowd?'

'Of course! They are bindaas and actually very smart. They know if you are found chatting with someone in a crowd, no one suspects you.'

'Bloody hell. What chalu girls we have, bhenchod,' Surya said. 'I never imagined Rairikar would have an affair.'

'She's so quiet in class,' Bhaishetye commented.

'The ones who are quiet are the ones who do all these things,' Surya said.

He was silent for a while. Then he jumped down and said, 'Hey, each one will declare his secret love today!'

For a moment, I did not understand what he meant.

'Hey, listen to me, guys! Each one has to reveal his secret love interest. No one should hide anything. I love Kevda. Kevda meri jaan!' he said, throwing kisses in the air, and then turning towards us, said, 'Now guys! Tell me.'

Chitre and I looked at each other. We did not know how to respond. We kept quiet. I was hoping no one would say anything, but Dashrath volunteered, 'You know mine; the one in the village.'

'That Kanchan? You call her your sweetheart? Bhenchod, you are fingering her all the time. What about you, Santya?'

'Don't you know her? She stays in the same lane as yours.'

'That Shobha? She's a bloody kid. You will have to carry her around on your shoulders. What about you, Phawdya?'

'Mine is studying in Tope,' Phawdya said. 'You know who I am talking about? Vaishali Kadam. She comes to buy vegetables every evening.'

My chest was pounding now. Next would be Chitre and then me. Surya loves to start such discussions. One cannot make him change his mind then. I was in a spot now. For a brief moment I was tempted to reveal Shirodkar's name, but then I realized the whole school would be talking about it in no time. Life would then be impossible for me and her. And anyway, I had no idea what she thought of me. I waited for Chitre to say something. I knew that he had fallen for Kevda, but I knew he would never reveal that in public.

'Chitre, you tell me!' Surya said.

'Mine stays in Bandra,' Chitre said, fiddling with a grass stalk. 'She stays in mavshi's building. Her name is Naina. Naina Thakur.'

'Does she fancy you?' Surya asked.

'She will in some time. What's the hurry? I am going to attend college there, after all.'

'Joshi? What about you?'

My mind was racing in search of the right answer while Chitre spoke.

'Mine stays in Aaji's town,' I said. 'She's the daughter of Naru mama's colleague...'

'What is her name?'

'Sangeeta,' I said. 'Sangeeta Kulkarni.'

Chitre smiled. He knew I was lying through my teeth, just like him. But Surya could not see him smile as his back was turned towards him.

'Kulkarni, is it?' Surya quipped. 'Joshi and Kulkarni... You guys won't change, bhenchod. Same caste! Saale, how do I know you are not bluffing?'

'Why should I bluff?' I asked. 'If you don't believe me, go and ask Naru mama on your own. Or come with me to Aaji's place in the holidays.'

That silenced him. He turned to Shetye and asked, 'Shetya, what about you?'

'I don't have anyone,' Bhaishetye said.

'Come on! What do you mean no one? Bhenchod, don't act smart.'

'I mean it. I really don't have anyone.'

'Shetye, I don't want anyone trying to act smart, okay?' Surya said, walking towards him. 'Tell me the truth.'

'What do I tell? I cannot create one.'

Surya lunged forward and twisted his hand.

'Are you going to tell me or not, bhenchod?' Surya said, twisting his hand further. 'Joshi told us without any fuss, but you are acting pricey. Each one of us spoke the truth. Why are you hiding?'

'Arre! What do I tell you? I don't have anyone. I cannot create one, I told you so. Aah! Don't twist my hand. It is hurting.'

'Tell me. Tell me else I'll break your hand,' Surya said, twisting it further. 'I will break your legs too.'

We looked at each other. Bhaishetye was in trouble. Surya was hell-bent. We were hoping for the bell to ring announcing end of the period, but that did not happen. We indicated to Dashrath to intervene.

He stepped forward saying, 'Leave him alone. Just assume that Bhaween in his village is his love interest, okay? Come on now. Leave him alone.'

Surya would not have relented, but seeing Dashrath, he released Bhaishetye's hand. But his eyes burned with anger. Bhaishetye was scared to death. He had not seen Surya behave so. The bell rang and we were all relieved.

The next period was PT and all the students came out into the playground. There was no teacher in sight and we mingled with the crowd.

'Adhav ma'am had come in the off-period,' Teredesai

said. 'She took attendance too. You guys were marked absent. You had pushed off, isn't it? Now you are going to be summoned soon!'

As if a bomb fell on us! Adhav ma'am had come in that period. We had never expected that. Her responsibility is the PT class and is thus free most of the time. She's always on the lookout to take over a free period.

'If someone has bitched about us, I will make sure he pays for it,' Surya threatened.

'No one had to bitch,' Misal said. 'You guys left together. It was evident. Those benches were vacant.'

Despite it being a games period we could not enjoy the hour. We went back to the class when the bell rang. The next period was Rajguru sir 's. We got busy with the given task. For a moment, we thought nothing would happen. Perhaps Adhav ma'am had ignored our absence.

But soon Ganoba appeared with a paper in hand and said, 'The following students have been called in by the Headmaster.' He read out our names, 'Chitre, Joshi, Mhatre, Pawar and Bhaishetye.'

Santya and Dashrath were not named. They had come in late that morning and hence they had already been marked absent for the day. It was clear no one had bitched about us. We stood up from our benches.

'Come on, Princes!' Ganoba quipped.

We followed him in a line to Appa's room. Adhav ma'am was already present there.

Appa's room is half the size of our classroom. The room is covered with a carpet which is old and torn in many a places. You need to be careful while walking over it, else you are likely to trip and fall. There is a centre-table covered with a glass top. It shines and reflects everything. We are used to standing there with our heads bent low and that's how we see the table most of the time. There are two cupboards on both sides of the table. One of them has a glass door. It has all the trophies, shields, cups and other medals earned by the school. The other, in all likelihood, must be for keeping the school files. A dust-laden globe sits on top of one of the cupboards. Three walls of the room are covered with photos of the national leaders—Mahatma Gandhi, Nehru, Vallabhbhai, Rajendra Prasad, Maulana Azad, Subhash babu, Sarojini Naidu, Lokmanya Tilak, and others. There are Shivaji and Lakshmibai too. Of course, Warhadkar dada, our founder, has to be there. All of them look down at you from the walls, except for Subhash babu and Shivaji Maharaj, who seem to be looking far away. The ones who should be looking at you ignore you. Imagine Gandhiji smiling at you while you stand before Appa! Iron chairs, without any armrests, are lined against the walls. A list displays the number of students in each class while a board lists the names of all the headmasters till date. There are just two names there—Appa has been the headmaster for the past seventeen years and will continue to be so for another seventeen! There is another list with the names of all the teachers. It also lists their qualifications and the date of retirement. It is good that the board is put up there—it tells us that Bendre ma'am will retire in another twenty-two years. It serves as a warning for any new student joining school. Normally, we wouldn't get a chance to stand here and observe all this, but we are smart! Last year we volunteered during 'clean the school week' to clean Appa's room. That was the time we saw all this.

'These are the students—' Adhav ma'am said, the moment we walked in, our heads bent as usual.

'Oh, I see,' Appa said, nodding his head. He never shouts but his tone is pointed enough to scare the shit out of students.

'Running away from school, eh?' Appa said. 'Don't feel like staying in school, is it? Why do you come to school then?'

We stood without saying a word. Everyone knew that staying quiet was the best thing for one to do at such times.

'No, Sir. We thought it was an off-period, Sir,' Bhaishetye said, trying to justify the deed.

'You thought, is it? How did that 'thought' occur?' Appa asked, his tone getting sharper. 'So school runs as per your thoughts, huh?'

'And the other students did not think likewise?' Adhav ma'am asked, looking at us and then turning towards Appa for his approval. But there was no need for her to interrupt. Appa continued. Ma'ams in our school have this habit of supplementing when Appa is talking. They try to impress him by repeating whatever he says.

'What are your names?' Appa asked. The hollow in the pit of my stomach deepened. I was sure the others were nervous too. We were hoping Appa would cane us twice and let us go. But he did not get up from the chair, and asking for names spelt trouble. Appa has a terrific memory. He remembers each and every student's name.

Surya stood in the corner. Appa asked, looking into his eyes, 'Who are you?'

'Mhatre,' Surya answered.

'Mhatre?' Appa asked, his forehead furrowed a little. 'Are you Mhatre sheth's son?'

'Yes, Sir,' he said, nodding his head.

'Madam, do you see? He is our Mhatre sheth's son. Look what he is up to!'

Ma'am looked at Appa in acknowledgement.

'And you?' Appa asked Chitre.

'Chitre, Sir.'

Appa narrowed his eyes and asked,

'What does your father do?'

'He is an architect, Sir.'

'I see! So you are architect Chitre's son. Waah! Shabbash!'

I knew I was next. Appa looked at me and raised his eyebrows questioningly.

'Joshi, Sir.' I said. Appa pondered for a moment.

'Sachivalaya?' he asked.

'Yes, Sir,' I said.

'Madam, do you see?' Appa repeated. 'His father is in the state secretariat—that too in the education department. Good, good! Next?'

'Prasad Vinayak Bhaishetye.'

Appa was lost. He had not recognized him.

'He is a new student, sir,' Ma'am clarified.

'Oh, I see! That's why he is not aware of the rules here. And what about you?'

'Pawar,' Phawdya answered, without raising his head.

Appa did not know him. But he did not bother to enquire.

'Do one thing,' Appa said, his voice low but stern as before. 'You don't want to sit in the class, is it? No problem. Get a letter from your parents stating you don't want to attend school. I will issue the leaving certificates immediately. Okay?'

We stood there, mutely. As if we had not heard him.

'It seems you didn't hear me. Come on, get going. Get the letters from your parents tomorrow.'

We knew it was wise to keep looking down at the floor. We did not say a word, but Bhaishetye took it literally and was scared. He knew his brother-in-law was just waiting for any sort of complaint from school to send him back to Konkan. He started crying.

'What are you crying for? Don't make a fool of yourself,' Appa said, his voice taking on a edge.

'You didn't think of the consequences when you ran away from the class. Now get lost! You guys don't deserve to be in this school. We do so much for you, but you think of running away, isn't it?'

Bhaishetye again took Appa's words literally and was about to turn around and leave the room, but Chitre held his wrist.

'Sir, we promise this won't happen again.' Chitre had his usual defence in place.

'We won't do it again, Sir,' Surya chorused.

'Not do it again?' Appa asked. 'I am ensuring that you *never* do it again. Got it? You need not come to school—ever.'

'Sir, we waited for almost fifteen minutes. No teacher had come to substitute for the free period. We went to drink water and go to the toilet,' Chitre said, putting on his most earnest voice. 'We did not run away.'

This was news to Appa. He turned to look at ma'am.

'Well...I was a little late by the time I reached their class...', Ma'am hesitated. 'We were discussing who would take the free period. Pethkar ma'am had agreed first but then...then I took the class.'

'Why did you not return to the class then?' Appa asked, looking at us.

'We thought it would upset her,' Chitre explained. 'So we decided to wait in the playground. We had not run away. We were sitting in the ground as the next period was PT. Then we returned to the class. Else, how would Ganoba have found us in the class, sir?'

'And…' Bhaishetye began, getting a little emboldened. I immediately squeezed his hand hard to shut him up. He would blabber something and spoil the scenario so beautifully created by Chitre. It is good to allow Chitre to speak. He speaks logically and, being a fair-complexioned fellow, he is trusted by most.

'But we agree we made a mistake, Sir,' Chitre continued. 'We will never repeat this. Give us any punishment you wish but don't ask us to get letters from our parents, Sir.'

I was tempted to fetch the cane saying, 'If you so wish, cane us twice or perhaps four times each, but don't ask us to get that letter.'

I sensed a flicker of smile cross Appa's face, but he kept it stern. He knew it was a huge deterrent—asking the children to get a letter from their parents. Quite obviously, no parent was going to give a letter stating that they are fine with their children being thrown out of school. This was Appa's way of scaring us. Frankly, our crime did not deserve such a punishment. And if ever the parents had to send a letter, they would send a plea stating the child would not commit such an offence again. They would never ask for the child to be removed from school. Surya would get a thrashing at home. Ambabai and Aaisaheb would give me a double-barrel verbal treatment. Chitre's father would probably gently tap him on his head and then proceed to write a beautifully worded letter in English. Phawdya would have to write the letter himself. I was not sure of Bhaishetye—he may not tell his brother-in-law but ask his sister to write it; what could the poor soul do? She would write not just a page but an entire book for the sake of her younger brother!

'Come in early tomorrow morning and water all the plants in the playground,' Appa said, pronouncing his punishment.

'*All* the plants, Sir?' Chitre asked.

'Yes. All of them. You deserve this punishment. Now get going!'

We quietly walked out of the room. The only thing we did not do was to jump with joy when we came out. Watering all the plants was a huge task as the trees were spread out wide. But Phawdya and Surya would finish off most of the task. In any case, it was better than getting a letter from home.

'I was worried I would be hanged,' Bhaishetye said.

'What were you crying for, you asshole?' Surya said, punching him in the back. 'You should never be scared. I prefer Appa any day to that Bendre.'

We walked back to the class with our heads held high. The girls had seen us being taken away. Now they saw us come in. I caught Shirodkar looking at me. The girls must have expected us to come with our heads hanging.

'What happened?' The boys started off the moment we sat down. 'What did Appa say? Did he shout? Did he cane you?'

'Appa? He can't do a fuck!' Surya said, as usual. 'He has

asked us to water the plants tomorrow morning. That's not a big deal. We will do it!'

The fallout of the episode was Bhaishetye's decision to stay away from our group. That was a real loss! We used to enjoy his stories about Bhaween. Surya's truant behaviour had spoilt the show.

The next Saturday was earmarked for the science exhibition. We were not given the day off but the classes were held early in the morning. Normally Saturday school begins at 9:30. The laboratory hall was prepared for the exhibition. Chitre was to display his railway signalling system. We were given a few free periods on Friday afternoon for us to arrange the stuff. Chitre had carried his things in the morning and I was the obvious choice to help him put up his experiment. Phawdya was not interested but Surya wanted to volunteer for help—to excuse himself from attending class. But Zende sir refused. It was good in a way—the parts were delicate and Surya might have damaged some. The other students had created a variety of experiments. One guy from tenth standard had made a water tank. The tap would stop flowing when the tank was full. Another girl had made a design showing the details of the functioning of a radio. But they were just drawings. No moving parts. There were many experiments on display—a brano, a trolley running on a motor, a dynamo, properties of a magnet, etc. But Chitre's model was the best. Two trains approached a crossing; if there was a train ahead, the signal would not allow the other train to go. The trains ran on battery cells. Two people were required to demonstrate the experiment. We arranged all our things and then left when Zende sir locked the laboratory hall.

We were at our adda the next morning. Phawdya and Surya had arrived early. Chitre came in with a long face. He seemed to have cried a lot and quietly sat down in one corner.

'What happened?' I asked.

He just shook his head.

'What happened? Why the long face?' I asked again. He did not answer.

'Ichibhana, what is the problem?' Surya asked. 'Did someone confront you while coming here? Tell me. I will go bash him up right away.'

'Was there an argument at home?' I asked.

That was the reason. He nodded his head in the affirmative but did not say anything. He was trying to hold back his tears.

'So what's new?' Phawdya said.

'Aai is threatening to leave the house,' he said. And then the tears flowed.

We were stunned. We had never seen him cry. It was a known fact that his parents argued, every now and then. I mean, that was the case everywhere. Baba would keep quiet in my house, else every argument would have led to a fight. Chitre would often talk of the arguments but had never broken down like this.

'There was a bad argument this morning,' Chitre said. 'Aai did not even bother to make tea this morning. I prepared the milk for Raju. The arguments were going on since morning. I left without eating anything.'

'Ichibhana, why didn't you say that earlier?' Surya asked. 'Come, let us go and have a wada pav.'

'Don't worry,' I added. 'Things will be okay by evening.'

'I don't think so,' he said, wiping his tears on his sleeve. 'Aai said she's sick of this bickering and that she will leave the house. She has never spoken like this earlier.'

I did not say anything. Chitre's aai was very nice but stubborn. Not like Aaisaheb. Aaisaheb would say a lot but not do anything. I could not say the same about Chitre's mother.

'They were least bothered about the science exhibition today,' Chitre added, his eyes filling up again. 'They did not even bother to ask. They were busy arguing.'

'But why was your aai so upset?' Surya asked.

'She does not like it when Daddy drinks.'

'Ichibhana, you should ask her to have a look at my house,' Surya said. 'The other day my father came in drunk and then he did not care to see where he was hitting my mother. He broke her bangles, you know?'

'It was the same story in our home too,' Phawdya said. 'That's why my father died early.'

'All parents are the same,'Surya said. 'They care a fuck about the children. Why do they produce them in the first place, bhenchod?'

'I don't feel like doing anything now,' Chitre said. 'I don't want anything—this house, this school, this exhibition.'

I kept quiet for a while and then glanced at my watch. Zende sir had asked us to come in early. He would allow one class at a time to see the exhibition. But Chitre seemed to be in no mood to go to school.

'Come, let us go. Sir has asked us to come early.'

Chitre finally relented when everyone coaxed him. Surya and Phawdya went to the class and we entered the laboratory hall. We were to stand behind the counter and explain the experiment to the students. Everyone seemed excited and was waiting expectantly for the crowds to stream in. Only Chitre's face was downcast.

The exhibition opened in some time and the students started coming in. Chitre perked up a little when he saw a large crowd entering. Luckily this time, Appa had not arranged any 'opening ceremony'. There were no guests and hence no speeches, else people like Prem Chopra and Narvekar ma'am would get a chance to show off. Each class got half an hour to see the display. The other classes continued as usual.

'The railway signal is a complex system,' Chitre began explaining his set-up. 'This prevents trains from colliding with each other. Imagine a train stopping at a station while another one is coming in, close behind.'

We would then get one engine into the station and the signal would automatically turn red. We would move the engine out of the station and the signal would turn green. We had to place the engines with our hands, but the other things happened automatically. Chitre's mama had got the railway set from one of his trips abroad. The students enjoyed our display so much they were reluctant to move away from our table.

Then Kevda came in with her class. She stood at the back and allowed the other girls to gather at the table. I saw her smiling to herself when Chitre was busy explaining the set up to the girls. She must have seen the set-up at Chitre's place. Chitre must have shown it to her. Chitre did not bother to glance in her direction, but it was clear to me that something was brewing between them.

'Line clear?' Chitre said, taking the engine on to one side.

'Line clear,' I repeated, trying to suppress my smile.

The pun was lost on the eighth standard girls, who were busy gawking at the engine and the experiment.

Then the boys and girls from our class streamed in. Quite obviously, the boys gathered around our table. Bibikar and Ghasu Gokhale were jealous of Chitre and deliberately went around looking at other experiments. Surya picked up the engine and Phawdya poked around trying to check the lights. The boys refused to move and crowded around the place. The girls were left behind until Barve ma'am came to their rescue.

When the girls gathered around our table, Chitre said, 'Joshi, you explain everything. I will have a glass of water in the meanwhile.'

'No! It is your experiment. You need to explain. I will take a break instead.'

But the girls were there before either of us could move. We explained the set-up without meeting their eyes. Shirodkar stood a little behind. I dared not look at her. The birdies had many questions. Mirikar asked, 'What happens if the signal does not function properly?'

'Then there will be an accident,' Chitre said, a little irritated. 'Just ensure that you are not on that train, okay?'

Mirikar was upset, but the other girls laughed out loud. Finally ma'am had to come to shoo them away. While leaving, Sukdi managed to snidely remark, 'The engines are fine, but the drivers seem to be shy.'

The girls were streaming out one by one. Chitre was busy fixing some screw, which had come loose. I saw Shirodkar leave at the end. She slowed down a bit and then said, almost in a whisper, 'Very nice!'

I looked around. Chitre was bent below the table finding the loose screw, which had fallen off the table. The other groups were busy with their own experiments. No one had noticed our brief exchange. I was stunned. I had not expected her to speak to me. It meant that she was not at all angry with me. I was shivering from head to toe.

I floated on air the rest of the day. Our throats were parched having spoken the whole day and our legs were aching. Luckily they gave us some snacks at noon. We were dead tired by evening. But I imagined a totally different scenario—only Kevda and Shirodkar had come to see the exhibition. We then took them for a ride in the two engines, through dense jungles, by the bank of rivers, over the empty plains. Our engines ran fast, bellowing smoke and letting out shrill whistles. We did not stop at any station or halt at any signal. The whole world spread out before us welcoming us, into its arms.

Until the science exhibition, I had not dared to look at Shirodkar. Not that I had not seen her at all but not in the way I used to do earlier. I would try to find an opportunity and quickly glance at her. But when she spoke to me at the exhibition I realized that she was not angry with me. In fact, she had been looking at me when I was not aware. I had caught her a few times doing that. Girls, in any case, do not look at boys directly. They look through the corner of their eyes. I had seen Shirodkar do that. Not looking in the general direction of the boys—but specifically at me. But the moment I caught her doing that, she would look straight ahead.

But I could not meet her again near the peepal tree. I

was scared of the darkness now. If she saw me there again she was likely to get very upset. And then the whole thing might end. I did not want that. I had worked hard to get it to this level and could not afford to ruin it. As Naru mama says, one needs to cultivate patience.

Then the days of matches arrived. Classes are not held during those days. We have cricket and kabaddi matches. No one plays kho-kho. Our girls play kabaddi, but we don't have any guys good enough for the game. It is fun to watch the girls play. There are more boys than girls watching whenever there is a girls' match. The girls wear shorts and those who do not have brothers borrow the shorts from the other boys in the class. Normally the request is made in the presence of a teacher so there is no way the boys can refuse. Those who have to lend their shorts feel it would have been better for the earth to have swallowed them than face the embarrassment of lending one's shorts to the girls. Surya is the first person to grab his place whenever there is a girls' match. His favourite fantasy is to see a kabaddi match between the girls and boys.

The individual competitions are held in the playground. Surya and Phawdya participate in the races. Bibikar, Ghasu Gokhale, Teredesai and other nerds do not participate in the games. In a bid to impress Zende sir, Bibikar asked, 'Sir, when are the matches starting?' Zende sir looked at him and commented, 'Bibikar, never ask directions for the town you don't intend to visit.'

Bibikar got upset and decided to participate in every event. The chess tournament was being held this year too, but I decided not to participate. Bibikar has learnt it recently and thinks he is another Bobby Fischer. He was the first one to volunteer. The only girl to participate was Mirikar.

'Joshi, why don't you participate?' Chitre asked.

'Leave it!' I said. 'I don't want to compete against those smarties.'

'Ichibhana, Joshi, why don't you play, saale? You play so well,' Surya said, poking me with his pencil tip and then got up and announced, 'Ma'am, Joshi wants to participate.'

'Why are you proposing his name?' Ma'am asked. 'Can't he speak for himself?'

I was planning to decline when I glanced at Shirodkar. Her eyes seemed to be saying, 'go ahead'. The phrase, 'fame is the fragrance of heroic deeds' rang in my mind. I imagined Bibikar playing against me. The decision was simple. I raised my hand.

'Joshi,' Ma'am said, noting down my name in her register. 'Anyone else?'

The matches began. We may not win in kabaddi, but no one can lay a hand on us in cricket. Chitre and Phawdya began to practise in right earnest. We were up against Nine-C in the first round. Phawdya took two wickets in the very first over and another one in the next. That was the beginning of the end. We bowled them out at a mere twenty-six runs.

Halbe sir supervises the chess tournaments. He took out the draw as per international rules and then put up the chart on the notice board. Most of the participants were boys; there were very few girls. They did not have separate draws. I had Ninave from class ten in the first round and then Tivre from eight for the next. Ninave did not know how to play and I routed him in fifteen minutes. Tivre was a smart guy and I initially assumed that he did not know the game. But when he threatened my bishop in the fourth move, I was alert. He was on the verge of tears when he lost. 'How did you, of all people, land up against me?' he asked. I was feeling bad. Had it been someone other than me, he would have reached the semi-finals.

The next round was against Mirikar. She had won the earlier round against a girl from eighth standard. She got a walkover in the next round as Keluskar from nine-d did not turn up. I was stunned. So were the other boys. 'Where did this female land up from?' Phawdya muttered. Her confidence level was high and she was now dreaming of becoming the champion. The girls were there to cheer her.

'I'll play white,' she said the moment we sat down to play. It was to be decided by a toss but I let it be.

We began to play.

The moment she moved the knight pawn as an opening gambit, I knew that she did not know the game. She made more mindless moves.

'Gokhale has not come in, yaar,' Surya observed, throwing a glance at her. I glanced up to look at the girls. Shirodkar was there amongst the crowd. She must have been watching me, but the moment I looked up, she lowered her eyes.

'Your bishop is in danger,' I warned Mirikar.

'Really?'

'Look where my knight is,' I said, tapping on the knight's head.

'Aiyaa! I did not notice,' she said, biting her tongue. 'Can I take it back?'

'Okay,' I said.

She then made another blunder moving it to B7. I thought one warning would be enough, but she had no clue and moved her bishop ahead.

'Don't move it there,' I said. 'If I take your pawn, it would be a check to your King and you will have to lose your bishop.'

'Aiyaa! You are right,' she repeated, biting her tongue again. 'Can I take it back, please?'

I nodded and then glanced at the girls. Had I finished the game in ten or fifteen moves, they would have got disappointed and left in a huff. I had no plans to make such blunders, not when Shirodkar was watching.

I allowed her to play a little more. She copied me when I castled, but she had left a gaping hole. 'Do you realize if I sacrifice my knight after taking yours, you stand to lose you bishop?' I asked her and then glanced at the crowd.

'Chhi! What am I doing?' she muttered.

'Hey, play properly,' one of the birdies chirped.

'Hey, call Gokhale quickly,' Surya commented.

Mirikar put her bishop back, but she had no idea how to progress. My defence was strong.

'What shall I do now?' she asked me.

'Move your pawn forward,' I said, thinking for a moment. 'Then either my knight or bishop would be threatened.'

'Yes, yes. That's correct,' she said. 'I wonder why I never thought of it.'

She was clueless and I could have easily routed her. But I decided to let her continue. Everyone, except Mirikar, knew that I was playing along. I glanced up to see Shirodkar smiling.

I allowed Mirikar to take my knight and another

pawn. I was enjoying the game now. I was no more part of the chess game. I felt like a large-hearted emperor who believed in forgiving rather than killing those who surrendered before him. 'Go! I give your kingdom back to you.' The emperor in me would dismiss the surrendered foe with a wave of the hand. I would return to the capital with my huge army. There would be someone waiting for me, with her eyes shining like two lamps—waiting for me with a traditional tray and an oil lamp to welcome me home!

Shirodkar stood with a smile playing on her lips. Had it been Shirodkar instead of Mirikar, I would have sacrificed everything!

Chitre realized I was whiling away my time and said,

'Joshi, come on. Let us finish the game. We have a match with Eight-B at three p.m. Do you want to come or shall I take Shembe along?'

'You go ahead and take the toss,' I said. 'If you win, opt for batting. I will join you soon. If you lose, take Shembe for fielding.'

But the girls caught on and told Mirikar, 'Enough of this game now! He has allowed you to survive many times now.'

'Wait, wait,' Mirikar said, 'My game is improving. Isn't that so?'

I just smiled and looked up to see Shirodkar too smiling quietly. I played along for a while but then realized everyone was getting bored. Then I decided to checkmate her. Mirikar took the defeat sportingly.

'Congratulations,' she said, jutting her hand out for a handshake.

The birdies too chorused, 'Congratulations!' Shirodkar

did not say anything. But that hardly mattered. She had conveyed what she had to.

I moved out, floating on air. As expected, we won the cricket match. The other team was good, but we were at our best. All the girls had come out and were standing in a shaded area cheering us. I was moved to a slip position during Surve's spin bowling and managed a catch that had eluded Chitre. I also managed to score six runs—a record for me.

I played the rest of the chess games with zeal. I *had* to win. Bibikar was against me in the semis. There were no girls to watch the game.

'I read Bobby Fischer's book recently,' Bibikar said, trying to impress me. 'I am going to use some of those techniques.'

I was silent. I knew that Bibikar was not Mirikar. He had brains. I played with white. I started with Baba's favourite opening moves, allowing the game to progress at a slow pace. Bibikar was impatient and made the mistake of exposing his knight early in the game. I was ruthless and decided to rout him. I had many chances to challenge for a checkmate, but I deliberately allowed him to escape in order to trap him at some other place. I wanted to destroy his entire board and let the king run for his life. I won with a loss of just two pawns, a bishop and a knight. Bibikar somehow managed not to cry.

I played against Mehendale from tenth standard in the finals. He was a bright lad and was expected to get a board rank. But I was in form, on my way to becoming the chess champion! I could clearly see the crown. I could have defeated Fischer and Spasky had they played against me that day! Mehendale made the mistake of attempting the Nimzovich defence. I routed him in less than twenty minutes.

Our classes continued while the sports meet was on. But I bunked most of the times much to chagrin of Ambabai. 'All this is fine only this year, okay?' was her constant refrain. They would not allow me to be anywhere near the sports meet next year. I told myself I would cross the bridge when I came to it.

I went to the class the next day because I knew they would announce the names of the winners of individual sporting events on the huge board at the entrance. Anyone entering school could see my name written in large letters. I also went to the tuition classes that evening, but Shirodkar was absent.

She came in the next day and I thought she smiled shyly on seeing me. I caught her watching me again after some time. Naru mama says girls speak with their eyes. I knew she was watching me. For the first time, the tuition classes seemed worth the effort.

Deshmane sir announced tuitions the next morning. He was taking some extra classes. It suited us as the next day was a Saturday and we were to be handed out our prizes that evening. There was no school that morning. I went back home chatting with Pingle, but then an idea struck me.

I reckoned Shirodkar may not be comfortable talking to me under the peepal tree in the late hours of the evening. It seemed inappropriate. But then she may not mind talking to me in the morning. I could bunk the tuition class and wait for her. But then she might guess I would be waiting for her and take a different route back home. I had to think of some other plan.

I went over to Deshmane sir and requested to be allowed to leave a little early. 'Sir, we have a puja at home. Can I leave a little early?' He agreed saying, 'You may leave fifteen minutes early, but be careful not to disturb others.' I ensured Shirodkar saw me entering the class and then left quietly without anyone noticing me. I walked slowly towards the peepal tree.

I had never been there in the daytime and noticed the tree was quite green. There was a lot of greenery around. The sun was bright and I realized I should have carried a cap, but the tree's shade was adequate. The lane was quiet and I did not see anyone passing by. Winter was setting in and the air was cool.

I waited there in anticipation. There was a chikoo tree on the opposite side and I saw a lovely bird flitting by. I could not see it clearly, but I was sure it was the Bharadwaj bird. It was a lucky sign.

I did not need the lucky sign though. I was feeling very good despite the mild shivering. But soon an unknown fear gripped me. It was a strange, heady feeling, a mixture of fear and excitement. I was sure Shirodkar would come by this route. I glanced at my watch. The class must have got over and she would be seeing her friend off near the temple.

It was fifteen minutes to eleven when I saw her. She was wearing a buff-coloured skirt with a light yellow blouse. I had seen her in the class, but she looked completely different in the bright sun. I stood there, enthralled by her beauty, not realizing I should be walking towards her.

Seeing me there, she asked, 'What are you doing here?' She did not seem surprised; her eyes, when they met mine, had a glint.

Not a word escaped my lips.

'You were there attending the class, isn't it? How did you reach here so fast?'

'I left a little early,' I said, finally finding my voice. My heart was beating hard.

'Why?'

'I wanted to speak to you,' I said.

What for?'

I did not know how to answer that. What can you say to a question like that? I was scared she may start walking away. She stood there and glanced once in both directions.

'You won the chess championship, isn't it?' she said.

'Yes.'

'Mirikar does not know how to play at all, isn't it?'

'She's okay; not that bad.'

'We had asked her to practise daily; but she wouldn't listen. You must be practising daily, I suppose?'

'Yes… No… I mean, sometimes.' I wanted to tell her I won because she was there, but the words eluded me. I was unable to believe my eyes that she was still there.

She fumbled for words. She looked again at both the sides of the lane. I knew if I did not continue the conversation, she would walk away. My mind was whirling fast.

'Who all are there at home?' I asked.

She raised her eyebrows quizzically and said, 'Aai, Pappa, two sisters and a brother. What about you?'

'I have an elder sister. She's in college.'

I knew, but asked nevertheless, 'How old is your brother?'

'He is in class four,' she replied. 'My elder sister goes to college. Little One is in class seven.'

Little One! That was a new term. We never use that word to address a younger sibling. But I liked it.

'What does your dad do?' I asked.

'He works in a bank,' she said and then started laughing. 'Why are you asking all these questions?'

What could I say? Time was ticking by. I should have asked Naru mama how to take the conversation further. My chest continued to pound away.

'The tuition teacher teaches well, isn't it?' I said.

'Yes. But we don't like him much. We feel sleepy in the class. I prefer Zende sir.'

'Then why did you join this class?' I asked.

'It is close by,' she said. 'But it is so boring to attend classes in the evening. What made you join this class?'

I was tempted to say I joined because of her, but I was worried it may upset her.

'Just like that,' I said. But I knew that she knew. She smiled a sweet knowing smile.

'What is the name of that girl? The one who walks with you back home?'

'Oh, that one? She's Juvekar. She's at Subhash. What about her?'

'No, I just wanted to know her name,' I said. 'Most of the students here are from Subhash, isn't it?'

'Yes. Deshmane sir is from the same school, you know.'

'If any sir from our school starts a class no one will attend.'

'True! No one knows how to teach well. Look at that Redkar sir and Bendre ma'am!'

'Zende and Manjrekar sir are nice.'

'Right,' she said.

I did not know that the girls had the same opinion as the boys. The conversation was progressing well. I was feeling better and my chest had calmed down a little.

'Why did you not participate in any competition?' I asked.

'I don't know any games. I can play games like carrom. We have a board at home. Do you play carrom?'

'Yes,' I said confidently. I had played a few times with Ponkshe kaka. 'People play carrom every evening in our building.'

'How nice! We are forced to play at home.'

'Our building is a lot of fun in the evenings,' I said, warming up. 'All the people assemble in the courtyard after dinner to play or watch chess games, carrom, and exchange some gossip!'

'Aiyaa! How nice!' she repeated. 'It must be fun. We don't have any neighbours.'

'Who stays on the first floor then?'

'Our landlord,' she said. 'He is a grumpy, old fellow, can't tolerate even a little noise from our house. Immediately comes down to complain.'

I was enjoying the talk. No one had passed by—it was as if they had wanted us to be alone and had made a collective resolution not to come this way. Not that I would have bothered if they did. She had stayed back and spoken to me. That was enough. I was floating in the air, and all I could see was the blue sky with pure white clouds.

But this could not go on for eternity. She must have seen someone enter the lane when she said, 'May I go?'

I wanted to ask her to stay back, but then I realized this was enough for one day.

'When will you meet again?' I asked, steeling myself.

'Na re baba. I cannot manage all this.' She started moving away. 'And don't wait for me over here. There are a lot of people who know me in this area.'

'But will you meet me again?'

'Let me see,' she said, but I could see her eyes had a flicker of a smile.

I could have spent my entire life standing there, but I saw two plump ladies coming my way. One of them looked like the one staying in the Devgiri bungalow and I quickly walked away with rapid steps. Once out of the lane, I spread my wings and gently floated all the way back home.

That evening we had the prize distribution ceremony. It was the happiest day of my life. We had an ex-student as our chief guest. He regaled us with stories of his school days, which were not very different from ours. We doubled up with laughter hearing them. He said those who shine on the school playground would shine in the playground of life too. We loved that statement. Phawdya said we should use that as our school's motto. We got our medals—Phawdya received one for the best bowler and Surya for this two hundred metre sprint. Chitre got the second prize in the science exhibition and I got an award for the chess championship. The girls received a shield for the kabaddi match.

Holding the silver cups in our hands, we congratulated each other. Chitre had a certificate of appreciation too. We congratulated the girls. Surya and Phawdya did not want to let go of their cups. My cup was larger than theirs. Chess has a special place of honour in our school. The cup exchanged many hands as it went around the crowd. The lid fell off a few times, but I did not mind. I had received my prize in the morning itself! It was bigger than all the cups and shields, and much more beautiful. I was not going to show it to anyone, and no one could take it away from me.

I felt there was no need to meet Shirodkar again. I was happy and contented. I would meet her whenever the situation arose naturally. There was no need to try hard for it. I started attending the tuition classes again. She would look straight ahead, as always, but I knew she would be watching me now and then. I kept a straight face and did not try to catch her. We had some sort of a secret pact now and both of us had to adhere to it without fail.

But I got restless after five or six days. I was desperate to meet her. Her memories were as strong as before—from the moment I woke up till I dozed off in the night. But they were not sufficient, afterall. I had to meet and speak to her.

I could have bunked the tuition class but was not sure whether Shirodkar would take the same route back home. Also, she may not stop and talk at that place in the dark. It was not a convenient spot for us to meet. I would not have agreed to meet someone in the lane next to our building. In fact, I would have found it difficult to stand there for more than five minutes. I would have been mortally scared of coming across someone known to me.

I needed to find another place for us to meet, where

we could sit and chat undisturbed. There are a few places in our town where girls and boys stand and talk—the lane near Shrinath Laundry, the lane near Korde ma'am's crèche or the road leading to the Municipal Hospital. These places are quiet with lots of trees and the houses are spread apart. The boys who meet girls there are older to us, but sometimes there are school boys too. The boys come on bicycles and the girls walk alongside. The boys then sit on the front rod holding the handle with their hands. They don't look around; they are busy staring at the girls' face, but the girls are conscious and keep glancing this way and that, lest they see a known person. Or sometimes, they fiddle with a pebble lying on the ground with their toes. Most of the times the couples are giggling to themselves, but once in a while one can see the girl sulking while the boy tries to humour her.

Last year, Surya had taken it upon himself to tease these couples. We would pace the lanes a few times. Some of the timid ones would push off, but the shameless ones like Sukdi-Mahesh would not bother. We would tire and leave, without any success. But since Surya began lusting after Kevda, he had not found time for anything else.

That said, it was foolish to stand there in those desolate lanes. I wonder why those stupid girls and boys never realized it. Naru mama would have said the same. Anyone passing by, especially a regular, was bound to notice. You need to change places every day. That's why it was important to search for a proper place to meet.

I visited Chitre the following Sunday on the pretext of exchanging some notebooks, and then spent time roaming the lanes and bylanes around his place. There were quite a few desolate ones, but none that appealed to me. The one behind the Parasnis Dispensary seemed appropriate, but unfortunately there was a cobbler sitting under a tree who would keep staring at me. The lane next to the Tilak statue too was lonely, but there was an open drain on one side and a lot of garbage dumped along the lane. The lane next to Faiyyaz garage was fine, but there was a row of trucks parked back to back. I did not venture beyond that lane as the area was quite isolated. There was a danger of the rowdies from Akurli troubling us.

I realized my search for quiet lanes was proving futile. I then went in search of crowded places. The station area was fine, but there was a constant din of vegetable vendors there and cows roamed around freely the whole day. As was the case with Om Market, which has embroidery and tailoring shops and a constant stream of women going in and out. The lanes are narrow and any passer-by will have to brush against you to move ahead. And one has to stand there all the time. There is no place to sit. The only place to sit is in the park near our house, but Phawdya says only the chalu couples visit that place and one has to tip the watchman there. Who wants to have such transactions? The cemented platform behind Sawarkar statue was spacious and the shops there were closed in the afternoon. One could sit there without being seen, but only in the afternoon. I was not keen to sit in such a place. Even if you sat with your sister, people would think otherwise.

It suddenly dawned on me that the Ganesh temple was a good place to meet. It was the only temple in the town and was quite spacious. The main hall had a big chandelier and the floor tiles were smooth and cool. There was a peepal tree with a cement platform all around it. The other small temples around the main one were those of Maruti, Devi and Vitthal. The temple was busy and yet strangely quiet. You could see young children playing hide and seek there. The best part of the temple was the fact that one could stand there and talk to anyone without anyone raising an eyebrow.

I wondered how to convey this idea to Shirodkar. There was no question of standing below the peepal tree waiting for her. Similarly, speaking to her in school was ruled out. The boys would suspect me if I so much as glanced in her direction. The only option was to speak to her when the tuition classes got over. But there was the problem of Mande and the other girl accompanying her. I would be dead meat if I were to speak to her in their presence. Mande would tell the whole school the very next day. It was probably okay if Juvekar came to know of it. She was her best friend in any case.

It then dawned on me—the main reason behind people sending letters. There is some danger in putting things in writing, but at least the contents are not revealed to anyone except the person who reads it. One can convey one's thoughts, otherwise difficult to articulate, through letters. No wonder girls and boys exchange letters. Naru mama may have a different opinion, but I didn't have much choice. I would ask her to destroy the letter after reading it. There would be no danger of any evidence then.

The next day was Saturday. There was school in the morning and Scouts in the evening. I went home and hurriedly finished my tea and toast. I tore off half a page from my notebook and wrote a line, changing my handwriting a bit. The line was simple: 'Will you meet me at the Ganesh temple tomorrow morning at ten?' No one would identify my handwriting. I further added that the letter had to be destroyed after reading.

I attended the tuition class as usual.

Pingle asked me whether I would accompany him on the way back home, but I said, 'I have to return a book to Misal. Do you want to come along?'

I knew he would refuse because he got bored of our talk. Shirodkar, as usual, left with her two friends. I followed them. Mande turned to enter Dedhiya Kirana, much to my relief. It would have been difficult had she continued to walk along. Juvekar and Shirodkar turned towards Juvekar's lane. I knew they would chat there for a while. I was right.

They stood chatting when I slowly walked towards them. I managed to say, 'I got the grammar book you had asked for.'

She was lost for a moment. They both looked askance at me and Juvekar seemed a little suspicious. Shirodkar did not understand my ploy but accepted the book, and I left immediately.

I was fine until I reached home. And then my heart began to pound miserably. There was some time for dinner and, lest Ambabai start talking, I quickly went over to the corner table and opened my Maths book. But I could not concentrate on the book at hand. I had managed to perform the daring task but wondered whether it would yield the desired result. Would Shirodkar understand my ploy? Would she open the book and read my note? The fact that I gave it to her was cue enough. She was sure to find it.

There was a possibility that Juvekar, in her excitement to take a look, might open it and find the note. It was a risk I had to take. At the most, she would come to know of our affair. So what? She might tease Shirodkar—big deal! She might, in all probability, even help her. That would be great! I just hoped the book was not discovered at home. Her younger sister could borrow the book to clear her doubts in grammar. That would be disastrous!

I had asked her to destroy my note. But what if it was discovered before she could destroy it? Imagine her elder sister or mother or her father seeing the note! Luckily, I had not written my name in it, but then she would be forced to tell my name, if asked. Imagine if her father were to land at the temple instead of her! Or, what if she read the note but decided not to visit the temple? Or her mother gave her some errand to run just as she stepped out to meet me?

I could not sleep that night. A strange fear enveloped me. But I had a lovely dream—Shirodkar had come to meet me; I took her for a ride on my cycle and reached the temple meandering through the lanes and bylanes. Everyone stood waiting for us there—Surya, Phawdya, Chitre, Sukdi, all the boys and girls, all the teachers, Appa, Aaisaheb, Ambabai, Juvekar and Pingle. The old lady from Devgiri bungalow too was present. We were welcomed with a round of applause. Surya garlanded us. We were nervous and did not know how to react.

Next morning I got up and prepared to leave. But I couldn't decide which shirt to wear. My favourite almond-coloured shirt—my lucky shirt—was unwashed. The grey T-shirt was a little crumpled. I had never been in such a quandary.

There was a new shirt which we had got for Diwali, but it was meant for special occasions like weddings. Ambabai would get suspicious if she were to see me wearing a new shirt for a casual visit to a friend's house. I finally wore the grey T-shirt, ironing out its creases with my hand.

I reached the temple at quarter to ten. It was a Sunday, so there was quite a crowd. People here visit the temple as a place to go to and not just for worship. All kinds of people come there—young, old, even college-going people like Ambabai. I saw some of the college girls praying earnestly as they made the ritualistic pradakshina around the temple. Our gang is never seen anywhere near the temple; hence this was the most suitable meeting place for me.

Finishing my darshan, I sat outside on the parapet near the Vithoba idol. I don't like to ask for favours while praying. I remember Aaisaheb bringing me here before the results of the seventh standard scholarship exam were to be announced. She had asked me to recite '*pramanya shirasa devam*' and had made me take a vow that I would offer a tray of twenty-one modaks if I were to get the scholarship.

I had tried my best to stifle my laughter then. I'm sure Ganapati too would have wanted to laugh. Why would he fall for such bribes? He would know Aaisaheb would not make the steamed modaks but somehow dish up fried ones made from wheat flour and dry coconut. I was not keen on appearing for the exam, but Ambabai was insistent and I did not want to argue. Bibikar was the only person from our class to get the scholarship. He goes to the school office every two or three months and, after getting a princely sum of twenty or thirty rupees, goes around showing off the whole day. Aaisaheb later felt we should have prayed to the family deity. She's planning to do that when I get to class ten.

I know the Ganesh Atharvashirsha shlokas. Ponkshe kaka organizes a programme every year where the shlokas are recited a thousand times. He manages to inform every one and collects quite a crowd. The attendees get to eat homemade sabudana khichdi and bananas. Even if one person from the group recites the shlokas, Ponkshe kaka conveniently assumes that each one has recited them, thus multiplying the count by as many times. We are thus able to complete the task within a few hours. It is naïve to assume that Ganesh does not understand our ploy. But kaka cheerfully continues with his cheating.

I waited for her. It was one thing to meet on the road and talk for some time and another to actually have my wish fulfilled. Perhaps she did not like the way I had invited her. My chest was throbbing hard. I was hoping I wouldn't meet any known faces here in the temple. I prayed for the same, sitting outside. I then tried my usual ploy of thinking of just the opposite—she would not come, she would not come...she would definitely not come!

At quarter past ten, I lost patience. I was not sure how long I would have to wait. I could see the main gate clearly, but there was a side gate too. She was unlikely to come that way, but I still went around and had a look. She was not to be seen. I took a round of the temple and then returned to sit at the same spot.

She came in at twenty-five minutes past ten. I saw her much before she entered the temple premises. She was wearing that frock with yellow flowers. It was probably her lucky dress. The usual pit of fear in my stomach was replaced by a lump of excitement, which rose right up to my chest. I sprang up. I did not know what to do next. I could not believe my eyes. She had come!

It then dawned on me she was accompanied by someone— a girl younger to her. I figured it must be her younger sister. Oh, no. I felt let down.

She came in and looked around, but I did not move from my spot. Her sister's presence had stumped me. They walked towards the shoe stand. I started walking towards them, lest she assume I had not come.

We stood near each other at the stand, but she acted as if she did not know me. They went into the temple and I followed them as if I too was going in for the first time. They went and stood before the Ganesh idol and prayed. They had brought some flowers, which they offered to the Lord. Then they put some coins in the donation box. I stood behind them with my hands folded, but my entire attention was focused on her. She had worn her hair in two plaits, with aboli flowers adding to her beauty.

They went around the sanctum sanctorum doing the pradakshinas. She darted a quick look in my direction to confirm whether I was still there. I could not, obviously, do the pradakshinas in the counter-clockwise direction in order to see her, so I stood a little away so that I could watch her as they went around.

They crossed me after finishing one round, the younger sister ahead of Shirodkar. She was in seventh standard and must have been coached not to look at boys. She continued to walk with her head bent low. Shirodkar followed her a few steps behind. They did three rounds and each time she crossed me, she gave me a sweet, shy smile.

Then they went around for the darshan of other idols. I followed them into the Vithoba temple, but when they went into the Devi temple, I did not go in. I did not want her younger sister to notice me, and so I spent the time praying to the idol of Hanuman. I was sure Shirodkar approved of my ploy. She continued to give me that shy smile.

Then they went and sat outside. I too took my place a few feet away. I thought Shirodkar had decided not to speak to me. Else she could have easily said, 'Aiyaa, how come you are here?' or something to that effect. But that moment had passed.

I was dumbstruck. It was clear that she had got my message and hence come at my behest. She must have taken her sister along on her mother's insistence. But the question was—how do I speak to her? I should have spoken to her the moment they had entered. Trying to speak now would make her sister suspicious. She may have been younger to her but was old enough to understand a few things.

I was feeling restless. She continued to chat with her sister and glance in my direction once in a while. But then it dawned on me after a while that simply sitting there was bliss. The courtyard was neat and clean, the tiles cool and soothing. There was a pleasant smell of flowers and incense sticks while the temple bells rang intermittently. The people coming in to pray were neatly dressed and freshly bathed. There was an air of purity and happiness all around and, more importantly, Shirodkar was there with me! She may be sitting a few feet away, but there was something holding us together—like the stars in the Milky Way. There was a connection that bound us together, invisible to others—her sister, the people there. It was visible only to the both of us and the gods up there. They must have been smiling down at us and giving us their blessings. Shirodkar must have realized this early and thus sat there without looking perturbed. The smile continued to play on her lips.

I realized this is what I had been looking for. This indescribable something between us. It wasn't slave to words. All of us were searching for the same thing—Surya, Phawdya, Chitre, Ambekar, Sukdi, Naru mama and I. It could not be named and there was no need to do so either. We both had found it and a strange sense of delight filled the very core of my being. I felt happy, pure and complete.

They got up after a while and walked towards the gate. I was sure she would turn around at the gate to look at me, and she did. I gave her a knowing smile.

Afterwards, I went over to Chitre's house. I would have recounted the entire episode if only he had been free, but they were leaving for Bandra. I did not feel like going back home. I roamed around the lanes and by-lanes of our town. I was feeling so good I did not notice the passage of time. Finally when my legs were tired, I walked back home.

My favourite dish of spicy dumplings had been cooked. Its smell pervaded the house. I suddenly felt very hungry. I washed my feet and hands, and sat down to eat.

The food was good. I was feeling contented. When I complemented Aaisaheb, she said, 'Then why don't you take some more?'

Ambabai was silent for a while and then halfway through the meal, with her trademark, naughty smile, she asked, 'So what did you ask Lord Ganapati for?'

Oh fuck! I was lucky not to have anything in my mouth, else I would have choked. She sat there giving her wry smile, twisting her lips a little. A knowing smile which only an elder sister can give. My mind was racing. She knew I had been there. Denying it would be of no use. I wondered whether she had seen me herself or had been told about it.

If she had seen me, she would surely have me there. Which meant she had been told about my visit by one of her friends. But I had not seen anyone there.

'I prayed that you may get some common sense,' I said.

'Oh really?' she asked. 'For me? Or for your own self?'

'You. Who else?'

'What is going on here?' Aaisaheb asked.

'Our prince paid a visit to the Ganesh temple today,' she said, smiling. 'Isn't that strange?'

'Who told you so?' Aaisaheb asked.

'Sunita had come a while back to return the embroidery kit. She saw him there.'

'Strange indeed!' Aaisaheb said, smiling. I saw Baba smiling too. I felt like hiding beneath the table.

'You won't recite *Atharvashirsha* at home when asked to,' Aaisaheb said. 'Then why go visiting temples?'

'All this happens when one does not study,' Ambabai added. 'Please remember, one does not get marks just by visiting temples. Got that, sir? One needs to study hard.'

Thank God! I said to myself, the way Naru mama would have said. Then I mentally bowed low before Lord Ganesh.

It was divine intervention that prevented Shirodkar and me from talking to each other. Else that Sunita, or whoever that friend of Ambabai's was, would have spotted us chatting. I would have been a dead duck then.

Nothing had changed—the classrooms, the tables, the chairs and the playground—it was all the same, yet I felt different. I felt light and floated my way to school and back and to the tuition classes. I could not define my feelings. A constant, pleasant tune played inside me. Biology, Physics, Chemistry or Geometry— everything felt friendly and easy to understand. Nothing seemed difficult. Even the hot afternoon breeze seemed soothing, and the barren paddy fields seemed full of water and the sweet smell of ice-candy hung in the air. The mountains beyond Sonarpada seemed enveloped in majestic blue coats. It was a sight to behold.

We continued to assemble regularly at our adda and our pranks continued as before. Surya would get restless seeing Kevda and was worried about the days slipping by without his making a headway. To add to his agony, Phawdya announced that he and his heartthrob, Vaishali Kadam, had met in a lane near the railway station. This meant that he too was on his way.

One Saturday morning, while returning from school, he said, 'Come on. We will follow Kevda today. What say?'

For a moment, I could not grasp what he meant. The other students were slowly streaming out of the class. Chitre was absent that day.

'Chaila! It has been too long now, bhenchod. There is

no point in simply waiting,' Surya said. 'We will follow her. Let us see what she does!'

Phawdya was quick to wriggle out.

'I have to go and pick up vegetables. I can come with you till the station if you wish.'

'Joshi, come with me,' Surya said.

I was scared. Follow Kevda! This was unexpected. And if Chitre came to know about it, I would be in trouble.

'No, yaar. I have some work to finish at home,' I began.

'Come on, saale! Why are you acting pricey?' Surya threatened.

One look at him and I knew I had no choice. I *had* to go with him.

'I don't have much time, okay? I need to get back home by eleven,' I tried.

'We will see. Come, let us go,' he persisted.

Holding his bundle of books between his thighs, he quickly combed his hair, all the while keeping an eye out for the girls from class eight. Shortly, Kevda came out with her friends and they walked by, laughing and chatting away.

We followed them. My chest was pounding wildly. It was one thing to tease the girls hiding behind a wall, and another to brazenly follow them. Some of the boys looked at us. Surya followed the girls at close quarters and I had to pull him back by his shirt.

'Don't be a fool! Don't follow them so closely,' I said. 'We need to maintain a respectable distance.'

We then allowed a reasonable distance between us. The girls had probably realized we were following them as a couple of them turned to look at us and then murmured something amongst them. Everyone in school knew that Surya was hell-bent on impressing Kevda.

After a while, most of the girls went their respective ways. It was only Kevda and her other friend now. Chitre had mentioned she stayed somewhere on the other side of the railway line but, instead of crossing the railway gate, she turned towards Chiplunkar lane.

'Come on, let us get a little closer,' Surya said.

'Why?'

'What do you mean why? We need to let her know.'

'She knows,' I said. 'The whole school knows. What will you get by going closer?'

'I want to speak to her,' Surya said. 'What do you expect me to do otherwise? Just go on pining for her?'

Kevda's friend turned into a lane and Kevda walked alone now. There was no crowd and the lane seemed quiet.

'Come on, let us move a little closer,' Surya said, pulling my hand. 'We will go speak to her.'

'Wait a moment. Let us see what she's up to. Why is she going that way? That's not the way to her house.'

We got the answer to our question shortly. She entered a shop in the lane. It must have been a ladies' garments and tailoring shop; we could see a lot of coloured blouses hanging outside. We did not notice her entering the shop and walked past. Kevda was inside the shop talking to the person at the counter. She looked straight at us. Surya continued to stare and then gave a goofy smile. I pulled him and we continued to walk. I could see Kevda was taken aback and was looking at us with suspicion. The tailoring master, with the measuring tape hanging from his neck, also looked at us.

We had to stop and wait for a while. We were not sure where she would go after finishing at the shop. We realized the lane ended a little ahead and we turned back. I told Surya,

'Let us stand a little further on the other side. We will be able to see where she goes.'

We walked back. Kevda was still in the shop. I was sure Surya would stare at her as we passed by and hence took the precaution of keeping him on the other side. Kevda continued to look out, her eyes full of suspicion and anger.

We came on to the main road and stood below the transformer put up by the electricity board. My guess was right—Kevda came out and then retraced her steps, turning into a lane near Syndicate Bank. She had not seen us. The lane led to the railway gate.

'Come on,' I said, pulling Surya.

We kept a safe distance. Kevda must have assumed we had left and walked at a relaxed pace without turning to look out for us. We felt relieved. There was a vegetable market near the gate followed by the Octroi naka. The railway gate would be closed most of the time, but that did not deter people from going beneath or from the side of it. Kevda suddenly turned around when she reached the gate. We were caught unawares. She looked at us for a brief moment and continued in the direction of her house. My chest was pounding now. Surya, optimistic as ever, said, 'Ichibhana, she saw us!'

Kevda crossed the gate and then the railway lines. She turned to see us crossing the lines. A local train from Mumbai was coming our way. We crossed over while she moved ahead and quickly crossed over to the other side beyond the vegetable and fruit sellers. I tried to hold back Surya who seemed eager to close the distance. She turned once more to look at us. I could clearly see that she was angry.

'She's angry,' I said. 'Let us go back.'

Surya stopped for a moment but was not willing to give up the chase.

'She's not angry or anything,' he insisted. 'Let us see what she's up to.'

We continued walking. A makeshift police chowki straddled the crossroads. It had been set up when people had complained about the rowdyism of boys from Akurli village The chowki was a small one, with no space to sit inside. Two havaldars sat on steel chairs outside. A thousand bulbs lit up in my mind the moment I saw her going by the chowki.

'Surya, wait!' I shouted, pulling him back. 'See that havaldar sitting there? If Kevda complains to him, we are dead meat.'

Surya took some time before he came back to his senses. Kevda was near the chowki and all she had to do was to point out a finger towards us. I turned and started walking back without waiting for Surya. He, quite obviously, followed me.

'Ichibhana, why the hell have they set up that chowki?' he asked.

'For the havaldars to sit and sunbathe!' I taunted. 'Come on, let us scoot!'

I left him at the turn towards Mokshadham and took the road home, breathing a sigh of relief.

The real question for me was how to get the grammar textbook back from Shirodkar. Not that I needed it—for I knew most of the stuff in it. I did not use it every day.

I wondered what she would do. I watched her constantly in class. I thought I had seen the book with her a couple of times. She could have passed on the book to me in Rajguru sir's class when we have the permission to roam around the room. But she did not.

We were busy chatting before the tuition classes began. I had made friends with most of the boys. Though they were from Subhash. It was fun talking to them. They would gossip about the affairs in their school; the most talked about being one Madgaokar's. She was a bombshell and many boys from other schools had an eye on her.

We stood near the compound wall. The boys and girls stood near each other chatting away. I would never look at Shirodkar when Mande was around. But my ears strained to hear every word they spoke.

The earlier batch streamed out. We picked up our books and started walking into the class when Shirodkar said, a tad loudly, 'Juvekar is not coming in today.'

'Why so?' Mande asked.

'She's not well,' Shirodkar answered, loudly as before.

No one spoke further and we entered the class and sat down.

The class began and the teacher started teaching Algebra. It did not strike me for a while but then I realized the reason behind Shirodkar's loud voice. They normally spoke in whispers. But she had suddenly raised her voice today to announce Juvekar's absence.

My mind was racing away. I could not follow Deshmane

sir. Shirodkar had loudly said, Juvekar would not be coming in today. How did it matter if she did not come in?

It then dawned on my stupid mind. She wanted me to know! For it meant she would be walking down that lane alone. It was a message to me so she could return my book.

I smiled to myself and then looked at her. She was looking down at her notebook. I nodded with a slight tilt of my head to indicate I had understood. Naru mama says girls are very perceptive and they would know. I had got the message. I knew what to do.

It happened the way I had anticipated. I spent some time to find a way to excuse myself from Pingle. Shirodkar and Mande started walking back home and I followed them at a safe distance. As expected, she glanced back when they reached the temple. It was a little dark, but I was sure she would have seen me. She must have been happy to see me. I was not an idiot not to have recognized her message. Mande went her way and Shirodkar started walking towards her lane. She glanced back once more in my direction.

I followed her and when we met, she smiled knowingly. She took out the book from her bundle and said, 'Your book!'

I took the book but was unable to speak. My heart was beating hard, and I did not know what to say now that we had met.

She quickly glanced in both the directions. The lane was silent. The street lights had come on. We stood below a street lamp. It seemed dark despite the glow of the lamps.

'Why did you give me the book?' she started. 'I could not find a way to return it.'

I did not answer. I could not straightaway say it was only for the purpose of hiding that note. That purpose had been served in any case.

'You could have kept it,' I said.

'Aha! What do you mean kept it? I have mine,' she said.

I realized that I had to say something else to keep the conversation going. We were losing precious time.

'It was good you came to the temple the other day,' I said.

She smiled but did not reply.

'Why did you get your younger sister along?' I asked.

'What could I have done? It was not possible to come alone.'

She was right and it had not made much difference. I had to find another topic for our conversation. There was no point in discussing old issues.

'We are going to have the khari kamai session soon, isn't it?' she asked.

'Yes.'

'I feel very embarrassed going for it,' she said. 'Especially to those who know us. Doing errands is all right but how to ask for money? Don't you feel the same?'

'Yes, me too.'

'And the people here are so stuck up! That Bhole aaji made me sift a whole tin of rice. And the money I got in return was a mere four annas. Aai was really upset because I don't work at home but can go and slog in someone else's house. It was lucky I was not asked to wash their dirty utensils.'

I laughed out loud imagining all the girls in our Guides' team going out and washing utensils in people's homes.

'What are you laughing for?' she asked. 'Perhaps you are not asked to do any work.'

'We never do anything,' I said. 'They give us money to get us out of their hair as soon as possible!'

'Aiyaa! That's not khari kamai. That is jhooti kamai.'

I had no answer. I could not tell her that many families look at the card we carry from school and assume we are collecting some donation for some thing or the other. Last year Chitre, Surya, Phawdya and I had collected money in this fashion. Most of the people would not even open their door fully but look at the card and give us some money. They would not even bother to sign the card. We would, of course, go to places a little away from our homes where people would not recognize us. But I could not tell her all this, and the fact that we had used that unaccounted money to enjoy some hot dosas in Anand Ashram Hotel.

I couldn't say much, but I was enjoying our little chat there.

'Shall I come to your place for khari kamai?' I said, a little emboldened.

'My home?' she asked, a little surprised. 'Why not? We will give you some work. I am sure Aai will pay you well.'

'Really?'

'Yes, surely!'

'You mean it? Shall I come? What will you tell your Aai?'

'What is there to tell her?' she asked. 'She knows about khari kamai.'

'Won't she have any problems?'

'No. Why would she have any problems? I will tell her you are my classmate.'

I was knocked out cold. I had never expected Shirodkar to be so bold. A feeling of lightness pervaded me. I realized I had been scared all along for no reason at all. I needed to be bolder now, I told myself.

'I need to go. It is getting late now,' she said.

The lane was desolate and it was getting dark. But I did not have the heart to let her go. I wished we could stand there and keep talking for ever.

'Please wait for some more time,' I pleaded.

'Why?' she asked, glancing around.

I could not answer. My heart kept thumping away. I did not know why I wanted her to stay.

She smiled, seeing me lost in my thoughts. But she did not leave. We looked at each other. It was dark, but the moment our eyes met, she looked away.

'Let me go now,' she said.

'When shall we meet again?' I blurted.

She did not say a word and then, glancing at me once more, walked away smiling to herself. I stood there rooted to the ground.

The next week started with khari kamai. I did not have the guts to visit Shirodkar's house. Like last year, Chitre and I had the card where we could note down the amount received from each family. Chitre's father gave him a five-rupee note. Chitre was smart enough to break down the amount into small change, showing receipts from different households: Wandrekar—fifty paise, Shetty—one rupee, Shah—fifty paise, Upadhyay—twenty-five paise, and so on, scribbling each signature in a different ink.

'I am done,' Chitre said. 'You may go and earn your

own way.' Surya was ready to join us, but I did not want to take him along. Last year he had collected the money as if it were the Ganesh festival and used most of it to enjoy dosas and buy Cadbury's chocolates for all of us. He had returned the balance amount of a mere thirty-five paise. Luckily, this time, his father had given him some errand to run, which kept him busy and he did not trouble us.

Aaisaheb gave me fifty paise while Ambabai gave me another twenty, but she made me trace three drawings on her handkerchief in return. I went to Upasni Aaji, who was pleased to see me and said, 'Wah! It is nice that they teach you good values in your school.' She then asked me to deliver some dabba to the Gogates in Dattawadi and I had to get her atta dabba from the neighbourhood atta chakki. When I asked her for my tip she got upset and said, 'What do you mean asking for money? Is that what they teach you in school? I cannot give you any money.' And then, plonking one laddoo on my palm, she said, 'Here, take this.' I was not interested in her disgusting laddoo, which was nothing but a big lump of sugar. I left in a huff.

Ponkshe kaka, as usual, had a hundred questions. 'How am I to know how these people would use the money? What is all this fuss about khari kamai? I kept listening quietly as I knew that after the speech, he would take out a fifty-paise coin and hand it over to me saying, 'Why do you want to do any task; here, take this.' And that's what happened. Nikam kaka was on his way to the cycle repair shop and was looking for someone to wheel the bicycle. I volunteered and he then put a twenty-paise coin in my hand. Mayekar kaku from the neighbouring house was listening to our conversation and she took out a four-anna coin, but I declined saying I would not take it for free. I then bought a loaf of bread for her from the shop.

I went upstairs to KT, Ashok and Vijay's room too. KT was busy chopping onions while Vijay was washing clothes and Ashok was shaving. He asked, 'Why don't you attend our meetings these days?'

'I don't get time. I have tuition classes in the evening.'

'Has anyone benefited from attending these classes?' KT asked. 'Why do you waste your time there?'

I would have agreed, but I could not tell them the real reason. I told them the reason for my visit.

'What is all this?' Vijay asked, reducing the radio volume.

'This is khari kamai.'

'So are you saying others are not earning their own bread?' KT asked.

'Your teachers are bloody smart!' Vijay said. 'They don't work and make the children earn for them.'

Vijay took the clothes out to hang them to dry. He said, 'Good. It is good to learn these things in childhood. You should know how to earn your own bread.'

'And then let the leaders loot you of what you earn with toil and sweat!'

I was used to their comments and did not react. I looked around the room. A poster of a bearded man with long hair seemed fresh on the wall

'Who is he?' I asked.

'He is Che,' Vijay said. 'Che Guevara. Do you want to read his book?'

'Not now. Later,' I said. 'First I have to earn my own bread.'

'Why are you wasting your time earning money for someone else?' KT asked. 'Instead, read this book.'

'Don't pester him,' Ashok interjected. 'Hey, Vijay. See if I have some coins in my pant pocket. Give it to him.'

'No. I don't want it that way,' I objected. 'Give me an errand to run.'

'Forget it, yaar. You are our friend. Take it.'

'No, no,' I objected again. 'I have to earn it.'

'What can we give him to do...' KT pondered and then suddenly an idea dawned on him. He stopped chopping the onions and looked at Vijay and Ashok. They waited for him to say something.

'Wait! I have a task for you.' He looked at his partners and said, 'Will you do it? It is a small task.'

'Yes, I will do it,' I said. 'What is it?'

KT wiped his hands on a towel and bent down to take out a cloth bag from under the bed. There was a small parcel in the bag. It was wrapped in paper. He took it out and asked,

'What is the time now?'

'Ten-thirty,' Vijay said.

'Then it is fine,' KT said. He turned towards me and asked, 'Do you know Gomantak?'

I nodded.

'There is a paanwallah there. All you have to do is to deliver this parcel there.'

'What's in it?' I asked. I realized that I should not have asked. I was sure he would not tell me.

'There are a few papers in it,' he said. 'Just hand these over to the paanwallah. Tell him KT has sent you. Don't speak anything else, okay? Not a word more.'

'And don't speak to anyone on the road,' Vijay added.

'No one will ask you anything,' KT added. 'Will you do this for us? You'll get two rupees!'

I would have done the work even otherwise. It sounded thrilling. The way KT put it made it sound like an important task. I left immediately. The bag was a little heavy. The three of them came out and stood in the balcony. For a moment, I wanted to duck into my house to pick up my cap, but then I decided otherwise. Ambabai was at the door and asked, 'Where are you off to?'

'I have some work,' I said, avoiding any further questions.

I looked up to see the three boys waiting for me to leave. KT gave me a thumbs-up signal.

I walked along the road, a little alert. I looked around to see if anyone had noticed me but realized I should walk casually. I was curious to open the bag and tried to feel the packet with my fingers. It had something rolled up in it. Suddenly I missed Shirodkar. It would have been fun to have her accompany me.

The paanwallah was there, sitting on a high seat inside his shop. There were a few customers and he was busy making paans for them. I stood for a while hoping that the customers would leave, but they seemed to be in no hurry. Seeing me, the paanwallah raised his eyebrows questioningly. Pointing at the bag, I said, 'KT has sent this.'

He nodded and, with a jerk of his head, asked me to come in from the back door. I went in and was hoping to hide the bag somewhere, but he casually asked me to drop it on the floor and continued his work. There was no point in hanging around there any more, so I left.

I got a pat on my back when I returned and informed

KT of the mission being successful. He filled up my card and signed it with a flourish. I pocketed the two rupees he gave me. Ashok gave me a new deck of cards.

Ambabai was curious as always and asked me what I had delivered in that bag for KT. I casually mentioned that he wanted some books to be given to a friend of his. She did not believe me.

School resumed, as usual, after the sports meet, but had not picked up steam as the annual gathering was yet to take place. The gathering would have the usual fare of dance, plays, songs etc. The girls in our class felt a bit shy, having grown up a bit, and did not put up a dance performance this time. Desai, as always, had plans for a solo dance. Deodhar would sing while Kulkarni and Dongre would sing a duet based on two sisters-in-law. Bibikar, among boys, participated in a play titled, 'The Stage Is Being Set.' He may be a smartass otherwise, but acts well and hence is popular among the girls and teachers. Teredesai would have his usual comedy act, cracking cheap jokes. Surya came up with the funny idea of reciting Gangu's ribald song.

His idea was scoffed at and everyone doubled up with laughter, so he dropped it and chose to volunteer. We had to select five volunteers from each class. In our class, other than the four of us, Santu and Harishchandra agreed to volunteer while among the girls, Sukdi, Ambekar and Mane came forward. Shembekar put forth his name seeing others participate when Zende sir commented, 'Wah! It seems your class is quite keen on social service.' He had, in fact, asked Shembekar and me to withdraw, but Surya insisted on our names and he agreed. That fatso was happy to be part of our group again, but he did not know that Surya had plans to slog his ass off.

It was also time for our annual trip but somehow the teachers were unable to find free days as they were asked to attend some training programme. To make matters worse, a bus carrying school children from Buldhana fell into a valley. The report was splashed across the front pages of all the newspapers. That silenced the issue of the trip for a while.

The trip was cancelled, but the annual Scouts and Guides camp was finalized. The NCC camp too was being held at the same time. Last year our school had saved time and money by organizing the Scouts and Guides camp in a temple in the adjoining village. The temple premises were large and the facilities were good. While the camp was fun, the fact that it was so close by took some of the excitement out of it. We pleaded with Rajguru sir to take us somewhere else this time. He may not have agreed on his own, but Manjrekar sir agreed to take us to Sule village. There is a huge dam in Sule next to which there is a school. We would have to take a local train and then a state transport bus to reach there. The best part was that the Scouts and Guides would camp in the same place.

It took an entire day to plan for the camp. We had to get everything—salt, rice, turmeric and chilly powder, onions, potatoes, vessels, spoons, blankets, sweaters, knives, rope, torch, what not. Luckily the teachers were getting tea, sugar and milk. It was my camp, but for a change Ambabai was excited and helped me pack, as if she herself were going. We had Sadu Kale with us, which was a great relief. He had lost his mother in childhood and knew how to cook; his chapattis were particularly good. So cooking would not be an issue.

We reached the railway station in the afternoon. The train was at half past four. Sir had booked the tickets in advance. We were in our uniform and everyone at the station stared at us. Adhav ma'am made the girls sit in the ladies compartment. I searched for Shirodkar and our eyes met. We all boarded the train. It would have been fun, though, to have them in our compartment as it wasn't crowded. We sang songs all the way to our destination.

Kamat from Nine-C was with us. He is a very good singer. He is in the Lion team now, but was earlier in our group. He started singing songs, beginning with the Scouts' songs and then as the crowd thinned he began singing Hindi film songs. Manjrekar sir sat on the bench next to us and raised his eyebrows when he sang '*Aaj kal tere mere pyar ke charche*.' It was unfortunate that we reached our destination in the middle of the song. I loved that song. Chitre too was enjoying it. We decided to request Kamat to sing it again later.

The red and yellow state transport bus was waiting outside the station. We rushed to get in despite the teachers asking us to go in a line. Everyone tried to get in at the same time. The girls were not far behind. I barely managed not to collide with Shirodkar.

We had reached the steps at the same time and could not enter as the luggage on our backs came in the way. She giggled. The boys and girls were pushing us from behind and I laughed as well. I wished we could stand there stuck at the footboard forever. But then someone from behind gave us a push and we stumbled into the bus.

The bus was cramped and full. The locals did not find a seat as the boys and girls were all over. Most of the boys were sitting on someone's lap. Many of us were standing. Shirodkar was standing next to me at the rear end of the bus. I was holding on to the rod above and her hand was very close to mine. Her face was partially hidden by her arm, but each time our eyes met, a sweet smile played on her lips. I tried to be nonchalant but could not avoid returning the smile each time. The road was bad and we would bump into each other every time the bus suffered a jerk. The boys and girls would laugh and we would join the laughter, for reasons known only to us.

'Why are you smiling so?' Chitre asked suspiciously.

'Just like that,' I said.

I wished the journey would go on forever. I was willing to travel all the way to Kanyakumari in this fashion, but we reached the village within fifteen or twenty minutes. The school was large—a huge playground surrounded by flat rows of classrooms on three sides. We were allotted the classrooms for our stay. Our teachers were wise; they had allotted the rooms on one side to the girls and the boys on the opposite. The girls could use the school toilets, but we would have to go outdoors into the fields.

The day passed by cleaning the rooms and arranging our things. We had carried food hence there was no need to cook that night. We were asked to sit on the ground. The girls were on the opposite side. It was getting dark, but I could see Shirodkar clearly. The teachers gave us a lot of instructions. No one was supposed to venture out anywhere near the dam. Anyone found doing so would be promptly sent back home. It was good that we did not have boys like Surya in the Scouts' team. He would have been the first one to break the rules. There was a small pond behind the school, which was not out of bounds. We would have to collect water from there. We had plans for a bonfire after dinner, but we could not collect firewood and the plan had to be dropped.

The real camp began in the morning. Unfortunately the Guides' team was away from us. Manjrekar sir went over with two boys to Sule village in the morning and got pao buns for all of us to have with tea. The tea was served in plastic cups giving out a faint plasticky smell. The morning was spent in classes where they taught us ways of tying different types of knots, using the whistle to signal, and so on, but we spent most of the time cooking.

The place was beautiful. The school was built on a hilly slope, with a pond in one corner. A huge dam lay on the other side of the hill. The entire area was wooded and, when we went to the hilltop to collect dry wood for our bonfire, we got a clear view of the dam. The blue water seemed cool despite the bright sun. We could see far into the distance. The entire area was barren, with a small tiled roof village on one side. The area was so huge and spread out that I wanted to go for a long walk around it. The hill was full of small shrubs with wild flowers. I plucked a bunch. Chitre was curious about whom I planned to give it to, but I said it was for the purpose of decoration. He too picked up a few bunches.

The girls' rooms were a little far away, but the cooking done at a common place. The area near the pond was flat with a few large trees giving a cool shade in the hot afternoon. We roamed around the pond, picking up large stones for the chulhas. Chitre had the common sense to pick up some bricks from a construction site which we use to quickly set up our chulha. He then lit up the fire. We had Sadu Kale with us so we were not worried. We cut onions and potatoes while he made rotis. We then set up rice to cook on one stove while the other was used to make curry. Chitre managed to grind some chutney on a flat stone. By the time the girls got their stoves going, we were almost ready with our meal. Rajguru sir, walking around with his hands behind his back, told the girls, 'Look at them! They have finished cooking.'

'Huh! What's so great about that? We too shall cook a nice meal,' one of the birdies, Dongre, chirped. 'Anybody can cook a meal, but what about taste?'

'Why don't you taste it and see?' Chitre challenged, removing the plate covering one of the vessels.

'No need to,' she said, gruffly turning away.

We were free to roam around now. The atmosphere was really relaxed. We were not in our uniforms and, although teachers were around, there were no classes to attend. Adhav and Pethe ma'am sat there, sipping endless cups of tea since morning. Manjrekar sir was talking to the teachers from that school and Rajguru sir roamed around the camp. No one bothered us.

The boys were cool as always, but the girls too had let their guard down. I could see the boys and girls of Nine-C talking to each other. The boys had helped them get a few buckets of water from the pond. There were more girls in nine-a as compared to the boys. Our class girls too were now interacting with the boys. I had seen that on the bus last evening. Teredesai and Shembekar had stood up and offered their seats to the birdies and they had given them some lemon flavoured hard-boiled toffees in return. They found some excuse or the other to chat with the boys since morning. One of the groups was short of dry wood and requested us to give them some for our cooking. Bibikar in the Tiger group was, as usual, trying to act smart. He borrowed some washing powder from the girls to clean the vessels.

The girls from Nine-C had set the ball rolling by speaking to the boys. Each one in the school wanted to mingle with the other sex, but the question was who would take the first step. No one wanted to get teased to death. No one knows who created such stupid rules. Naru mama says, in countries like England and America, no one bothers. Girls and boys talk to each other without a care. They can even sit on the same bench if they like. Boys like Surya would love to do that. I am sure the girls too feel the same, but who would bell the cat?

We sat down for lunch and the boys and girls exchanged their dishes, urging the other groups to taste. Our chutney was immensely popular and we had hardly any left for our own selves. Kamat's group had made besan curry and all hell broke loose when the birdies announced that they had got some pickles from home. Dongre was on the verge of tears seeing her pickle disappear in minutes. Shirodkar stood up and handed over a plate to us without saying a word. It had some vegetable curry, similar to the one we had prepared. Sadu, Gaitonde, Memane and some boys were clueless, but Chitre gave me a knowing smile. The curry tasted divine. She had added some fresh coconut to it. Their group must have brought some freshly grated coconut from home.

There was a decoration competition in the afternoon and Chitre came up with a bright idea to pluck small branches from trees and label them as per their botanical names. Bibikar tried copying the same but fell flat. We bagged the first prize. The girls roamed around in groups inspecting what the other groups had done. We had free time in the evening and there were some matches between the boys and girls. We played the langdi game, with one leg folded. I was hoping Shirodkar would play against me, but I was up against that long-legged Pandhre from Nine-C who pulled me down in a matter of seconds.

That evening Manjrekar sir came up with the idea of preparing a common meal. We borrowed some huge vessels from the school and the chowkidar helped us light a big fire. The boys were given the task of making rice while the girls opted for dal. Chitre casually announced that we need not be a part of the process and could excuse ourselves. We asked Kamat to come along and enjoyed his songs sitting on the bank of the canal.

In the evening, all the girls and boys sat around the campfire in a huge circle. Sir had noticed that we had managed to slip out of the meal duty and promptly ordered us to wash the vessels. We were a little late by the time we finished and joined the group around the bonfire. There was no place in the ring. Chitre and I were forced to sit next to Adhav ma'am. I was fuming but had no choice but to sit quietly. The bonfire was bright, but the circle around it was so big I could not see people's faces clearly.

The girls started some stupid 'chain song' game wherein you go on adding one line every time and repeating the whole song at the same time. The boys soon got bored of it and Sir asked us to stop. We then sang a few other songs. Sir sang one sung by the local fishermen. The tune was catchy and the chorus '*jhim gale gale jhim…jhim gale gale….*' was soothing making one drowsy. I could imagine myself swaying gently as the fishermen rowed the boat back to the shore after a hard day's work.

Adhav ma'am got up and returned in a while with the teachers from the local school. We were asked to squeeze in closer to make space for them. The teachers sang a local song for us. The bonfire was burning, but the brightness had reduced considerably now. I looked up to see the sky. It was filled with stars. It was not cold, but a pleasant wind was blowing gently. I felt something fall near my thighs. It seemed to have been thrown from the side where the girls sat. I looked down to see a Ravalgaon toffee lying there. I glanced up and was shocked to death to see Shirodkar sitting next to me. When I looked, she continued to stare at the bonfire as if nothing had happened. But I could see her faint smile in the mild light of the fire.

I grabbed the toffee and looked around to see if anyone had noticed. The boys were busy listening to the teachers singing, but Chitre had noticed. He said, 'What is it, buddy? What's going on?'

I was forced to show him the toffee. He exclaimed, 'Good progress!'

I was terribly embarrassed. But I was feeling good too.

I did not know what to do. On one hand I was keen to preserve the toffee and keep it in my pocket, but on the other there was a danger of being caught by the others.

'Do you want to share it?' I asked Chitre.

'No. You eat it,' he said, smiling.

The next day we were to depart after lunch, but no one felt like leaving. Sir had called for a feedback session an hour before departure. Teredesai was the first to speak up.

'Sir, what if we have our school permanently based here? It would be so much fun,' he said.

'Yes, Sir,' the birdies chirped in. 'We don't want to go back. Teach us here.'

Everyone felt the same. No one was teasing anyone else. We were happily chatting with everyone. Even when Deosthale threw up in the morning, no one sniggered and, in fact, when Phatak from Nine-C got some cloves for her to chew on, no one teased him. The distance between the boys and girls had disappeared, and we felt as if we all knew each other for ages.

'Sir, why can't we have a school without walls?' Kamat asked. 'We don't mind cooking.'

'It is so nice and open here,' Gaitonde commented.

'Yes Sir,' the birdies chirped. 'We should have a school like this one. We will never trouble you.'

Manjrekar sir smiled.

'I agree with you, but my hands are tied,' he said. 'When you grow up, you should build a school like this one.'

The next day I was in a dual mood wanting to go and yet felt like staying back alone. It was a Monday and we had decided to meet at our adda. Surya and others would have returned from their NCC camp, and we were waiting to hear their exploits.

I left a little before eleven. I was planning to take the route through the paddy fields but changed my mind and went by the main road. Walking past Shriram Flour Mill I noticed some posters stuck high up on the wall above it. The message was loud and clear—'Emergency Murdabad! Down With Dictatorship!' The black and red letters on the white paper were clearly visible from a distance. The bhaiya managing the flour mill was oblivious to the posters and was busy grinding wheat in the mill. I then understood the meaning of Ambabai's whisperings this morning. She had spotted the posters while returning from a friend's place. 'They are everywhere,' she was telling Aaisaheb in a low voice. When I asked her what she meant, she snubbed me saying, 'Why are you so curious? It's none of your business.'

The posters were in many prominent places—on the dustcart, on the electric transformer, on the wall near the shops, on some fences, and one on the wall of Chowdhary bungalow. Someone had tried tearing it off. There was one on Surya's building too.

When I reached our adda, I saw Chitre and Surya looking at the poster. Surya said, 'Just see these posters—Emergency Murdabad! Down With Dictatorship! It is fun, bhenchod!'

'They are up all over town—even near the station,' Chitre said. 'The police are removing them.'

'But who put them up?' asked Surya.

"Who knows?' Chitre said. 'Someone has dared to.'

'There are a few on the wall of Mokshadham too,' I added.

'What does it say?'

'The same message—Emergency Murdabad!'

'They should stick them everywhere, bhenchod,' Surya said. 'I would have put them up if I had them.'

'The police will put you in jail, understand?' Chitre explained. 'Take these out before your dad thinks you put them up.'

Phawdya came in and told us that the posters were all over the marketplace and that the police were removing them.

'How do we remove them?' Surya asked, looking around. 'They are so high up. How did they put them up in the first place?'

'They must have used your ladder,' Chitre said. 'Look, I can see the ladder there.'

Surya put the ladder against the wall and we stood looking at the posters when I said, leave it. People may think you are putting up the posters. Why bother?'

Surya agreed and got down the ladder keeping it on one side.

'Leave it, bhenchod,' he said. 'My dad will take care of it. Come, let us go and sit upstairs. How was your camp? Our camp, Ichibhana, was fabulous!'

We bounded up the stairs. The work was almost complete and the floor tiles had been set. The bamboo poles had been removed and now one could not hide behind them. The dampness of the walls was gone and the room was not as cool as before. But there was a lot of space for us to move around.

'We had such fun, you know,' Surya said.

'We teased the eighth standard boys a lot,' Phawdya said. 'That stupid Vichare had got some laddoos in a dabba. We found that out, ate the laddoos, and replaced them with small stones.'

'I tell you, bhenchod,' Surya said. 'And tell them what we did to that Pendse.'

'Chaila! Unfortunately for him, he was in our barrack. That night, Surya took his toothpaste and emptied the entire tube into his trousers after unzipping them.'

'Oh boy!'

'You bet! He started crying and was quite sure Surya must have played that prank. But we kept our mouths shut. He could not prove it.'

'Wasn't your sergeant present?' I asked.

'He was. Pendse went crying to him, but he shooed him away saying, "tum kuch bhi karo, bhosadike."'

'And those guys from Shivaji High School? They had got a bottle of brandy, you know?' Surya said. 'They offered us some too.'

'Were there students from other schools too?'

'What do you mean other schools? There were three thousand students!' Phawdya said.

'You have no idea! We could do whatever we felt like. It was total ruckus.'

'But was there no one supervising you guys?' I asked.

'Yes. There were supervisors. But they were bothered about discipline on the ground. In the tents, no one bothered. That havaldar would kick us if we tried some prank on the ground. There we would behave well. And we had mutton four times. It was total dhamaal!'

'Anyway! Forget our tales. Tell us, how was your camp?' Surya asked.

Chitre and I looked at each other. We did not know what to say. We had not had their kind of fun. We were with our own schoolmates and teachers. We had made khichdi and onion-potato curry.

'Tell them,' Chitre nudged me.

'No. Why don't you tell,' I said.

Chitre thought for a while. He had to make our camp experience feel better than the NCC one.

'The boys and girls stayed together in our camp,' he said.

'What!' Surya and Phawdya exclaimed at the same time.

'Together, meaning next to each other. Not exactly staying in the same room,' Chitre explained 'It was like being at home. We were all bindaas—all the girls and boys.'

Phawdya and Surya were all ears now.

'What are you saying?' Surya asked, not believing what he heard.

'You bet! We went for walks together. We cooked together; someone would make chutney; the other person would make subji. The girls were really free and chatting with everyone. We all sat close together on the bus.'

'Ichibhana, it must have been fun, isn't it?' Surya exclaimed.

'Of course! Joshi was in his true spirits. He was busy chopping vegetables, running errands for them. He even got a toffee in return for his efforts.'

'Hey, shut up!' I said.

'Why are you asking me to shut up? Didn't that Shirodkar give you a toffee? That too, at the camp fire, when no one was looking, isn't it?'

'That's nothing special. The girls were giving many people such toffees.'

'Chaila! You guys had all the fun,' Surya said. 'Phawdya, we too should join the Scouts now.'

'What is so exciting about this?' Phawdya asked. 'All girlish activities!'

'Wasn't Kevda there?' Surya asked.

'No. The girls from eighth standard were not there.'

'Then it is fine. But tell me, were the girls really interacting with you guys? You should have taken one of them into the woods in the dark of the night.'

'Don't talk crap!'

'What do you mean crap? Were there no woods around? If I was there, I would have taken one of them out. But I am sure you sissies must have sat and just talked the whole night.'

We did not comment. Surya would not appreciate the kind of fun we had there and it was useless trying to make him understand.

There was not much discussion on the posters in school as most of the idiots would not have understood or even seen them. But during our mid-break, when we were standing near the water taps, we heard Redkar sir saying, 'This is going to increase now!' Prem Chopra commented, 'These people are not going to keep quiet.' Unfortunately Manjrekar sir did not have a class else we would have encouraged Bibikar to ask him some questions in this regards.

But Appa gave a lecture during the last period when the entire school had gathered in the ground for PT. We were made to sing the song, '*Anushasan parva shuru aaj se*'. Someone got the harmonium down from the office. Sontakke from class ten is always ready to play it and she sang, '*Ma tere beeson sapne pure karenge hum*'. Appa's lecture, as always, lamented on the lack of discipline, how indiscipline was rampant and why people do not like discipline, how the country moves ahead only when there is discipline, and then he gave examples of Japan and Germany and their discipline! He espoused discipline all over, be it in school, at home, on the roads, in railway stations and in queues. The students had no choice but to endure the lecture.

We were hoping Appa would stop after five minutes. We would gladly do ten hours of PT in lieu of listening to him for ten minutes. But Appa was relentless. He went on and on and on. The teachers, zealously patrolling the crowd, too got bored. The boys were restless and a mild murmur started in the crowd. Someone commented, 'Please note; it is PT period.' Whoever said it had said so in a low but deliberate voice, clear enough to be heard by everyone. It must have been someone from the tenth standard. But Appa did not hear it. We tried to stifle our laughter. The same voice said, 'Children need exercise.' The teachers were now alert and looked around trying to spot the culprit. Appa's lecture finally got over. He was in consultation with the teachers over the next steps, with his back towards us, when someone from the crowd shouted, 'Emergency Murdabad!'

Appa turned around sharply. The teachers were taken by surprise. We too were surprised but we continued to stare ahead. The rule was to either look straight ahead or look down. One should never turn back or look around.

There was a chance someone may bash you up later if you were found doing so.

'Who is it? Who is it?' Appa shouted angrily. Sycophants like Prem Chopra immediately came down to investigate. Bendre ma'am, standing near the girls, came towards the boys' side. But there was nothing to be gained. And frankly speaking, there was nothing to get angry about. But Appa was angry at the indiscipline of the students.

'These fellows will not listen! Let them run around the ground. Right now!'

The whole school was then made to go round the ground in a line. It looked like a long train. The girls too were asked to run. It was good that boys like Surya were not leading the train, else they would have deliberately taken a zigzag route. But the boys from tenth standard managed to break the line and then within moments, there were a few trains running around the ground. The boys were having fun. Prem Chopra tried running along with us for a while but gave up soon. Someone shouted, 'Emergency Zindabad!' The whole crowd started shouting, 'Emergency Zindabad, Emergency Zindabad!' Appa had no choice but to ask Ganoba to ring the bell, thus ending the day.

The classes began in earnest after the school gathering. The fun was over. All that remained were the months leading to the final examinations. The road ahead was stark. It grew hot in the afternoons. The grass in the playground had dried up long back and it was dry and dusty.

The atmosphere in the classroom was back to normal; boys and girls kept to themselves. We exchanged a few words during the gathering, but in the classroom we did not talk to each other. It was as if the intermittent period when we spoke did not exist. Bendre ma'am continued her torture as before and so did Redkar sir. He had become even more boring than before. The Maths classes were getting tougher. Luckily, Zende sir's and Manjrekar sir's classes were fun, as usual.

But that day in the fifth period, when Manjrekar sir came into the class, Ambekar stood up and said rightaway in English, in a clear, loud voice, 'Sir, these girls are talking about you and me.'

Most of the class did not get the drift of it. They were yet to settle down after the break, and many had just managed to enter the class after a last minute dash to drink water and were wiping their mouths with the back of their hands. I had managed to steal a glance at Shirodkar while looking around. But I had noticed Ambekar getting up and had heard her clearly.

Sir was trying to figure out what she was hinting at when she repeated in English, 'Sir, these girls are talking about you and me.'

Surya poked me with his pen asking what she meant. I indicated to him with a wave of my hand to keep quiet.

'Who?' Sir asked.

'Those four on the first two benches,' Ambekar said, pointing to the birdies in the front row. 'And Mane.'

The birdies realized they had been targeted and murmured, 'Aiyaa, aiyaa, what have we done?' amongst themselves while Mane joined the chorus. Everyone by now was fully clued into the situation. They looked at sir, waiting for his response.

'Sit down,' Sir said, without showing any emotion. He then opened the textbook and said, 'Please turn to chapter four—types of weather.'

Ambekar was not convinced, but getting no reaction from Sir, she was forced to sit down. Sir continued teaching as if nothing extraordinary had happened, but his sense of humour was missing. He would normally crack a few jokes. We patiently listened to him, but most of us did not understand a word of what he spoke that day.

The next class was Rajguru sir's. Manjrekar sir continued his class a few minutes beyond the time while Rajguru sir waited outside. When he got up to leave, Ambekar followed him. We heard her saying, 'Excuse me, Sir' to Rajguru sir as she exited the class to talk to Manjrekar sir.

We then came to know that all the girls teased Ambekar. They believed she had a crush on Manjrekar sir. It was not without reason—while Manjrekar sir did not take any tuition at home, Ambekar would go over to his house to clear her doubts. Dongre, one of the birdies, stayed close to sir's house and had seen Ambekar coming there. The birdies needed a reason to gossip. Sir had refused to take tuitions when the girls had requested him earlier. Mane had been waiting for a chance to get even ever since the sports' meet. And people like Sukdi would happily join in whenever they got a chance to tease Ambekar.

Ambekar returned to the classroom and sat down quietly. She did not look up throughout the drawing class. She had stopped talking to us boys ever since the girls teased her. The boys too were not showing any interest since they had found out that she was not responsive. Even the boys from the senior classes had realized that.

Deshmane sir had taken leave on Friday and Saturday and hence we had a Sunday morning class from ten to eleven. It was too good an opportunity to lose. It was becoming impossible to speak to Shirodkar these days. It got dark early in the evenings and she did not have the courage to bunk classes and talk, standing in that desolate lane, for long.

I followed them the moment the class got over when Pingle caught me and asked, 'What buddy? Off to meet Misal again?'

His tone suggested he was in the know. He winked at me. I said coolly, 'Yes. Do you want to come along?'

'I would, if you were really going to his place.'

'What do you mean by that?'

'Nothing really,' he said. 'You carry on. Do you think we don't know you are following those girls?'

I did not say anything.

'Which of those three are you after?' Pingle asked.

I felt relieved. It meant he did not really know. He was trying a shot in the dark. I had my answer ready, 'I am trying to get any one of those—whosoever falls for me. Want to come along?'

'Huh! I am not into all this,' he said.

'Bloody scaredy cat!' I said, hitting him on his back. 'It is easy to tease others. You need guts to do something.'

I had managed to silence Pingle, but I needed to be careful henceforth. Juvekar was already in the know and it was natural for Pingle to harbour a doubt. He was a little naïve, but any other person would have quietly followed me to check. And God help me if that Mande came to know! The whole school would know of it the very next day. As it is, Chitre had already guessed.

For a moment, I was in two minds whether to follow Shirodkar and fuel the suspicion of these people or not care a damn. I remembered Naru mama's words—one should never be scared. You are dead if you are scared. Let things happen. I had a brainwave. While Shirodkar and Juvekar were still chatting and had not left, I moved ahead to wait for them en route. That would kill two birds with one stone: guys like Pingle would not think that I was following the girls and Shirodkar would know that I was already on my way.

I waited for her below the peepal tree. I knew Shirodkar may while away some time with Juvekar but was bound to come that way. My chest was not pounding as it normally would. I felt relaxed.

It was half past eleven by the time she arrived. I was expecting her to ask me what I was doing there, but she did not. Instead she came by smiling.

'What took you so long?' I asked.

'Juvekar wouldn't leave me,' she said, glancing around.

'Did she have a doubt?' I blurted out.

'Doubt?' she laughed. She probably does not use that word and was amused at the expression. 'What doubt?'

I did not answer. I should not have asked. In all probability, she may have confessed to Juvekar.

'She knows,' she said, giving me a quick glance.

We both smiled.

This time I was not worried about finding ways to stretch the conversation. I was going to talk about our camp. It had been a week since we returned from the camp, but its memory was fresh in my mind.

'The camp was fun, wasn't it?'

'Yes. Very nice. I was hoping it would never end. Manjrekar sir is really bindaas, no?'

'Pethkar ma'am too,' I said. 'Manjrekar sir mingles with us boys a lot, but Pethkar ma'am was a revelation.'

'But she's partial,' she said. 'She favours that Hibiscus team a lot.'

'You mean the birdies group?'

'Birdies?'

'We call the four of them birdies. They chatter away all the time.'

'Aiyaa, really? I didn't know that. Come to think of it, they *are* birdies. They chat a lot and try to impress ma'am all the time.'

'They are always acting smart in class,' I added.

I did not know what to say further. My chest was not pounding, but I was at a loss for words. I saw a man entering the lane. She glanced in that direction and we fell silent for a while. The man came walking down and I expected him to look at us, but he merely glanced and went past, lost in his own thoughts. Our town has many nosy people, and I was preparing myself to answer in case he asked something.

'We should not stand here,' she said. 'I have to give a shopping list to the kiranawallah. Will you come along?'

I was tempted to decline. To be seen walking with her in broad daylight! It was a huge risk, but I decided it was worth it.

We turned back and went towards the tamarind tree. The usual crowd of people reading newspapers sat under it. A few cycles were parked there. I could spot some familiar faces, but no one bothered to look at me. It was a busy road. The sun burnt brightly. We moved to a shop next to the tree.

It dawned on me that no one bothers you when you are not bothered! No one in the world can bring any harm to the confident man. He is almost invisible. I used to assume people on the road are waiting to stare at us, gossip about us, point fingers at and tease us. But nothing of the sort happened. The world was busy doing its own thing. People were busy reading newspapers, the banana seller was selling bananas, and bullock carts moved along the road carrying their loads. We walked on our own—Shirodkar and I—but no one cared to glance at us. As if we did not exist! We could see everything, but no one could see us!

I stood outside while she went into the kirana store. The store was crowded. It was probably a ration store as I could see a row of tin drums lined up and people waiting to buy kerosene. Sacks filled with grains, coconuts, wheat, peanuts and what not were stacked outside. Huge drums of kerosene were kept on the steps while plastic buckets hung from the top. A strange, mixed smell of oil and jaggery tinged with that of kerosene pervaded the air.

Shirodkar stepped out after handing over the shopping list. 'Let us wait here,' she said. 'He is packing a few things. He will deliver the rest later at home.'

We stood under the tree. It felt good standing there.

'We haven't played the word game in some time,' she said.

'Yes. No one gives us a free period.'

'How come you know the names of so many films?' she asked.

For a moment, I did not know how to answer. My secret

was not known to anyone. But then I realized there was no need for secrets between us. Whatever was mine was hers as well.

'Well, I have a book,' I began. 'It is actually a book of songs, but it lists the names of all the old movies. I will lend it to you someday.'

'Aiyaa, really? No wonder you know all the names.'

The very thought of lending the book to her made me happy. I wondered what else I could give her.

'Are you not getting late?' she asked.

'No, it is fine. They know that I am at the tuition class.'

'But the class got over long back. Won't your Aai be waiting for you?'

'Aai won't be waiting but Ambabai would be for sure.'

'Ambabai?'

'My elder sister.'

'Aiyaa! You call her Ambabai?' she said, laughing.

'Yes,' I said. 'She's a real Ambabai—fussy and nagging all the time.'

'My Akka is not like that,' she said. 'She's very nice. She used to help me with my homework earlier but nowadays she does not have time.'

'Don't you fight?' I asked. 'Ambabai and I are constantly at loggerheads.'

'Little One and Raju fight all the time,' she said. 'But Akka and I don't. I have an argument with Little One once a while. But then we form two groups—Akka and I on one side and Little One and Raju on the other. We have two parties.'

The very thought tickled me. It must be such fun to have two parties! I was itching to ask whether her Akka had a boyfriend, but then I checked myself. She wouldn't have liked it. She may be called Akka, but I was sure that she was good-looking and had many boys pining for her. It would make our life much easier if she set the trend of having a boyfriend.

It was fun talking of home, but that wasn't enough. I knew I had to come up with something better. But words eluded me. I looked at her and saw the lovely light in her eyes. She was with me, but that was not enough. I had to say something different. But then keeping quiet was better than idle prattle. I could have stood there for eternity without saying a word. The way we had sat in the temple the other day.

Just then, Ambabai's friend Marathe—the one with the long, sharp nose—walked up. I had not seen her coming. Not that I could have done anything about it.

'Aiyaa! Mukund! What are you doing here?' she said, looking at me once and then at Shirodkar.

'Nothing, really. I was just chatting,' I said in a calm and composed voice. 'How come you are this side of town? Is *this* your ration store?'

'Yes,' she said. 'But I have not come for ration right now. Wanted to buy some sewai.'

She smiled at Shirodkar. I wondered how Shirodkar would respond, but she smiled sweetly in return—as if they had known each other all along. Shirodkar asked me later who she was.

'Ambabai's friend,' I answered, the moment she stepped into the store. 'You know her?'

'No!' she said. 'Isn't she beautiful?'

'Yes,' I said. I was eager to tell her she was the only

one among Ambabai's friends whom I liked, but I checked myself.

'Ambabai's friends are spread out all over town.'

'Really?' she asked. 'It is not the case with our Akka. She has a few select friends.'

'That's good,' I said. 'Ambabai's friends are a real pain.'

'Why?'

'They roam around the town acting like spies.'

'Spying on whom?' she asked, a smile playing on her lips.

'Who else but me?' I said, angrily.

'Hutt! How you exaggerate!' she said.

Her words were music to my ears, like the sound of coins tumbling out of Naru mama's trousers. I wanted to hear their melody again and again. We say *Tchah*! It sounds crude. But the way she said it! *Hutt*!

'We should not be standing here,' I said.

'Why? Because you may bump into another one of your sister's friends here?' she asked, with a teasing smile.

'Yes.'

'Then where shall we stand?'

I was silent for a moment.

'I will find a suitable place.'

'No, no,' she said. 'You had better come home.'

'Home?'

'Why? What's wrong with that?'

My chest started pounding again. The idea seemed good, but I was not sure whether I would have the guts to go there. I wondered why she was calling me home. In such situations, no one invited the other person to their homes.

Just then, Marathe came out of the shop. She probably

did not have much to buy and hence was out quickly. She smiled sweetly looking at both of us and said, 'Tell Tai to get my book when she comes to college tomorrow.'

'Sure.'

That's it! I muttered to myself, mentally slapping my forehead. Had it been someone else I may not have bothered, but I could not afford to ignore Marathe. And now she had given me the task of informing Ambabai, which meant she would surely know of my meeting with Shirodkar. I was tempted to run behind her and request her to keep my little secret safe. She seemed to be reasonable. After all, she had smiled seeing Shirodkar. She could be trusted. But I did nothing of the sort. I just stood there while Marathe turned and went her way.

'Hey, girl. Come and take your bag,' the shopkeeper called out to Shirodkar coming out of the shop.

She went in to collect her bag. We had to leave now.

'Shall we?' she asked, looking at me. 'Which way are you going?'

'The same way,' I said. I then steeled myself and asked what I had wanted to for a long time, 'Will you bunk class one of these days?'

She was lost for a moment and then, realizing what it meant, said, 'Let me see.' She gave a knowing smile and said, 'Achha.'

I had to decide what to tell Ambabai. It was clear Marathe would tell her everything, so there was no point in hiding anything.

Ambabai sat near the dining table reading a book. I washed my feet and then came into the room.

'I met Marathe today,' I said. 'She has asked me to tell you to get her book to college tomorrow.'

'Where did you meet her?'

'While returning from my tuition class. I was talking to a girl from my class when she came into the ration store to buy some sewai…'

Ambabai looked at me for a moment. She would never have expected me to openly state that I had been chatting up a girl from my class. She kept looking incredulously at me for a while but did not say anything. She continued reading her book. My ploy had worked. I decided—it was best to be bindaas. There was no need to fear anyone.

The next day when I reached our adda there was no one except Chitre. He was not busy with his experiments as usual, but seemed to be lost in thoughts, his head resting against the wall. I sensed something was amiss. There must have been some fight at home.

'What yaar! Some fight at home, huh?' I asked.

He shook his head in the negative.

'Then?'

He did not reply. He kept his bag down. The window grills had already been put. The doors were ready and the tiles had been laid in most of the rooms. The plastering work was complete. Surya's father had visited a few days back and mentioned that the work would be complete soon and that we would have just one room to ourselves. The rest would be rented out.

I sat near the window. I knew Chitre would confide sooner or later.

'My bottle burst, yaar,' Chitre said, without a preamble.

'Don't tell me!' I said, getting up.

'Yes!'

'How come?'

He did not reply for a while. He wiped his lips with the back of his palm and then said, 'I was studying Science this morning. There was no one at home. Aai-Daddy had left for office and Raju was in school. It was just me and that Devaki. She came out after having a bath and asked me to help her hook her bra.'

'Then?'

'She was in her petticoat. She stood with her back to me and asked me to hook it up.'

'Then? Did you?'

'What else could I do? It was a little tight. She then thanked me smiling and went and wore her saree.'

'Then what happened?'

'What else was to happen? My bottle burst then and there. I could not even stand. I went straight into Daddy's room and closed the door.'

My chest was pounding. The way it pounded while reading *Apsara* magazine during the Diwali holidays.

'I went and changed my underwear,' Chitre continued. 'And then I left.'

I heaved a sigh of relief. Thankfully Surya and Phawdya were not present. They would have asked a thousand questions. Chitre looked miserable.

'Not much leaked,' Chitre said, 'but I am really scared.'

'Let it be,' I said. 'You were the one who used to say there is nothing to be scared of.'

'That's true. But this Devaki is there all the time. What

if she comes and stands before me like that again? My studies will go for a toss!'

'Why don't you go and tell your mother?' I asked.

'Tell what?'

'Tell her what she does.'

'Are you mad? One does not discuss all this with mothers!'

I was at a loss of words. Chitre was looking dejected.

'Do you get such feelings while talking to Kevda?' I asked.

'Tchah! It really feels nice when I talk to her,' he said.

I wanted to probe him more and, if asked, would have told him about Shirodkar but Surya entered.

'Ichibhana, what are you guys discussing?'

'Nothing really. Just talking about some girls,' Chitre said, winking at me. It worked. Anything else and Surya would not have believed us.

'Which girl are you talking of?'

'Sakhardande. Look at the way her breasts are popping out!'

'She must have found someone to fondle her,' Surya said. 'It is damn easy for girls to find someone. It is us who are unlucky.'

Surya needed just a small cue to get started. He went and sat by the window looking out. Phawdya came in as usual, running up the stairs.

Surya was hoping to see Sakhardande, but she did not turn up. Soon Gumaste from class eleven passed by. She had recently joined school. Most of the girls wore a saree and blouse, but some wore trousers and a shirt.

Gumaste is on the fatter side and wears the shirt one size too small; it hugs her plump body. Surya *had* to make a comment.

'Bhaji lo...bhaji...' he shouted the moment she came closer and then added, 'Pumpkins....Buy some pumpkins!'

We all burst out laughing. Two other girls accompanying Gumaste looked up. They would not have seen us as Surya had ducked by then. When they were right below the building Surya shouted again, 'Bring the pumpkins! We have some customers here!'

Sukdi and Bakre followed. I had promised not to tease Sukdi hence kept quiet, but Surya was in the mood and shouted, modulating his voice a bit, 'Hey, Mahesh!'

Sukdi is normally alert but was probably unprepared and looked up, falling for Surya's falsetto voice.

'Mahesh is not here!' Surya continued. 'He is in the market!'

Sukdi left in a huff, gesticulating in the air as she spoke to Bakre. Chitre was quiet till now but seemed eager to participate. The road was crowded and we could see groups of school children walking by.

Bendre ma'am came in. She was wearing a figure-hugging blue saree with a matching blouse. She sported sunglasses and walked straight on without looking around. We had no option but to keep quiet. Phawdya whispered,

'Look at the way she walks!'

'She won't change, bhenchod,' Surya muttered.

'One bloody nuisance for us,' Chitre commented. 'Miss Sunanda Bendre!'

'Somebody should kidnap her and take her to the jungle,' Surya cursed.

'Who will kidnap her?' I asked. 'No one will, even if she requests!'

'Right,' Phawdya agreed. 'It is our misfortune.'

Havaldar from our class followed Bendre. She was accompanied by Deosthale. We would normally leave such girls to themselves, but Surya was in form and shouted, 'Hey, Pandu Havaldar!'

We ducked quickly though we were sure the girls would continue walking down the road without looking up. But we saw them talking to Bendre ma'am who had stopped hearing Surya's voice. The girls went and said something to her and they all looked in the direction of the building.

'Surya, we are going to be roasted, saale,' Phawdya said, looking out of the window. 'Bendre is talking to Havaldar.'

Surya peeped out to see them chatting.

'Get ready to scoot,' Chitre said, casually.

But luckily they continued walking towards school. Bendre did not know it was us playing the prank, but it would not take her long to figure that out. All she needed to do was to ask anyone in class and they would have squealed on us. It was clear that she would investigate.

'Surya, be careful,' I warned. 'If Bendre comes to know, we are dead.'

'What can she do, Ichibhana?' Surya asked. 'This is not school.'

It was evident that he was scared, but he was not going to admit to it. Phawdya and I sat down tired. Chitre almost lay down.

'Joshi, your heartthrob!' Surya said, looking out.

'Who?' I blurted out. I should have kept my mouth shut.

'Who else but Shirodkar!' Surya said.

I got the shock of my life. I quickly glanced at Chitre. He was busy packing his bag. Phawdya seemed to be watching me closely. I wondered how Surya had got wind of it. He was capable of blurting out whatever came to his mind but the fact he took Shirodkar's name came as a rude shock.

'What do you mean, my heartthrob?' I said. 'What are you blabbering?'

'Saale, don't we know?'

Phawdya started laughing and Chitre joined in. I wondered whether they really knew or were trying to shoot in the dark.

'Joshi, tell me honestly,' Surya asked. 'Are you not pining for her?'

I was tempted to admit to my feelings and end the debate forever. In any case, if the class knew of it, there was no way I could stop others from knowing it. But there was an element of doubt that they were trying their luck and did not have any concrete proof. In which case, confessing here would fetch nothing. But I had to say something. I could not keep quiet. Surya had raised a doubt and it needed to be addressed. My mind raced against time, looking for the appropriate reply.

'Yes,' I replied, without showing any anxiety. 'I am chasing Shirodkar—and Dongre, Mirikar, Rege, Deodhar, Kulkarni, Sarwate and even Rairikar. What do you have to say now?'

That shut him up. But he was upto some mischief and the moment Shirodkar passed by, he let out a cat call.

'Hey, Joshi!' he shouted, cupping his mouth.

Fuck! I cursed him under my breath. But I was helpless. I prayed she would not look up. She was not Sukdi, who was used to such cat calls. It would be a deadly arsenal in Surya's hands if she looked up. My prayers were answered. She walked by without reacting.

'Saali! Does not respond,' Surya said, disappointed.

The classes began as usual, but my mind was elsewhere. If the whole school knew of my affair, it would be a disaster. Shirodkar would not like it at all. She would lose all respect for me if she came to know that I too was there in the building. She may even assume that I had provoked my friends to tease her. I would be a dead duck then.

A cold sweat broke out. She never glanced at me even once that day. Quite obviously—no girl would like the fact that she was being teased in such a manner. I needed to clarify that it was Surya's prank and that she should not give credence to such calls. But the question still remained—how did Surya come to know of it?

I caught up with Chitre at the water tap.

'Saale, Chitre. You told Surya, isn't it?'

'What?'

'What what? That I am chasing Shirodkar.'

'Why should I tell him that?'

'Tell me the truth. Are you betraying me?'

'Come on, yaar. I did not tell him. Don't be foolish.'

'Listen, Chitre,' I began. 'Let us be honest with each other. Else, I will tell Surya about you and Kevda. Then you see!'

'Arre, I really did not tell him. Believe me!'

'Then how come he suddenly decided to tease me?'

'That Misal had blurted out once—that you had joined the tuition classes to be with Shirodkar. That got him thinking and he deduced rightly.'

I was silent. The connection *had* to be established some day. Juvekar must have told Mande and she would have told Misal. I was aware of this risk.

'Is she really yours?' Chitre asked.

I wasn't sure to what extent I should confide. To be fair, he had been honest about his feelings for Kevda. I was in a dilemma. I had to choose between the devil and the deep sea.

'What is the point in my having any feelings?' I said. I let it open ended. There was no point in telling him about our secret meetings.

He did not ask further. He was smart enough to guess.

'How do we reign in Surya?' he asked.

'We need to do something.' I said. 'He blurts out whatever comes to his mind.'

'I had warned you earlier,' he said. 'There is no point in hanging around with him. We need to stop going to that building.'

'We will tell him he should not tease his friends.'

'That would only reinforce his belief further. At least now, he is not so sure.'

'Then?'

'Wait. I will tell Phawdya. We will tell him if Surya plays such cheap pranks, we will not be a party to it.'

I don't know what Chitre told Phawdya but he asked me not to go to the adda for the next few days. He also asked me to ignore Surya in school and not speak to him. I agreed. Phawdya must have counselled Surya. He came over and said,

'Why don't you guys come over to the building these days, eh?'

'We can't. Saale, you are resorting to mischief now!' Chitre said.

'You are out to screw your friends,' I added.

'Why do you tease the girls?' Phawdya joined in.

That quietened him. He then pleaded saying, 'no, no, it is not really so.' We had been given a lot of homework that week in Maths and English and the offenders were to get a letter of explanation from their parents. Surya desperately needed our help. He remembered the day Bendre ma'am had stopped near the building and was worried she might investigate. He promised not to tease the girls henceforth. As an added assurance, he went and threatened Misal against spreading rumours.

Pethkar ma'am was absent and the girls requested Rajguru sir, who was taking the off period, to allow us to play the word game with movie titles. I had not got a chance to give the book to Shirodkar as promised. Sir was not agreeable at first—there was a lot of pressure to complete the syllabus before the final exams. 'Take out your books and read them,' he said. 'These are the Principal's instructions.' The boys were fine as they could continue with their stupid pranks. Santu and Harishchandra were already preparing to sneak out of the door. But the birdies stuck to their demands.

'Sir, let us play the word game. Pleeeaaaase.... they cajoled, surrounding him. 'Just for this period.'

Rajguru sir does not know how to turn down a request. Had it been some other teacher, he would have started teaching right away and the birdies would have shut up. But Rajguru sir could not do that. Surve had started reading, 'Kala Pahaad' while Patil and fatso Shembekar cried out, 'ground, Sir, ground.' They repeated their demands a few times, but in the end the birdies won.

They eagerly took the chalk piece and wrote the first word on the blackboard,

'*Phu…ti.*'

That was lame. Ghasu Gokhale took one look and answered, '*Phool Ban Gaye Moti.*' Then Teredesai tried '*Aaye Din Bahaar Ke*,' which did not take Sukdi more than a minute to decipher. Same was the case with Mirikar's *Hare Ram Hare Krishna,* and Bibikar's *Mera Gaon Mera Desh*. Sarwate wrote '*si*'. She fumbled trying to count the number of words when Surve looked up from his reading and said, 'Don't bother; it is *Seeta Aur Geeta*.' Sarwate threw the chalk piece away in disgust and stomped back to her desk.

I had decided not to be a part of this tomfoolery and sat silent. I had told Surya and Phawdya that I was not playing the game. Sir had guessed Santu's idea of easing out of the class and went and stood near him, resting his hand on his shoulder. That put cold water on Santya and Harishchandra's plans.

Teredesai's '*Ek Phool Chaar Kante*' did not last more than a few seconds when Shirodkar stood up and wrote '*aa….m*' with four blanks in between.

I had made up my mind not to participate. Let Shirodkar win. I had guessed the movie *Anand Ashram* but kept my mouth shut. Fatso Shembekar looked at me for help, but I turned my gaze away to stare at the playground. The eighth standard boys were out there and pitching in their stumps. It would be good to watch them play cricket. Teredesai looked at me saying, 'Joshi, come on!'

'I am not participating,' I said, continuing to look out of the window.

The boys were silent when one of the birdies chirped, 'Why don't you accept that you don't know?'

I was tempted to say the answer, but seeing Shirodkar standing there, with a smile on her lips, decided to continue staring out of the door.

'Sir, they lose, they lose,' the birdies chirped.

'Wait a moment, Sir. We may get it,' Bibikar said.

'We cannot wait for so long. Loser! Loser!' they chorused.

The boys turned to look at me. I continued staring out.

'Ichibhana, we will lose,' Surya pleaded, poking me with his pen.

'Let it be,' I said. 'I know, but I am not participating.'

The boys tried for some time and had to give up. They lost that point. Shirodkar had glanced at me once while writing on the board. I wanted to smile but I checked myself.

It was the girls' turn again. There was a lot of clamour amongst them as to who would volunteer. Sarwate wanted to, when Dongre said, 'Hey, wait! You would write something lame. Let her write.'

Shirodkar went to her bench, glanced at her notebook and then returned to the board and wrote, *'Ki...ra.'*

I observed her. For a moment, I was confident that I would get the answer quickly. My mind was racing but the name eluded me. I knew all the names from the book, but this seemed to be new.

My mind went blank—totally blank. I could not think of anything.

The boys in the front benches were stumped. The class was silent. Ghasu Gokhale asked, raising a doubt, 'Is there a movie like this?'

'Looks like she's trying to create a new name, Sir.' Teredesai said.

Sir turned to look at the board. Had it been Zende sir or Manjrekar sir, they would have tried to guess the answer.

'It must be right if she has written it on the board,' Sir surmised.

'There is no movie by this name,' Bibikar said. 'Is that not so, Surve?'

Surve looked up and seeing the letters on the board, put his head down and continued to read. Shembekar looked at me and raised his eyebrows. But I refused to answer.

'Loser! Loser!' The birdies were now singing in chorus. The boys were restless. These girls are capable of shouting in the most irritating voice.

'Joshi, come on!' Teredesai said.

I ignored his comment and continued to look out of the door. The wheels in my mind were turning, but there was no movement. It was like those tyres were caught up in mud.

'He does not know,' Mirikar said.

'Joshi, come on. Show them,' Surya said. 'Don't be so adamant. We will lose otherwise.'

I could not afford to tell at this stage that I did not know. It would have meant a loss of face. I continued to look out.

'Loser! Loser!' The chirping continued.

'Joshi, why don't you just say the answer?' Bibikar cajoled.

'I am not playing, yaar,' I explained.

'Then play, saale,' Phawdya said. Sir heard him.

'Who is this using foul language?' Sir said, looking in his direction. 'Can't you guys speak without using expletives?'

'Sir, they have lost,' the birdies continued.

'Wait, Sir. We are thinking,' Shembekar said. He conferred with Bibikar and Teredesai.

'Hey, you can't leave your seats, okay?' Sir said.

I glanced at Shirodkar. She ignored me as if she had not seen me. A faint smile played on her lips. She seemed to be challenging me. She must have caught hold of some other book with rare movie titles.

'Sir, they should declare now,' Dongre shouted. 'No one is allowed so much time.'

'Loser! Loser!' the birdies were back. 'Tell them the answer.'

'*Kitne Pass Kitne Door*,' Shirodkar said. I mentally slapped my forehead with my hand. It wasn't difficult, come to think of it. Sir smiled and put a mark against our team.

'Let me try now,' Sarwate volunteered.

'Shut up!' the girls jumped on her. 'Let her write. We need to win with a huge margin today.'

Shirodkar consulted her notebook and returned to write. My chest was pounding now. This was unexpected. It was one thing to sit back and not participate despite knowing the answer and another not to know. I was at a loss!

She wrote,

'*Aa....ya.*'

The room was silent again. It was clear she had managed

to get hold of some book. I had not given my book to her. Her book seemed to have names of movies we had never heard of.

The boys were silent and the girls realized we were stumped. They normally don't need a reason to celebrate and now we had handed them one on a platter. They teased us to death. We had no choice but to listen to their taunts.

Teredesai looked at me, then Bibikar and finally, Ghasu Gokhale. They could not tolerate the insults. I continued with my act of looking out of the door. Fatso Shembekar caught my eye and said, 'Joshi, why don't you play? Stop acting pricey.'

'Ichibhana, Joshi! Enough! Speak up now!' Surya added.

They thought I was trying to avoid playing not knowing that I was stumped. My mind raced hard. I had a feeling I knew the name, but it was eluding me at the moment.

'What, Joshi sahib?' Sir asked, smiling. 'Looks like your brain is not working today.'

No one responded to his comment but Bibikar said, in a voice loud and clear, 'We know why Joshi is not playing.'

It created ripples across the classroom. The boys gave a knowing smile and the birdies giggled, 'Aiyaa, really?' I wished the earth would swallow me up and that I would disappear. My body had hot flushes. I glanced at the board to see Shirodkar pursing her lips. Her face was flushed red. But she did not seem angry. There was a twinkle in her eyes. She stood for a while and then walked back to her place.

I was angry at Bibikar. I glared at him and made a face indicating, 'Wait, I will take care of you!' But he was least bothered. He laughed, looking at other boys. They too joined in the laughter.

'We will hammer Bibikar once the class is over,' I told Surya.

'Why? Just because he pointed out the truth?' Surya retorted. 'Saale, you are not playing because she's your sweetheart. Don't we know?'

'Sir, they have lost. Put a point against them,' Sarwate shouted.

Sir looked at us. The boys were dejected knowing they would lose a point. My mind continued to race. It was imperative that I find the answer. That was the only way to silence the boys.

'Hey, Shirodkar. Go and write and answer on the board,'Dongre urged.

'That's it! Loser! Loser!' the birdies chorused.

She seemed reluctant to get up, but the girls urged her. My mind was whirling now. She glanced at the boys' side for a brief moment and our eyes met. She seemed to be saying, 'Idiot! Say the answer. Do it now!' My chest was pounding wildly now. A million light bulbs flickered in my mind.

'*Aapki Parchaiyan*,' I blurted out loudly.

Shirodkar stopped dead in her tracks. She looked at me and smiled, as if it was her own victory. She then dropped the chalk piece on the desk and walked back to her seat.

'Yes!' the boys chorused. I knew what I had to do now. We were two points down. I stood up brushing Misal aside. That idiot Teredesai was planning to attempt the next round, but the boys pulled him back. I picked up the chalk piece. I had selected an English movie. I had never tried this before. It was a weapon I had saved for a special occasion—for the final battle.

'*La...s*,' I wrote.

I knew there was no way the girls would be able to decipher this; even their fathers wouldn't know! I then wrote another one. I was about to write a third one and then a fourth one. I wanted to rout the enemy completely.

'Only one at a time, Sir!' Mirikar complained.

'Yes, Sir,' Dongre added.

Sir did not interrupt. I completed my task and returned to sit on my bench. I was proud of my job.

The girls racked their brains, but in vain. Shirodkar was silent. She did not know and, even if she did, she would not have volunteered. We won that point without any resistance.

'Joshi, tell the answer,' Teredesai said.

'*Lighthouse*,' I said. Then I stood up to write another one. But before I could reach the board, the bell rang. The girls couldn't keep quiet. They started shouting, 'Two points down, two points down.'

'Girls! Don't shout, please. You are creating a racket,' Sir said, getting up from the chair. But the birdies continued to make noise.

The next class was Redkar sir's. He had given some difficult problems on logarithms to solve. But Bibikar's words rankled in my mind. I was sure the other boys in class would surmise what he meant and if I did not take immediate action the word would spread. I was wild at Bibikar. It was evident he had deliberately made that remark.

'We have to hammer Bibikar after school,' I told Surya, turning back.

'Ichibhana, let us solve this problem first,' he said,

looking at his notebook. 'I am unable to understand anything.'

The problem at hand was a difficult one. Chitre solved it quickly and Surya copied it from him. I glanced at Shirodkar, but she was busy working the logarithms.

School got over and the children started streaming out. We came out through the back door—Chitre, Surya, Phawdya and I.

'We have to teach Bibikar a lesson, okay?' I reminded them.

'Leave it, yaar,' Chitre said. 'Don't take it to heart.'

'No! He has deliberately provoked us. We need to teach him a lesson.'

'Go ahead,' Surya suggested.

'Why don't you come along, saale?' I asked. 'Don't try to act pricey.'

'You go ahead. We will follow you,' Phawdya said.

Bibikar came out and walked through the ground with other children. He tried avoiding us.

'Hey, Bibya. Wait!' I shouted.

He stopped.

'So trying to act smart, eh?' I said, grabbing his collar. I knew the rule: hold the collar first.

He was a strong guy and probably aware of the technique, and immediately brushed my hand off.

'What? What do you mean smart?' he said. He glanced behind me to check whether anyone else followed me. But he did not seem scared.

'You really want to know?'

'What can you do?' he challenged with a straight face.

'Tell me whether you want to know,' I said, glancing back. Surya and Phawdya were closing in.

He did not reply.

'Don't try to mess with me, okay,' I warned him. 'I will break your teeth.'

'You? What can you do?' he challenged.

'You want to see?' I said, trying to punch him. He ducked at the last moment and the punch was wasted.

'What's going on?' Surya asked, coming near us.

Bibikar was a little worried seeing Surya but held his ground.

'What do you want?' he said.

Surya may have, in some other circumstances, not got into a fight. But seeing his attitude, he shifted his books from his right hand to left and said, 'You want to know that, huh?' and before Bibikar could reply, punched him in his stomach. Bibikar buckled down in pain. He stood up, challenging Surya.

'He is our friend, understood?' Surya said. 'If you try crossing his path, I will break your jaw.'

Bibikar was silent. A few boys had gathered around us. There was no point in hanging out there any more.

'Go. Go home now,' I said and we started walking towards the gate. 'Else you will get hammered unnecessarily.'

'Come alone, if you have the guts,' he said. 'Why are you hiding behind him?'

'Go. Go now,' I said.

I took the route through the paddy fields. I had to go home and then leave for tuition, but I stopped when I reached the woods. The fields were barren. A few stubs were all that were left of the harvested rice. There were no children playing there today. I stood near the trees. Bibikar's comment rang in my ears. The other boys and girls would easily surmise the meaning.

He must have suspected this for long. No doubt he spoke the moment he got an opportunity. It was likely that the others would tease us as well. But there was no point in getting angry. Shirodkar had not got angry. I realized I should not have got into a fight with Bibikar. He was not a bad guy after all. He may try to act smart, but he had been nice to me. Chitre was right—I should have ignored him. I had picked up a fight for no reason. The boys would know I get upset when teased.

It was getting late, but I stood there lost in my thoughts. I realized that deep down I wasn't really angry with Bibikar. In fact, I had felt good. It was a great relief in some sense. He would not tease me any more and I was feeling relieved. It felt like a spring erupting forth, after being stuck under the rocks for a long time. I felt free—bindaas!

I had to find a way of bunking tuition now. There was no point in meeting after the classes. It got dark soon. And no girl would have liked to stand and chat in a dark lane. We could not even see each other well so the whole point was lost. But luck was on my side that day. On the blackboard was written in large letters—'There will be no classes today and tomorrow due to unforeseen circumstances'. The earlier batch was expectedly not around, but a few students from our batch had come. No one knew the reason till someone found out that Sir's mother had been admitted to the hospital.

I whiled away some time talking to the guys from Subhash. Pingle had not come. He may have probably seen the notice earlier and left. I glanced at the girls. Shirodkar stood chatting with Mande and Juvekar. It was a golden opportunity. We had an entire hour to ourselves. But the question was—how to let her know. She looked at me once. The next time she glanced at me, I looked at the watch. I was keen to somehow let her know. Mande saw me looking at her. I was getting restless.

I decided to go and wait near the peepal tree. I was hoping she would come that way. I decided I would wait there for a while and then head back home. Had the girls not been there, I would have told her to meet me. But I could not do that. Lucky that Pingle was absent! I said, a tad loudly, addressing to no one in particular, 'Hey, guys. Bye,' and then moved on. There was no need to shout, but I was hoping Shirodkar would hear me. She would have seen me walk in the direction of her house.

I was prepared to wait for long, but I was lucky. I glanced at the watch. It had taken her thirteen minutes. The street lamps were on. There was enough light and yet adequate shadow under the peepal tree. The lane seemed desolate as usual. A few municipality workers hurried past, followed by a man on a bicycle, a young boy returning from tuition and then a couple of college girls. I looked at them carefully; one of them could be Shirodkar's Akka. If we were spotted together we could land in trouble.

'Lucky that Juvekar let you off early,' I said, the moment she arrived.

'Yes,' she said, smiling as usual. 'But Mande was not willing to leave me. She, in fact, wanted to come along to my house.'

'Then?'

'I managed to wriggle out somehow,' she said, glancing in both the directions.

I was silent for a while. We didn't have to worry about the topic of discussion. The events of the earlier class were fresh in my mind.

'Where did you get the names of all those movies from?' I asked.

She did not reply but smiled. I waited.

'Tell me, please!'

'My Pappa got me a book.'

'Which one? The one with songs?'

'No. Not a book of songs,' she clarified. 'I had asked Pappa to get me a list of movie names and he borrowed this book from someone in his office. It is called *History of Hindi Cinema.*. It has a list of all the movies at the end.'

'Really?' I asked, surprised. '*All* the names?'

'Yes. The complete list, right till date,' she said. 'Till last year that is—so it does not have Sholay, but the rest are there.'

So that's that, I thought. I had a few names in my book, but here she had the entire list. And it covered the history of cinema, so it would have names which I had never heard of. No wonder she won.

'Then… the movie which I wrote—you must have guessed their names,' I said.

'Yes!' she said. 'I was planning to use the same in my turn. I had copied the name into my notebook actually.'

'Then?'

'Then what? I kept quiet!'

'Why?' I asked. Like an idiot!

She glanced at me once and then looked away, smiling mysteriously.

Her smile was lovely. There was no need to speak. It was like the time when we sat in the Ganesh temple. I felt the same invisible connection between us. We could not see it but it was there. And the darkness around added to its allure. I felt I could stand there forever, without saying a word. The invisible connection would keep us there. We would stand there, fixed, like statues. We would just move our eyelids once in a while. The time would stand still.

'I gave that Bibikar a solid warning,' I said.

'Don't get into fights,' she said.

'You know, the boys in the class now know.'

'What?' she asked. She laughed in her sweet way.

I was about to explain, but seeing her laugh I too joined in.

An old man came our way, interrupting our laughter. I was hoping he would walk by without saying anything, but he stared at her as he crossed by. Luckily he left without saying a word.

'It is good that we got a break from tuition,' I said.

'Yes,' she said, 'but we can't miss our studies now. Maths is so difficult.'

'Redkar sir is a pain,' I said. 'Lucky that Bendre ma'am does not teach us Maths. Else, we would have been dead by now.'

'You bet!'

I discussed the teachers, but that was not what I wanted to talk to her about. I wanted to say something else, something sweet.

'What shall we do going forward?' I blurted.

'Meaning?' she asked. I could clearly see her eyes twinkling despite the darkness around.

How do I explain! She may not have got the drift of my question.

'Going forward means…ahead, you know!' I tried explaining.

She laughed again. She must have understood.

'I don't understand all this,' she said.

I wondered how I could elaborate. I wanted to tell her that we were still in class nine and we had quite a few years to go. We needed to be together. There were a hundred things I wanted to say. But the question was—how to say?

'How is your Akka?' I asked, changing the topic.

'Akka? She's fine. Why?'

'I mean, what is she like?'

'She's fine,' she said. 'But why do you ask?'

'No. Just like that,' I said.

'There was a singing competition in her college. She got a prize there.'

'Really? That's great,' I said. 'Our Ambabai is no good. If she starts singing, everyone will run away.'

'Why do you ridicule your sister so?'

I could have spoken about Ambabai for hours. But then seeing her reaction, I shut up. I wondered how to continue the conversation.

'Your dress suits you,' I said.

'Aiyaa! It is such an old one,' she said, smiling.

I realized while speaking to her that I was trying to grasp that elusive 'something' which enveloped us. We stood there surrounded by a fog binding us together. I could sense it but not catch it.

We were lost in our own world and I did not notice an old woman walking towards us. She was holding a bag which seemed pretty heavy as she walked with slow steps. I decided to ignore her keeping my head down. But she was watching us as she walked towards us. It was Ponkshe kaku! She recognized me the moment she came near us. She would recognize me in the middle of the night in pitch darkness too.

'It's Mukund, is it?' she asked, coming closer. 'What are you doing here?'

'Nothing. Just chatting,' I said.

'Chatting? And who is she?' she asked, looking at Shirodkar carefully.

Where the hell did this Ponkshe kaku land up from? And what was she doing here so far away from home in the evening?

'She's in my class,' I said. 'And what brought you this side of the town?'

'In your class? Arre, but what are you both doing here—that too in this darkness?'

'Nothing. Just talking. Where are you returning from?' I tried changing the topic.

'I had gone visiting the Gharpures. Their daughter-in-law gave me some fresh vegetables. She asked me to take this route. So where are you headed?'

'Home,' I blurted.

'Going home, is it? Beta, then carry this bag home for me. I have to drop in at Khatavkar Aaji's place on the way. I don't want to carry this and answer her barrage of questions.'

Oh god! I was now being forced to carry her bag home. I looked at Shirodkar, but her face did not betray any emotion.

'No, Kaku. I have to go a friend's house from here. I would be late.'

'Let it be. You are going home from here, isn't it?'

I was desperately looking for an escape route.

'No. I have to visit another friend from here. I will be very late.'

'Look at today's children,' she mumbled to herself. 'They have time to chat standing in this darkness but not help an old lady like me. Now I have to lug this bag around.'

She walked away towards the Devgiri bungalow. I kept looking at her for a while.

'Who was she?' Shirodkar asked.

'Our neighbour Ponkshe kaku.'

'What's wrong with carrying her bag?'

It then dawned on me. I had committed a blunder I should have volunteered to take the bag home. She would complain to Aaisaheb now and would report to her about my standing here and talking to some girl. She would exaggerate and make a mountain out of a molehill. Shirodkar was right. I should have taken the bag. For a moment, I thought of running after her and asking for the bag. But it was too late. She was already far away.

'It's fine. She's quite a nag, actually,' I said, putting an end to the discussion.

But her arrival had broken our chain of conversation.

'We should not stand here,' she said. 'Shall I go now?'

'Wait,' I said. 'If you reach early, won't your mother get suspicious?'

'Suspicious?' she asked, and started laughing. 'I will tell her my class got over early.'

'What if she asks what took you so long?'

'So what? I will tell her I was chatting.'

'With whom?'

'What do you mean "with whom"? I will say with Juvekar; and then with you.'

I was jealous of her. There was no way I could have told this so casually to Aaisaheb and Ambabai. They would make my life hell.

'What is the plan tomorrow?'

'Tomorrow? What about tomorrow?'

'There is no class tomorrow,' I said. 'Will you meet me?'

She thought for a moment.

'But there is no class tomorrow, isn't it?' she asked.

I wondered how to tell her, the very fact that there was no class made it easy for us to meet.

'I won't be able to come tomorrow,' she said. 'And we should not stand here and talk.'

'Then where?'

'Will you come home?'

'Home?' I felt I was floating in air.

'Yes. Why not? Come home and we can sit and talk.'

My chest was pounding away. Land up at her home! She had asked me earlier too. And isn't that what Naru mama used to advise all the time? But listening to his advice was different from actually following it. I could take the chance, but if the school mates come to know of it, I would be dead meat. I was at a loss for words. But I could not refuse.

'What will you tell your mother?'

'I will tell her you are my class fellow.'

'Won't she object?'

'What do you mean? My Akka's friends come home. What is so different?'

My chest continued to pound. The feeling of emptiness in the pit of my stomach grew deeper. The very thought of visiting her home was beautiful. I could not believe my ears.

'So, will you come?' she asked.

'Yes,' I said, finally getting the courage to say so.

'What time?'

'Same time as our class?'

'That's fine,' she said. 'I will go now.'

'Will you wait for me outside?' I said. I did not want her to leave.

She nodded and smiled again, without saying a word.

'Wait a little more,' I said. I had to say much more. I had not yet said what I wanted to. I had frittered away all the time.

'I think of you all the time at home,' I said, steeling myself. My heart was beating hard when I said that, but then there was also an enormous sense of relief.

I knew her response. She would give me that knowing smile and then leave immediately. And that smile would be heavenly. And that's what happened!

I was floating high up in the air. I felt like I was on top of the Everest. Everything below was hidden in the mist. I did not go home immediately. I looked at my watch—there were twenty minutes for the class to get over. Ambabai would be suspicious if I reached early. I could not tell her the class had been cancelled. I normally reach home a little late, hanging out with friends after class. For a moment, I thought of spending time at Phawdya's vegetable shop, but there was a danger of being spotted there by Ambabai or one of her many friends. I decided to visit Chitre. He was busy experimenting with some gears from a wristwatch. I went home after spending some time with him.

I was nervous when I reached home. I was not sure what Ponkshe kaku would have told Aaisaheb. She may not have come and complained immediately but the danger remained. I was lost in thought when Aaisaheb served me dinner. When she asked me whether I wanted some more subji, I nodded yes, much to Ambabai's surprise. The vegetable in question was the mushy bottlegourd, which otherwise I don't care much for. I spent some time outside, watching a few chess games. I had kept my Algebra textbook open as an alibi for my studies.

The next day at school was what I was really worried about. We had taken care of Bibikar, so I was sure the boys would not dare to tease me, but there was no guarantee of what the girls would do. There was no way of stopping them. They had earlier teased Ambekar and Sukdi. And girls like Mande would be waiting for a chance to tease Shirodkar. They would not allow such a golden opportunity to go by.

I decided to keep a low profile in the first three periods. The birdies were chattering away as usual while some of the smarties like Bibikar and Ghasu Gokhale were in their elements but, much to my relief, no untoward incident happened. But in the next class, which was Zende sir's, when Sir asked Shirodkar a question and she took a little time to answer, Surya loudly shouted out 'Joshi!' much to the amusement of the entire class. Quite obviously, Sir did not understand the context, but there was a general murmur in the class. Surya, of course, got an immediate snub when Sir asked him a question and, when he could not reply, taunted, 'You are the sheth of Kanhe village. What's the need for *you* to study?'

I was expecting Shirodkar to get angry at Surya's comment, but she did not react. In fact, when I tried glancing at her in the mid-break, she returned my glance with a slight smile. I was not sure whether her friends had teased her. I decided not to respond to Surya's comments and add fuel to the fire. I deliberately started a conversation involving Sakhardande, Ambekar and Bendre ma'am in the mid-break to divert their attention.

I knew I was going to do something no one else was aware of. It was our little secret, mine and Shirodkar's. I wanted to laugh out loud just thinking of it. No one in class would ever know. I glanced in the direction of the playground and the hills beyond Sonarpada shining brightly in the hot sun. In the next period, Halbe sir droned in his usual monotone while I gazed out and enjoyed the scenery.

That day I realized where the real fun lay. There may be classrooms, benches, girls, boys, teachers, Maths, Physics - even Social Studies. But I am not a part of any of them. I am a free soul, like the white egret sitting on a cow's back. I may be physically present in this school, but there is a different school which I hold in my mind - one that is just mine. That school has no walls, no blackboards, no teachers, but it teaches something truly beautiful.

I reached her house that evening and was disappointed to find no one at the gate. I was expecting her. I waited for a few moments, unsure of the next steps. The gate had a wooden latch, but I did not dare enter. I looked around, but there wasn't anyone in sight. Luckily, no one walked by. I waited for sometime. I could not call out for anyone. Finally, I steeled myself and opened the gate. I turned to put the latch back when she came out into the verandah. She smiled brightly.

She was wearing a white frock which had lace all over—the kind of frock girls wear in school when dressed as a fairy in a dance programme. She looked like a freshly blossomed flower. I realized I should have worn a new shirt.

'Come,' she said. 'I was wondering whether you would come or not.'

I did not know what to say. I continued to look at her, smiling. The verandah had two large stone pillars supporting the roof—the kind I had seen in the temple. There was a grill window covered with a floral curtain. Near the entrance was a jute doormat similar to the one in my house. I removed my sandals and stood there.

'Why don't you come in?' she asked and then, turning towards the room, shouted, 'Aai, come and see—Joshi from my class is here.'

The drawing hall was quite large, almost the size of two of our rooms put together. There were two more windows on the left side covered with similar curtains but light filtered through, brightening up the room. A door led to the kitchen. There was another door through which I could see a few hibiscus plants in the backyard. Two more doors in the corner led to other rooms. I could not see what lay inside as they had curtains.

Her mother came out of one of the inner rooms followed by her younger brother, who ran into the hall.

'This is Joshi from my class,' she said. 'I told you the other day, remember? He is the one who beats everyone at word games.'

I kept looking at her mother. She was beautiful and fair like Chitre's mother. She was wearing a bright yellow saree—the kind I had seen on the Goddess during Gauri puja. She wore a huge red bindi on her forehead. She had tied her hair into a large bun and decorated it with aboli flowers.

I kept staring like an idiot for a while and then it dawned on me! Despite the notebooks, I quickly folded my hands in a smart namaskar. She laughed. Her laughter was sweeter than Shirodkar's.

'Is that so?' she said. 'And where do you stay?'

'Kudalkar chawl,' I said.

'Where is it?'

How was I to answer that? She would not know where Kudalkar chawl was. Most people staying in their part of the town would not know.

'It is a little before Dhaparewadi,' I tried explaining. 'On Devpada road.'

She probably did not get it, but she nodded saying, 'Oh I see, I see.' My chest was pounding loudly. I was struggling to speak. Her younger sister came into the hall from another room.

'This is my brother Sandeep,' Shirodkar said. 'And this is my sister.'

I knew them and there was no need to get them introduced. For some reason, I assumed that her brother's name would be Raju. I was worried that her younger sister may recognize me as she had come to the temple the other day. But she did not. They both looked at me as if they were meeting me for the first time.

'Sit down,' her Aai said. She noticed the books in my hand and asked, 'Did you have tuition today?'

'No. I had to return these to Misal,' I said, looking at my books.

I had thought of it when I left home. Carrying notebooks would make her mother wonder whether we had bunked, but then I had no choice. Not carrying notebooks was worse; Aaisaheb would have smelt a rat.

I was about to sit down when Shirodkar asked, 'Do you want to see our garden?'

I kept the notebooks on the teapoy and followed her out into the garden. Sandeep and her sister followed us. There wasn't much grass in the garden, but there were a lot of small shrubs and bushes. Most of them seemed to be some kind of flowering plants. The flower beds were neatly lined with half-cut bricks. There were a lot of aboli shrubs.

'This is a rose creeper,' she said. 'And this one is mogra. This is bramhakamal. It flowers only once a year. This is jai creeper and that one is green champa. Do you want to take some flowers for your sister?'

I looked at her, my mouth agape. Ambabai would love to have these flowers, but there was no way I could take them. Firstly, she would not believe I got flowers for her. And if I were to tell her where I got them from, both Aaisaheb and Ambabai would fall off their seats.

'No,' I lied. 'She doesn't wear flowers.'

We walked around the garden for a while. Her sister and Sandeep were in tow, but the very act of walking around with her was a pleasant one. Naru mama was right;

one should not try meeting a girl anywhere outside. One should simply go over to her house. And if the house is a bungalow with a garden like this one, I could go there every day.

'Tai! Show him the rose buds,' her younger sister piped up.

'Look at this one,' she said, pointing to a rose sapling in a pot. 'It is her work. They have been taught grafting in their school.'

We too had had such gardening lessons in our school. She had grafted a thin stem to a thick one and wrapped a plastic sheet around the joint.

'Shall I show you my snail?' Sandeep asked.

'Sure,' I said.

Sandeep got a matchbox kept in one corner. There was a snail inside, curled up in the shell. Sandeep lifted the snail and put it on the floor, but it would not come out. He tried poking it with a twig.

'Don't trouble it,' Shirodkar said. 'Leave it be. We will see it later.'

We walked around the garden and then went inside.

'Hey, what shall we play?' her sister popped a question.

I was taken aback. Did they think I was visiting to play with them? I looked askance at Shirodkar.

'Wait a while,' she said. 'We'll see later.'

I was hoping her sister and Sandeep would get busy with their own games and leave us alone, but they continued to sit there. There was a couch on one side with two chairs. They had cotton cushions on them, with some embroidery work on the covers. I had seen Ambabai do such work. There was a teapoy and another low cot to sit on. The walls were lined with big boxes, which doubled as additional seats. The boxes were covered with bedcovers. I noticed her father's name painted on the boxes.

'What will you have?' her mother asked, coming into the hall. 'Tea or coffee?'

'No. I am good,' I said.

'Why? What do you have at home? Milk?'

'No. I have tea.'

'Then have tea here,' she said. 'Why are you saying no?'

We sat in the hall. I wasn't sure what to talk about when Sandeep came out of the room carrying a bat. He dumped a ball in my lap and then went and stood near the wall.

'Throw the ball,' he said.

'Arre! Why are you playing inside the house?' Shirodkar shouted.

'Five. Just five balls,' he pleaded.

I was tempted to bowl him out, spinning the ball the way Phawdya does, but then I decided to gently lob the ball. But he still missed it. I then let the ball bounce twice and he was able to hit it. The younger sister sat in one corner with a long face.

'Go, get your stamp notebook,' Shirodkar told her. She brightened up and then went inside to get her notebook. There were stamps stuck on each page. She then sat next to me and showed me each page indicating the country—this is Nepal, this is Norway, this is Canada, and so on. I managed to snatch a glance at Shirodkar when she had gone in to get the notebook, and we exchanged a knowing smile.

I remembered I too used to collect stamps earlier. We had one Mr Potnis as our neighbour and he would get letters from some of his relatives staying abroad. I would remove the stamps from the envelopes and store them in a packet.

'I too have some stamps. I will give them to you,' I said.

'Aiyaa, really? How nice!' she exclaimed. 'Tai, remind him.'

Her mother came in with tea. I was sure that it would not be just a cup of tea. There would be some snacks too. She carried a large cake in another plate.

'Here. See if you like this cake,' she said, handing me the tea cup.

The cake was home-made and it tasted really nice. Aaisaheb tries making a cake, putting some sand on a tawa and a baking vessel over it, but it does not turn out as well. It invariably gets burnt at the bottom. But this one was uniformly soft and nice. I was quite sure it would be good.

'What are these boxes for?' I asked, indicating at the row of boxes along the wall.

'Arre! Her father you know! He gets transferred every now and then. We use them to pack our stuff,' her mother said. 'Did you like the cake?'

'Yes.'

'Then have some more,' she said. 'Sandu, you too have some.'

I heard footsteps at the door and then her Akka walked in. I was quite sure it was her Akka by the way she walked in. She glanced at me and would have understood that I was Shirodkar's classmate.

'Classmate,' her mother said.

'Oh, is that so?' she said, smiling and then asked me, 'What is your name?'

I told her my name and she smiled. She was as beautiful as Marathe—in fact, a little taller. One look at her and I knew all the boys in her college must pine for her.

'His sister's in college too,' Shirodkar said.

'Which one?'

I told her the name, but she was not aware of it. She was in a Commerce college, so it was unlikely that they would know each other.

'He calls his sister Ambabai,' Shirodkar said.

'Really!' she exclaimed and both of them burst out laughing.

I wanted the ground to swallow me up. I looked at her and she was still laughing. Then I too joined in their laughter.

'Will you have tea?' her mother asked her sister. 'There is some left. Your father is expected any minute.'

'No. I had a cup at Kedare's place,' she said and then went inside.

We then talked for some more time. Sandeep would ask me to throw the ball at him once in a while. The younger sister tried playing the word game with me. I knew all the words. I then tested her by giving a few easy ones. When I tried a difficult one, she was stumped. Even Shirodkar could not guess the answer. Her Akka came out once to attempt and then gave up. I was eager and at the same time a little nervous about her father coming in. I prayed that his local train may get late, but then I was also eager to see what he looked like.

He came after a while. Sandeep dropped his bat and jumped on to him. He exclaimed, 'Arre, arre' but then caught him mid-air. He was, as I had imagined—fair, bespectacled, a little bald and clean-shaven. He was wearing a yellow shirt with some floral design and it was tucked inside his trousers unlike my Baba who never tucks in his half-sleeved shirt. He seemed a little tired. He sat down on the sofa to remove his shoes when he saw me. My heart was beating hard.

'Who is this?' he asked. He did not seem irritated.

'He is my classmate,' Shirodkar said. 'Joshi.'

I knew what I had to do when introduced. I was ready with a smile and a namaskar with folded hands. He was pleased.

'Namaskar, namaskar!' he said, smiling. He then asked the next question, as expected, 'What does your father do?'

'He is in the Sachivalaya,' I said

'Oh, is that so? Which department?'

I was going to say 'Shikshan' in Marathi but managed to say 'Education'.

'Nice!' he said, as expected. He then looked at her mother and asked, 'So have you offered tea to Joshi saheb? I wouldn't mind a cup either; if there is any.'

They laughed at his comment. I was blushing and wanted to hide my face. He then walked out of the room patting my back. Shirodkar smiled, enjoying the banter.

I knew it was time for me to leave. That's the norm in most households—you leave when the friend's dad arrives. Everyone gets busy after that. Ambabai's friends start leaving the moment Baba arrives.

I stood up after a while.

'Do come again,' her mother said.

'And don't forget the stamps,' the younger one reminded.

'Next time we will play in the garden,' Sandeep added.

Shirodkar and her Akka did not say anything but smiled. I looked back while opening the latch at the gate and she waved. I took a little extra time to put the latch back.

I was absolutely at peace with myself. I had nothing more to desire. I had got what I had wanted. Walking back home, I could clearly see everything on the road despite the darkness—the stone well, Urban Bank building, Vaishali Cloth stores, Pendse Doodh Mandir, Khoja Bakery, Om Market and so on. There was nothing to fear any more. There were no worries. All my troubles were over. I could now be peaceful and carefree. There was no need to be worried of the boys teasing me. And even if they did, there was no need to react or hide things.

I decided I needed to tell everything at home. I would wait for an opportune moment to tell—'Aai, there is this girl in my class. She has two sisters and a brother. Her father is a bank manager. They are all very decent folks and you need not be worried. I will study well and try to get the first rank too. I will also do engineering as you want me to.'

I was sure that she would not get upset if I told her all this. She was quite nice, after all. And I was the only son, her pet. Everything was taken care of. All I had to do now was to clear my ninth and then tenth standard. And then once I passed twelfth standard and reached college, the whole world would be mine. I would be an adult. No one would bother me any more.

I reached home at dinnertime. Aaisaheb was giving finishing touches to the dinner and Baba was just back from office and removing his shirt. Ambabai's friends had gone back. I went in, had a quick wash, and then took my place at the table to study. I opened up the Algebra book. The chapter on linear equations was a difficult one but I was able to solve them.

When we sat down to dinner, Baba said, 'Mahajan from my office has suggested an alliance for Naru. She's a B.Com and has a part-time job. Her father works in our office.'

'What is their surname?' Aaisaheb asked.

'I am told they are Deshmukhs.'

'Deshmukh?' Aaisaheb wondered.

'Yes. Yajurvedi.'

'Yajurvedi! No way!' Aaisaheb retorted. 'Are there no girls left in our caste?'

'Aai!' Ambabai exclaimed.

'You shut up! Don't try to give your smart opinions.'

'Naru mama is going to marry a Christian girl,' I said casually.

It took a while for Aaisaheb to register what I said and then she exploded.

'Christian? Let him do that,' she challenged. 'I won't ever see his face. Then I am dead as far as he is concerned and he is dead as far as I am. I don't care if the girl is blind, dark, short, handicapped or squint-eyed. She *has* to be from our caste.'

She then continued serving us while she muttered different examples. Someone she knew had married a person from a different caste; how the CKPs behave and how the Saraswats do. This is what they probably discuss in their meetings in the chawl and in their ladies' club. Her best friend here is Nikam kaku. She has never had an argument with her. She's constantly at loggerheads with Ponkshe kaku, but when it comes to inviting a married woman to dinner, she always calls Ponkshe kaku, just because she's from the same caste as ours. And if there is a need to invite a boy for the function it's always their son Kiran. That Kiran has no manners—he fills up his plate like a greedy pig and then wastes most of the food. Aaisaheb gets irritated and curses him, but then the next time she invites the same fellow again. We tolerate all this. Ambabai, otherwise ready to argue at the drop of a hat, was silent. The discussion was over as far as Baba was concerned. He does not like to interfere in her family matters beyond a point. He went and sat outside after washing his hands.

But a creeping fear filled me. I had never thought along these lines.

On Monday morning, Surya was waiting for us at our adda.

'Ichibhana, Joshi, you know what Ambekar has done?' he asked the moment I stepped in.

'What happened?'

'That Ambekar—she popped sleeping pills.'

I looked at Chitre and Phawdya. I knew what Surya was saying, but one could never trust him completely. He may have invented the whole thing and one could not afford to have such rumours floating around.

'But why?' I asked, looking at Chitre.

'She tried to commit suicide,' Chitre said, his voice taking on a serious tone.

I looked at all of them. I wanted to be sure they were not pulling my leg. But that did not seem to be the case.

'She popped in a whole bottle of sleeping pills last afternoon,' Surya said. 'She's in the hospital now. What guts, Ichibhana!'

'Saale, why don't you tell me the whole thing properly,' I said. 'Who told you all this?'

'No one needs to. The whole town knows. What a scene there was last evening!' Surya said. 'Police, ambulance—and the note she had written! You know who she named?'

'Who?'

'Manjrekar sir!'

'Don't tell me!'

'You bet, Ichibhana! And do you know what she wrote in the note? "Manjrekar sir does not love me. That's why I am committing suicide."'

The whole thing was unbelievable. But it was true. I put down my bag, sat next to Surya and said, 'Surya, tell me everything properly.'

Surya then recounted the story. Ambekar's family had decided to go for the afternoon show of *Sholay*. She had already seen the movie and declined to go, staying back at home. Her mother is in the habit of taking sleeping pills as she cannot sleep at night. There were a few tablets left in the bottle. She wrote her note, popped the remaining pills and went to sleep. When the family returned they were shocked to find her unconscious with the note by her side. The municipal ambulance was called for. Apparently, the number of pills was not large and she survived. The police came in the next morning.

I was stunned. Chitre and Phawdya were quiet.

'I had a hunch, bhenchod,' Surya said. 'She was trying to woo sir.'

'Where's the hunch?' Chitre said. 'It was evident. She was after him from day one.'

'Fuck!' Phawdya said. 'She had complained that the girls were teasing her, remember?'

'What will happen now?' Surya asked.

'What will happen? Sir will be forced to marry her,' Chitre said. 'These girls are very shrewd.'

'Fuck!' Phawdya repeated. 'So that's the plan, is it? She must have got the idea from some movie.'

'Ichibhana, she's really clever,' Surya said. 'And look at her guts! To pop pills like that!'

'That's no big deal,' Chitre said. 'One of the girls near my mavshi's place in Bandra drank Tik-20.'

'What is that?' Surya asked.

'It is an insecticide. It burns like hell. The girl was screaming and writhing all over.'

'Did she die?'

'No. The doctor saved her.'

'Some people slit their wrists,' I added.

'That's easy, bhenchod,' Surya said. 'Take the blade and *khachakk*!'

'Hey, come on! Let us go. Let us see what's happening in school,' Phawdya said.

To our surprise, most students, seemed to have got the news. They stood huddled in groups whispering to each other. Then everyone gathered around Teredesai as his house was right across Ambekar's. He was in his elements recounting the episode, exaggerating the events.

School started as usual, but no one seemed to be attentive. Ambekar's vacant bench seemed to stand out. The first period was Paranjpe ma'am's for Marathi. She seemed a little tense, but did not say anything. She went through the motions of teaching the chapter, but no one paid any attention. Everyone had the same question in their mind—what would happen now? Marathi was followed by Hindi and English. We could speak a little in the Hindi class, but there was pin-drop silence in the English period. The next class was taken by Zende sir and we expected him to say something, but he too kept quiet. He did not crack his usual jokes. We all waited for the mid-break.

Surya had a brainwave in the fourth period—to go and have a look at Ambekar's house in the break. It was a great idea. Her house was a little far away, but we could reach there in time if we ran all the way. We ran out the moment the bell rang. Fatso Shembekar and Teredesai joined us. We could not refuse Teredesai as his house was in the same area.

We reached Ambekar's house to find the doors and windows shut. A few bedsheets hung out in the balcony to dry. The houses around too seemed to be shut. We expected a crowd there, but there was none. Teredesai went to his house. There were a saloon and a presswallah nearby.

'I don't think anybody's home,' Chitre said.

'They must be at home, but they would have shut the door,' Phawdya remarked.

'She must not have returned from the hospital,' Surya said.

Someone stepped out of the saloon with a pair of scissors and a comb in his hand, chewing on paan. Letting out a stream of spit, he asked, 'What do you want, eh?'

'Nothing,' Surya answered and then putting his arm

around my shoulders said, 'Ichibhana, let us go. There is nothing to see here.'

By the time we returned, we got the news that Manjrekar sir had been arrested by the police. Ganoba had got the news. He did not tell us, but he had told Thombre from eleventh standard. Apparently Appa had got the phone call. Manjrekar sir had not come to school that day. We did not have his class that day, but no one else seemed to have seen him. Appa called for a meeting of all the teachers after the mid-break. They assembled in his room. It was ten minutes since the bell rang, but no one came out. The tension in the air was palpable. No one said anything, but there was a lurking fear in everyone's minds.

The atmosphere in the afternoon, after the break, was tense. The fact that they had arrested Manjrekar sir meant that the matter was serious. The class was nervous and alert. We went through the motions of attending the other classes. We could hear the other classes going on as usual. The eighth standard guys were reciting a poem loudly and the tenth standard chaps came out into the playground. But our class was silent. Halbe sir explained a few theorems, but no one could pay any attention. Even he seemed a little distraught.

I broke the news to Pingle in the tuition class and he went and relayed it to the boys from Subhash. They exclaimed, 'Aila, really!' Shirodkar must have told Mande. I looked at Shirodkar a couple of times but did not smile. There was no question of meeting her after the class that day.

The air was tense the next day too at school, and much more than the previous day. Everyone in school knew the chain of events. The police had arrested Manjrekar sir. Ambekar's family had handed over the note to the police and he was kept in custody.

We were shaken to the bones.

'They would hammer him badly,' Santya said. 'They would burn him with cigarette ends and pound his knees with a rod. My Ba was made to lie down on slabs of ice.'

'They would not do anything like that to Sir,' Chitre said. 'They would not have put him behind bars.'

'What do you mean?' Surya said. 'There is no guarantee when dealing with the police. They may break his legs.'

'Bloody hell! What a pity that Manjrekar sir has become a victim of all this,' Phawdya cursed.

We all echoed his sentiments. We may not have felt so bad had it happened to someone else—Prem Chopra, Kendalkar sir, Redkar—anyone. But Manjrekar sir! And that too in police custody! It was too much to bear.

'Ichibhana, sir is not at fault, you know,' Surya said. 'It's Ambekar who was interested in him.'

'That's true,' Phawdya said. 'Sir never encouraged her!'

'But, bhenchod, why should she write Sir's name,' Surya asked. 'She was going to die in any case.'

'That was precisely her plan,' Chitre said. 'This is what people attempting suicide do to make the others listen to them.'

'But what if she had died?'

'She wouldn't have. She's too shrewd. She knew the safe number of tablets!'

'Chaila!' Surya exclaimed. 'But Sir is trapped in this whole mess!'

There was no way to know what action was being taken

against Manjrekar sir. He was the only person with whom we could afford to be free. But we could not have asked him anything in this case. All we could do was discuss amongst ourselves. The girls who had teased Ambekar, especially Mane and the birdies, were tense too.

Someone commented that Mane might get arrested if Ambekar did not recover. That scared the hell out of her and she started crying. When Barve ma'am entered the class, she was sobbing into her handkerchief. When asked for the reason, one of the birdies said, 'She's feeling bad for Ambekar.' Barve ma'am was silent for a while and then shot off, 'I don't understand what is wrong with all you girls? Do you even understand the meaning of love? What is all this nonsense about love and letters and all that? You watch some movies and try to emulate them. Now see what this has led to!'

She then lectured us for the entire hour. They must have been discussing it in the staff room and she was waiting for a cue to let it out. She was one of the seniormost and on the verge of retirement. That gave her the authority to lecture us. She continued to sermonize for a long time. She was primarily addressing the girls, and they listened to her quietly with their heads down. The boys were silent though we kept exchanging glances.

Chitre, in a low voice, interrupted her saying, 'The syllabus is yet not complete.' The way he said it was interesting; everyone could hear it, yet no one knew who had said it. We all wanted to burst out laughing but kept a straight face. It was not clear whether ma'am had heard him, but then she stopped her sermon and started teaching.

The next few days were tense as before. Teredesai got

news the next day that Ambekar had returned home. The boys continued to let their imagination run wild. Ambekar, quite expectedly, did not come to school. She wouldn't have dared to. Teredesai tried to impress others telling them how he had seen her standing in the balcony when Phadtare from class eleven asked, 'Is she having bouts of vomiting?'

Everyone laughed hearing that. Teredesai is a little dull-witted and took some time to get the meaning. But when he did, he quickly disappeared.

We saw Manjrekar sir after a couple of days. We were standing outside the office room to collect cricket gear. It was a free period. We saw him walk down the corridor past us. For a moment we did not recognize him. His hair was dishevelled and there was stubble on his chin. He would normally wear a neatly ironed shirt and trousers, but his clothes looked shabby today. The shirt was not tucked in. The sleeves were not buttoned. We thought the police might have tortured him in custody. He did not even glance in our direction. He would normally talk to us with his arm around our shoulders. But today he did not look at us and walked out of the school.

I was getting ready for the tuition class when Aaisaheb came in and asked, 'What time does your class get over?'

'Seven,' I said.

'I want you here by 7:15, okay? I don't want you to stand there chatting with anyone.'

I was stumped. Aaisaheb stood at the door with her hands behind her back. Ambabai was reading a magazine sitting on the chair. I looked at her but she ignored me.

It then dawned on me; it must have been Ponkshe kaku's doing.

'I have things to discuss with my friends.'

'Boys or girls?' Ambabai wanted to know.

'How does it matter? And why are you bothered? And what is wrong with talking to girls? Don't you talk to boys in your college?'

'I don't.'

'Who'll talk to you anyway? Have you seen your face in the mirror?'

'Mukund!' Aaisaheb shouted. 'I will pull your tongue out. Don't argue. I want you home by 7:15. Is that understood?'

I was already dressed up. I put on my sandals and left immediately. I was expecting this to happen sooner than later. Ponkshe kaku must have complained. Not carrying her bag was a huge mistake. I was paying for it now. I looked back. Ambabai's face was crestfallen. I felt bad but she had no business to poke her nose into my affairs. I had decided to come home early that day. In fact, I could have come at ten past seven had I wished to, but I whiled away my time chatting with some friends and entered home only at half-past seven. Baba was already home and no one said a word to me.

We came to know after two days that Manjrekar sir had been asked to leave. School would not be fun any more. His class would be taken by Pethkar ma'am now. His was the only class we used to look forward to. The only other person whose class was enjoyable was Zende sir's, but he too seemed quieter now. Manjrekar sir used to make the class entertaining and he was the only reason we had enjoyed the Scouts' camp. All the boys were depressed.

'Ichibhana, this does not portend well for us,' Surya said.

'Now people like Bendre ma'am will sit on our head's,' Phawdya said.

'It is Emergency all over,' Chitre added.

'Shall we collect a petition from all the students?' Bibikar suggested. 'We can also go on strike. Those school boys in Vikroli had done that.'

It was a great idea, especially since Manjrekar sir was not at fault. But we could not take the idea to fruition. We did discuss it, but the lead should have been taken by the eleventh and twelfth standard boys. We were told that Thombre from eleventh had spoken to Zende sir, but he was informed that the management was not willing to take any steps as this case involved a girl. The teachers had taken up the cause but to no avail. He also mentioned that since Manjrekar sir had not been made permanent they did not have a good reason to oppose his termination. We had no choice but to give up.

But the event shook up everyone. Bindaas girls like Sukdi walked with their heads down and girls like Sakhardande had mellowed a lot. Boys like Chawre, who would openly flirt in the playground, were not to be seen now. I remember we had a rare cold wave once in the winters when everyone walked around as if frozen. Shirodkar had stopped glancing in my direction now. Our eyes never met.

At home, too, Aaisaheb came to know of Manjrekar sir's episode. She must have heard about it from Ambabai; by then, it was the talk of the town.

'Is it true?' Aaisaheb asked me that evening.

'Yes,' I said, casually.

'Was she the same girl with whom you stand there chatting?'

I didn't know what to say. I was tempted not to answer but then that would have been worse.

'I don't stand anywhere *talking* to a girl,' I insisted. 'This is a different girl.'

Aaisaheb was not convinced.

'Forget studies and do other tamasha,' she said. 'Is this a school or a drama company? Just see the antics of these young children! And the teachers? If they themselves behave so, what can you expect from the students?'

'That's why I said you should not put him in that school,' Ambabai added. 'We should have admitted him in Subhash. They don't allow all this nonsense there.'

I was tempted to tell her about the famous Subhash affair, but it would have served no purpose. There was no point in defending Manjrekar sir either.

'And I am warning you,' Aaisaheb said, wagging a finger at me. 'Beware! Don't get into any of these affairs. You have your tenth boards next year. I hope you remember.'

Yes, I remember! I muttered to myself. I had realized that all this was not going to be easy. The soft cloud floating around me had vanished long back, and like the dry wind blowing through my classroom windows, I could feel the heat on me now. There was no point in letting them know. I had to be careful.

That evening there was a satyanarayan puja in KT and Vijay's room. They had invited each and every resident. It was quite a surprise to hear they were holding a puja; they did not have a single picture of any god in their room and KT had once argued with Ponkshe kaka that there was no point in worshipping a stone idol. Aaisaheb concluded that one of them was getting engaged. I returned from my tuition and was planning to visit them when Ambabai said, 'Come, let's go. I was waiting for you.'

'What work do you have there?' Aaisaheb shouted. 'Have you no sense? There is no need for you to go anywhere.'

Ambabai had put on her sandals. She discarded them now, making a face. Served her right! She had been acting oversmart these days. To add insult to injury, I thumbed my nose at her before going out.

I went upstairs. Their house was full. They had invited a lot of people from outside. A large number of chappals and shoes lay outside the door. I looked at the crowd. There was no one from our building. They were all outsiders. Some of the women had bob-cut. I was about to go back when KT spotted me and said, 'Come, Mukund. Come and sit next to me.'

I then realized that they were actually holding a meeting. They had performed the puja earlier, but in reality they were holding a meeting to discuss the Emergency. Vijay clarified that they were not allowed to hold a meeting openly, hence the ploy. He then reeled out statistics of the number of people arrested all over the country. He spoke about how people were not allowed freedom of speech and how stacks of magazines were being confiscated. The room was crowded, but I was enjoying the discussion. Nikam kaka came in and quickly realized that a meeting was in progress. He took the prasad, but when Vijay requested him to sit down he refused, asking them to carry on. He cautioned them to be careful.

I came down after nearly three quarters of an hour. Aaisaheb asked, the moment I stepped in, 'What took you so long?'

'Aai, they were singing songs and cracking jokes,' I said. 'Real good jokes. It was fun.'

She did not question me further. Of course, I was prepared to recount a few jokes from the many Chitre had told me.

I was pleasantly surprised to see Naru mama sprawled on the cot when I came back from school the next day. He had not sent a letter nor called up Baba's office. But I was very happy to see him. I had so much to tell him and many things to ask.

'Arre! Naru mama!' I exclaimed.

'You bet!' he said, punching me lightly on my stomach. 'See! Here I am!'

'Damn good! Hope you are going to stay for a while?'

'He is not staying,' Aaisaheb said. 'It's a flying visit.'

'Mama is getting married,' Ambabai added.

'Don't tell me!' I said. 'Who is she?'

Naru mama did not answer. A smile played on his lips.

'Tell me please, Naru mama,' I repeated.

He did not reply but pointed towards the table.

'Look at this photo here,' Aaisaheb said. 'Take it carefully. There is a horoscope along with the photograph.'

I eagerly opened the envelope but was disappointed to find that the girl wore a big bindi on her forehead. She looked like one of our many relatives. She was quite ordinary to look at, nothing to write home about.

'So? How do you find your mami?' Aaisaheb asked.

'Nice,' I said. I knew the correct things to say. 'But what is her name?'

'See the horoscope. It is mentioned there,' Ambabai said.

I unfolded the paper containing the horoscope and saw that there was a host of information in it, along with the star sign, date of birth etcetera, and the name—Pratibha Ramchandra Kulkarni.

I felt cheated and was about to ask Naru mama whatever happened to his plans of marrying a Christian girl, but I kept quiet in Aaisaheb's presence. I soon got the other details. The marriage was not fixed yet. The girl lived near Naru mama's town. He had liked her and their horoscopes had matched, but the marriage would not be fixed without Aaisaheb's permission. Aaisaheb and Naru mama would visit the place to meet the bride's family. Aaisaheb would return after two days. 'He has finalized everything. He just needs me to give the official stamp of approval,' I heard Aaisaheb telling Baba that evening.

I bunked the tuition hoping to spend time with Naru mama, but in vain. Aaisaheb insisted on buying a saree for Aaji and she had to shop for other things. Ambabai too joined the bandwagon. Naru mama wanted me to come along. We finally left after Baba returned from office and had had his cup of tea. Aaisaheb decided to buy a saree for the prospective bride in advance in case things progressed well at the meeting. We then made the customary visit to Pethe ice-cream parlour. Aaisaheb went into the bangles shop next door and I got a chance to ask Naru mama, 'Naru mama, you were to marry a Christian girl— what happened?'

He smiled and did not reply. After a moment he said, 'That's what my plan was. But what to do, I found her first!'

I did not believe him but had no other option than to keep quiet.

Aaisaheb left the next day and returned after finalizing everything. The wedding was fixed for a date after my final exams.

I decided to meet Shirodkar the day Aaisaheb left with Naru mama. Luckily, Mande and Juvekar were both absent that day. I did not sit next to Pingle but on the last row so that I could slip away the moment the class got over. I walked briskly in the direction of Shirodkar's house and went and stood near Dedhiya Kirana Store.

She came in early as there were no friends to chat with. We did not stop and chat near the grocery but continued walking and then taking a turn into another lane, stood near the peepal tree.

'Did Juvekar not come today?' I asked.

'No. It seems she's unwell.'

'Mande too did not come, I believe.'

'I don't know why.'

'Good that they both were absent.'

She merely smiled in reply. I was quiet for a while, but I knew what I had to discuss. The Ambekar episode was a huge one to talk about.

'It was sad for Manjrekar sir, no?' I asked.

She nodded wordlessly.

'That Ambekar is amazing!' I said sarcastically. 'Why did she have to take sleeping pills?'

She look uncomfortable. 'We should not stand here and chat.'

'Then where shall we go?'

'Nowhere,' she said. 'I will go home now.'

She said so but did not move. I realized that I had made a mistake by talking about Ambekar. No girl in the class was comfortable talking about her. I changed the topic.

'Naru mama's marriage has been fixed,' I said and then realized that she may not know who Naru mama is.

'My Naru mama is a bindaas character, you know,' I said. 'He teaches English in a college but is like a friend to me.'

'Aiyaa, really?' she said. 'Where will the wedding happen?'

'In his town.' I said. 'After the exams. We'll go and stay in Aaji's house. In fact, Naru mama wanted to marry a Christian girl, you know?'

'Really? A Christian?'

'You bet! He had planned so but could not somehow manage it. He then found someone from our caste.'

I had deliberately stressed on the caste factor hoping she would get the hint. It was not going to be smooth sailing for us. But she just nodded her head. I was struggling to find things to talk about.

'What shall we do going forward?' I asked.

I had expected her to respond in her usual manner asking 'What do you mean?', and I would be at my wits' end to explain. But she said nothing and simply looked at me. She then started to look the other way, without saying a word.

It was getting dark and the lane was silent. There was no sound either, of a radio or any children playing. The lamp at the end of the lane burnt while darkness crept up slowly. The peepal tree stood still without a leaf moving. Everything stood still.

'Tell me,' I urged her.

'What do you mean?' her voice took on a serious tone.

I realized that the stillness had changed to something deeper. The tension in the air was palpable.

'I mean, in future,' I repeated.

'I don't know,' she said, looking down at the ground.

I realized that she was not avoiding my question; she genuinely did not know the answer. The feeling of emptiness in the pit of my stomach grew deeper and my heart began to throb hard. The darkness around us seemed to be getting darker. Suddenly, a deep sense of anger enveloped me. I was angry at the world, angry at our town, my school, Appa, Bendre, Ambekar—even Manjrekar sir! And then a strange fear gripped.

She did not stay for long. Using the excuse of someone entering the lane, she briskly walked away in the direction of her house. I wanted to say we shall meet at the same place the next day, but it was too late. She had already left.

I walked back home slowly, thinking of the question I had asked. I realized that the world was a difficult place. It had its own rules; and one had to follow them if one had to live in it. The world was huge and I was too small to challenge it.

I sized up the situation with a cool head. I had to clear class ten first. I could then leave home and take up any job. Naru mama says if one is willing one can get any job. I could take up a job and then join night school to pass class twelve. I could then continue higher studies. Shirodkar would continue with her studies as usual. It was a question of five or six years, seven at the most. And no one can stop you once you are eighteen.

I could depend on people like KT and Vijay for help. I could take up a room or share it with some friend. I remembered my kaka's son Prakash had done something similar. He did not frequent our house much, but we had heard of his leaving home. He was not keen on studies and wanted to pursue theatre. When his family objected, he left home and took up residence in a small room in Byculla. He was apparently doing fine now. He had once sent us a few passes for his play. I too would have to take the same route. There was no choice.

I enquired about night school next. It was in Vakhar lane. The board said, Adarsh Night School. A yellow lamp burnt brightly. The office was in the verandah and a fat man sporting a huge moustache sat behind a desk. The board indicated he was the principal. He was probably responsible for everything. I did not see anyone else there. The wall behind the desk was adorned with photographs of national leaders.

I stood before him when he looked up from the papers he seemed to be studying.

'I wanted to enquire regarding the night school,' I said. 'I have a cousin who is coming over from the village. I am enquiring on his behalf.'

'What is your name?'

I told him.

'Which school?'

'Warhadkar High School.'

'Which class?'

'Ninth.'

'Where do you stay?'

'Near Dhaparewadi. Kudalkar chawl.'

'Achha. Near Majgaonkar dispensary, is it?'

'Yes,' I said, a little surprised. He seemed to know every lane in town.

'Who wants to attend night school?'

'My cousin from the village.'

'Then get him here,' he said, getting back to his papers.

'He is not here at the moment.'

'Get him when he comes,' he said. 'Now you may go.'

'Do you have eleventh science here?' I persisted.

He did not answer but pointed to a board in the room. It said in bold letters—Arts and Commerce only. There were other instructions like the school starting at seven pm and attendance being compulsory, prior permission needed for taking leave etcetera. I stood there reading the board for a few minutes and then left.

There were no Science classes here and it was unlikely this moustachioed fellow would take me even if I opted for Commerce. There was only one night school in town. But then if I went over to Mumbai, there would be many options. I would cross the bridge when I came to it. I decided that for now I needed to focus on passing class ten.

The year was coming to an end and most of the syllabus was over. Bendre ma'am had, in fact, started revising the chapters. More importantly, Halbe sir had completed his Geometry and Algebra portion. A few experiments in Physics remained, but they were easy. The matriculation exams would begin from twelfth of March, but luckily our school was not an examination centre. Subhash and Tope are designated centres each year and they have to suspend classes during that time.

The tenth standard guys were not attending school these days. The school seemed a little empty without them. There was a palpable tension across town. It happens each year during the exam time. There is invariably someone or the other appearing for the exam known to each person and the only discussion in town is centred around exams. There is no disturbance during that period. The theatres don't dare put up a good movie during that time. The atmosphere in school is ominous.

Surya's building was near completion now. They had painted the inside walls and were now painting the exterior. A brick wall had come up around the building. The building looked bright and shiny, but it was no fun sitting there now. The earlier damp, cool and dark atmosphere was long gone. The labourer couple had moved away and the shack was occupied by a watchman, presumably from the same group. The ground floor was likely to be occupied soon and the plumber was busy fitting the taps.

Surya's father had not asked us to move out yet. In fact, Surya mentioned once that his father had designated two rooms on the second floor for us, so that we may use them for our studies in tenth standard. It was a good idea. But we had to clear ninth first! There was no point in joint studies as Phawdya and Surya would while away their time, not allowing anyone to study. This place was good to hang out—as we had for a whole year—but not for studies.

The tuition classes too were likely to end soon. Everyone winds up their activities once the matriculation examination begins. I wondered where I would meet Shirodkar after this. In class ten in the coming year, we would be swamped with tuition classes in all our free time. In fact, some of the classes start in the summer holidays itself! I was not against classes now. I did not mind joining tuitions next year. Ambabai had made it clear that I should not continue with Deshmane sir 's classes next year. Someone had suggested Chaitanya classes. But I had decided—I would join the same class as Shirodkars. And if Chaitanya was good, I would ask her to join the same. That's it! Then I could spend the whole day at tuition centres; even whole nights, if required.

There was a discussion on which teacher would teach what subject next year. We had no favourites other than Zende sir. Bendre would continue with English and we wondered whether Halbe sir or Kendalkar sir would teach Maths. We would be dead if it were to be the latter. Pethkar ma'am would continue with Social Science while Chemistry would be taught by the boring and oversmart Prem Chopra. We had heard that Appa would take Hindi. So we could forget about fun in that period. Phawdya did not mind Paranjpe ma'am teaching us Marathi so long as she continued wearing sleeveless blouses. All of us agreed with him. Any teacher was fine so long as she wore sleeveless! Surya thought it was a nice way to begin the day.

The paddy fields were barren and dry now. The grass had been grazed upon by the cows and they too were nowhere to be seen. There was a bit of enthusiasm while the England team played, but now, with the exams looming, the children playing cricket too had vanished. The only greenery left was in the adjoining woods.

But then soon Shankar's father would come over in the summer holidays to start tilling the fields. He would collect the dry twigs and leaves and burn them in one corner of the field. The planting would start in the rainy season. The fields would be full of rain water then. It was a sight to behold. The smell of ice-candy and the cool breeze were intoxicating. If there was heaven on earth, it was here, it was here, it was here! I needed to get Shirodkar here next year, even if it means bunking school. My favourite rock had a big flat space enough for both of us to sit on. We could sit there the whole day without getting bored.

The playground too would be green and beautiful. I would try and grab a seat near the door. But I was not sure of the classroom being allotted to us. Currently tenth standard was in a good room at the corner of the school building, and with a great view. One could see the woods from there. We would be dead if we were to be allotted the other room inside. It is behind the iron railing. The passage is busy with someone or the other constantly walking by. I wished we would get a room facing the playground. I would spend time watching the lovely hills beyond Sonarpada outside and the beautiful Shirodkar inside! Whether I was taught Maths or Physics would be irrelevant. I would not be worried about either. The school could go on forever.

That day Nikam kaka bought a television. We were aware of its impending arrival because we had seen the antenna being installed the previous day. It was a black-and-white TV and everyone gathered to see the evening news. Nikam kaka has a lot of furniture in his room, but people managed to fit in. Ponkshe kaka and Sukhtankar kaka grabbed the two chairs while Shenvi and Barve kaka occupied the cot. The children sat right in the front along with Upasni aaji.

KT and Vijay stood outside the door but came in when the news began. I could see the TV sitting on the edge of the sofa. Nikam kaka stood with his back to the wall while kaku watched it standing near the inner door. She was able to hear the news but not see it.

We watched the news followed by announcements for the next day's programmes. There was a lot of static disturbance along with the black horizontal lines constantly running by the screen. But the sound quality was good. Chayageet was the next programme. By then the Mayekar couple, Aai-Baba, Ambabai, and many of the other residents had joined in. Nikam kaka had to slide the window curtain, allowing the people standing outside to get a glimpse. Mayekar kaka asked me to keep my head low and I developed a crick in my neck as a result.

As expected, there were no games that evening. The Nikams were carrom lovers, but they did not bring out the board from that day onwards. Kiran got addicted to the television. The crowds continued to gather each evening. There was a musical programme on Saturday while Sunday evenings was movie time. No one was interested in playing games any more.

Baba went in the first day. Nikam kaka welcomed him with 'Come in, come in, Joshisaheb!' Baba was not interested in watching TV, but he must have gone not finding any partners for chess. Sukhtankar kaka joined in for chess one day but left the moment he heard the 'Dinu chhi sasubai' serial being aired. 'Joshi sahib, please excuse me,' he said, getting up hurriedly. 'I am willing to concede this board, but I cannot afford to miss my favourite serial.'

Baba had no choice. He wound up the game. 'Chess is over!' he said, resigning himself to the change.

We had a general idea of the tentative dates for our exams. It became clear when the timetable was put up on the notice board. It was good that they had not been postponed as they would have clashed with Naru mama's wedding. The exams were to start on the second of April and would get over on the tenth. The wedding was on the nineteenth. Results would be announced on twenty-eighth, two days earlier than usual. Pethkar ma'am said this had been done to allow students to start their tuition classes in time.

Surya's way of mugging up things was to hold the notebook in his hand and pace the room reading out loudly. Chitre had told him it would not do, but he would not listen. It was impossible to study in that situation. We did not need him for our studies. Chitre was, as always, upto date with his preparation. He could write the exams any day. He used to come there as he did not want to stay back at home alone. Devaki continued her flirtation much to his dislike. Chitre said that she had tried the same trick once again. She would also drop her pallu whenever she got a chance.

Phawdya had no respite from the vegetable business. He had to sort the vegetables in the morning and then sit at the shop in the evening. He wanted to come over the building at nine in the morning but could reach only at quarter to twelve, running all the way. He was desperate to study and pass the exams because his mother had warned him that she would pull him out of the school if he failed.

There was still a week or ten days to go for the tuition

classes to get over, but Deshmane sir had started winding up his portions. He gave us a sample test which we had to attempt at home. We were out of the class in no time.

We had enough time. It was still bright outside and no one was in a hurry to go home. The boys and girls stood there talking. I looked at Shirodkar and her eyes told me that we had enough time to chat. I was not going to let such an opportunity go by. Pingle deliberately asked me in a loud voice whether I was visiting Misal. Juvekar laughed at his comment, but I ignored him.

I went and stood under the peepal tree. It was bright and the place looked clean and dry. The lane was desolate as usual. A few leaves fell down from the tree intermittently. I then remembered that the peepal leaf formed a lovely design once dried in between the pages of a book. For a moment, I thought of picking up two leaves; one for me and the other for her. It would be a memento for both of us. But I brushed away the thought. The peepal tree was going to be here forever and the leaves would continue to fall in heaps.

She came in after ten minutes. She must have managed to escape from her friends, but it seemed that she had been teased by them. She came in smiling to herself.

'What happened?' I asked.

'Nothing,' she said.

'That Juvekar must not be letting you go,' I said.

'That's right. In fact, we had decided to study together till the exams.'

'When are their exams?'

'At the same time as ours,' she said.

'Why doesn't Mande come these days?'

'She has to help her mother in the kitchen.'

'We are going to start studying in the building.'

'That adda of yours? Chhi! You guys just sit there and rag the passers-by. What studies can you do there? *You* don't go there.'

I kept quiet. The fact that we assembled there was known to everyone now. And our pranks were considered ragging now. There was no point in discussing that.

'The classes will end soon,' I said.

'Yes. On twentieth.'

'What next?'

'Next?' she asked.

I was not sure whether she had understood what I meant or whether she was just acting innocent. My heart was beating louder.

'Then where shall we meet?' I asked.

'Why do we need to meet?' she asked, laughing.

'I enquired regarding night school,' I said, changing the topic.

'Night school?'

I realized she would not know the context. She was not aware of my plan.

'I have decided to join night school if I take up a job after class ten. My kaka's son Prakash did the same.'

She did not understand and looked at me, glancing once in both the directions.

'Which class are you planning to join next year?' I asked.

'I have not decided yet,' she said.

'Ambabai says, Chaitanya classes are good,' I said.

'Aiyaa, really? Juvekar said the same thing. But it would be a little far away.'

'Not that far, really. And it is better that way.'

That was good news. And Juvekar's presence would not be a hindrance. She knew, and it was good that she was in a different school. She could come along with Shirodkar. Two birds with one stone!

'The exams are approaching,' she said.

'Yes.'

'We need to study now,' she said. She glanced around once. 'We cannot meet here any more.'

I did not say anything. She was right. The classes would end and the exams would begin. There was no way we could meet here. It was just a matter of a few weeks actually. Then the tuition classes would begin in May and school too would start.

'After the exams, we are going to Naru mama's wedding.'

'Right after?'

'No. A few days later. I will return a day before the results are announced. Are you guys going anywhere?'

'Nothing fixed yet,' she said. 'We may visit our Aaji.'

'Will we meet in the vacations?'

'Let us see,' she said, looking away from me.

I did not know what to say further. The air was still and the lane was quiet. It was as if the wind had stopped blowing in order not to disturb the silence. The hollow in my stomach was growing. For a brief moment, I thought of popping the question—will you marry me? But the words did not escape my lips.

'Which college will you join?' I asked.

'College? It is too early,' she said. 'We still have class ten to get past. Who knows whether I will pass or not.'

'What is there to worry about? Are you taking Arts or Commerce?'

'I have not decided anything yet.'

'I will have to take Science,' I said. 'The folks at home have decided that I am going to be an engineer.'

'What's wrong with that?'

'Will you join that college?' I asked.

'Me? Why me?' she asked, smiling. 'I don't like engineering!'

'Then what do you like?'

'Nothing,' she replied like most girls do.

This conversation was not going anywhere. There was an air of urgency all around. I could feel the tension in the air. I wanted to speak out what I wanted to but did not. The emptiness in my stomach continued to grow. I could not understand. What was it? Was it because the year was ending? or was it because the exams were approaching?

'This year went off well, isn't it?' I said. I had to say something.

'Yes,' she said. 'But that Bendre ma'am made life hell for me. It will be good if she does not teach us next year.'

'Bendre will be there for sure,' I said. 'Maths will be taught by Kendalkar. And Appa is going to be there too.'

'Oh God! That's terrible!'

'We cannot play word games next year.'

'Aiyaa, really? Why?'

'They have decided so.'

'Issh! That will be really boring,' she said. 'Who wants to study all the time?'

I wanted to say the only solace is your presence, but she would not have liked that. I could not afford to say anything stupid.

We stood there without speaking for a while. It was nice to stand there like that. Like that day in the Ganesh temple. But time was slipping by. I wished I could hold it in my hand.

'Shall I go?' she asked.

I knew she would say that sooner than later. But I felt I was losing something precious.

'No,' I said.

She smiled at me. Her smile was lovely. I was happy that I had dared.

'I need to go,' she said. 'Aai had asked me to come home immediately after class. She will get upset if she comes to know that the class got over early.'

'Will you come tomorrow? 'I asked.

'No. Only after the exams,' she said.

'But there are no classes then.'

'You can come home. I will leave now.'

She started walking away. I too had to go home and could have walked along with her till the end of the lane, but I could not move from my place. My legs felt weak and I felt empty. She walked a few steps and then waved at me, smiling. There was enough light, and the moment she stepped out of the shade of the tree, I could see her face clearly. I felt an acute sense of loss; something inexplicable. We had school tomorrow and there were a few tuition classes left to attend, but a strange fear gripped me. For a moment, I was tempted to run after and walk her home, or perhaps take her to my home. But my legs refused to move and I kept watching her as she walked away.

When I reached our adda I found that Surya had arrived before me. He came in early these days. Ever since the building had been made ready, he spent most of his time there. He had spread out his books on the floor. We had homework to submit that day—an experiment in Physics and some equations in Chemistry. Predictably, he had not been able to complete them. I gave him my notebook, which he copied from hurriedly. Chitre was not expected as he was in Bandra. One could not be sure of Phawdya. Surya wanted to understand some Maths problems, but he lost interest by the time he copied the Physics and Chemistry homework. He then lay down on the floor looking at the ceiling. I too sat down and stretched my legs.

'Ichibhana, you know what I dreamt of last night?' he asked.

'What?'

'Kevda and I were sitting in a garden. There was a big crowd around us but we did not care. Chitre asked me whether I was enjoying alone with us, and then you said you should leave us alone. You boys went away and I held Kevda's hand. But I don't remember what happened next.'

I stifled my laughter. Chitre would have burst out laughing. Surya was describing his dream in all honesty. He was dreaming of Kevda and it was obvious that we would land up in his dream. I was surprised that Phawdya was absent!

'Dreams are a good sign, especially if you see them early in the morning,' I said. 'Did you dream of this early morning?'

'Ichibhana, what is the point in dreaming?' Surya answered, turning prone. 'No dreams materialize in reality. And now the exams are approaching. All I have achieved is nothing.'

He was right. He had followed her once, but that had yielded nothing. While Chitre was going steady with Kevda. Chitre had mentioned that they were, in fact, spending time studying together.

'Why don't you ask that mama of yours? We need some good ideas. We have to find a way to woo that Kevda, yaar.'

I pitied him. He was not aware that Chitre had already beaten him in the game. But there was no point in telling him. It was Kevda who would have to tell him that. Chitre had said he was planning to advise her to tell Surya clearly that she was not interested.

'There is no point in following her,' Surya said, sitting up. 'She does not say a word!'

'Why don't you ask her directly?' I suggested.

'What can I ask her?'

'Whether she's interested or not. That way you would know it once and for all.'

Surya was silent for a while. He probably mulled over my suggestion. Then he stood up and went near the window. He could see the road from there. There was still time; we had reached early. The morning batch was yet to get over.

'Ichibhana, are you a soothsayer or what?' he shouted.

'Why, what happened?'

'Come over here. See.'

I went over to the window. I could see the road right upto Mokshadham. There was no one on the road. And Kevda was walking by, alone.

Surya kept looking at her as she approached the building.

'Hey Joshi, come on bhenchod,' Surya said, hurriedly.

'You suggested I should ask her directly, isn't it? Come on, I will ask her today.'

I did not know what to say. I had casually mentioned but did not know he would put that into action right away. The moment was opportune. Kevda was alone. There was no one else in sight.

'Don't rush,' I said.

'Why not? We won't get a chance like this.'

'But here? Near our school?'

'So what? Let us go down. I will ask her right away.'

Surya was in high spirits.

'You go alone,' I said.

'No. You come along, saale. Just stand there next to me.'

'No. You go alone. I will wait here.'

'Come on bhenchod. Don't be stubborn,' he shouted angrily. 'It was *your* idea and now *you* are shying away.'

He literally dragged me down. We went and stood near the building wall. Kevda walked alone in the bright sunlight. She had a scarf on her head. She was wearing a well ironed skirt and blouse. A cyclist crossed her, but there were no other students on the road.

She spotted us the moment she came near the building. She glanced at Surya and then at me. Then she started walking in the middle of the road. Surya took out a comb from his hip pocket and arranged his hair into a buff.

My chest was pounding.

The moment she came near us, Surya stepped on to the road and, trying to block her way said, 'Apne ko line deti kya?'

She stopped and then, pursing her lips, simply nodded in the negative, making a '*chkk*' sound.

'That's all you can say?' Surya persisted.

'Yes,' she said. 'Now let me go.'

She walked away without bothering to even glance at me. Surya kept staring at her for a while.

'Chaila! She refused,' Surya said, looking at her go by.

I was expecting that. We stood there for a while and then climbed back the stairs.

'Ichibhana, she refused,' Surya repeated, sitting down.

'Let it be, yaar,' I said. 'Let her go to hell.'

Surya did not say anything. It was evident that he was sad. But it was good that he knew her feelings now. Phawdya came in after a while and seeing us glum realized that something was amiss. Surya was silent and I persisted, 'Let it be, yaar. Don't take it to heart.'

'You guys are having a great time with your sweethearts,' Surya said. '*We* are the unlucky ones.'

I kept quiet. School went off as usual. Zende sir was absent and his class was taken by Halbe sir. We were not free in the PT period either. The tuition class also went off uneventfully.

Chitre came in the next day, but we did not sit there for long as we were busy doing Biology homework. We did not get time to peep outside and reached school just in time.

Ganoba came into the class during the Marathi period. 'Mhatre and Joshi,' he announced, searching for us. 'Headmaster has summoned you.'

Ma'am stopped teaching and the entire class looked at us. No one knew the reason. We stood up and Ganoba said, 'Come on.'

We had no idea why we were being called. Ma'am

simply stared at us and then indicated with a nod of her head for us to go.

I glanced at Shirodkar as I left the room. She had a surprised look on her face. My mind was racing. It dawned on me—only Surya and I had been summoned. Not Chitre or Phawdya or Santya or Harishchandra. It had to be Kewda!

'Ganoba, why has sir called us?' Surya asked.

You will know soon,' he said.

'Your prank yesterday—that's the reason,' I told Surya.

I spotted Kevda the moment we entered Appa's room. A fair person sat on a chair. It did not require divine intervention to know that he was her father. The school supervisor, Jangam sir, sat on a chair next to Bendre ma'am. Appa was waiting for us. He addressed us with his usual, 'Welcome, please come in', the moment we entered.

Ganoba made us stand near the table.

'Are these the same boys?' Appa asked Kevda.

She nodded.

'Which of them accosted you yesterday?' he asked.

'This fellow,' she said, pointing at Surya.

'Oh, is that so? Step forward!'

Surya stepped forward gingerly. Appa picked up the cane and spanked him fiercely. The cane made a whip-like sound as it cut through the air.

'What is my mistake, Sir?' Surya screamed as the cane hit his arm.

'What do you mean? Nalayak! What temerity!' Appa shouted and continued caning him. Surya turned his back to Appa, trying to avoid the cane and took the beatings on his back. My legs were shivering now. I had never seen Appa in this avatar.

'I did not do anything, Sir,' Surya shouted.

'Besharam! You hold a girl's hand, and then say you did nothing!' Appa screamed while another blow landed on Surya's back.

Surya shuddered hearing Appa's words. I stood shivering in my place. It was not true. Surya had accosted her but he had not held her hand.

'I did not hold her hand, Sir,' Surya pleaded. He was trying to protect his face with his palms.

'Shut up! Not a word more,' Appa growled, caning him once more. He then turned his attention to me.

'Come forward. You!' he indicated with his cane.

'I did nothing, Sir,' I pleaded, not moving from my place.

'What was he doing?' Appa asked Kevda.

I looked at her. She was at a loss for a moment and then said, 'He was just standing there.'

'Oh, I see. Accomplice!' I did not understand the meaning of the word, but Appa continued, 'Put your hand forward!'

I put my hand forward and Appa let the cane land on my palm with all the force he could gather. This was not Bendre ma'am. This was Appa in all his fury. I convulsed and took my hand back. My eyes were bursting with tears.

'Why are you scared now?' Appa asked, holding his cane. 'Why are you pulling your hand back? You enjoy mawaligiri, isn't it? Put your hand forward!'

I put my left hand out; and then the right one; then the left one. Hot flashes raced through my body. The mind went gone numb. My palms were singed.

Appa stopped after a while. The other people present in the room had not said a word. I realized what must have happened. Kevda had not said a word in school yesterday, but she must have gone home and complained to her father. We had not bothered to notice this morning when we were in the building else we would have seen her with her father. Or perhaps she came in later.

'This boy was following her earlier too,' her father said. 'Isn't that so?' he asked, looking at Kevda.

Kevda nodded without speaking.

'He had followed her right upto our house once,' her father continued.

'Oh, I see. Brilliant!' Appa exclaimed.

'And these boys sit there in the building and tease the girls going by,' Bendre ma'am added. 'I have seen it myself.'

'Oh, I see!' Appa said. 'I am getting to know my students better now.'

We are in for a huge trouble. If Bendre ma'am enquired in the class, more than twenty girls would speak up against us. Appa sat there nodding his head, muttering, 'Oh, I see.' His cane rested on the table. Appa's posture spelt danger. It was better for him to cane us. We stood there with our heads hung. My palms were hurting badly. Surya's body must have been burning all over.

'Sir, how are we to send our girls to school if we have such boys around?' her father asked. 'This boy accosts her in broad daylight and that too on the way to school.'

We were looking down, but I glanced at Jangam sir who seemed be nodding in acknowledgement.

'These boys are beyond redemption,' he said.

'There is no discipline,' Bendre ma'am added.

'Whose son is he?' Kevda's father asked.

Appa asked, 'Aren't you Mhatre sheth's son?'

Surya nodded.

'See! His father is one of the donors to this school. We started this school for their convenience and look at what these guys are upto!'

'Sir, don't just sit and watch. We need to take some action,' Kevda's father continued. 'These guys have accosted my daughter. They may do something else tomorrow. How can we allow our girls to study here?'

'They need to be given a strict punishment,' Jangam sir said.

'Punishment? What are you saying?' Kevda's father interrupted. 'These boys need to be rusticated and sent to a remand home. What do you think—these guys will improve if punished? They need to be handed over to the police. Just look at the way they stand there with their mawali faces!'

I was taken aback. Surya too must have been taken by surprise. We had not expected this. We were expecting Appa to spank us and Bendre ma'am to add fuel to the fire at the most. We were prepared for some more caning. We did not mind that. But Kevda's father seemed to be on a different track. Rusticated! Surya would not have understood the meaning of the word. And police! Remand home! This was getting too dangerous.

Kevda's father's request took Appa and Jangam sir by surprise. They were quiet for a while.

'We need to punish them for sure,' Appa continued and then, turning towards Jangam sir, said, 'Call their parents. Prepare a letter and let them know what their children are upto!'

'No. There is no point in just calling their parents,'

Kevda's father erupted. 'You must complain to the police. If you don't want to, I will do it. We cannot allow them to go scot-free. This is no ordinary matter.'

'I agree,' Appa said. 'But their parents need to be informed first. Jangam sir, please get the letter drafted right away and give it to these boys. Ask them to come with their father tomorrow morning at eleven. Gupte saheb, you too come at that time.'

'I will come, but we need to register a complaint with the police.'

Appa nodded but did not say anything. He then looked at us and growled, 'Go home and give the letter to your fathers. If you lose or do not give it, there will be no one worse than me. Understood? I will throw you in jail. And come with your fathers here tomorrow at eleven. Okay?'

We both nodded our heads.

'Now go back to your class,' he said. 'Ganoba will hand over the letter to you.'

We came out of the room but did not dare go back to the classroom immediately. We stood in one corner. My hands were hurting and I was sure that Surya's body was burning badly. Surya looked at me and, rubbing his shoulders, asked, 'Ichibhana, what crime did we commit?'

'You asked her out,' I said.

'But I never touched her. She's lying.'

I kept quiet. Surya was right; these people had misunderstood the whole episode.

'What will happen now?' Surya asked.

'Let us go back to the class now. We will see later,' I said.

The class was on. We stood near the door when ma'am

indicated with her head for us to come in. We went and sat down at our places. I looked at my palms. There were thick, red lines on them. I was desperate to run my hands under cold water. I wished I could cut them off.

The boys around us murmured, but no one dared ask us anything. I glanced at Shirodkar. She continued to look down at her notebook. No one knew what had happened. Teredesai raised his eyebrows, but I nodded, indicating nothing had happened. Phawdya asked Surya and he mumbled, 'Will tell you later.' Chitre looked askance and I indicated the same. Ma'am continued to teach.

The boys' curiosity got the better of them the moment the class was over. They gathered around us and asked, 'What happened? Why did Appa call you?'

I did not know what to say. We would have to say something. But I decided to keep quiet. Then Surya said, 'We spoke to Kevda yesterday. She went and complained to Appa.'

'We?'

'Surya,' I clarified.

'What?' Chitre asked.

Surya fumbled for a moment. He looked around. Barve ma'am was likely to come in any moment.

'I went and asked her whether she would come out with me,' Surya said. 'That's it! She promptly went and complained to Appa.'

'Chaila! That's all?' Phawdya asked. 'What did Appa say?'

'Appa was wild with rage, bhenchod,' Surya said. 'Look at this! He literally tore my shirt. There are red marks all over. Ichibhana, we will teach him a lesson one day.'

'I too got caned,' I said, showing my palms.

'Fuck! You got beaten black and blue,' Santya exclaimed.

'You were trying to act smart, bhenchod,' Harishchandra said. 'Who asked you to go and accost her?'

'Joshi asked me to. So I did that!'

Chitre stared at me. I clarified, hurriedly, 'I never asked him to go and accost her right there on the road. I got sucked in because of your foolishness.'

'Did you not tell me to ask her?' Surya challenged.

Barve ma'am entered the class before I could answer. She banged the duster on the table to disperse the crowd around our bench. Chitre gave me a look, which made me want to hide my face under the table.

Barve ma'am's class got over without any untoward incident. The next class was Bendre ma'am's. She was at the door even before Barve ma'am left and we did not get a chance to continue our discussion. She looked at us as she entered, but we kept our heads down.

But that ploy did not work. She was explaining the meaning of the word 'smart' and she got a chance to hit back at us.

'Smart means someone who thinks beyond his capabilities. For example take, some of the boys in our class! They try to act smart. They accost girls on the road and ask them whether they would reciprocate their love. But they get their reward. What do you say, Mhatre? Joshi, am I right?'

I wished I could disappear. It was out now. The girls in my class may have been a little stupid, but ma'am's comments said it all. A murmur rippled across the class. Some of the girls stared at us.

In the next period, Halbe sir was teaching us when Ganoba came in and spoke to him. Halbe sir looked at us. Ganoba handed over the envelopes to us and took our signatures in the outgoing register. I had assumed that Appa would probably not send the letters. He would manage to pacify Kevda's father. After all he had already spanked us. But the threat was for real. There was no escape.

The boys stared at us but I casually kept the envelope in my bag, as if it was nothing important. Then I continued to concentrate on what Sir was writing on the blackboard. When he turned his back to us, I opened the envelope and quickly took out the letter and hid it in my notebook. Teredesai raised his eyebrows, but I signalled to him to look ahead. Then I opened my notebook and read the letter.

The letter was typed on the school letterhead. Only my father's name was written in ink. The letter began with the usual salutations and then went on to state, 'your ward…followed by my name in ink…has been found to be seriously misbehaving with a school girl. In this regard, you are requested to meet the Headmaster tomorrow, eleventh March, at eleven o'clock in his office.' It was then signed by Appa followed by a seal of the headmaster. Surya too must have received a similar letter as this was a carbon copy.

My legs were shivering after reading the letter. I was sweating the way I once did when I had taken some medicines for fever. My body was wet. My palms stained the pages of the notebook. Seriously misbehaved! And that too with a school girl! Earlier I was a little relaxed that I was not party to the crime. I was not happy that I had been subjected to the caning, but the letter made me look like a criminal.

I tried wiping my face, but the sweat continued to pour. I knew that phrases like 'serious misbehaviour' were dangerous and the event may even get reported in the local newspaper. The police would arrive in no time then. This is what had happened to Manjrekar Sir. The police then take you into custody and hammer you black and blue. They must have done the same to sir despite him being innocent. A few days back some of the boys had made cat calls seeing the girls from Tope High School near Anand Talkies. The local faujdar had rounded up the boys and beat them up. He had made them shave their heads. We may be sent to the remand home as we were juveniles. That's it! We would be housed there with criminals—pickpockets, thieves and so on. Then I might as well forget school or anything else in future.

I turned around to see Surya looking at me. I knew he too had read the letter. His situation was worse than mine.

The boys gathered around us in mid-break. I had kept the letter back into the bag, but Surya's letter lay on the table. Phawdya read it, followed by Santya and then Harishchandra. Teredesai and Bibikar came in to enquire, followed by Ghasu Gokhale, but Phawdya threatened them and shooed them off saying, 'Get lost, you all! There is nothing for you to know'. They left. Sarwate and Deshpande were sitting in the classroom, eating from their tiffin boxes, but there was no one else.

'My dad will kill me,' Surya said in a hoarse voice. He then put his head on table and started sobbing.

We did not know how to react. We had never seen Surya cry. But it was true. Anyone in his place would be scared like him. Surya's father was a terror. I realized there would be chaos when I showed the letter at home. Baba may not spank me but he would be very upset. Aaisaheb would make a hue and cry. I was not sure how I would raise the topic. I would have to explain everything to them. I had done nothing wrong, but I would have to tell them everything; why we assembled at the building, who Kevda was and so on and so forth. I started sweating again. I tried using my handkerchief to wipe my face, but it was already drenched.

'I will have to run away from home,' Surya said, wiping his face with his shirt sleeve.

His comment made us sit up. We knew that he was really scared.

'Come on. Let us not sit here,' Phawdya said. 'Let us go and sit in the woods.'

We went and sat in the shade of the trees.

'Don't show him the letter,' Santya suggested.

'Appa would send Ganoba immediately,' Surya said. 'I cannot avoid showing him that.'

'You tell your father that you did not do anything.'

'My father is not a chutiya. He would not bother to ask why he has been called,' Surya explained. 'Ichibhana, I can't go home.'

'Then where will you go?' Harishchandra asked.

'I will go and stay with my mavshi in Kharpada.'

'Sure! Go! That mavshi's husband will be the first one to bring you here.'

That shut him up for a while. He had no place to hide.

'What made Appa get so wild?' Harishchandra asked.

'That's what is surprising,' Surya said. He looked at me

and asked, 'Yaar, what crime did we commit? We did not touch her. She's lying through her teeth that I held her hand.'

'That's right. But Appa never hears us out first.'

'But what do I tell my father? He won't believe me one bit. I cannot escape the beating today.'

I was silent for a while. We needed to do something. There *had* to be a way for Surya to escape his father's wrath. But the matter would become more complex if he ran away.

'Do one thing,' I said, my mind racing in circles. 'Don't mention the letter at all. Tell him Appa has called him for some discussion.'

'But won't he get to know when Appa tells him that? He would beat me up then and there.'

'Then do one thing,' I continued. 'Tell him that a girl is falsely accusing you and that you never did anything, but Appa has called him to discuss the case.'

'Yes! That's a good idea,' Phawdya agreed. 'You say that he needs to come to the school and when he asks you why, say that Appa wants to discuss this matter.'

'My father is not like yours,' Surya said. 'He will not believe me.'

'But you need to explain the situation to reduce the punishment,' I said.

Surya was not convinced.

'I think I will run away,' he said. 'I will hide somewhere and return after a few days.'

'Very good!' I said. 'These people will inform the police that you are absconding. Your family will lodge a complaint with the police that you have gone missing. The police will be searching for you all over. It is better that you tell your father the truth.'

'He is right!' Harishchandra said. 'It is not good to land the tag of an absconding criminal.'

'What do you mean he is right?' Surya said. 'I am in this situation thanks to *his* advice.'

'What do you mean my advice?' I asked. 'Did I not say let us not rush?'

'But the idea was yours to begin with.'

'Yes, but that does not mean you have to implement it immediately. I too am stuck. I too have got the letter.'

'Hey, don't fight, okay?' Phawdya said. 'We need to plan the next steps.'

'Next steps?' Surya asked. 'Ichibhana, the next step is to get hammered. I got bashed up today and will get beaten up tomorrow too.'

We were quiet for a while. Despite the shade in the woods, it was getting hot. My palms were not hurting as much but the marks showed. Surya's body must be aching, but he was more worried about what he would undergo next.

'Joshi, let us go and drink some water,' Chitre said.

It was a good excuse and I stood up immediately.

'Joshi, saale! Why did you have to act so smart?' he said, the moment we got to the playground. 'Look what you have got yourself into?'

'Arre! We did not do anything. He just asked her out.'

'But did you not advise him to ask her?'

'What else could I do? You know how he is. I thought if he asks her once and she refuses, he won't bother her any more.'

'Don't tell me! You screwed up the whole thing.'

'No. I mean it. I felt it would end the issue forever.'

I was being honest, but Chitre did not believe me. We drank water at the taps.

'You are lucky that you were absent. Had you been there, he would have you come along too. Imagine, what would have happened then!'

He did not reply for a while.

'Now pay for your crimes, you bloody fools!' he muttered. 'You don't know Gupte's father. He is going to teach you a lesson. Surya was trying to act too smart.'

For a moment, I was tempted to request Chitre to go and plead on my behalf to her father stating that I was innocent. But then I realized that it would not help. I had to face the consequences now. Our fathers had been called. Chitre's visit may go against him.

The mid-break was over, but Surya wanted to bunk the remaining classes. We asked him not to do so. He may get caught and that would give Appa one more reason to pull him up. No one could concentrate in the next class. The sun shone intensely and the playground reflected the harsh sunlight. I could clearly see the hills beyond Sonarpada. I kept looking at them for a long time. I dared not look at Shirodkar. I had seen her glance at me once, but the look was not the same as before. She must have been angry with me. The girls meet near the water taps and it was likely that the girls in our class had got the details of the entire episode. In any case, the birdies in our class would be more than curious to find out the gory details. And there was no way to know whether what Shirodkar had heard was the true version or an exaggerated one. I would have to clarify when I met her next.

Time crawled slowly. I was worried of the impending tamasha at home. And what if they handed us over to the police? All kinds of weird images floated before my eyes—of the police taking us away while the school boys stood watching us; of us handcuffed in Appa's office and then being taken home; of everyone in the building coming out to see the spectacle; of Baba, Aaisaheb and Ambabai looking at me with despondent eyes; of them looking helpless; of us being taken to the police station; of Surya getting beaten to pulp in the prison; of me trying to intervene and getting a few blows; of us being asked to confess our crime; of us being taken away to a distant remand home with a huge wall with iron barbs; of us being pushed inside and the door shutting with a bang forever! The thoughts made me shudder.

School got over and I took the path through the fields. I sat down on the rock the moment I reached the paddy fields. I did not have the heart to go home. I was better off in school. I did not feel like going for the tuition either. I dare not look at Shirodkar. Then I realized that it was the last day tuitions and the only chance to meet Shirodkar. I had to meet her and tell her the truth. I had to tell her that I was not at fault. I was merely standing next to Surya. She would otherwise believe that I had accosted Kevda on the road.

I hurriedly stood up. I did not have much time. Luckily, Ambabai was not at home and Aaisaheb was waiting for me; she had to go somewhere. That prevented any discussion and I quickly changed my clothes and left after gulping down a cup of tea.

But Shirodkar had not come to the class. Juvekar and Mande were present but she wasn't.

I could not concentrate in the class. I could have bunked, but it was too late. I could not walk out now. And there was no point in bunking. I could not go to her house. There must have been a reason why she did not come. And going home was out of the question. It was better to postpone death as much as possible.

The class got over a little early. Sir wished us luck for the forthcoming exams and announced that the classes would start again in May. Those already attending classes would be given preference over others, and early birds would get a ten percent discount. Most of the boys had plans to continue there. Pingle asked, 'Are you planning to continue?' I did not answer. He smiled and said, 'Ask her and then let me know. But I hope you come. It will be fun.' The boys were saying their goodbyes and took advantage of the last day to wish the girls too. Juvekar looked at me while leaving and smiled at me muttering 'okay then' as she walked by. I was tempted to ask her why Shirodkar had not come but realized that she too may not know. I could not spot Mande in the crowd. I wondered whether Shirodkar had deliberately bunked the class today to avoid meeting me. Perhaps she did not want to speak to me. Why would she bunk on the last day of the class otherwise? The remaining hope had vanished and I felt completely drained. My legs felt like wax. I somehow managed to reach home.

Baba had returned from office and was having his tea. He was reading the newspaper sitting on the bed. Aaisaheb was busy inside the kitchen while Ambabai was immersed in a book. There was no point in delaying the inevitable. I washed my hands and feet. Then I drank some water but my mouth felt dry. I steeled myself and, going near the bed, said, 'Baba, you have been asked to come to the school tomorrow.'

He looked at me and raised his eyebrows enquiringly.

'You have been called,' I repeated.

'What is the reason?' he asked.

'That Suresh Mhatre from our class—he teased a girl last morning while she was on the way to school.'

'Then?'

'Her father has complained to the headmaster.'

'So? How are we concerned?'

'I was standing next to him. She mentioned my name too. Mhatre's father has been asked to come and you too.'

Baba must have got the jist of the problem. His frown suggested he was lost in thought. Listening to our conversation, Ambabai shouted, 'Aai! Did you hear that?'

Aaisaheb walked in. There was no need to shout. Her ears were too sharp in any case.

'What happened?' she asked, wiping her hands on a towel.

'Listen to our prince's exploits!'

'What happened? Tell me.'

'Nothing. Baba has been asked to come to school tomorrow,' I said.

'Tell her what for?' Ambabai said.

I kept quiet. I knew she would say it on her own accord. She said, 'They have teased one of the girls from school. The headmaster has called father to meet him.'

'I did not do anything,' I said. 'Surya did.'

'Then what were you doing there?'

'I was just standing next to him.'

Baba raised his hand for me to stop. I feared the next question. He asked, 'Have they sent a letter?'

'Yes.'

'Show it to me.'

I took out the letter from my bag and handed it to him. My chest was pounding and legs were shivering. Baba was in the education department. He had correctly surmised that the school would have issued a letter. He read the letter, and his face turned grim.

'Show me,' Aaisaheb said.

Baba handed over the letter without saying a word. Ambabai promptly peeped over to read it out.

'Rascal! Is that why we put you in that school?' Aaisaheb screamed after reading the letter. I was expecting that, but it still took me by surprise.

'What have you done!' she exclaimed.

'Aai, I have done nothing wrong,' I said.

'Nothing wrong? Then why are they writing all this? Serious misbehaviour! Tell me the whole thing from the start.'

I then recounted the entire episode without, obviously, mentioning Surya's dialogue.

'But you were in school, isn't it? Where were you guys standing then?'

'At Mhatre's building.'

'What were you doing there?'

'We assemble there every day before school begins.'

'Assemble? What for?'

I kept quiet. I could not tell her the real reason. As

expected, Ambabai interjected, 'They sit there and tease the girls passing by.'

I did not want to respond to her comment but then I realized that silence would tantamount to admission of guilt.

'Don't blabber,' I said.

'Why? Is she wrong? What did that boy tell her?'

'He asked whether she loves him or not?' I said in a muted voice.

'Oh God! Look at today's children!' Aaisaheb said wide-eyed. It looked like she had seen a ghost. 'Arre! You are so young and you talk of love? Do you even understand the meaning of the word? Or are you imagining yourself to be avatars of Lord Krishna teasing the maids!'

I was tempted to smile. She would have erupted like a volcano had I smiled. I had not expected her to use such an appropriate simile despite her rage. We had not realized that we were behaving like Krishna teasing the gopis. Surya and Phawdya would have been tickled with this comparison. The only thing left to do was throwing stones and breaking their water pots.

Then Aaisaheb opened her canons. It was due for a long time and now she got a golden opportunity. How I was not interested in studies these days; I was in the company of rowdy boys; I was going to the classes to waste time on girls; how I was becoming a brute and a rascal day by day; how we were living in difficult times; how the parents were put to shame thanks to the actions of their sons and how we would be ridiculed by the entire samaj; how the school was to be blamed for bad behaviour including the behaviour displayed by some of the teachers; I was getting everything at home without having to ask for it and had not understood the value of hard earned money and was taking advantage of their goodness; how there was no chance of me becoming an engineer and how the deeds of today were an indication of the marks I was likely to get in matriculation. I felt like a soldier caught in a crossfire. Ambabai continued her job of adding fuel to the fire. She had the official sanction to do so. Baba, as usual, was quiet.

When Aaisaheb's arsenal finally seemed to have emptied, he said, 'What time are we to reach school?'

'Eleven,' I said.

'I will have to take leave,' he muttered. 'Do one thing; go over to Chandorkar's and give him my leave application. Tell him to hand it over in the office. He took out a blank sheet of paper and wrote an application for leave. I handed over the same to Chandorkar kaka when he asked, 'Any problem?'

'No. Just some house work,' I said.

I could not sleep after dinner. Before lying down, I surreptitiously took out the dictionary to see the meaning of the word 'accomplice'. It stated 'partner in crime', 'a person who assits the criminal', 'an assistant'. My legs started to shake again. I was innocent, but they would assume I was helping Surya in committing the crime. And I was aware that if the main accused got life imprisonment, the accomplice was awarded rigorous imprisonment. They would love to teach both of us a lesson. On top of it, Baba would have to listen to the barbs of having bought up a criminal at home. He was a government official and would have no option but to listen quietly. I remember once Aaisaheb had asked Baba not to join the agitation against the lack of drinking water supply because he was a government officer and it was not right for him to take part in such morchas. The thought made me feel worse.

I woke up the next morning to find Baba, Aaisaheb and Ambabai having tea at the table and talking. I continued to pretend I was sleeping.

'I am unable to understand what Mukund is upto,' Aaisaheb said.

'He is in bad company,' Ambabai added. 'I had told you—not to put him in that school.'

'All schools are the same. They are involved in every activity but studies.'

'This school is a little too much,' Ambabai added.

'Next year is critical,' Aaisaheb continued. 'If this fellow continues to behave so, I shudder to think what will happen. Perhaps we should change his school.'

'Will you please listen?' Baba said. 'There is nothing so dramatic about it. Boys at this age behave so. One need not fear the worst.'

'The problem is he does not fear you,' Aaisaheb said. 'You need to take action at the right time. Else it will be too late.'

We left at half past ten. We could have left ten minutes before eleven, but Baba decided to leave early. We took the route through the paddy fields. There was no danger of meeting anyone known to us had we taken the main road, but I wanted to play safe. I walked a few steps ahead of Baba. I used to walk next to him and, in fact, when I was small I would hold his hand. But that was a long time back.

We reached the fields. The sun was bright. There was

no grass anywhere. There was no one in the fields. The woods seemed quiet too. I walked along the rocks when Baba called out to me. I stopped and Baba came near me. He put his arm around my shoulders and asked in a quiet voice, 'Mukund, tell me honestly. Tell me exactly what happened?'

I looked around for a moment and then recounted the entire episode without hiding anything. I repeated what Surya had told Kevda.

'What did the headmaster say?' he asked.

'He called us because her father had complained.'

'And then?'

'He caned us.'

'You too?'

'Yes. I was caned on my palms. Surya took the blows on his back, arms, everywhere. His shirt was torn.'

'And what else did he say?'

'He said, "accosting girls on the road? Aren't you ashamed?"' He then suggested that we get our fathers to school. But Gupte's father was insistent on lodging a complaint with the police. But Baba, it is not true that Surya held her hand. He did nothing of the sort. He was standing a few feet away from her. He just asked her out and when she refused, he turned back and went away. And these guys are talking about handing us over to the police.'

I started sobbing. The tears flowed freely. I had not felt like crying when Appa berated us or when Aaisaheb scolded me. But in the middle of the paddy fields, with silence all around, I was unable to hold back my tears. I could not speak. I realized I was missing Shirodkar as I walked through the paddy fields.

'Don't cry,' Baba said, hugging me. He then took out his handkerchief and wiped my tears. We stood there for a while and then walked to school.

The morning batch was yet to get over and the classes were in full swing. I could hear the students reciting a poem in one class. The playground was empty. It felt like I had walked into a different school.

While walking towards Appa's room, we met Prem Chopra on the way. He was probably not aware of the issue and arched his eyebrows enquiringly seeing me with Baba. Baba did not react and I kept my head down. Ganoba was sitting outside Appa's room on a bench.

'Is the Headmaster in?' Appa asked.

'Yes. He is in,' Ganoba said. That fellow knew what had happened, in any case.

Kevda's father was present when we stepped in. She stood in one corner. Appa stood up seeing Baba and said, 'Joshi saheb, please come in. Take a seat.'

I was not sure what I was supposed to do—whether to stand there or wait outside. But I did not want to go out on my own. My heart was beating hard. Luckily Baba rescued me saying, 'You wait outside.'

I went out. There was space on Ganoba's bench, but I did not sit there. I stood reading the notices on the bulletin board. Luckily Appa's door is covered with a curtain. Earlier there was a swinging wooden door, which would squeak every time someone passed through. They later replaced it with a curtain.

Surya came in soon, followed by his father. I could not recognize him! His face was swollen and looked black and blue. His eyes were half-shut and there was a bump on his forehead. He had applied some kind of cream on the swollen area. He was limping and looked weak. I was scared to death seeing his condition. His father was wearing his usual white shirt and trousers. The shirt buttons near the neck were open, as always. A gold chain hung around his neck. His eyes, as usual, were red.

'Is the master in?' he asked in his gruff voice.

'Yes, yes,' Ganoba said, getting up hurriedly. He moved the curtain aside for him to step in. He did not step in immediately. He stood there and folded his hands in namaskar when Appa responded, 'Come in, come in, Mhatre sheth'. He then removed his chappals and walked in.

Surya stayed back outside with me. Kevda joined us soon. She was taken aback seeing Surya's condition. She looked at us, but we did not say anything. She then went and sat next to Ganoba, fiddling with the handkerchief.

We could hear snatches of the conversation inside. Appa was recounting the episode while Kevda's father intervened a few times. The voices were not very clear. Then Surya's father said in a loud voice, 'But, Sir, do you know the punishment I have given to that fellow? I bashed him well and proper. You have not seen him?' He shouted looking at the door, 'Come in!'

We heard him but did not move. Appa rang the bell on his table. Ganoba stood up saying, 'You have been asked to go in.' My chest was pounding. To be fair, Surya alone had been summoned, but I accompanied him.

'See! I have given him a nice treatment with my fists and legs,' Surya's father said, nudging Kevda's father ahead to observe Surya clearly. 'Teasing girls, eh? If you want I will hammer him again. Sir, give me your cane.'

Appa did not oblige.

'Leave it.'

'Don't leave it. We cannot leave it. I will kill this bastard.'

'Leave it, Mhatre sheth. Leave it,' Appa repeated.

Surya's state was evident. He stood there, his head down and legs bent a little.

'There is no point in beating him up,' Kevda's father said. 'These boys are thick-skinned. They are used to beatings. We need to hand them over to the police. They can be cured only in a remand home.'

Baba was silent until then, but hearing Kevda's father, he said in a clear voice, 'Gupte saheb, do you think our boys are orphans?'

That stopped Kevda's father in his tracks. Appa and Surya's father looked at Baba.

'Then what do you suggest?' Kevda's father was agitated. 'These guys dare to hold a girl's hand in broad daylight. What should one do? Should that not be taken care of?'

'Just a moment!' Baba said. His voice was clear and steady. 'I agree the boy made a mistake. But he did not hold her hand. Ask her.'

Kevda was called in. She went and stood near her father, her head bent.

'Beti, don't be afraid.' Appa said. 'Tell me clearly. What happened there?'

'I was on the way to school when I saw him standing on the road. He asked me whether I would come out with him and I said no.'

'Then what happened?'

'He turned back and went away.'

'Did he hold your hand?' Baba asked.

'No.'

'Was he standing a few feet away?'

'Yes.'

'See?' Baba remarked. 'It is not what you are making it out to be.'

'Did he not hold your hand?' Appa asked.

Kevda shook her head.

'Then why did you say he held her hand?' Appa asked her father.

'Perhaps he did not hold her hand. But it does not change the situation.'

'No. I don't think so,' Baba said, his voice steady. He turned towards us and said, 'You go and stand outside.'

We went out but stood near the curtain. We could hear everything being discussed inside.

'I agree the boys have made a mistake,' Baba said. 'But we need to clearly understand the mistake. He asked whether she loves him. She said no. That's it! Did he trouble her further? No.'

'It is not as flippant as you are making it out to be,' Kevda's father said, his voice loud and angry.

'I agree,' Baba said. 'But there is no point in stretching it further. They are at a confused age. Children err, but that does not mean we throw them into jail for such mistakes.'

We wanted to hear more, but Ganoba realized what we were up to and asked us to move away. Kevda too had come out of the room. Ganoba indicated to the bench and said, 'Sit there.'

We could not hear the discussion any further.

Baba and Surya's father came out after quite a wait. We stood up on seeing them. They walked down the corridor and stepped down into the playground. We followed them. Baba walked a few steps and then said, as we approached them, 'What time does your school begin?'

'Twelve-forty,' I said.

'You are carrying your books, aren't you? Go and sit in your class. And focus on your studies, okay? You cannot be pardoned every time, understood?'

We nodded and continued to look down. Baba looked at Surya and then, putting his arm around Surya's father's shoulder, said, 'Mhatre sheth, you should not beat up your son like this. We need to explain things to them. Your son is a tiger. Don't treat him like dirt.'

Surya's father looked at Surya for a while and suddenly burst out crying. 'Saheb, what can I tell you?' he said. 'I lost my mind last night. I did not know what to do. Luckily his mother stepped in, else I might have killed him.'

'Please pull yourself together. Things cannot be resolved with physical punishment alone.'

'He is my only son,' Surya's father said, wiping his tears. 'I never went to school. Should he not study sincerely? But look at his antics!'

'He will learn to study,' Baba said. 'But don't beat him up unnecessarily. Else you will lose him forever. Go, both of you. And go to your class directly, okay?'

They left. Kevda and her father came out. She was wearing her school uniform but was not carrying her books. We ignored her. We went and sat down in the wooded area. The morning batch was yet to get over. The shade felt cool. We both sat there for a while without saying a word.

'Did you get a lot of beating?' I asked. 'What did you tell your father?'

'He was out to kill me,' Surya said. 'I went home and told him that he had been asked to come to school. That's it! He started beating me up. He stopped when a customer came to buy some sand. I thought I had a lucky escape, but he beat me up again at night.'

I inspected his hands and feet. He must have been in great pain. He had red marks all over his arms and legs.

'He beat me with whatever he could lay his hands on,' Surya said. 'First he hit me with his hands and then with his belt. Then he picked up a stick and then a bamboo. Aai intervened, but she too got a few kicks. Luckily kaka came in and saved both of us. I was lucky not to have broken any bones.'

I did not know what to say. There was a bitter taste in my mouth. The whole thing had turned ugly.

'What will Appa do now?' Surya asked.

'Nothing. What else is there to do now?'

'Won't he throw us out of school?'

'Tchah! Nothing of that sort.'

'Ichibhana, why did Kevda's father get so angry?'

I had no answer. He had asked a valid question, but I had no way of knowing why.

'I am confused. I don't know what mistake we made, Ichibhana? We had just asked her. What is wrong with asking?'

I had no answer to his question. He was absolutely right. But there was no way to know a girl's mind. We sat there for a while, lost in our own thoughts. I felt sad for Surya. I could see the school boys on the ground now, but I did not feel like mingling with them. I did not feel like attending classes either. But there was no choice. It was sad that this had to happen at the fag end of the year. A deep sense of sadness filled me.

The morning batch got over. The boys had already gone into the classrooms. We did not feel like getting up.

'I don't feel like attending school today,' Surya said. 'I wish I could lie down here.'

I felt the same but knew it was not possible. All the teachers would be looking out for us. And if we bunked, that would be the end of it.

The bell rang and we reluctantly stood up, dusting our trousers.

Surya said, 'Ichibhana, your advice turned out to be expensive.'

I felt a lump in my throat.

We knew what to expect in the class. Most of the boys were shocked to see Surya's condition. Paranjpe ma'am came in and the boys did not get a chance to talk. The girls saw him and began whispering amongst themselves. Shirodkar too joined them. She turned back to glance and our eyes met briefly. I thought she wanted to ascertain whether I too had been beaten up. But I could see no hint of recognition in her eyes. Surya sat hiding behind the boys, but ma'am spotted him when she saw the girls turning back to look at him. She asked, 'What happened? Did you have a fight?' The poor soul had no idea what Surya had gone through.

Surya had no answer. He sat there with his head down. Bendre ma'am came in next. All the teachers asked the same question of Surya. Later, during the mid-break, they must have got the details in the staff room. Zende sir came near him to inspect the wounds but did not comment.

The next few classes continued as usual, but our mind was elsewhere. Everything seemed lost—like a painting spoilt when you spill water on it accidentally. Earlier we used to be relaxed in the class. No one would dare answer back at us. But now we felt like hiding our faces. Zende sir cracked some jokes and Halbe sir, as usual, lost track of himself trying to solve some equations, but we did not feel like laughing. I sat there like a criminal, trying to avoid the teachers. I could see the hills beyond the playground, but they seemed to have taken on a dull, grey haze, like a rainless cloud. I was dreading the mid-break. All the boys would surround us and bombard us with umpteen questions. Guys like Bibikar, Ghasu Gokhale and Teredesai would express false sympathies but would be secretly happy about our pathetic state. They would be pleased that we had been taught a lesson. We went and sat in the wooded area but did not enjoy sitting there. Surya started describing the way his father beat him up, but no one encouraged him to continue. I was eager to go back to the class so that I could escape talking to anyone. I somehow managed to spend the next few hours and then walked back home through the paddy fields. I realized that Chitre had not spoken a word to me on his own and that Shirodkar had not once glanced at me.

When I reached home I found that Aaisaheb had kept the tea and biscuits ready on the table. Ambabai had gone off somewhere. Baba was not there. Aaisaheb seemed to be in a decent mood. Baba must have told her everything. He must have asked her not to trouble me any more. She did not say anything while I finished my tea but then stood up saying,

'Take your books and get down to studying right away. You don't have tuition, isn't it? There is no need to go out anywhere. Study till dinner time, understood?'

She did not seem angry, but her tone prevented me from saying anything. I wanted to step out and walk around Shirodkar's house on the pretext of meeting Chitre. But I dropped the idea. Luckily Aaisaheb had not told me which subject to study. I put my head down keeping the History book open. I could not concentrate. Nikam kaka's TV was blaring away at full volume. But then Napoleon took the better of me and I concentrated on the task at hand.

School ran for another week. There was no question of going to the adda now. Surya's father had locked the room upstairs and the teacher who had taken the lower room on rent had now started taking tuitions there. We walked on our own to school without any pranks on the way. Chitre and Phawdya often came in together. We had the Scouts' exam on Saturday. The Guides' had their exams too on the same day, but the girls sat far away.

The teachers completed their syllabus and started revisions. Appa announced a free period once and made the entire school sing songs dedicated to Emergency. Then he gave us the usual lecture on how we should focus on our studies because the exams were approaching. It was the last period and everyone was bored. So we tolerated it in silence. The tension of the impending exams was evident. The birdies were spending the mid-breaks immersed in textbooks. Shirodkar continued to be indifferent. No one played any pranks. We had decided to spend the rest of the days quietly.

On the last day of school, I stepped out of home on an excuse to visit Chitre. I reached the lane leading to Shirodkar's house and walked about slowly. The window in her verandah was open, but I could not see anyone. I was taking another round when I saw Sandeep. He had probably come out to collect some stones. But he did not look at the gate. For a moment I thought of visiting them. After all, I had already been there once. No one would object and I would be able to meet her. I could spend some time talking to her mother even if Shirodkar was not there. I was sure she would not have mentioned the Kevda episode to anyone at home. But I could not get myself to open the gate and step in. My heart was beating wildly and the hollow in my stomach grew. I had to meet her—at least once before the exams. I had to tell her what exactly had happened—that I was not at fault. But I could not see her. I walked up and down her lane a few times and, when darkness fell, I walked back home.

School was over and I was under the constant supervision of Aaisaheb and Ambabai. They would not allow me to leave the house. I had the permission to sit in the verandah in the evenings. But there was no one to play with. Nikam kaka's TV would be on all the time, which I would watch for a while. But I was not comfortable sitting in that crowd. KT and Vijay would have visitors. They held their meeting once, but they did not call me. Ambabai would be on guard after returning from college and Aaisaheb would take charge of me in the morning. She had decided to stay put and had stopped going out, except to buy vegetables in the evening.

I was unable to concentrate on the first day. But then I realized that there was no escaping this and I might as well concentrate on my studies. I would be able to extricate myself from their grip only if I secured a rank among the top five. They would not spare me if I got low marks and my rank slipped. They would not only change my school but put me under house arrest. I would be tortured to death. In any case, it was just a matter of another year. I need not bother about anyone once I clear class ten. I decided not to think of Shirodkar. Let her not speak to me. I would now focus on getting my rank. If possible, I would try for the first rank. It would put Bibikar and Ghasu Gokhale back in their place. I would collect my results proudly, and then she would be forced to look at me. It is said that fame is the fragrance of heroic deeds, isn't it? Let me try that!

That spurred me on. I was reminded of a poem we had in school last year—'a lone star to reach for and fire below the feet.' I focused my attention on nothing but my studies. I would wake up in the morning and immediately sit down to study. I did not ask for tea or breakfast or lunch. I had forgotten everything—Baba, Aaisaheb, Ambabai, the people in the building, Surya, Phawdya, Chitre—even Shirodkar. My focus was to revise one chapter after another—whether Napoleon or Magna Carta. I was lost in the different types of winds in Geography and the process of making Hydrogen Sulphide in Chemistry. Archimedes and Newton gave me company while various insects fascinated me in Biology. I was engrossed in linear equations, Trigonometry and Algebra.

The examinations began. We had a paper each day between eleven and two. We had the eighth standard children for company. Shirodkar was not in my room. We had a few girls like Achrekar, Dongre, and Ambekar, who had come in only to appear for the exams. I was hoping to meet and wish her luck for the exams, but she was with other girls in the next room and I dared not speak to her in their presence. Mirikar came in to wish Achrekar and, while going out, she wished Bibikar too. Ghasu Gokhale was busy poring into his book, so she did not speak to him. She would have wished me too, but I avoided her eyes. Surya sat in the row ahead of me, so there was no question of him anything during the exams. Phawdya was in the rows behind me, but he did not bother me. At the most, he would ask for answers to 'match the following'. Chitre was in the same row as Surya, but it was upto him to help.

I attacked the paper the moment the teacher handed it to us. Usually, I was the first person to ask for supplements. In fact, Ghasu Gokhale and Bibikar gave me a surprised look, seeing me ask for the additional sheets so early in the hour. I would have enjoyed writing the paper had Shirodkar been in our class. The Chemistry and Physics papers were a bit tough and so was Geometry. Hindi was difficult, but on the whole the exams went off well. At home, I would be asked the same question every day and I would say, 'I have done well'. Obviously, they would not believe me, but I did not care.

We would rush home after every paper. But, as per our ritual, we did meet after the last exam. No one refused Bhaishetye when he joined in.

'I am not sure of my performance,' Phawdya said the

moment we sat down. 'I got screwed in Algebra and Geometry.'

'Me too,' Harishchandra said.

'I am dead in History,' Santya said.

'And I am dead in everything,' Surya said.

'Chemistry was a little tough,' I said in order to add to the conversation.

'Joshi, saale, you had no time to look around. You were scribbling away with your head down,' Surya said. 'Looks like you had been nicely bambooed at home.'

I kept quiet and did not answer.

'Aai has warned me—if I fail I will have to quit school,' Phawdya said. 'I will have to sit at the shop then. We have been given a permanent shed in the vegetable market now.'

'Good for you,' Surya said. 'My dad is forcing me to attend school at least until the tenth standard. Even if I fail, he will not allow me to quit.'

'My dad does not bother at all,' Santya said. 'They are planning to marry off Sundri next month.'

'Sundri's wedding?' I asked.

'You bet! I will invite all of you. You will get to eat some mutton. Joshi, will you eat?'

'I will eat Joshi's share,' Surya said. 'Just ensure that we are invited.'

'Naru mama is getting married too,' I said. 'We are leaving next week.'

'Aila, so he is finally getting married, is it?' Phawdya said. 'Are we not invited?'

'Why do you need a formal invitation?'

'Who are the teachers next year, yaar?' Harishchandra asked.

'Next year? Kendalkar will surely take Maths,' Chitre surmised. 'And Bendre, English.'

'We are screwed, bhenchod,' Surya said.

'What about Zende sir?' Harishchandra asked.

'Zende sir will be there,' Surya said. 'But what can he do alone? Manjrekar sir is gone.'

'And that pain-in-the-neck Prem Chopra will be there. Kendalkar sir is tolerable, but Prem Chopra is bad news.'

'We won't have Rajguru sir. No Drawing classes next year.'

'What about Paranjpe ma'am? 'Surya asked. 'Hope she's there; at least something to look forward to.'

'We have all the difficult teachers next year,' Chitre said. 'Appa—to start with.'

'Which classroom are we being allotted?' Santya asked. 'Hope not that bloody caged one inside.'

'Exactly that,' I said. 'The current Ten-B is there. One cannot see anything outside from it.'

'Next year is going to be a pain in the ass, saala,' Phawdya said. 'Tenth! Each and everyone will be sitting on our heads.'

We were relaxed as the exams were over now, but the very thought of the next year was suffocating. But I was fine. Until the time Shirodkar was around, I did not care whether the classes were held here or in Andamans!

'Screw the next year,' Surya said. 'First we have to clear this year. Hey, how many subjects are we allowed to fail in, without losing the whole year?'

'Three,' Chitre answered. 'I think they should promote everyone to tenth standard. We have studied for ten years.

Is that not enough? Whoever wants to go ahead can appear for the exams.'

'I agree, Ichibhana,' Surya added.

'But who is going to listen to us?' Phawdya asked. 'They don't run schools based on our recommendations.'

'You start a school when you grow up,' Santya advised. 'You can take Chitre as an advisor.'

That broke the tension. We all laughed out loud. Then Surya started singing one of his ribald songs and Santya joined in. We asked Bhaishetye to recount his tales of Bhaween, and Phawdya later sang an abhang. The atmosphere was gay and light. Time, like the rapidly receding sunlight, flew without notice.

Ambabai and Aaisaheb had no excuse to hold me back at home now that the exams were over. Besides they got busy with the preparations for Naru mama's wedding. Luckily Aaisaheb was on the groom's side, so the responsibilities were fewer. She would leave five or six days in advance. At first, I was not keen to accompany her. I had already made my plans for those days. It was an ideal time to visit Shirodkar, but ever since Surya's prank, I had decided to take it easy. A good rank in the exams was sure to make things easier for me. I had the entire month of May to myself. Aaisaheb would leave within a few days and the results would be announced by the end of the month. So I changed my mind and decided to accompany her. Naru mama's company was fun and I had Ashok, Gaikwad's son, as a companion. There was a sugar factory there and, adjacent to the professor's colony, there were sugarcane fields.

I had, of course, not stopped going over to Shirodkar's lane. The very first day I spotted Misal and quickly made up the excuse of coming over to meet him. He had come out to buy some groceries and I had to accompany him to the shop. I spent a little time with him and then returned home. The next day, I walked through the lane to find no activity around the house. They were, in all likelihood, not at home. Another day, I spotted her walking the verandah and was tempted to visit them but somehow could not get myself to do so. I would not have minded meeting her outside. But the opportunity never arose.

I visited Chitre a few times and once Phawdya's stall too. Chitre seemed very quiet. He told me that Kevda's father had decided to put her in a different school. Chitre's mother was planning to move to Bandra near their mavshi's house. It would suit her as her office was much closer from Bandra. The arguments between his parents continued and her mother had made up her mind to move to Bandra irrespective of whether Chitre's father joined them or not. Chitre had spoken to Devaki about his mother and she had fired her. Chitre seemed a little uncertain of his future.

That day, while returning from Chitre's house, I met KT, Ashok and Vijay at the Gyanjyoti library. They had another friend with them. They seemed to be waiting for someone. It was not yet dark and I could see the road clearly. They stood in one corner. I saw them and stopped.

'What, Mukund? Returning from your usual bird watching?' Vijay asked.

'Yes,' I said. 'What are you guys doing here?'

'The same,' he said, laughing. 'There is lots to see here.'

'Are your exams over?' KT asked.

'Yes.'

'Then what's the plan?'

'We have to go for Naru mama's wedding,' I said.

'Aila, he is finally getting married, is it? Where is the girl from?'

'From his town.'

'How come he has not invited us?' KT asked. 'We need to catch him when he comes next.'

'The invitation will follow,' I said. 'Else I will hand it over to you. But you should come.'

'No. We will accept the invitation only from Narya.'

They spoke to me, but their eyes were on the road. They seemed to be waiting for something or someone important. KT glanced at his watch a couple of times.

'Are they coming?' their friend asked. 'It is already ten minutes late. Hope there is no problem.'

'They will come,' KT said.

'Are you waiting for someone?' I asked.

'Our friends,' Vijay said.

'Off to a movie?' I asked.

'Yes.'

I stood there with them. It felt good, standing there like an adult, without a care in the world. We could watch the people pass by. A couple of college girls went by, looking at us and giggling. It was getting a little dark and the lights in the shops were coming on one by one.

'Mukund, you carry on,' Ashok said, his tone a little serious. 'We are busy. You go home. Don't wait here.'

I looked at Vijay and KT and they nodded their heads. They looked a little tense. Their friend seemed anxious and had raised himself on his toes to look at the other end of the road. There seemed to be some sort of noise coming from the other end of the road.

I was about to move when KT said, looking at Vijay, 'Ask him to convey the message. You may not be able to.'

'How can I tell?' Vijay asked. 'Why don't you tell?'

KT thought for a moment. He then put his arms around my shoulder and said, his voice assuming a serious tone,

'Mukund, ask your sister not to fancy Vijay. We are not sure of our future. She should not waste her time.'

For a moment, I did not register the meaning of his words. Then it struck me. Ambabai liked Vijay. Ambabai! I could not believe my ears. I looked at Vijay. He glanced at his watch and then smiled at me.

I was about to ask a question when their friend said, 'Let him go. I think they have arrived.'

'Okay, you go,' KT said. They were watching the other end of the road. The buzzing noise increased in its intensity.

I moved away a little but stood near Parsekar's shop watching the road, hiding behind a few oil barrels kept on the footpath. Soon I could hear slogans.

'Emergency Murdabad!'

'Murdabad, murdabad!'

'Hatao, Hatao. Emergency Hatao!'

A group of five or six men walked by, shouting the slogans loudly. Everyone stopped to look at them. I could recognize two of them though their names eluded me. I had seen them in our building.

Ashok, KT, Vijay and their friend joined the group. Their slogans got louder. They urged the men on the road, 'What are you staring at? Join us.'

'Emergency murdabad!'

Vijay pumped his fists in the air and shouted. I had never seen him shout loudly. The others repeated the lines. They stood near the library shouting for a while and then moved ahead. The slogans continued.

I was tempted for a moment to join them. I may not know their slogans, but I could always shout, 'Bharat mata ki jay', or something like that. But I stood rooted there. I was a bit scared. Their voices faded as they moved away. It was dark and the lights were on all over now. I remembered they had asked me to go home.

KT's words rang in my ears. Ambabai had fallen for Vijay! No one knew about this except Vijay, KT and Ashok. She had turned out to be a chupa rustam! I had been fooled. Then I remembered instances that connected the dots—she would come out and watch whenever Vijay played carrom or chess. She would often visit Jyoti vahini upstairs and they would stand in the gallery and talk. Now her secret was out! She could not try her dadagiri on me any more.

I met Ponkshe kaka's son Kiran on the way and told him what Vijay, KT and Ashok were upto. He was surprised and said, 'Aila, really? Let us go and inform Appa.' Ponkshe kaka was watching TV, sitting bare-chested as usual. Kiran and I described what I had just seen. Others had gathered by then.

'These guys have finally decided to take the matter in their own hands!' Ponkshe kaka exclaimed. 'I had been telling them—don't get involved in all this. But they won't listen to me. We are scared but they are young. If they don't take up these issues, who else will? Shabbash! But shouting slogans will not help. We need to burst bombs! Bombs!'

Ambabai stood at the door. Aaisaheb joined her.

'What happened?' she asked the moment I stepped in.

I went in and gave an exaggerated version of the entire episode. I described it in great detail, adding unnecessary drama to it. I deliberately mentioned Vijay four or five times. I was keen to see Ambabai's reaction. She seemed scared. I realized that I was overdoing it. This knowledge was an ace up my sleeve. My trump card! I had to use it once and at the most opportune moment. Trying to be oversmart, haan? Telling me how to behave? I will teach her a lesson now!

Aaisaheb heard the whole thing but did not comment.

'Such young guys! Why do they get into all this?' she muttered.

Ambabai did not respond and continued with her work.

I could not sleep. I was surprised at the recent discovery of Ambabai's affair. I was angry at myself for having not discovered it on my own. I thought her a simpleton, but she had turned out to be smarter than all of us! The unsaid rule was not to try and have a fling with anyone in the building, but she had boldly gone and tried to woo the guy one floor above. But now I had a weapon in my hands. I would use Vijay's name and gauge her reaction. It was one thing to be seen chatting with girls in the class and another to flirt with the boy next door! Ambabai would be willing to allow me any liberties to prevent me from telling Aaisaheb. I could stop her from troubling me once and for all. She would be forever a slave to me.

I thought of ways to trap her, but then I realized there was nothing wrong with liking someone. I should be, in fact, helping her. Vijay was a good fellow and a friend to boot. Ambabai had two more years of college left. Aaisaheb would start searching for a suitable groom for her. I had heard her tell Ponkshe kaku to be on the lookout. If things boded well for Ambabai, it would clear a path for me too. I needed to find a way to help her rather than tease her. She was nice except for her constant nagging. But now she would not nag. She would be my friend.

I dozed off dreaming of nice times.

The police came in the morning. I was sitting in the verandah reading a newspaper while Ponkshe kaka had just finished his bath and was roaming around bare-chested, rubbing his sacred thread against his back. Nikam kaku had stepped out to clear the garbage and Upasni aaji had spread out a dhurrie to dry out the sewais. Sudhakar Mayekar stood at the door step, sipping tea.

They were three of them in plain clothes. We did not recognize them immediately. They dismounted from their bicycles and stood there watching. For a moment, I thought they had come visiting Nikam kaka. I had seen such men come to his house, but Nikam kaka did not seem to know them. Ponkshe kaka had a doubt and asked, 'Whom do you want?'

'Those boys who stay here—where are they?' one of them asked. He was wearing a striped shirt, which hung outside his trousers.

'Which boys?' Ponkshe kaka asked.

'They hold meetings here.'

'We don't know,' Ponkshe kaka said, fiddling with his sacred thread. 'No one holds meetings here.'

'Please watch how you speak,' the man said. 'We are policemen.'

'If you are policemen, why do you ask us?' Ponkshe kaka shouted. 'Why don't you find out yourselves?'

'Sir, please don't shout,' the other man said.

'Why? What will you do? Will you arrest me?' Ponkshe kaka said, his voice taking on an edge. Then go ahead. Arrest me. I am ready. Take me and throw me into a jail as you are doing to many others. Huh!'

'Arre, kaka; just tell us one thing,' the striped shirt fellow said. 'Just point us to the room where K T Dhawade, Vijay Deshmukh and Ashok Sutar stay. That's all. They were arrested last night for shouting slogans against the government. We have to search their room. Show us their room.'

'It is in the corner on the first floor,' Ponkshe kaka said. 'But do you have a search warrant?'

'Yes, we do. Here, we will open it in your presence.'

By then all the residents had come out. Ambabai was combing her hair and Baba was putting on his office clothes. Aaisaheb asked him not to go out. Nikam kaka, Sukhtankar, Shenvi, Upadhye, Karadkar and our neighbour Mandke had all gathered. Everyone was home as it was still early.

'We need two witnesses,' the man with the striped shirt said. He told Ponkshe kaka, 'You come along, kaka. I will open the door in your presence. Who else will come?'

He turned and spotted Sudhakar Mayekar. He wanted to duck, but Ponkshe kaka said, 'Sure, come on. I am not scared. Sudhakar, you come.'

'No, I am getting late,' he said.

'Arre, come on! What are you scared of? These boys are in jail and you are scared to be a witness? Come on.'

They climbed to the first floor. We followed them. The man in the striped shirt unlocked the door and got in without removing his shoes, followed by Ponkshe kaka and Sudhakar. We stood outside. I could see everything from the door.

They turned everything upside down but could not find anything. There was nothing to be found. The room was sparse—two iron cots, a few mattresses, some clothes hung on a rope, a few novels, a few suitcases under the bed and a few cooking items like the stove, spoons, pots and utensils on the kitchen counter.

'Come on, there is nothing here,' the man in the striped shirt said. He took out a pad, which had some papers clipped on to it. He wrote something after putting in a carbon paper and asked Ponkshe kaka and Sudhakar to sign.

'Why have you not got one of the boys here along with you?' Ponkshe kaka asked.

'They are not here. They are far away,' he said.

'What are you going to do next?'

'We don't know all that, kaka. We are just doing our job. Government will take care of their hospitality. Don't worry. Nothing will happen to them.'

'Yes. Government will take care of them. Why should we be worried?' Ponkshe kaka retorted.

The man then locked the door and, tying a paper around the lock, sealed it with some sort of wax. The entire procession then went down to the ground floor.

The men cycled away. The other people in the building

too did not speak much. Everyone knew what had happened and expressed their sympathies. Baba finished his meal and left for office. Ambabai's face was pale. She went for a bath and I suspected she may have cried in there, for her eyes were red and swollen when she came out. I pitied her. I felt like telling her that I knew and that she should not be worried. I wanted to tell her that I will help her, but I could not bring myself to say so. She would have got upset. Then she left for college.

I was very upset with the fact that they were arrested and that Ambabai had cried. Ponkshe kaka later told me that the government can keep them in custody for as long as it wishes. The rules were such. There was no telling when they would return. That depressed me further. What would happen to Ambabai and Vijay now?

As planned, Aaisaheb and I left for Naru mama's place. The state transport bus was a direct one. Baba and Ambabai had come to drop us off at the bus station as we had a lot of luggage. We had booked tickets in advance, but we got separate seats. It turned out to be a blessing otherwise I would have been subjected to her sermons all the way. The person sitting next to me offered his window seat to me. Aaisaheb found a talkative co-passenger. She was in a good mood. After all her younger brother was getting married. She kept buying things to eat all through the way. Baba had given me money and I could have bought things on my own, but the situation did not arise.

The bus driver drove well and the bus moved at a good speed. We crossed the industrial area near our town after which the bus entered the hilly area and we crossed a few mountains and valleys. There were farms on both sides of the road and the breeze put me to sleep.

Naru mama received us at the station. He was busy. The relatives were arriving one by one and Aaisaheb was busy exchanging snacks and showing them the things she had got for the wedding. Naru mama took me to one of the bigger shops there and asked me to select cloth for a pair of trousers and a shirt. We gave it for stitching right away, but the tailor there cut the bellbottoms a little too wide and we got the clothes a day after the wedding!

I spent most of the time with Gaikwad's son Ashok. He was a friend and we spent time cycling down to the Shankar temple. One of his friend's father worked in a sugar factory and he took us there. We climbed up the Kanifnath hill. There were sugarcane fields adjacent to the Professors' colony. We discovered a huge stone well over there. Ashok taught me to swim, initially with a tyre around my waist. Within two days, I was able to swim without any support. He introduced me to his girlfriend Sujata Bhosale. Her father too was a professor and they stayed in the same colony. She was good looking but a little short. She was in class eight and now going into ninth standard. Ashok knew her since he was a child and they visited each other's houses often. Ashok had asked me to entertain her with tales of a big city like Mumbai so that he would get to spend more time with her. But I somehow could not do so.

One day, while sitting at the edge of the well drying ourselves, I told him everything about Shirodkar. Everything since the beginning—how I had tried to get to know her, how we used to play word games in the class, how I got caned by Bendre ma'am, how I defeated Mirikar in the chess tournament, the reason for joining tuition classes, the way we used to chat under the peepal tree and how I went over to her house.

'You are a lucky fellow,' he said after listening to me.

'Why? Aren't you lucky?' I asked. 'You are, after all, staying in the same colony.'

'But things are not yet set.'

'Why? What is the problem?'

'We are BC, backward caste, yaar,' he said with a sad face.

I did not answer. The lovely blue sky reflected in the well. Shirodkar's thoughts floated through my mind, leaving a pleasant feeling. I could feel her presence everywhere—while climbing down the Kanifnath hill; while cycling on the road; while pulling sugarcane from the truck passing by; while seeing the hot, bubbling sugarcane juice in the factory boiler; while listening to the shehnai in the wedding hall and while sitting next to Naru mama collecting gift packets. I would smile for no reason and the whole world around me smelt fragrant like rose water.

Aaisaheb had worked for the wedding with great gusto, but her enthusiasm had waned after mami arrived. She had not liked the folks from mami's family. In fact, she was not too appreciative of mami either and, to add fuel to the fire, the saree given by her family to Aaisaheb was quite ordinary. That made her grumpy. What's worse, they had not gifted any saree to Ambabai. I did not find mami remarkable at all. He had introduced me to her praising me—that this nephew was more like a friend; that I was a chess champion and so on. But all she said was a meek

'Is that so?' Naru mama spent all his time in her company. They belonged to the same town and Naru mama had been visiting her every evening until the wedding. After the wedding, he was sure to just stay tied to her pallu. 'Naru is no more one of us,' remarked Aaisaheb. Later, while taking leave, she told Aaji in a resigned voice, 'So that's it! No more "mother's house" for me.'

The three of us came back together. Baba had attended the wedding and left immediately. We had got a three-seater row. Aaisaheb and Ambabai discussed the wedding for a long time—how those folks were street-smart and Naru was a simpleton; how they did this and did not do that; how Aaji would manage now, and many such family matters. I spent my time enjoying the scenery outside. I was feeling good. We were returning home, but the journey and the route seemed new. The results would be announced the next day. And then a month long holiday!

But then Ambabai started her lecture. She started off with describing a dam as we crossed it, and then the discussion moved to her favourite topic. 'Next year is critical—tenth standard,' she began. 'Now you need to forget everything else and focus on studies alone. The syllabus may seem easy, but it is not easy to score marks. You should start tuitions from the day after. I have enquired. We have one Kaduskar in my class. Her father teaches all the subjects. He takes only five students per class, but he has agreed to take you. He teaches at home for two hours daily. You have to join that class immediately. There was no one to guide me like this, but you are lucky to have someone,' and so on.

I looked outside the window to admire the lovely green

sugarcane fields. A few bullock carts passed by. But her sermons continued. I had to find a way to shut her up.

'That Vijay from our building is a nice guy, isn't he?' I said. 'I wonder where he is now.'

She stayed silent for the rest of the journey.

I reached home, washed my hands and feet, had a quick cup of tea, and left. I walked around Shirodkar's lane. Aaisaheb was feeling a bit unsteady after the bus journey and was lying in bed. There was no need to bother about Ambabai, though I took care to give her the excuse of visiting Chitre.

It was evening, but there was still enough light. The lane was silent as usual and there was no activity outside her bungalow. I could not see the door from the lane, but I may have walked in casually had the window been open. I paced the lane a few times, but I could not find any indication of anyone around. Later the landlord upstairs switched on the lamp when it became dark. But the house on the ground floor seemed silent. I was convinced they were not at home. I was keen to visit Chitre, but my feet were aching, so I decided to head back home.

It was vacation time and there would normally be a many people around the carrom and chess boards, but there was no one today. Baba commented that everything had changed. The Shenvis had bought a TV following Nikam kaka's purchase. The crowds assembled in his house these days to watch programmes. Kiran was out of town for some exam or the other while Sudhakar kaka and his wife were out on holiday. The first floor seemed desolate. One of the tubelights was not working and no one had bothered to replace it. In a matter of a fortnight, the building seemed to have lost its soul. Someone had dumped garbage in one corner of the open space.

The results were to be announced at ten, but I got ready much earlier and walked merrily through the paddy fields. It was time for the fields to be ploughed. Shankar's father would be there; I could chat with him for a while. But I was in for a surprise when I reached the paddy fields. Shankar's father was there with several other men, but they were not ploughing. Instead, I saw a truck dumping heaps of gravel and sand. Men and women worked with shovels to dig up huge square blocks and there were white lines in the field, marking squares and rectangles. A man wearing a cloth cap was taking some sort of measurement with a metal tape.

I stood there dumbfounded. When Shankar's father came near me, I asked, 'Kaka, what's up? Won't you be planting rice this time?'

'Rice? No rice any more,' he said, throwing up his hands. 'Now we are building chawls, you know.'

I stood there for a while, but clearly he was busy. There was a fine dust in the air as the truck dumped the gravel. Shankar's father was not wearing his usual striped shorts. He had put on a white pyjama and kurta today. Someone called for him from the other end. I paused near my favourite rock for a while and then walked on.

The playground was basking in bright sunshine. All the boys—Phawdya, Surya, Chitre, Harishchandra and others—stood outside. I quickly scanned the group but could not spot Shirodkar. We stood around, chatting, until Ganoba rang the bell and we walked into our class.

I scanned the group again. Most of the girls were present, except Shirodkar.

Paranjpe ma'am walked in with a register and the bundle of report cards. My chest began to pound. I was sure everyone else too was nervous, for an eerie silence descended on the class.

Ma'am engaged us in some small talk as usual before handing over the results—you guys have not attempted the papers well enough; you need to be more serious next year; and so on and so forth. But no one seemed to be in the mood to listen to her. We waited with bated breath.

Ma'am took out her register and untied the bundle of report cards. They were arranged in the usual alphabetical order—boys first and then girls. But before distributing the report cards, she announced the top five ranks. I could not believe my ears—I had come fifth! Bibikar stood first, followed by Ghasu Gokhale, Surve, Mirikar and then myself. Ma'am taught us Marathi and hence specifically mentioned that I had got the highest marks in her subject.

She then read out the results. Chitre had stood eleventh while Bhaishetye had managed to pass. Misal too had passed but Surya had failed, along with Phawdya. Santya had managed to pass but Harishchandra had not. Two other students had failed.

Ma'am took out the girls' list after that. My mind was numb while my chest continued to pound. The birdies had passed as expected and so had Ambekar. Sukdi had failed, along with Sundri. Ma'am announced Shirodkar's name and my heart leapt up. She had secured the thirteenth rank. Ma'am looked around, holding her report card.

'She's absent, ma'am,' Mande shouted. 'Her father got

transferred. He said he will come and collect the report card later.'

My mind went blank, as if someone had hit me on the head. I sat there transfixed. My eyes were open, but I could see nothing. I could hear nothing. Ma'am was announcing a few details related to the next year, the names of teachers, etc. The girls were making a din, chattering away. But our group was silent. Phawdya sat there with his head in his hands. Chitre was silent. Surya was on the verge of tears.

We left the classroom in the same state of numbness, each one lost in thought. The boys and girls were saying their goodbyes. 'Joshi, congratulations. I need to be careful about you next year!' Bibikar called out. I did not reply. Surya and Harishchandra began to walk away without saying a word to anyone. Santya joined them. Chitre and Phawdya took the main road while I walked back through the paddy fields. I managed to reach the rocks and then my legs gave way. I plonked down on my rock.

The sun burnt brightly. The fields looked barren and dry. Shankar's father was nowhere to be seen, but the other men continued working. A huge mound of gravel stood in one corner while another truck made its way slowly into the field, leaving behind a trail of dust. The fields resounded with the growl of the engine struggling under its load.

I sat there stunned for a long time. Slowly things started dawning on me. Her father must have got transferred while we were away to Naru mama's wedding; or perhaps a little earlier. They must have decided to move houses after the exams got over, but I hadn't met her, so I did not get to know. I was desperate to tell her that I was innocent and had nothing to do with that episode between Kevda and Surya. But there was no way I could tell her now. I had no idea where she was.

I felt like sprinting across to Mande's house to ask her. Where had she gone? To which town? I was sure Mande would have her address. Else Juvekar was sure to have it. I could continue to be in touch through letters. I would join college here. She would join hers wherever she was. And then one day...

But I knew that this was not to happen. Nothing of this sort ever happens. Everything was over now. My fears, which I had been trying to stifle for a long time, were turning out to be true. I had always dreaded this. I somehow knew that one day it would all slip out of my hands. And that's exactly what had happened.

I wanted to wail out loud and let the tears wash it all away. That would have helped. But not a teardrop escaped my eyes. Everything had dried up—my heart felt barren, hard and empty.

I sat there for a long time. Then reality seeped into me. The results had been announced. Surya and Phawdya had failed. Surya would have to repeat the class while Phawdya would have to leave school. Chitre would probably move to Bandra. We would never assemble again for an adda in the building next year. Bendre ma'am would be there to teach us next year and so would Appa, Halbe and Kendalkar. But Zende sir would not be there. Manjrekar sir had left long ago. We had been allotted a classroom without a view. I would not be able to see the playground or the hills beyond Sonarpada. Kaduskar sir's tuition would begin tomorrow.

The Emergency continued as usual, but Vijay and KT were not around. Naru mama had got married. No more chess matches in our courtyard every evening. They were building chawls in the fields. No more water-filled paddy fields. The rest of the wide world around me remained as before—but Shirodkar was lost, unknown to me in the vast expanse somewhere.

School days were over. All that remained was a dreadful year called Class Ten.

About the Writer and His Body of Work
Vikrant Pande

My Conversations with Milind Bokil
Vikrant Pande

On Translating *Shala*
Vikrant Pande

P.S.

Insights
Interviews
& More...

About the Writer and His Body of Work

Vikrant Pande

Milind Bokil (born 1960) is one of the most important Marathi writers today. A sociologist by profession, Bokil has written extensively on rural and tribal communities and developmental issues related to them. His novels urge the reader to look for a deeper meaning in life. His ability to present personal emotions and social relationships without sacrificing the craft of writing makes him a popular writer.

Reared in a middle-class family, Bokil spent his childhood in a suburban town near Mumbai and studied in a commonplace Marathi school. This experience provided the material for his much acclaimed novel *Shala* (शाळा meaning 'school'). Bokil has a graduate degree in electronics and radio engineering, but he left the field after doing a couple of jobs, which were not to his liking. During this time, he was strongly influenced by the Sampoorna Kranti movement led by Jayprakash Narayan in the mid-seventies. . The students' and youth movement led by the veteran freedom-fighter was aimed at eradicating corruption and reforming Indian polity and society. The Indira Gandhi-led Congress government tried to crush the agitation by imposing internal emergency, but it was overthrown in 1977 by a coalition of opposition parties. As a result of this awakening, many Indian youths and professionals left their vocations to pursue social reconstruction and development. Bokil too left his job to work as a volunteer in a tribal development project in the coastal area of Maharashtra. The echoes of internal emergency and people's resistance are evident in *Shala*.

Bokil's writing career began in 1981 with the publication of a short story based on his experiences in the industrial sector. It was titled 'Punha Surya, Punha Prakash' and was published in February, 1981. It was a hair-raising tale about an engineer caught in a chemical tank. After that, he wrote about a dozen short stories, which were published in leading Marathi periodicals. His first book *Udakachiya Arti,* a collection of short stories, was published in 1994. The book derives its title from a much acclaimed story included in the book. It is a story about the emotional ordeal of a woman who is an anti-dam activist, and has been made into a short-film by the same name. The story earned the Katha Prize in 1992 and its English translation, 'Thirsting for Water', was included in Katha Prize Stories Vol. II published by Katha, New Delhi. Other stories in the collection also centre around the life and emotional experiences of social activists torn between personal existence and social priorities.

Bokil's themes and sensibilities were new to Marathi literature when he started writing. However, he later moved on to analyzing personal relationships. His second book of short stories, *Zen Garden*(2000), illustrates the shift. Here, Bokil appears to be more concerned with the feelings and emotional struggles of men and women, individually as well as in relationships. His style becomes subtle, and he focuses on the artistic balances implicit in a work of art.

Although his previous works were well received, Bokil became popular with his novel *Shala*. Running into several editions since its publication, *Shala* evokes a compelling sense of nostalgia, and has been popular across generations of Marathi readership. It has twice been adapted into films; *Humne Jeena Seekh Liya* (Hindi) and *Shala* (Marathi). The Marathi adaptation won the Silver Lotus Award at the 59th National Film Awards in the Best Feature Film in Marathi category. A theatre adaptation of the novel has appeared as a two-act play called *Ga Ma Bha Na*, and has run for more than a hundred and fifty performances.

Bokil's novella *Ekam*(2008) is the story of a writer who explores the meaning of solitude in her life against the backdrop of her family, friends, readers and the society at large. Bokil's treatment of the subject is both emotionally disturbing and enriching. In *Samudra*(2009), Bokil takes up the strains and stresses of a marital relationship against the background of a sea resort. An unconventional and refreshing novel, it has been translated into Hindi as *Samandar*.

Runn/Durg, published in 2011, is a compilation of two novellas, both of which revolve around the self-realization of women. *Runn* portrays the realization of the latent potential of a divorced woman who is involved in an earthquake relief operation. The novel, cast against the backdrop of an Indian desert, deftly combines environmental imagery with human emotions. *Durg* is the story of a young woman who experiences self-liberation atop a mountainous fort. The rugged, elevated setting is portrayed vividly by Bokil and subtly merged with the protagonist's stream of consciousness. In both the novels, the environmental and experiential aspects of the plot blend smoothly and create a feeling of oneness. This has been a distinguishing feature of Bokil's writing and is visible in all his works.

Bokil's professional experience and concerns are directly reflected in his non-fiction and sociological works. *Samudraparche*

Samaj(2000) is a collection of sociological travelogues. Here, Bokil writes about societies abroad from a comparative sociology perspective. There is an element of travel writing in it, but Bokil is primarily concerned with social issues. In "Mabuhai Ifugao', he sketches the plight of the indigenous people in the Mindanao province of Philippines, whereas in 'Costa Rica', he describes the trade-off between development and environmental conservation. In 'Amsterdam', he takes a look at the so called 'red light' area and analyzes sex trafficking in Europe. This analysis is further carried on in 'Amazing Thailand'. Bokil's concern for the deprived and marginalized are reflected in his writing about the dalits in Japan and the blacks in Zimbabwe.

Janache Anubhav Pusata(2000) is a collection of articles on people, natural resources and livelihood linkages. Here Bokil studies the developmental issues India is facing, with respect to local communities negotiating with the changing environmental and socio-political situation in the wake of globalization. While Bokil does not compromise with analytical rigour, the spotlight is always on the disadvantaged sections like dalits, tribal people, cowherds, fishermen, small farmers and women.

A detailed socio-anthropological account of a tribal community is found in Bokil's *Katkari: Vikas Ki Visthapan* published in 2006. Bokil studies the plight of a so-called primitive tribal community called Katkari living in the hilly, coastal area of Maharashtra. Bokil traces the community's history, analyzing how it lost its traditional occupation of extracting catechu due to colonial laws, and describes how at present they are facing the danger of displacement from their traditional abode. He makes a strong case for the development of this community by highlighting the tenacity, tolerance and developmental aspirations of its members. This book represents Bokil's continuous association with tribal communities and his deep concern regarding their well-being. Another book in the same genre is *Gosht Mendha Gawachi*, wherein Bokil documents the heroic struggle of a small Gond village in the Gadchiroli district of Maharashtra in acquiring community rights over surrounding forests and ushering a process of self-governance.

Bokil has co-authored *Wataani Mukkam*(2009) along with three other Marathi writers—Asha Bage, Bharat Sasne and Saniya. These four contemporary Marathi writers jointly undertook an innovative venture for literary discourse. They discuss around forty questions about life, literature and society, and present a comprehensive and interesting symposium for students, readers and critics.

Bokil has also compiled and edited the works of two important figures. The first is *UdakChalwaweUkti* (2003), a collection of articles by Vilasrao Salunkhe, the technocrat crusader of equitable distribution of water and initiator of the *Pani Panchayat* movement. The second one is a collection of articles by Vinoba Bhave, the luminary disciple of Mahatma Gandhi and the world-famous originator of *Bhoodan* Movement. This compilation is titled *GyanTeSangtoPunha* (2004) and makes available Vinoba Bhave's rich social, political and spiritual thought in an easy to read language.

Coming back to fiction, his latest novel *Gawatya* tells the story of a young man from Mumbai who is not happy with his job and life, and in his quest for peace and knowledge goes to work in a Gandhian ashram in a remote tribal area, where the mountain 'Gawatya' is his constant companion. He meets many individuals and communities, and through this interaction, an understanding dawns on him. His ultimate realization is the sense of connectedness with his own self and his surroundings. He also understands the meaning of love and its unity with knowledge.

My Conversations with Milind Bokil

Vikrant Pande

I had many a conversation and exchange of notes with Milind Bokil before he agreed that I was the right person to take up the task of translating *Shala*. I was curious to know how he got into writing working, as he was, in the area of social development. 'Since my childhood, I knew that I was going to be a writer or rather I *was* a writer,' he says. 'I do not know how that feeling arose in me, but it has been part of my consciousness right from the beginning. I used to read a lot. We didn't have many books at home; we were a humble middle-class family, but our town had a good municipal library. I used to virtually go there every day and had read most of the important books in Marathi literature by the time I passed matriculation. I think that was a decisive influence. Reading taught me how to write, and I strongly believe that books are food, clothing and shelter for a writer. Being and becoming a writer, both are valid processes.'

There are several literary giants in Marathi and it is easy to be influenced by them. I asked Milind if he followed in the footsteps of any writer. He likes the short stories published in the 1940's and the '50s, and his favourites are Gangadhar Gadgil and Vyankatesh Madgular. 'Gadgil portrayed the parochial, chawl-dwelling, middle-class ethos of Mumbai whereas Madgulkar painted the rustic, rural communities and individual characters. His *Banagarwadi*, the tale of a shepherd community, has had a lasting impact on me,' Milind says. The other authors who have influenced him are G.A. Kulkarni, who expanded the horizons of the Marathi short story by exhibiting the unhappiness and the disappointments underlying the lives of the middle-class. 'I love G.N. Dandekar for his simple and humane portrayal of his subjects, Bhalchandra Nemade for his existential treatment and C.T. Khanolkar for his passionate and lyrical depiction of Konkani life,' he adds. Some of the Marathi poets like Mardhekar, Anil, Arati Prabhu and Narayan Surve are also Bokil's favourites.

Most authors are shaped by the times they grow up in, the social milieu around them. Milind Bokil says, he was strongly attracted to Jayprakash Narayan and his appeal to the youth. He joined the Chhatra Yuva Sangharsh Vahini founded by JP. Bokil was also going through an existential crisis, working in the electronics industry but getting disenchanted with it. Then he quit and went to work as a volunteer in the tribal area of Western Ghats. 'We can see glimpses of the Emergency in *Shala* while in *Gawatya*, the protagonist leaves a Mumbai job to work in the tribal areas of Maharashtra searching for his own self. Bokil's love for sociology and rural development led him to do a Ph.D in Development Sociology and become a full-time sociologist. All these experiences colour his writing. 'From a writer's point of view, these things are important. They break the parochial boundaries, change your worldview, and that shift is reflected in your writing. If as a writer you are not bogged down by isms and philosophies, it becomes a very liberating process. JP movement instilled caste and gender equality in our minds. It also put me in touch with the deprived sections of society like dalits, adiwasis and nomadic communities. And that was a very humbling experience. Thirdly, I became associated with grassroots activists and their organizations committed to social change. Their world then began to appear in my stories. If I had to summarize the journey in a single phrase, I would say "enrichment of worldview". I believe writers are recognized not just by their content and style but also by their worldviews,' Bokil says.

Shala is the story of adolescence. I was curious whether he had a particular view which he wanted to portray. 'One doesn't write fiction to impress any particular point of view upon the readers. The view emanates from the work,' he says. 'So in this case, the point of view is the search for love. Not just the protagonist but most of the characters in the novel are searching for love. I believe it is a primary human need but not always satisfied. During adolescence, this need assumes an altogether different dimension. Children are in search of love and affection, but when they become adolescents they realize that they also can give love. And this feeling comes naturally with biological changes in the body. Unfortunately our society doesn't respect this change, which is the natural scheme of things.Moreover, school has become a severe and competitive institution and the morals of our caste-based society are still very constricting. We do not raise our children in a liberal atmosphere. The situation might be changing in metropolitan areas, but in villages and smaller towns it is still suffocating. And this causes considerable psychological and social stress,' the author says.

While translating *Shala*, I found that the writer has left the end open to interpretation. Does the protagonist meet his love later? Do they unite? I asked whether a slightly melancholic style was a trademark of his. I had observed the same in *Gawatya*. Despite a strain of melancholy, the author leaves the reader with a subtle hope in the end.

Bokil thinks, it is a part of human nature. 'I believe, a writer is basically a melancholy person and although he or she may have moments of exhilaration, good literature often ends on a melancholic note. This is because you realize that life is not perfect. As a human being, you try to make it perfect, try to find harmony in your existence, but you cannot control life. The imperfection stays. The fact that you cannot do anything about it and you have to be just a spectator brings on the sadness. However, in literature, the melancholic feeling is also triggered by realization—the happy awareness of having understood something. It is true that this realization is tinged with sadness, but it is knowledge nonetheless. Literature, therefore, has this soothing or cathartic effect. And when the subject matter is 'love', then the effect is multiplied. Love is one element which is intrinsically loaded with joy and sadness. Love and literature make a great mix because they understand each other well. Understanding the meaning of terms like love, truth, knowledge and endearment is an all-time literary endeavour. In *Gawatya*, it is done more explicitly and from a more philosophical angle, but that striving is there in other works too.'

On Translating *Shala*

Vikrant Pande

Shala is a deceptively simple novel. In the first reading, it appears to be a straightforward love story of a school boy who pines for his classmate despite the social milieu he occupies, which does not allow him to express his feelings openly. I realized that I needed to get under the skin of Mukund to get the voice of the teenager right, and, more importantly, maintain the consistency of the tone and tenor throughout the book. I had to avoid the temptation of using a language which would sound alien when spoken by a school boy. I say 'temptation', because a translator is often tempted to enrich the script with his own style, which can possibly enhance the beauty of the text but take it away from the original. Another challenge was to convert the local idiom and slang into acceptable English and yet convey the originally intended meaning. One of the characters, Surya, is a rustic fellow who speaks in the local dialect. There is no English equivalent of the local Marathi dialect and it proved to be a difficult task. I had many conversations with Milind Bokil in order to understand the social context, the physical descriptions of the town and the background against which he had set the book. I saw the film adaptation to understand how its director had transferred Bokil's characters into the movie. Bokil mentioned that the director had made a sincere effort to understand and assimilate the book because he was very passionate about making the film. For me as the translator, the film gave faces to names and helped me construct the characters in a new language.

Milind Bokil's writing is realistic and, even though it is tinged with melancholy at times, he always leaves the reader with hope in the end. The entire story is appealing for its simplicity, its uncluttered, aesthetic nature, and dialogues which are natural and heartfelt. Having been in school in the mid-1970's, I was able to connect with and understand the protagonist's feelings and reactions. I enjoyed the challenging but enjoyable process of translating this charming novel.

Lastly, my editor Minakshi Thakur's inputs were extremely valuable. They helped make the text eminently readable.

HARPER**PERENNIAL**

Harper Perennial presents special editions of its finest books in translation

Age of Frenzy
Mahabaleshwar Sail
Translated from the Konkani by Vidya Pai

A Life Incomplete
Nanak Singh
Translated from the Punjabi by Navdeep Suri

Mohanaswamy
Vasudhendra
Translated from the Kannada by Rashmi Terdal

The Music of Solitude
Krishna Sobti
Translated from the Hindi by Vasudha Dalmia

No Presents Please: Mumbai Stories
Jayant Kaikini
Translated from the Kannada by Tejaswini Niranjana

A Preface to Man
Subhash Chandran
Translated from the Malayalam by Fathima E.V.

The Secret Garland
Andal
Translated from the Tamil by Archana Venkatesan

Shala
Milind Bokil
Translated from the Marathi by Vikrant Pande

The Weary Generations
Abdullah Hussein
Translated from the Urdu by the author

Written in Tears
Arupa Patangia Kalita
Translated from the Assamese by Ranjita Biswas

HARPERPERENNIAL

Bhima: Lone Warrior
M.T. Vasudevan Nair
Translated from the Malayalam by Gita Krishnankutty

Chemmeen
Thakazhi Sivasankara Pillai
Translated from the Malayalam by Anita Nair

Ghachar Ghochar
Vivek Shanbhag
Translated from the Kannada by Srinath Perur

Hindutva or Hind Swaraj
U.R. Ananthamurthy
Translated from the Kannada by Keerti Ramachandra & Vivek Shanbhag

The Liberation of Sita
Volga
Translated from the Telugu by T. Vijay Kumar & C. Vijayasree

A Life Misspent
Suryakant Tripathi Nirala
Translated from the Hindi by Satti Khanna

The Sea Lies Ahead
Intizar Husain
Translated from the Urdu by Rakhshanda Jalil

Selected Poems
Joy Goswami
Translated from the Bengali by Sampurna Chattarji

Wild Animals Prohibited: Stories/Anti-stories
Subimal Misra
Translated from the Bengali by V. Ramaswamy

Wild Words: Four Tamil Poets
Malathi Maithri, Salma, Kutti Revathi and Sukirtharani
Translated from the Tamil by Lakshmi Holmström